ONCE
&
FUTURE

PRAISE FOR *ONCE & FUTURE*

"A rip-roaring, no holds-barred, gloriously queer reinvention of Arthurian legend."

Malinda Lo, author of *Ash*

"All hail this worthier-than-ever, fresh, and affirming reincarnation of the legendary king and her round table of knights which dazzles with heroic flair, humor, and suspense."

Kirkus starred review

"Fun and fearless, this story romps right across the galaxy and into your heart."

Amie Kaufman, author of the bestselling Illuminae Files series

"If a gender-bent retelling of King Arthur sounds as good to you as it does to me, then you'll definitely want to add this one to your list."

Book Riot

"The inclusive, gender-bent King Arthur retelling that your bookshelf has been missing… An adventure of epic scale."

B & N Teen Blog

"Pointedly funny and deftly topical; an effortless Arthurian update with heart in all the right places."

E.K. Johnston, author of *Ahsoka*

"A sizzling, bold exploration of gender, power, and revolution. Its dynamic and diverse cast will inspire and delight readers. I loved every second!"

Jessica Khoury, author of *The Forbidden Wish*

"An utterly delightful romp, full of witty voice, imaginative adventures, and *deeply* lovable characters. It kept me up into the wee hours of the morning. I couldn't put it down!"

Katherine Locke, author of *The Girl with the Red Balloon*

"Oh my goodness, I loved it so much! Utterly compelling, brilliantly witty, and delightfully queer, I absolutely raced through it and loved every second. It was so refreshing to see LGBTQIA characters front and centre of the plot, being the heroes and saving the day. And the humour is sharp and genuinely funny—who doesn't love a barbed Spice Girls reference?!"

Simon James Green, author of *Noah Can't Even*

ONCE
&
FUTURE

**AMY ROSE CAPETTA
AND
CORI McCARTHY**

ROCK THE BOAT

A Rock the Boat Book

First published in Great Britain and Australia by Rock the Boat,
an imprint of Oneworld Publications, 2019

Copyright © Amy Rose Capetta and Cori McCarthy, 2019
Foreword © 2019 by James Patterson

The moral right of Amy Rose Capetta and Cori McCarthy to be identified
as the Authors of this work has been asserted by them in accordance with
the Copyright, Designs and Patents Act 1988

ISBN 978-1-78607-696-0 (hardback)
ISBN 978-1-78607-654-0 (paperback)
ISBN 978-1-78607-655-7 (ebook)

Printed and bound in Great Britain by Clays Ltd, Elcograf S.p.A

This book is a work of fiction. Names, characters, businesses, organizations,
places, and events are either the product of the author's imagination or are
used fictitiously. Any resemblance to actual persons, living or dead, events,
or locales is entirely coincidental.

Oneworld Publications
10 Bloomsbury Street
London WC1B 3SR
England

Stay up to date with the latest books,
special offers, and exclusive content from
Rock the Boat with our monthly newsletter

Sign up on our website
www.rocktheboat.london

For SAGA,
with hope for a better future

"The destiny of Man is to unite, not to divide.
If you keep on dividing you end up as a collection of monkeys
throwing nuts at each other out of separate trees."

—T. H. White, *The Once and Future King*

Love. Death. Betrayal. Evil. Magic.

The story of King Arthur has it all. That's why *Le Morte d'Arthur* by Sir Thomas Malory could be called the Western world's first bestseller. And when I read *Once & Future,* a bold, unexpected retelling of King Arthur as an immigrant teenage girl, I knew it had all the same thrilling elements that would make the legend—first told sixteen hundred years ago—a modern favorite once again.

Amy Rose Capetta and Cori McCarthy have written an Arthur for the twenty-first century: a female king on a quest to overthrow a tyrannical corporate government. Ari is a girl who learns to live boldly and to fight fiercely for the right to be who she is—and to love who she loves. She's the hero we all need.

—James Patterson

ONCE
&
FUTURE

LOST
&
FOUND

Ari was hiding out in the Middle Ages.

The rubber knight's costume she wore squeaked with each movement and smelled like her brother—before he'd embraced deodorant.

"This is a weird secret spot, Kay," Ari said through the slits of the visor on the knight's helmet. She stiffly turned to take in the glass cases bursting with period drama: mannequins in knight regalia, sweating horses, and piercing swords. Off to the side, hook-nosed and formidable, was a lone figure labeled *MERLIN*.

"It's the best Old Earth myth," Kay muttered, going over the grocery list on his watch. "Don't you remember our classes on Lionel? Arthur was the one true king who saved his people from the Dark Ages. He gave a voice to all, righted the wrongs...made a round table."

"Round?"

"So that no single person would be at the head. An equal voice for all."

"An equal voice for all, plus he's the one true king? Sounds like delicious hypocrisy."

Kay blew out an annoyed breath. "No one comes in here, Ari. It *is* a good secret spot."

Ari let him have that one, reminding herself that while this place felt like a harmless museum in a forgotten wing of a giant floating mall, it was also ground zero for the Mercer Company. The starship *Heritage* was the galactic corporation's flagship, teeming with associates who would arrest her as soon as sell her a souvenir. She teetered back around in the stiff suit to face her brother. "How did you ever train in this thing at knight camp without peripheral vision?"

"Knights don't need peripheral vision. They need chivalry."

Ari snorted so hard her visor flew up.

Kay smacked it back down. "And the ability to realize when they should *not* draw attention to themselves."

"Really? That plaque over there says chivalry gave birth to toxic masculinity, which caused Old Earth a few millennia of bullshit patriarchy."

"Are you seriously picking fights right now?" Kay asked. "You've got to lie low. I've got to get supplies. Don't make me wish I left you on *Error*."

"You couldn't. Mercer is doing random spot checks in the parking docks."

"I could have left you stuffed in a trunk."

"The patrols would look there."

Her big brother picked up her rubber-gloved hand and slapped a coin in it. "Go. Over there. Let me think, will you?"

He pointed to a telescope by the nearest window. Ari squeak-walked toward it. She dropped the coin in the slot and pushed up the visor enough to peer out at the main attraction on *Heritage,* Mercer's most popular shopping and tourist destination: the view.

Ari squinted through the telescope. Up close, Old Earth was downright puny. Only a few thousand miles from the planet, and she could not figure out what was so sacred. She zoomed in, and the blue-and-white marble revealed green-brown clumps. When Kay stomped over on his magboots, she asked, "Is that *all* the land? Can't be."

"There were ice caps in its heyday," Kay said. "Less water, more land."

"Cradle of civilization, my ass."

"Hey." Her brother grinned at her, a maniacal, desperate, *Oh, my gods, just listen to me* look. "Keep your voice down, okay? That planet means a lot to most people."

Ari glanced at the crowds just outside of the museum wing, taking in Old Earth from the observation deck. The space rats were easy enough to rub elbows with, even if they were over-emotional at the sight of the retired planet. They were like Kay, born on ships and tailored in patchwork flight suits. The other humans, the crisp, smooth, elite Mercer Company patrons, were more unnerving.

And Ari? She didn't belong to either camp.

Kay eyed a pair of mall cops in stark white Mercer uniforms as they made their rounds.

"Help me finish the list. We need to get out of here." He pushed his silvery-gray hair from his scalp, and it arced damply over his brow. Her brother was doing what he always did under pressure: thinking with his stomach. "Did you like those protein preserves? The garlicky ones?"

"They made your breath stink up the entire ship for days."

"So, three cases?"

Ari side-eyed him, and he added, "Plus breath mints. And for the cake, chocolate this year?"

"I don't need a cake, Kay."

"Ten years is a big deal. I vote chocolate. I eat most of it, anyway." Kay hadn't even glanced out the window; Old Earth was old hat to Ari's adoptive brother. He'd been on board *Heritage* a bunch of times as a kid and claimed to be over the view. Still, whenever their provisions ran low, Kay set course for this exact starship no matter how far away they were.

"How many times did you come here with our parents?"

"Salt. Wounds," he gruffed, confirming Ari's theory that this place reminded him of better times, before his moms had taken in Ari and they'd all had to start dodging Mercer.

Ari turned her telescope to the motley, cratered moon. Unlike Old Earth, it had been overrun by domed colonies named after ancient vehicular gods. Each one featured its name and mascot in great, glowing letters. Even from this distance, a neon ram's head charged through a wall over and over, the letters DODGE blinking.

"Hey, we should stop there on our way out," she said, pointing to the overrun moon with its billboards more brilliant than stars. Live shows. Dance halls. Oxygen bars. Something called an *Elvis*. "When's the last time we went dancing, Kay?"

Kay snapped his fingers in front of the telescope, and for a second the automatic focus zoomed out dizzily and gave her a view of the powder granules of orange cheese from his favorite tortilla chips.

Ari lifted her face, watching a drop of sweat travel down Kay's cheek to his scruffy chin.

"Stop sweating. They'll think you're sick. Or hiding a secret Ketchan in the medieval times section."

"Hilarious, Ari. Truly." Kay wiped his face with his forearm. "Tell me, are you able to stop your body from sweating on command?"

Ari squinted. "I haven't tried. Maybe."

"Look, don't move from this spot while I pick up our supplies. Don't talk to a soul, and if you must? *Lie,* Ari. I want you speaking eloquent, exquisite, capitalistic lies. Repeat after me: 'Mercer is my king, my God, my salvation. I love to shop 'til I drop.'"

Ari's lips pruned; she'd make herself sick uttering such nonsense. "I'll stay put."

He put his hands on her shoulders. Worry folded his adorably brutish forehead into lines. "If something goes weird, run. Take off in *Error.* Don't wait. Promise?"

"I got it, Kay," she said, slipping past promises she'd never keep. Ari clapped Kay's shoulder, before he headed out of the museum exhibit and down the stairs that led to the heart of the mall. Ari moved to the balcony to watch him go, taking in a bird's-eye view of bleached consumerism. The ceramic tiled walls and floor were white. So were the identical Mercer storefronts: the symbols for grocery, pharmacy, clothes, and spaceship hardware among the most visible.

Worst of all, even the light pouring from the lofted ceiling was blinding and pale, the kind she couldn't look straight into without wincing—which was exactly what Mercer wanted.

"Don't look at us looking at you," Ari murmured, her nerves prickling. She couldn't blame Kay for sweating in this place. The Mercer Company didn't mess around. Ten years ago, the Mercer Company placed a barrier around planet Ketch, sealing everyone in—their response to the Ketchans, who had begun speaking out against the company's monopolistic tyranny. Not even communications could pass through. The Mercer Company proclaimed that the Ketchans had become hostile, that they were bad for the economy and therefore must be walled off. Mercer had become more than just a greedy corporation with a monopoly on goods and services for the entire galaxy— they *were* the galaxy. They controlled everything from people's food to healthcare to the freaking government.

Around the same time that Ketch got walled off, Kay's moms found seven-year-old Ari abandoned, starved, afloat in a piece of space trash. They'd taken her in, loved her. They'd even tried to find a way to get her through the barrier and back home to Ketch—and gotten arrested in the process. That was three years ago, when Ari was fourteen, and there hadn't been any word since. They could have died in a Mercer prison or on a factory planet. Kay said not knowing was the easiest part; that was his favorite lie.

"Welcome to Heritage Mall."

Ari managed not to shout. The words came from the image of the Mercer Company's CEO, known only as the Administrator, whose bust was now projected above her watch screen.

"We're so glad you could join us today on Heritage. *All pilgrimages to Old Earth are rewarded with a twenty percent*

discount on souvenirs and government documents." The man's blank eyes and digitally smooth skin hinted at intrigue, explicit knowledge, and caustic mischief. Ari wondered if he looked that way to everyone or just her. *"Whether you're in the market for a keepsake pebble from terra firma or a quickie divorce, the Mercer Company is at your service."*

The Administrator's face disappeared. Ari swore inside her smelly rubber knight's suit and silenced her watch. "It's just a pop-up ad," she murmured to herself. "He's not actually on this starship. It's just an ad...."

"Look, my sweets! A knight!" An elderly couple swept into the Middle Ages display, as swift as a pair of roaches. They were on top of her in a moment, groping her suit, all up in her personal space.

"Hey!" she shouted. "No touching!"

Unfazed, the old man with dyed dark hair held up his watch. "Can I take your picture with my wife? We honeymooned on Lionel more than fifty solar cycles ago, back when the planet was much more Mercer friendly, you understand."

The sprightly old lady posed on Ari's arm, and all of a sudden Ari was seeing spots from a brilliant bang of light.

"What the—"

"Spotlight flash. Erases all shadows and lines digitally before the picture is even taken." The woman chuckled. "It is a bit bright."

"Take mine now!" the elderly man yelled, handing off the watch to his wife, gripping Ari and repeating the blinding-by-luminescence. "Now let's do one with the sword!"

Ari snuck a fist inside her helmet to rub her stinging irises while he pulled her toward the only display in the museum that wasn't roped off. A golden, bejeweled sword stuck out of a stone in the center of the fake-cobble courtyard. Its handle was worn with smudges and dirty fingerprints. Gross. How many people had yanked on it since the last time it had been cleaned?

"Give it a tug! I'll stand by and act surprised, like, 'Oh, heavens, we've got ourselves a new King Arthur!' " he shouted.

Ari sighed and gripped the handle. At least the galaxy-worth of germs was only getting on Kay's old rubber armor. When the flash shattered the air once again, she gave the sword a heartless tug. It didn't budge. "Sorry, pal. Looks like we're stuck in the dark ages."

He waved her words away like they were annoying liberal chatter and beckoned for his wife to come over. "Now you take our picture," he ordered.

Ari held out her hand for their *seriously* large watch while they got in position. Her eyes caught the platinum diamond on the back that denoted elite Mercer status, the shining proof that this piece of tech had access to data that most people's did not. How easy would it be to type a few words and find out what kept both Kay and her awake in the endless night of deep space?

Ari glanced at the couple. They were discussing who should stand where, dissolving into a full-on argument. "Can I check out the photos you've taken?"

"Sure, hon," the woman said. She elbowed her husband out of the way in order to give the sword her own series of entitled tugs.

Ari opened up the universe-wide web and typed in the search bar. She didn't think about what kind of alarms might fly up when she entered her adoptive mothers' names; she didn't care. She would give anything to hand Kay some answers, a bandage for their wounds. Besides, what were the odds that Mercer was watching this particular platinum account at this exact moment?

She tapped ENTER, and the Mercer Company emblem spun lazily before blinking wide open with information on her parents' arrests. It listed their names, dates of birth, planet or spaceship of birth, and their joint status: *Incarcerated*. Deceased: *Blank*.

"They're still alive," Ari breathed, hardly believing it. She clicked on *LOCATION*, but a flaring red light darkened the screen. Ari dropped the watch, spun on her long legs, and ran from the blinking warning:

REMAIN STATIONARY.
MERCER ASSOCIATES ARE COMING TO ASSIST YOU.

&

Ari ripped off the knight costume and slid into the command chair on *Error*. She put her feet flat to the metal grating of the floor and engaged the ankle lock on her magboots. Hauling the crisscrossing safety belt across her chest, she pulled it more taut than usual. Only loose enough to breathe, and barely that.

Kay appeared in a flash of sweaty fear, his watch still buzzing from the alarm Ari had sent. He locked in, lording over the control panel. His frenetically moving fingers ticked against Ari's anxiety, a tally running ever higher against them.

If this were a normal takeoff, Kay would have wandered

into the cockpit five minutes after their preset hour, still in his boxers and clutching a mildly poisonous energy drink. This was entirely too reminiscent of the last time they'd run from Mercer—after their parents' arrest.

Kay pressed the anchor release once, twice, before hammering it with his fist. An echoing bang announced that their tiny lifeboat of a ship had disengaged from the mall parking dock. He wasted no time in gearing up the thrusters, pushing toward the bumper-to-bumper lane of compact spaceships waiting to pass through the parking booth.

"Don't suppose you paid for parking at the kiosk on your way out," Ari said with a badly timed chuckle.

Kay groaned and hit the accelerator. They shot over the lane of ships, over the security bar at the parking booth. The alarms blazed, and he hit max throttle. Ari and Kay could have been mirror images of each other, leaning forward, staring at the small mouth of an exit, willing it to stay open long enough to blast through. They were both holding their breath—until they burst out of the parking area and into the black of space.

"If they weren't suspicious of us before, they are now." Kay punched the speed while the floating mall shrank behind them, far enough to show off the threateningly large Mercer fleet orbiting the stationary starship.

"Are they following?" she asked.

Kay stared at the rearview screen. And stared. "No."

Ari scrubbed her face and let out a little scream.

"What happened, Ari? Or do I not want to know?"

She weighed her options. It didn't seem like the right moment to admit she'd found out that their parents were alive, but she'd never been good at right moments. "I'm not…sure?"

"My gods, you're the worst liar in the history of lies. Oh, *here* they come!" Kay throttled up while the rearview filled with Mercer pursuit cruisers, sirens blazing. "And the first thing they're going to do is hack the hard drive…" Kay's voice took on a sarcastic lyricism when he was riled, and now he was nearly singing. "I've got to drop her offline or we're going to be Mercer's ugliest new puppet ship!"

He thrust the steering console to the side—in front of Ari—and began digging in the wires under the panel. Ari reached for the controls, watching the Mercer vessels grow ever closer in the rearview. Too close. They'd overtake *Error*. Imprison Kay. Lock Ari away for merely existing in their galaxy without their permission.

No way.

She stopped staring at the rearview and looked ahead—at the blue-and-white marbled planet. Ari throttled all the way, beyond the red zone, leaning into the burst of speed.

Grunting, Kay slammed into his seat. "What are you doing? We can't outrun them!"

"We're not going to outrun them. We're going to hide."

"Where?" he yelled. Ari pointed through the windshield, where the blue planet grew larger with swift brilliance. *"Earth?* Even if we survive landing, Mercer will kill us!"

"Mercer won't follow. They can't. It's completely out of their jurisdiction. Earth is a protected nature preserve, predating Mercer's existence."

"How do you know that?"

"I read it on the freakin' observation deck!" Ari had to grit her teeth against the speed as their ship passed into the upper atmosphere and began reciting its own name.

"ERROR! ERROR!"

Kay hammered at the controls, yelling over the stilted voice of the ship's mainframe. Ari tried to slow them down with every trick, but they were hurtling through the cloudy atmosphere of the retired planet, rattling from the strain on the ship's joints. The view from the cockpit was all crystal-blue ocean and green, white-capped mountains.

Until they passed through a gray cloud, a digital smoke-screen, and were suddenly looking at the rusted, burnt-out shell of a wasteland. The whole planet was a garbage heap forgotten about long ago—apart from the dark strips where the land had been cleared to the bedrock.

"What the..." Ari mouthed, just as *Error* moved on to a new warning complete with flaring lights.

"ILLEGAL TRESPASS! ILLEGAL TRESPASS!"

"Sweet girl, gimme a break!" Kay yelled. He pounded the silencer, but the red alarm lights continued to wash the cockpit with chilling incandescence. Ari tightened her chest restraint as the smog gave way to a jungle mass of crumbling cities.

Kay took the controls back. "If I hit the emergency parachute, they'll know exactly where we land. If I don't, we have a tiny chance."

"Don't hit it," she said.

"We could die."

Ari gripped her brother's arm so tightly she wondered if their bones would fuse like melted plastic when the ship turned into a ball of flames. It made her feel better. There were worse ways to go than side-by-side with Kay.

He steered them toward a feral forest. The trees grew closer, and Kay managed to level out the ship, skipping across the canopy. Every single bash nailed Ari's teeth together, and yet they were slowing—sort of—until *Error* nose-dived into a break in the trees, plummeted through branches, and slammed into the ground. The viewscreen was filled with smashed earth until the ship's back end succumbed to gravity, falling with metal shrieks.

In the new quiet, Kay looked at Ari. "Hey, cheers. We're alive!"

Ari couldn't help herself. "They're alive."

"Who?"

"Our parents. I used some Mercer couple's watch to look up their status. They're alive, Kay. I don't know where, but they're still out there."

Kay unstrapped, shaking his head while his face turned a red shade of *punched*. His gray hair flopped in his face and he had to pull it away with both hands to stare at her. Ari needed him to say something. Instead he closed his eyes. "Okay, I'm not mad."

"Really? 'Cause you look mad."

"That's because I *am* mad. I told you not to do anything, so you *leaped* into Mercer's files. *Then* you crashed us on the birth planet of all humanity, *and* you damn near killed us."

"But you're also...not mad?"

"Let me have two feelings right now."

"No problem."

"They're both alive?" His eyes were still closed tight. "Are they together?"

"I don't know."

Kay's painful sigh ached through Ari. He shouldn't have to go through this. There had to be some way to make a stand against Mercer. To find their parents. To free them. To have hope.

"Thank the celestial gods." Her brother turned his glare at her, his voice rising sharply. "But the next time you want to wave your renegade flag and yell 'na-na-na-boo-boo,' could you please wait until after I've picked up supplies? Even if *Error* is in good enough shape to get off this rock, where are we going to go? We don't have food, Ari. Do you know what happens to people in the void without food? They eat each other."

"You can eat my left arm. I don't use it much."

"Ari."

"Can't we stop somewhere else? How about that lively moon up there?"

"Which will be overrun with Mercer patrols in less than a day. Patrols looking for *us* after you flagged our moms and we evaded arrest."

"Don't forget about the parking ticket," she added. He gave her a hard *I'm serious* look. "So we'll be discreet." Ari unstrapped her chest harness and unlocked her magboots. "Do you think Mercer will be able to locate us down here?"

"They won't catch our flight signature. We're too insignificant in this mess. Hopefully." He squeezed the command chair—Captain Mom's old chair—and Ari wondered if he was thinking about how she used to say, *Hope is the food of the foolish. Eat up, kiddos.*

Ari walked through the main cabin, toward the back of the ship, passing a half-smooshed cake in its box. Kay and Ari stopped, staring down at it. "I'm still eating it," her brother said. "Happy ten-year anniversary of being my pain in the ass. I mean, sister."

"Thanks." She tried not to laugh...or grimace. They crossed the cargo bay, and Ari hit the door release. Rotting dense undergrowth instantly wafted into the ship. "Gross. What the hell is going on with this planet? It didn't look this torn up from *Heritage*."

"No. It didn't." Kay stared at the foul, dead forest, skeletal skyscrapers lining the distance like broken teeth in a monster's mouth. His face turned dark before he pushed his feelings away. "Whatever is going on here is none of our business. Check the ship, especially the heat shields. I'm going to get the hard drive back online. If we have to run for that cheap excuse for a moon, we better do it before Mercer has taken over every square inch looking for us."

Ari stepped out onto surprisingly spongy ground, and Kay slapped the door closed behind her. She didn't blame him for being mad; her timing was historically the worst, her impulses a series of epic mistakes. Ari being adopted by Kay's family had only seemed to tear Kay's life apart, and yet he still wanted her around. He still loved her like family. She had to work harder to make it up to him.

She walked around *Error,* which wasn't in terrible shape for having dived through a hundred half-dead trees. For once, *Error*'s first life as a galaxy-class cruise ship lifeboat served her well; she was designed to crash.

Ari searched the skies for the off-white, boxy Mercer vessels that would arrest them on the spot, but the clouds were a solid dark gray. There was no Mercer. Her gamble had paid off. She needed to rub that in Kay's face—once they were safe, of course.

Ari stepped deeper into the forest, her curiosity piqued.

The gravity on this planet was heavy, and her whole body felt dense and stiff. The undergrowth thinned as she neared a clear-cut section, peering out at the madness of screeching, smoke-belching machines. No humans in sight.

Old Earth was supposed to be preserved. Who was leveling these trees? There wasn't even soil left, just strips of gray bedrock, which was also being laser-cut into cubes and hauled away by unmarked factory tanks with too many robotic arms. Someone was deforesting Old Earth, skinning it to its bones and then sucking out the planet's marrow.

Oh, who was she kidding? It was Mercer. It was always Mercer.

So they had crash-landed in the middle of a secret exploitation of the ancient home of all humanity. *Great*. Like she needed another reason for Mercer to come after her.

Ari took a few pictures with her watch and was about to double back to *Error* when she spotted a gorgeous stone wall. The machines were close. They would overtake it soon. She walked along the edge, brushing her fingers down the smooth, fitted rocks. So much had fallen—entire cities, mountains, countries—but not this. People had created it with their hands, bearing stones in their arms, leaving a mark on their world that lasted hundreds of years longer than any corporation or words or courage.

And the machines were about to eat it.

"Don't do it, Ari," she said in the same moment that she reached for the top of the stone wall, hauling herself up and over. She dropped down in a graveyard. Marble and granite headstones lay helter-skelter, mostly fallen, some crookedly half-sunk. And at the center of the darkly magical sight? A gigantic, ancient oak. Its gnarled arms were held up against the sky like a tribute to death. Ari jogged closer, her curiosity rewarded by an even stranger sight.

Buried in the trunk of the thousand-year-old oak was a sword.

"What the..."

Her eyes trailed along the silver pommel and the intricate crossbar. Unlike the sword on *Heritage,* this one looked real. She walked all the way around it. The shining point glinted on the other side like a question.

There were things in this universe that Ari didn't understand. Space travel for one, the segregation of Ketch for another, herself for the grand finale. But this sword—it needed to be set free. She'd never felt anything so strongly in her whole life, almost like someone was nudging her toward it. Almost as if that *someone* had been nudging for a lot longer than the last few minutes, and only now were they willing to tip their hand. She got her hands around the hilt and gave it a good tug.

The sword budged.

She tossed her long black hair behind her shoulder and set her stance wider. And pulled the sword. The blade came free with a ringing sound that didn't seem possible, and even though it had been lodged in that tree for however long, it was sharp and clean.

And no doubt worth a lot of money. Their parents' savings were running lean these days. Selling this sword could solve several problems....

"You're pretty enough to pay for a whole host of repairs to Kay's baby. Not to mention all the snacks his heart desires." Ari swung it with a loose wrist. It had the perfect weight. Like it was made for her. Already, she didn't want to trade it for tortilla chips, no matter how many it could buy. "Bad idea," she muttered, putting on her best Kay impression. *"So now you've got an impulse control problem* and *a sword."*

A cracking shriek sounded from the oak. Ari turned as the trunk gave way, a crumbling dark heart of bark where the sword had been. She ran as it snapped, snarled, and cascaded into a heartless fall.

Ari had to dive out from under the whipping branches. Rolling onto her back, she breathed in gasps on the soft ground, cradling her new treasure. "What *are* you?" she found herself mumbling, running her fingers over letters etched above the hilt. It wasn't in Ari's native tongue, but it was the same alphabet Mercer pumped through the galaxy along with their crappy goods. The only language she'd spoken during the decade she'd been forcibly separated from her home planet.

Ari thought she recognized the word. It was so regal she whispered the name aloud.

"Excalibur."

AGAIN
&
AGAIN

Merlin woke up.

The ceiling of the crystal cave glimmered. He could make out, in a fuzzy way, points that stabbed the air high above his head. He reached for his glasses, smacking around on the cold floor until he found the thin wafers of glass, the horn-rims. He settled them onto his face and everything danced into focus. Merlin sighed. He didn't know why he bothered correcting his eyesight when there was no one to look at.

At this point, he preferred his nightmares to being awake. Waking up meant caring about things like Morgana and magic. It meant the hamster wheel of tragedy was spinning, and it wouldn't stop until Arthur died—again.

The chivalrous fool must have pulled the sword out of something. It wasn't always a stone. Once it had been a sewer grate, another time, a beanbag chair. Let no one say that Morgana lacked a sense of the absurd.

And now that he was awake, it was time to work. Merlin

had to go through the same steps he did in every cycle. Find Arthur. Train Arthur. Relieve his bladder of centuries of pressure. Not in that order.

He stood up, knees springy. When he looked down, his skin was wrinkle-free and baby fresh. He caught sight of himself in the nearest crystal. He was no longer old and venerable, or even middle-aged and respectable. Merlin's cheeks were round, his glasses set over eyebrows that had been stripped of their bushy character. His lips frowned back at him, the color of English roses in springtime.

The glory of his beard? Reduced to a scratch of stubble.

"Stop," he muttered to his body. "Stop doing this."

Merlin remembered taking Arthur 37 to a Mexican restaurant for his thirteenth birthday, when over fried ice cream Arthur shouted that he, like Merlin, intended to get younger every year. Merlin had wanted to throttle that particular Arthur, in a friendly and informative sort of way.

Everyone assumed Merlin had done it on purpose, but he'd never *asked* to age backward. And now he was sliding into adolescence, with a sickening anticipation of what must be in store. How old would he be when he woke up for the next cycle? Ten? Five? Would Arthur listen to a tiny child who claimed to be his mentor?

And afterward—after babyhood—would Merlin merely blink out of existence?

He moved with a stewing sense of anger. He couldn't decide if the fuming was meant for Morgana, who kept them trapped in this cycle, or Arthur, who had woken it up. Again.

Merlin found an out-of-the-way cluster of crystals to use as a toilet before he made his way through the many paths of the cave. They all led one way. *Out.* Away from his hibernation spot and into the world—such a terrible place, the world, always needing to be saved.

When he reached the cave's entrance, the portal appeared like always, as reflective as a mirror, oily black instead of silver, ready to send Merlin wherever he needed to be. He touched his fingertips to the surface. It swirled like troubled ink. "Where are you, Arthur 42?"

That number. Merlin tried not to feel the weight of forty-one Arthurs, all dead before they fulfilled their great destiny. Mankind was never truly united. And so Merlin kept spinning through the cycle, hoping that the newest incarnation of an ancient king would do the job.

Merlin hummed a calming tone and sent his mind careering toward whatever came next. Being able to sense the vague shape of the future was one of his gifts. An ill-gotten one. He shook off thoughts of the past and tried to peer forward in time, but he couldn't see himself locating Arthur or the sword.

He tried clearing his mind like a junk drawer, rattling everything out. He hopped on one foot to regain equilibrium. He even ate a sandwich, which required an enormous amount of magic to summon. "Nothing worse for future workings than low blood sugar," he muttered, devouring the ham and cheese, mustard, bread, tomatoes, and pickles with wild abandon.

But when he'd done all of that, he still couldn't see a single tiny prophetic thing. Just the back of his own eyelids, which turned out to be a boring wash of reddish black. "Is this what normal people see when they close their eyes?" he muttered. "Ridiculous."

Merlin had gotten used to having a sense of the soon-to-be,

even if he couldn't fill in the details. It kept him one step ahead of the story, always able to help Arthur. In the end, though, it came back to stab him in the eye. Because eventually Merlin saw the *end* of the story and could do nothing to stop it.

Merlin ran his fingers over the surface of the portal. He had no idea where it would send him, and that was the first new thing he could remember in ages. The next breath he pulled in shivered with possibilities.

If Merlin couldn't see anything about this cycle, did that mean the ending was unwritten?

What if this Arthur finally united mankind, and brought the cycle to a close, ending the story as triumphantly as Arthur 12 had killed that giant with three eyes, or Arthur 40 had stopped the cyborg uprising?

Then—maybe—Merlin would be free.

Stranger things *had* happened.

Merlin cleared his throat and hummed a special set of notes. He would have to track Excalibur the old-fashioned way: using his magic to call out, waiting for Excalibur to respond, then going to fetch the sword and the young boy carrying it.

The sword hummed back, and Merlin smiled. "This time is different," he whispered to himself. "This time is *ours*."

With a purposeful wave, he drew the darkness like a curtain. Testing the ground with his slipper, he stepped out, inside the circle of a stone wall, facing a downed oak tree that had the same quality as a freshly robbed grave. Excalibur was gone. Arthur 42 had taken the sword. Morgana had fled, most likely while he'd been eating that sandwich. Typical.

Merlin stood on a ruined planet, under a tetchy gray sky. As he turned in a slow circle, the tang of smoke filled his mouth.

He remembered the earlier glories of this place, a time when everything was green, and a young Arthur—the first Arthur—climbed trees and learned the names of plants, becoming a squirrel with a little help from Merlin's magic. It had been the happiest time in Merlin's absurdly long life.

Fire tore through those memories as a spaceship shot away from the ground, rising through the atmosphere in a hurry. Merlin hummed so frantically it felt like a bee had gotten trapped in his mouth. A few moments later, the sword hummed back, confirming what Merlin feared. Excalibur was in that spaceship.

Headed away from Earth.

Stranger things had *not* happened.

&

When the hum of the sword and the roar of the spaceship had faded, Merlin heard something else. What could only be mechanical destruction.

A machine rolled in, looming above the stone wall as large as a building. He searched for windows in its face. A control room, perhaps. There were no humans to be seen. They had disappeared from the landscape, leaving behind machines programmed to devour mindlessly.

As if on cue, the mechanical jaws opened wide and bit down on the stone wall. Merlin wondered if it would crumble, but instead it disappeared, swallowed by the beast.

He ducked as the machine took out another bite and another. Next, its armlike protrusions aimed thin cannons and rapidly fired into the graveyard.

Bullets!

Merlin thought he would catch one in the chest or the shoulder, and braced for impact. But the bullets lodged in the trees around him, and each went down with a splitting crack.

"Interesting," Merlin said. The only bullets he'd ever seen killed creatures of the breathing, fleshy type. Was this some kind of fast-acting poison released on impact? A vibration that interfered with the tree on a molecular level?

What would it do to a few-thousand-year-old magician?

As if ready to find the answer to that question, the machine fired at him. Merlin hummed a frantic bit of magic. He split his hands apart and the bullet that was headed for his face broke into a hundred shards, which all flew wide. To prove that he still could, he wove his fingers back together and the bullet reformed behind him, hitting another trunk with a righteous *thump*. He neatly sidestepped the falling tree. It landed with a crash.

"I don't have time to be shot at right now," Merlin said to the machine. "Now would you please point me toward the nearest spaceship? I need to get off this, as they said in the last age I lived through, *hot mess* of a planet."

The machine had no answer, and he wasted no time slipping through the hole in the stone wall, and searching the skies for the remains of that spaceship. If only he could chase after it. His brain flicked through the steps of the cycle in a panicking rhythm.

> *Find Arthur*
> *Train Arthur*
> *Nudge Arthur onto the nearest throne*
> *Defeat the greatest evil in the world*
> *Unite all of mankind*

It was one thing to be stuck on that last bit, but he had never had trouble getting past the first step. Usually Arthur was more or less waiting for him when he stepped out of the crystal cave. It looked like this new Arthur would be a different sort of fellow, harder to pin down. A gust of irritation moved through him. Could he make a spaceship? That'd take too much magic and far too much time. If only he didn't need one. If only he could...

"Fly," Merlin muttered. *"I can fly."*

It felt like the sort of thing a person should remember, but to be fair, he hadn't flown in centuries. Medieval societies would have pestered him with witchcraft charges and modern ones would have simply shot him out of the sky. But ages ago he'd loved taking off like a roman candle. He had never left Earth's atmosphere, but if he had the chance to end the cycle, it was worth any risk.

Merlin felt himself heating, sparks gathering at his feet. His body became an engine, burning itself up. He rose at a speed that was equal parts thrilling and terrifying.

He passed through a layer of mean gray clouds and emerged, damp as a trout. He opened his mouth and could only manage a gasp. The atmosphere was growing thin; soon his breath would give out. He couldn't die—the cycle had proven that more than once when he'd been skewered or burnt or thrown out a window—but he *could* spend the rest of eternity spinning in space like a broken top.

"Not ideal," he muttered.

He flicked the moisture off his fingers and hummed a bit of an old ragtime song. A second spell formed a protective layer around him, sealing him into a sort of invisible spacesuit. Ice skittered off of it as he passed the highest, coldest reaches of the sky.

With a violent *pop* of the ears, he breached the atmosphere. He spun around, still hurtling backward, to say good-bye to the planet where he had spent so many ages. "You gave me toast slathered with jam," he said, starting with the best things. "You gave me magic, and some very nice views." He probably should have kept it to happy memories, but the not-so-happy ones elbowed their way in. "You let Morgana exist. You let Arthur die. Forty-one times."

Earth stared at him, unapologetic.

"I'm not going to miss you very much, either."

He turned, moving toward a gray fingernail in the distance. The moon grew larger and brighter as he approached, and though he didn't see the spaceship that took Excalibur, he hummed and felt that the sword was close. He saw long-dead seas and the skeletal remains of a rover that had landed on the moon. The flag with its faded stars and proud stripes, which made him think of Arthur 37.

Glass domes stood across the landscape, drawing him in. There were lights and sounds—civilization, even if it looked a bit crude at the edges. The new Arthur was down there waiting, whether he knew it or not. It was time for him to find the greatest hero that ever lived.

Again.

&

He landed in the chalky dust outside of one of the moon's many domes. He didn't see a way in, and the bit of Earth's atmosphere he'd brought along was all used up. Merlin wheezed the last of his exhausted magic to create a door through the glass, which dissolved the second after he'd walked through it. He got a few wide-eyed stares from people walking past, but they blinked the strangeness away and kept moving.

That told him a great deal. These people weren't necessarily used to magic, but they were willing to accept it as long as they didn't have to move their mental furniture around too much. He wondered if this was a side effect of leaving Earth: humans also had to leave behind the certainty that they understood the universe.

He left the spaceport and entered the moon proper, which was like a dusty version of Las Vegas in its heyday, sealed under a glass dome. Bright lights, big city, terrible music. He found himself drawn by the temptations of several diners, all of which claimed to serve the best and truest versions of Earth's comfort food. Tacos. Cheese fries. Pork buns. But not even the promise of a club sandwich with slightly burnt toast and actual bacon was stronger than the hum of Excalibur. He was getting close, and his excitement hummed to match.

It came to a fever pitch in front of a black-painted building with a sign that rose from the door in black letters. DARK MAT-TER. When the door opened, people in skimpy outfits stum-bled out, releasing the thump of too-loud bass. His Arthur had taken refuge in a nightclub. Was he apprentice to the owner? Being made to wash dishes and sticky floors? Perhaps Arthur had been adopted by someone on the moon. Was Kay—Arthur's boorish brother—here, too? The cycle did vary things up a bit, just to keep Merlin on his toes.

He walked in and found people of all descriptions huddled at a bar. It was a familiar sight, rows of shiny bottles gleam-ing down, though nobody seemed to be drinking. They all had tubes up their noses. He noticed a neon sign that declared PRE-MIUM OXYGEN.

Come to think of it, Merlin wasn't breathing much better than he had been outside of the glass dome. He thought about trying the wares but had more important matters to attend to. Looking over the dance floor, he hoped to find Arthur and get out as quickly as possible. His eyes met a veritable orgy, people wearing little more than a few atoms stitched together, pressing up against each other in twos, threes, and larger clusters.

In the center of it all, swinging dark hair like a mace, dancing with the fervor of a dying sun, was a teenage girl. Merlin wouldn't have noticed her, except that she was gyrating near a sword that had been stabbed into the heart of the dance floor. A sword that he would have recognized on any planet. He looked around for a smaller person in her company. Eight to twelve years old was the normal range for a new Arthur. And definitely, always, a *boy*. Merlin waited as patiently as he could, but no one fitting the description materialized. Arthur couldn't have gone far. Only he could lift the sword; certainly he would come back.

Merlin took off his glasses, rubbed them against his robe, and shoved them back up his nose. Everything danced into focus—and the girl was staring him down with dark-browed eyes.

Perhaps he should just ask her where Arthur was hiding.

He dance-walked toward the girl. His body felt different than the last time he'd been awake, which made dancing a minefield of new sensations. His limbs were looser, and not in a helpful sort of way. His hips jerked more than he would have liked. For some reason, he kept fist-pumping the air. It felt like stuttering the same word over and over.

Nervous. He was nervous. There was far too much riding on this cycle.

The girl had gone back to twisting her long dark hair in a rope, closing her eyes and murmuring the lyrics to a high-paced, techno abomination. Once he reached her, she turned her back, showing him the sweaty line that ran down her spine. He thought about using magic to get her attention, but he didn't want to startle her. Besides, he was spent from the act of getting here. He tapped her shoulder.

She flicked her eyes open. "Nope."

"Beg pardon?" he asked.

"I'm looking for someone to make out with," she yelled over the heart-grabbing beat. "It isn't you, pal."

Merlin stumbled. He didn't want to make out with her. His hands went up in a kind of surrender, and he backed right into Excalibur.

"Watch it," she said, sweeping him aside and lofting the sword out of the dance floor.

She.

She lofted the sword.

"Arthur!" he cried, his teenage voice jerking around as much as his teenage hips.

"Still not interested," the girl called out, her rejection saltier.

Merlin watched her tuck the long blade over her shoulder and inside the back of her shirt. "It really is different this time," Merlin announced blankly. He held out his arm to her. "Would you mind pinching me? I do believe I'm stuck in a very troubling dream."

She pinched him—hard—and his nerves forced him onto his tiptoes. "All right, I'm awake!" he shouted. "I'm awake!"

FRIENDS
&
ENEMIES

Dark Matter was swollen with music and shadows. The beat raged. The combination of sweat and perfume was intoxicating, and Ari's body ached from too many days pent up on *Error* over the last three years.

Ordinarily, sneaking into a seedy club on a wayward moon would have been the highlight of her month, but Ari didn't have enough credits to get even a minute of 60 percent oxygen, Mercer was infiltrating this colony in droves, and to be plain honest, she was furious with Kay. She might have risked too much on *Heritage*—and crashed them on Old Earth—but their parents were alive. *Alive*. And her brother didn't want to even talk about finding a way to help them.

"It's impossible," he'd said. "Case closed."

The last straw, however, was the squirmy, skinny boy yelling odd things at her.

"You've grown breasts!" he shouted, staring at her chest openly. His hair was a floppy, reddish mess, and his robe smacked of a religious affiliation or the worst hangover imaginable. He didn't even seem worried that she was packing a sword.

"Not cool, friend. Move along." She shoved past him at the same moment that half a dozen Mercer associates slunk through the doorway. Ari had to hand it to the people who hacked out an existence on this colony; they didn't bow out of the way of the uniforms or the riot sticks. The associates, on the other hand, glanced around in a strict pattern—searching for Ari.

Did they know what she looked like? Or were they simply profiling for Ketchans? She'd been ducking cameras and keeping her face hidden her whole life, but it was no secret that Mercer had unorthodox ways to track people. When they grabbed the elbow of a brown-skinned, tall girl with dark hair and took a picture of her features to run facial recognition, Ari had to accept that Mercer knew more about her than a rubber knight suit could cover.

She ducked along the shadows of the wall and pointed at the first decent-looking human in sight, a dark-haired, razor-edged fluid by the alleyway exit. The one who had tried hitting on her earlier. "You," she hollered over the music. "Come with me."

The fluid pushed off the wall and shoved a triumphant thumbs-up at the person standing next to them. They left the club, entering the alley together, and Ari inhaled the cool, yet too thin, air and dropped the sword point-down in the gravel. She grabbed the pretty fluid and hauled them against the wall, mouth to mouth.

Interesting. They had a piercing on their lip she hadn't noticed in the club.

Oh, and there was a second one on their tongue. Excellent.

In her mind, this person was also Ketchan. And they weren't kissing beneath the thermal shades of a lunar colony dome, which blocked out the searing sunlight of the day and the solid freeze of night. They were on the red sands of Ketch, buffeted by sweet, dry winds while the siren birds wrote a melody for the sunset.

It was her usual daydream, her happy place.

The fluid's hands roved down her chest, her belly, hooking into the lip of her pants just as someone entered the alleyway. Ari steeled herself for the congenial threat of a Mercer associate.

"I bet you think this is terribly clever, don't you?"

Oh, gods, her gangly stalker was back.

"You have no idea what 'no' means, huh?" She turned around and was only surprised to find him staring at the sword.

"I wasn't speaking to you. I was talking to Excalibur, but now that we're on the subject of *you*, how did you come by it?"

"Found it." Ari deflated. This guy had clearly come looking for his property, although how he was storing things on Old Earth was beside her. At least it seemed like she could beat him in a chase. He couldn't have been older than her, and Ari's legs were far longer. "Finders keepers," she said, lifting the sword and her leg at the same time, about to make a sprint for it. But Ari froze on the spot. One knee hitched in the air. Looking as ridiculous as she felt.

Frozen. As if by magic. Which *was* ridiculous.

The pretty fluid took off, and she didn't blame them. In the meantime, the scrawny guy had started talking and talking, but the only word that chimed in Ari's mind was, *Magic?*

"Oh, I'm being rude." He waved his hand and Ari unfroze.

She fell to one knee, her hand wrapping around Excalibur's handle for support. At that moment, the alley door whipped open and two Mercer associates stepped out. Ari grabbed the skinny guy and tossed him up against the wall—which was as dissatisfying as the previous time had been satisfying. He squirmed like Ari's body was the worst thing he'd ever touched, and she hissed in his ear, "They can't see me." She hoped this weirdo had enough sense to play along. "They'll arrest you simply for being with me as well."

"They can't see you? Oh, you don't *want* them to see you." He whistled three fine notes. Ari felt a stiffening in the air as if something between them and the associates had hardened. They passed by without so much as glancing at Ari.

Ari stared at the skinny stranger anew. "Who are you?"

"Merlin the magician. We've met. Forty-one times already. I've been hoping one of these days you'll remember me, but alas. Perhaps I look so different now that—"

"I've met you forty-one times?"

"Not *you*, per se, but Arthur has. The you that's inside of...you."

Ari stepped close to him again, gripping the sword and squinting. She wasn't going to run him through, but the temptation to pin his hideous robe to the brick was overwhelming. "Is there something different about you? I mean, are you translating from another language or are you part android or heavily medicated? Maybe you *should* be heavily medicated?"

The question folded his expression into a tight knot. "I'm Merlin. It's not easy to explain, but I'm here, Excalibur has chosen you, and we must get acquainted before..." His pale skin tinged with an almost blue shade of terror. "Before we meet the third wheel in the cycle," he finished icily, eyeing someone behind her.

Ari twisted around, immediately backing up, pressing both of them against the wall.

A slight woman was watching from the shadows—or perhaps her dress was made from shadows. She seemed *wrong* in some indefinable way. Even more, she seemed familiar. And slightly transparent. Merlin stepped around her in all of his bathrobed glory. His lips twisted, not a smile. More of a knowing grimace. "Hello darkness, my old friend."

"Merlin," the woman said, her voice a wisp of smoke, her body just as intangible. "Look at you! You're practically a child. Not a day older than your ill-fated little girl Arthur."

Merlin *tsk*ed. "You will let me train her first, Morgana. You've never jumped the gun before. It isn't your style."

"Haven't you noticed that nothing is the same this time?" She glanced around at the moon colony and smiled. "I think you've been away too long. Too much has changed, old wizard."

"You'll find, strangely enough, that I am in my prime," Merlin said.

This so-called Morgana's eyes sharpened. "Yes, you do look too well rested. It's only fair to give you a taste of what you missed." She rushed forward faster than light, startling Ari into dropping the sword in the ashy gravel. Morgana placed a single, semi-translucent finger against Merlin's temple. He slumped to the ground, writhing.

"No! *No!*" Merlin yelled before dissolving into the stifled screams of someone with a knife in their belly. Morgana hovered beside him, and Ari ran halfway down the alley before she stopped. She didn't want to run; she wanted to know what the hell was happening, and she wanted that gods damn sword—and that weird guy's ability to give the Mercer associates the slip.

Ari walked back toward them, keeping her distance from the ethereal woman, and stooped quickly to pick up the sword. "What are you doing to him?"

Morgana looked at her as though she was surprised by Ari's presence. "You should be running. That's what all the others did the first time they saw me."

"Are you killing him?"

Morgana laughed. "I'm letting him experience what I saw when I was that miserable oak. Catching him up on the latest Manifest Destiny fever, although I do not envy the headrush."

"You were the oak?" Ari felt the logic click—the odd moment that came after freeing the sword and the familiarity she'd felt when she saw Morgana. Merlin's screams turned to pealing groans. "What did you see on Earth? What's he seeing now?"

"The latest corrosion of mankind. The death of the planet. The exodus of the privileged classes in generation ships." She cocked her head at Ari, taking in her skin and hair. "Your people, the Arabs, were the first to leave, to turn their back on all that humanity had done to the earth. Not that I blamed them. Their lot on that planet was perpetual war and grief."

"My people are from Ketch."

"Revision." Her smile twitched. "One of the finest tools the human brain possesses."

Merlin's groans turned to whimpers, staining the entire alley with his pain.

Morgana watched with ferocious intensity. "I imagine he

thinks he's past the worst. The ruthless wars for the last of the fossil fuels. The collapse of western civilization. The plagues. You'd think that would be enough, wouldn't you? But while the rich immigrated to galaxies beyond comprehension, the poor stayed behind, their bodies as diseased as the soil and air."

Merlin's eyes were furiously shut, his hands in tight fists pinned over his heart while his whimpers melted into silent tears.

Morgana's voice dropped to a whisper. "They never died as fast as I hoped. They'd live long enough to stumble through hormones. To feel like they'd invented love. To have babies. And then the babies tried to raise themselves. To live on nothing." Morgana dragged her fingernails down her own arms, making Ari's skin sting. "They tried *so hard*."

Ari didn't know how to respond.

The woman slid her eyes over Ari's entire body. "I've longed for a female Arthur," she said, her voice like silt. "But you appear as foolhardy as the others. It will be your undoing." Morgana stepped closer, even more translucent in the streetlamp than she was in the shadows. "I'm here to set you free. We will find your death this time, Arthur. I promise."

"No more Arthur crap!" Ari raised the sword with one hand. If it had imprisoned this unnerving woman once, perhaps it could be done again. Morgana backed up with a snarl, and Ari used her free hand to haul the sobbing, skinny boy to his feet and secured his arm over her shoulder. He clung to her, and she felt a surge of protective feelings for this red-haired weirdo.

Morgana bared her white teeth, her eyes a fiery black. "You will listen to me this time. You will not fall for his chivalrous nonsense. I will *make* you listen!"

Merlin shuddered from Ari's side, his face pressed into her neck. *"Ashes, ashes,"* he sang softly, *"we all fall down."*

He pointed a finger upward. A bolt of lightning crackled forth, fracturing the dome.

Morgana shrieked and evaporated. Ari stared at the searing white lines high above. If the thermal shade broke, they had seconds before they were boiled in their skin. She ran, dragging Merlin. The evacuation alarms wailed, and Ari didn't have to worry about Mercer because the streets filled with the chaos of a few thousand lives on the brink of obliteration.

&

Error's cargo door opened with a mechanical gasp, and Ari dropped the still-faintish magician unceremoniously in the cabin. She placed the sword on the table and ran toward the cockpit.

"Kay! Time to get the hell out of Dodge!"

"You think?" Kay was already slamming controls, jarring them out of the lunar docks. Ordinarily, they'd have to request to leave the spaceport and receive a set time, but right now the entire colony was stuffed in tiny spaceships, bottlenecking the exit.

Although that wasn't what froze Ari in her tracks. "Lamarack?" she asked, her voice unsteady. Kay's childhood best friend twisted around in Ari's command chair, even more stunning than the last time she'd seen them, all magnificent cheekbones and perfect dreadlocks.

They gave her a small wink, flashing golden mauve eyeshadow. "Hey, kid."

She flung herself into a rather embarrassing back hug, not caring a bit, even when Lam chuckled. "What's going on? How are you here? Are you all right?" Ari's questions fought one another. Ari and Kay hadn't made contact with their friends since their parents' arrest; Mercer was always watching. "Is Val okay? What's happening?"

"Lock your boots, Ari. We're busting out of here," Kay hollered.

Ari's buzz of good feelings at seeing one of her favorite people turned to suspicion. She hit the lock on the ankle of her magboots, holding on to the emergency bar above her head. "Kay, what the hell are you up to?"

"Evacuations first, explanations second!" her brother yelled. Kay used *Error*'s odd canister-like shape to wedge them into the mass exodus, and a ship screeched into them from the left, and the right—and the top—as their little spaceship passed through several thrown-open gates and finally through a pinhole opening in the thermal shades.

"*Error,* my sweet girl, is the heat skin holding?" Kay asked.

"YES, KAY THE BEARDLESS WONDER," the ship said in a stilted voice.

Lam laughed, and Kay turned at Ari, looking more affronted than furious. "When did you have time to reprogram my baby?"

"You sleep more than I do," Ari said with a shrug, eyes on the commotion out the starboard window. The largest dome on the colony gave way to its Merlin-inspired fractures. Human paraphernalia expanded in a rush, only to tumble lazily in the vacuum—a slow-motion explosion.

"What now?" Lam asked, their voice as soothing as Ari remembered. Lyrical, sweet. It almost made up for whatever treachery Kay was peddling. Why hadn't he told her he was meeting one of their only friends in the cosmos?

"We hide in the pack of evacuees for now," Kay said. "We'll drop you off, and then Ari and I will head into the void."

Ari bit back rising anger, waiting for the right moment—and failing as usual. "*The void?* So we finally find out our parents are alive and you want to disappear into dead space?"

Kay swung around. "You want to know why Lam's here, Ari? Because I called them from Earth. I asked them to meet us. To bring us a few supplies and the latest Mercer chatter. Do you want to know what that might be?"

Kay was glaring so hard Ari was having a hard time not punching him in the face.

"That they're looking for me?"

"Looking? Oh, no, they're beyond looking. They've put out a bulletin about *Error.* Anyone who spots this ship can report it and collect a reward. We have to get out of Mercer territory now, or we're going to end up just like my moms."

My moms. He did that sometimes. Ari knew it was not a purposeful exclusion of her from their family, but that didn't make it hurt any less. Kay knew he'd hurt her, too, but instead of gearing down, he revved up. "Tell me you didn't have anything to do with that mess back there."

Ari folded her arms over her chest. *"Don't say anything,"* Mom used to tell her. *"If you can't lie and you don't know what else to do, just…say nothing."*

"Ari!"

"A little help, friends?" a voice called out from the main cabin.

Kay's face blanched to a gray that matched his hair. "You brought someone with you?"

He rushed out of the cockpit and Lamarack stood, giving Ari a one-armed hug. "Never boring with you two, is it?"

Ari smiled back but then hustled into the main cabin. Without magboots, Merlin was floating in the air, spinning slowly toward an upside-down position that would give them an unfortunate view of whatever he was—or wasn't—wearing under that bathrobe.

"Who is this?" Kay asked, incredulous.

"I found him in a nightclub."

"What were you doing in a nightclub?"

"You said to go somewhere Mercer wouldn't expect to find me. Who goes dancing when the largest corporation in the universe is after them?"

Kay growled and grabbed Merlin's leg, stuffing him into a chair and strapping him in.

"Greetings, latest Kay," Merlin said.

"He says he knows us," Ari added.

Kay stood back, studying him. "I don't know you. I would remember . . . you."

"I'm Merlin the magician, and I come to you now at the turn of the tides." Kay stared openmouthed at this attempt at dramatic grandeur. "Well, that's Gandalf's line, but I had to try it at least once."

Kay's face puckered with annoyance. "Is this because I made you wear the smelly rubber knight costume and hide in the Arthur exhibit? You find some wacko to pretend to be Merlin to taunt me?"

Ari remembered the miserable old figure listed as Merlin. "No, but that would have been a great idea. He's the reason the dome broke. I was merely a witness."

Kay swiveled at his sister. "He broke the dome and you brought him on my ship?"

"He can do magic, Kay."

Kay scoffed and spun at Merlin. "Right, sure, do some magic, then. Go ahead."

Merlin puckered a frown. "I'm a bit tired. Being tortured will do that."

"The fuck!" Kay's eyes had found Ari's newest love. Excalibur should have been floating along with Merlin, but somehow it was stabbed through the center of the crew table, rather majestically, Ari felt like adding.

"Huh. I didn't do that. I dropped it on the table. Promise."

"Do I look stupid?" Kay asked.

Oh, what a trap. Ari stared at Kay's livid expression, his shoulders hunched to match his eyebrows. Lam chuckled from the corner. "Not any more than usual."

Kay spun on Merlin. "So, *you* did that?"

"Not in the slightest," Merlin said unhelpfully. "Excalibur has its own ideas."

Kay yanked on the sword, first with one hand, and then with both. His face grew red and puffy, and Ari could tell he was about to bust something. "Excalibur only responds to the touch of King Arthur." Merlin looked at Ari knowingly, and she felt distinctly uncomfortable.

"Don't get your unders in a twist," she told Kay. "It's only a sword." She pushed him out of the way and lifted the sword with ease.

"I loosened it for you," Kay said, breathing heavily. "Everyone saw me loosen it."

"Told you," Merlin sang, a few sparks flicking from his fingers.

"Did you see that?" Ari said, shaking Kay's shoulder. "He duped the Mercer associates. Tricked them right out of seeing us like we were invisible. What if he could help us find our moms? What if he could help us save them?"

Ari stopped herself from the last piece, the unspoken, rushing desire beneath her muscles, hidden in her blood. The desire she'd only admitted to Captain Mom once—and yet it was so powerful it had cost her moms their freedom. *What if he could get me through the barrier, back to Ketch?*

"Ari, that's impossible." Kay placed a hand on her arm, highlighting how furiously she'd been talking. Her feelings toward her brother were tight and twisted. Ari refused to give up, and Kay had given up so long ago she was starting to hate him.

"Lam, tell him we can—" Ari cut herself off. Lam was leaning in the doorway of the cockpit, wearing a long leather coat and matching breeches. Their arms hung at their sides, one of them significantly abridged. Their left hand was missing. How had she not noticed it before? "What happened to your hand?"

Lam looked to Kay, who shook his head and nodded toward the crew quarters. Lam left obediently. "Lam had an accident a few years back. They don't want to talk about it."

Ari bit back a shout. She was going to kick the crap out of her brother. They hadn't had a full-on fistfight in years, but it was coming. And this time she had a sword.

"*Lam,*" Merlin said, interrupting. "Oh! Lamarack! He's an excellent knight."

"Dude!" Kay said. "Lam is fluid. *They.*"

"Oh, apologies." Merlin's face blotched with red. "I, um, come from a society with a history of gender assumptions based on physical markers, aesthetics...et cetera."

"*Ew,*" Ari said.

"That's wicked sad," Kay added.

Merlin, at least, looked deeply ashamed. "You've no idea."

"But Kay…" Ari faced her brother, only for him to duck into the cockpit and lock the door. Ari dug through the supply closet and found Captain Mom's old magboots. She brought them to Merlin, still strapped in the chair.

He lifted his head like a puppy while she shoved his feet into them. "Oh, space shoes!"

"They're magboots. They were my mom's," Ari said. "Our parents were arrested three years ago. For harboring me, a highly unwelcome Ketchan, in Mercer territory. Kay and I barely escaped." Merlin was staring at where her shirt buckled from her skin, revealing circular scars across her entire body like a constellation of old pain. She sat up, fixed her collar. "First you mess up Lam's pronouns, now you stare at someone's scars? We've got to work on you, Merlin the magician."

"Those are quite *a lot* of scars." His voice was so sad that Ari hated it.

"I know. I was there when I got them."

"Were you tortured?"

Ari allowed this question because she'd just seen this scrawny guy crumbled to his knees by that wisp of a nightmare. "It was a kind of torture. Tell me, will that woman come back for you?"

"Oh, not for some time. Most likely."

Ari unstrapped his chest, and Merlin stood up, eye-to-eye. "Until then you're going to help me find our parents and get them away from Mercer. That's why I brought you on this ship."

"Sounds like a quest," Merlin said hopefully. "I did see this

Mercer on the moon. Very imperial in my rough estimation. With a heaping of corporate slime."

"There's more going on here, but according to my brother, I'm not strong enough to handle it." She stopped pacing. "I need to know what Lamarack and Kay are hiding."

"I can help with that!" Merlin said. The magician had an almost embarrassing need to prove that he was useful—something Ari still doubted, no matter what she'd told Kay. His stomach growled loudly enough for them both to glance at it. "I'm much more magical when I'm not so hungry. Can I have something to eat?"

"We're on strict rations," Ari said. "The pantry only opens to Kay's iris scan. He's pretty protective of his food."

"Fine. I'll work on an empty stomach, but don't blame me if your first bit of training is subpar." He stared into the air, as if speaking to the molecules. "Arthurs usually delight in being turned into birds, fish, some variety of small furry mammal. Although none of that is conducive to spying on a spaceship. You need to blend in..." Merlin hummed a bit of an old song and spun his hands around in whirligigs. "Lamarack will tell Kay what they know."

"Of course Lam will tell Kay, but how am *I* supposed to find out when I've got all these butt-nosed protectors up in my busi..." Ari's voice disappeared as she looked at her hands.

Or rather, *Kay's* hands. She stared down at herself in the shiny tabletop, Kay's blue eyes bulging. She clutched herself across Kay's stomach. "This does not feel right."

When she looked up, she gasped. Merlin had turned himself into Kay as well. "Hey!"

Merlin nodded solemnly, a weird look on Kay's face. "Before

I let you go, you must promise you will use this visage for *no other purpose* than speaking to Lamarack."

"What else would I want to do as Kay?" Ari asked, her own voice bubbling out of his thick throat. "Scare people with my breath?"

Merlin glared. Ari got the feeling that this little exchange wasn't really about her.

"Okay. I promise."

Merlin nodded and resumed his perkiness, heading to the pantry and scanning his borrowed eyeball. "Off you go," he said. "This body will wear out in about thirty-three minutes, so do hurry."

&

Ari was Kay. Well, no. She was wearing his clothes...and his body. His whole body? It took her a few moments to gather the courage, but she poked the front of her pants and yelped. "Gross!"

She shot into the bunk room and went straight for the hammock pod that carried the wide shoulders and long frame of Lamarack. "Lam," she said, before remembering to drop her voice.

Lamarack unzipped the hammock and swung their legs out. "Did you find a place to drop me off?"

"We need to talk." God, she sounded foolish when she growled like Kay, but Lam didn't seem to notice. "Without Ari around, you know?"

Lam rubbed their face with their remaining hand. "She's damn curious, and oh, my heavens, that girl has grown up in three years. Not a kid anymore, huh? She's dynamite."

Ari let herself take that one in for a moment. Her childhood crush had just called her *dynamite*. She tried to lean back casually, but Kay's body was all bulkiness, and she knocked into three hammocks in the process.

Lam eyed her warily. "We can't keep her in the dark, Kay. No matter what your moms made you promise."

Ari sharpened. *What had they made him promise?*

"How about we don't lie to her?" Ari asked forcefully. "How about we trust her to handle whatever's going on?" Lamarack lifted an eyebrow. Wow, she was doing a terrible Kay. "Tell me what...Mercer did to you. You never told me the whole story," Ari guessed. Kay could be spineless; he'd rather have a snack than the harsh details.

Lam squinted, but they kept talking. "After your moms were arrested and you came to Pluto...and my parents turned you away, they allowed Mercer to lock down the docking bay until associates could pick you two up."

"Your parents called Mercer on us?" Ari asked, her voice tight. "Your *parents?*" She sat on the edge of the hammock, Kay's too-wide body making her bump into Lam.

"I was so mad, Kay. I snuck into the tower and hit the fuses so you could fly out. Mercer was going to send me to some work camp as punishment. My parents paid them off, and I ended up with a reminder of my disobedience." Lam rubbed their left wrist. "I was lucky."

Only Lam would look at the loss of their hand as luck. Always optimistic. Always looking for beauty, for hope. After all, that's why she'd set her young eyes on them. When everyone else was grumbling about water shortages at knight camp or static storms coming off the desert on Lionel, Lamarack would find an odd flower growing between the rock walls. They'd pull her over to see it. Proof of life, no matter what.

Lam squeezed Ari's Kay-shoulder. "The bounty on your head was part money, part violent threat. The worst one my parents ever saw come through the militarized associates."

"Oh." Ari had always known that they were marked, but this? They were being specifically—and expensively—hunted. "It's a miracle they haven't caught us yet."

"I bet they've been monitoring you." Lam folded their arms over their chest. "Waiting to see if Ari has contacts outside Ketch. Or inside."

Contacts? Ari would kill for a few Ketchan contacts. She kept that to herself.

"And now we have no choice but to run into the black," Ari said quietly.

Lam shook their head. "You promised to let me off first, man. I need to get to Lionel. They're going to track that call you made from Earth, and they know I helped you in the past. When they can't find me, they'll go after my brother, Kay. I have to warn him."

"Val?"

"He's a fancy type on Lionel now. An adviser to the queen. Can you believe that?"

"Yes." Ari imagined the boy who had been her favorite brand of childhood mischief. "He could rig any system by its own rules. It was his specialty."

"What if they take more than Val's hand, Kay? Can you live with that?"

"No," she said slowly, processing. No, she could not live with one of her very few friends being tracked down because Mercer had a renewed interest in her existence.

Lamarack put their hand on her shoulder. "You don't look so good. Your skin is grayer than your hair."

Ari blasted out of the room, terrified by how much her brother's boots crashed on the grated walkway with each step. She must have been a solid hundred pounds heavier than usual, but that wasn't important. She slammed her fist on the cockpit door. Over and over.

Her brother answered angrily—before he stared. And blinked. Then he started screaming. "I've lost it! I've lost my damn mind!"

"You haven't. Shut up. I'm Ari."

"Ari?" Lam asked. They'd followed from the bunk room and were now turning from Kay to Ari-Kay. "What the actual fuck…"

Merlin-Kay came running in, orange cheese flavoring stuck all over his face and hands. "Why are we screaming?"

Kay pointed to Merlin-Kay and started screaming all over again.

"Merlin!" Ari yelled over the sound. "Change us back."

"It takes less magic if it wears off," he said.

"Change us back, little wizard!" Ari cried.

"I prefer *magician*." Merlin wiggled his fingers and muttered. Ari felt the full body itch again, and then she relaxed into her slender and suddenly gangly frame. She took one deep breath, enjoying her own body before she pushed her brother in the chest with both hands, shoving him into the cockpit and shutting the door behind them.

"What in the hell just happened?" Kay blustered.

"I told you Merlin has magic. And you know I don't lie," Ari snapped. Kay opened his mouth, but she talked over him. "Val is in trouble, Kay. Because of me. We're going to Lionel. *Now*."

"We can't take on Mercer in a retired lifeboat. Our best bet is to escape. Val has people who will look out for him."

"What did our moms make you promise before they were arrested?" she asked. Kay looked over at her, a painfully slow move. "I want the truth. I can handle it."

"The truth is that you're reckless, and everyone who loves you gets punished," Kay blustered. Ari's face stung as though he'd slapped it. He squeezed his eyes shut. "I didn't tell you about Lamarack because I didn't want you to feel like it was your fault. All because you..."

Ari waited for a word that could possibly cap that sentence. When Kay couldn't find it, she finished for him. "Exist?"

"Yeah," he said sadly. "Lam thinks that going to Lionel will help Val, but it'll just prove to Mercer that Val is leverage. If we don't go, Val will be safer. Lam should understand that."

"You're being a coward, Kay."

Her brother punched her in the arm. Hard. "Mercer will arrest us. Send us to a work camp or prison. Or worse." Ari searched her brother's eyes. Desperation made them glow, or maybe that was just *Error*'s cockpit lights. "We've got four people on board and only enough supplies for two. We aren't going to get far. We have to make some choices."

"We eat Merlin."

Kay barked a surprised laugh. "Too gamey."

"So we don't run. We make a stand. We have a magician now. He can change our faces like he did a few minutes ago."

Kay's head jerked up. "Really?"

Ari stared out the window. Either the black of space or her frozen fear had finally gotten to her. "Or I'll go away. By myself. Maybe they'll follow me and leave you all alone."

"We're staying together, Ari." Her brother leaned closer, pulling her attention from the void outside…and the one inside. "Ten years ago, I had a dream that I could hear a kid crying. When I woke up, I told our moms that the junked ships we were passing weren't empty. Someone was on them. They listened to me because, well, you and I have the best parents in this damn universe."

Ari's heart beat wildly. Kay never talked about the day he'd found her. They didn't need to talk about it; the sharpness of the memory still cut.

"We flew to those junked ships, and I climbed through them until I found you in that empty water heater, all starving." He opened his hand to Ari, showing off the circular scar on his palm from one of the water heating coils. It matched the scars all over Ari, the lifelong souvenirs from her time trapped at the bottom of that barrel. "*That* was magic, Ari. We were meant to find you. To keep you safe."

Ari ran her fingers down Excalibur, aching to use it to make some sort of difference in this messed-up universe. "But I can't live knowing that our parents are suffering, Kay. Can you?" She took a shaky breath. "And we can't leave Val to face Mercer."

Kay shook his head, looking like Captain Mom. They had the same roughly blond hair that skewed gray. Captain Mom had been their leader, and now Kay was in charge, but he was too soft. Too much like Mom, a squishy hug of feelings. "Ari, before Mercer took them, they made me promise one thing. *One.* To keep you safe. They traded their freedom so we could get away." He leaned over the control panel. "If I jeopardize that, they'll never forgive me. *I* will never forgive myself. So we're going to Tanaka. Or the Ridges, if *Error* can make it."

"I love you, but you leave me no choice." Ari sighed deeply. And then she kicked her brother's ass, wrestled him out of the cockpit, and used Excalibur to wedge the door closed.

"No turning back," she muttered, laying in the course for Lionel.

MEAD
&
CONSEQUENCES

The winds blew strong on this new planet, and Merlin's robe nipped at his ankles like a terrier. When he turned in one direction, he saw *Error*, surrounded by desert of the tan, sandstone variety. When he turned the other, he saw a page ripped from his own past. Tournament rings. Pennants. Thatched houses, piping smoke, a lively marketplace.

Merlin grabbed Arthur—girl Arthur—no, *Ari*—as she passed him.

"This place..." He pointed to the city, then lapsed into song lyrics, a habit that bubbled up when he was nervous. " 'Is this the real life? Is this just fantasy?' "

"*This* is the place where medieval dreams come true, better known as Lionel. We used to come here every summer so that Lam and Kay could smash about like would-be heroes at knight camp." Ari rested a hand on Merlin's shoulder. "From the ecstatic look on your face, I'm guessing you'd like me to sign you up."

Merlin stammered, trying to figure out exactly what he felt. It was strong, if nothing else. This place tugged on inner strings that connected him to the first Arthur, the start of the cycle.

"I know you get mad at planets, but don't break this one, okay?" Ari thumped him twice.

"That was a moon!" he cried weakly.

"Well, Lionel has a delightful new reputation of incensing Mercer," Ari said, looking no small part proud. "Almost like home."

Merlin followed her across the sands, taking stock of what he knew about this universe. First, Mercer was the bad guy, obviously, run by an ominous figurehead known as the Administrator. He was so ominous, in fact, that Ari had caught Merlin chuckling along with him to one of his infectious pop-up ads and taken away the device he'd been screening. Second, Ari's home planet was called Ketch. Her people had bad-mouthed Mercer and were punished by an impenetrable barrier that kept everyone—including Ari—out. Merlin was no small part disappointed; it sounded like twenty-first-century buffoonery.

Kay trudged beside Merlin, one hand cupped over the eye Ari had blackened in their fight over control of the ship. He resembled a low-budget pirate. Lam, who had been nothing but easygoing on *Error*, exhibited nerves as they neared the grand painted gates of the city, right before sweeping up a figure who leaned against the left gate. Lam clasped their equally beautiful brother in a tight hug that pulsed out a few groans.

Ari wasn't far behind. She and Val curtsied—which made them both laugh—and then Ari rammed into him with another punishing hug. Kay's greeting made it clear the unnecessarily elaborate handshake had not died out. And then the one called Val came to the end of the line.

Merlin held out his arms in a tight, tentative V. "Are we hugging?"

Val laughed. "What have you brought with you?" he asked Ari, eyeing Merlin. "Is this a setup?"

"What? No. What?" Merlin's words were tiny, sharp cut-outs of panic.

"The stranger in robes doth protest too much," Val said.

"Shakespeare!" Merlin shouted, as if this were a tossed salad of embarrassment and quiz bowl.

Val's eyebrows inched up, lips quirking. Was he impressed? Amused? "I'm Val."

Merlin's cycle-driven brain filled in the rest of that name with ease. *Percival.* Lamarack's brother, and another of Arthur's knights, peerless and loyal. Merlin was glad to have him in the mix. Although, *him* might not be the right word. Merlin didn't want to make the same mistake he had with Lamarack. "Are you a young man or a young woman or...a fluid or...?"

"A set or a non?" Val filled in smoothly. "The first one, for the most part. He/him is fine. You?"

"The first one!" Merlin said, confident he'd gotten one thing right.

"Well then, welcome to Lionel, *young man*," Val said, his expression on the verge of laughter.

Merlin couldn't figure out what was so funny until he realized they were the same age. The idea stunned Merlin into studying Val more closely. He had Lam's smooth dark skin, but instead of Lam's dreadlocks, his tightly shaved black hair showcased the long line of his neck, the adorable protrusion of his ears. Merlin's blood fizzed in a dangerous and unpredictable manner. It took him a moment to realize he was having his first run-in with teenage hormones.

"This is the part where you tell me your name," Val said, layering the words with a smile.

"That's Merlin," Ari said, pulling Val's focus and making Merlin eternally grateful. "Now that we're all such good friends..."

Val put up a *stop-before-you-hurt-yourself* hand. "I know Mercer is after you, Ari. Do you honestly think that I work for the queen of this planet without knowing who is and isn't wanted by that vile corporation?" He pointed to a sign behind him, just inside the gates, hand-splashed with red lettering. ABSOLUTELY NO MERCER GOODS ON PREMISES.

"And I know you think you need to rescue me, but I can't run off and leave Lionel." Val rubbed his eyebrows. "I have a rare and exotic disease called *a job*. I know none of you've experienced that, so let me break it down. One of the symptoms of having a job is that I have to stay on the planet where the job is. Speaking of, I have an important tournament to work. I *should* send you back to *Error,* but you can stay. Just don't tell the queen I said that."

Merlin could tell from the way Ari nodded that she already had ideas about how to pry Val from the face of this planet.

Textbook Arthur.

Merlin followed everyone through the gates, not unhappy to stay. Step two—*train Arthur*—would have better results on a medieval planet than a miniature spaceship. He needed

Ari to embrace her destiny. Though after what he'd just been through, *embracing* seemed like a tall order. He would settle for an awkward handshake with destiny.

They wove around women who sold things to the incoming crowds. Corsets pushed their bosoms halfway to their chins, roses and daggers tucked into significant cleavage. "Nice robes," one said in a husky tone, and Merlin perked with delight. "You order those special?"

"They were made by the enchanted spiders of the Near Woods," Merlin said.

"Good for you," the woman said, tossing him a free map and a package of nuts. Merlin didn't recognize the half-moon shape, but they were browned and buttery. He ate them in handfuls as they reached a market lined with open-faced shops. The wind whipped from a new direction, bringing the tantalizing aromas of roasting meat, tangy mead, and spiced stews.

Best of all, a castle hewn from Lionel's tan stone sat at the far end of the market, swiped from one of Merlin's most nostalgic daydreams. And yet, as he studied the structure, he found it different from traditional castles. The framework of the towers and crenellations seemed to be metallic. The moat sloshed with a dark, queasy liquid—definitely not water. But the magician's old heart perked nonetheless. Merlin wanted to know who lived in that castle. He might be on step two of the cycle, but that didn't stop step three from pushing its way into his thoughts.

Nudge Arthur onto the nearest throne.

"Ari," he said, "do you happen to know who rules this planet?"

She shrugged. "Some queen they bring out on a palanquin. She's older than the sun."

"Not anymore," Lam said. "Val got a promotion when the new monarch took the throne."

"Who is it?" Kay asked, tipping a paper cone to pour roasted nuts into his mouth.

"You don't know?" Lam asked.

Kay crunched the nuts and shook his head.

"We've been a little busy hiding out to keep up with planetary politics," Ari said.

"You really don't know who the queen is?" Val asked. "Ohhhh, this is going to be fun."

Lam braced their hand on Ari's shoulder. "I'm putting her out of her misery. It's Gwen."

Merlin wished that Lam was holding *him* up. The weight of the past poured down on him, making it hard to breathe. His thoughts swam away, as if trying to escape that name—an emergency evacuation of sorts.

"My old girl?" Kay said whimsically, surprising Merlin out of his panic.

"*Your* girl?" he blustered.

"He asked her out once during knight camp," Lam added. "Not successfully. But it's hard to let go of the past." Merlin knew that all too well. He was the poster boy of knowing that. Ari's expression dragged him away from self-pity. She wasn't chewing her bottom lip; she was eating it. Lam noticed as well. "Ari and Gwen never did get on well. Talk about sparring, their verbal duels were majestic in intensity."

"We worked it out," Ari said, her voice cramped and odd. "No big deal."

"Personally, I love when Ari tries to lie," Kay interjected. "It's like watching a dog bite its own tail."

"Gwen," Merlin tried, in a last-ditch effort to avoid the worst of the cycle's pain. "Gwen...eth? Gwen...dolyn?"

"Gweneviere," Val said. "*Queen* Gweneviere."

"That's right up your game, huh, magician?" Kay asked, delighted. He turned to Val. "Is she in the market for a consort? I'll bet marrying Gwen would get Mercer off our back."

Val laughed heartily. "Oh, yes, Kay, do place yourself in the running. The sign-up for consideration is right over there." He pointed to the tournament ring. "All you'll have to do is defeat the queen's champion—who has destroyed a hundred and seventeen contenders to date—but I bet you're up for it. Tell me, how did you get that black eye?" Val winked in Ari's direction, as if he knew her handiwork a mile away.

Trumpets bayed, and a uniformed person announced that the tournament would begin in three hours' time.

"*Three hours?*" Kay cried. "We can't wait around that long. Mercer will eventually catch up to us. What are we going to do? Challenge them to a duel?"

"That'll be short enough," Ari said breezily. "You and Lam failed knight camp, what, four summers in a row?"

Merlin's hopes scattered like a cone of perfectly roasted nuts in the mud. "They *failed?*"

"Who needs to be a knight when you can be an outlaw?" Lam asked with a rueful laugh, spinning back to Val. "I know this is not your preferred life path, but you need to come with us. Mercer is not kidding." No one mentioned Lam's hand; no one had to.

As much as Merlin wanted to stay on Lionel, he didn't want Ari facing Mercer until she was ready.

That was how his Arthurs died.

Val sighed. "Come to the tournament. Mercer isn't invited, and if they do crash the party, Gwen will knock them out of the sky. *After,* I'll think about going with you. But only if my queen agrees. She might have given Ari a run for her money, and tossed handkerchiefs at Kay," he shuddered, "but she's the best damn sovereign Lionel's ever had. She needs me."

Ari clenched with determination. Merlin couldn't help thinking she'd need very different weapons to face this Gweneviere. He could see only one thing to be done: prevent them from interacting. Merlin could do that, couldn't he? He was a magician, after all. And Gweneviere breaking Arthur's heart was a repetition Merlin was most keen on avoiding. This cycle was already so different. This could be different, too.

No devastating heartbreak. No finding this Arthur on all fours, weeping so hard that not even one of Merlin's famous indoor downpours could conceal it. He imagined Ari's predecessors in that broken position; updating it with her image made him sick.

Of course, there had been one Arthur who had no interest in Gweneviere.

And Merlin had made him weep the hardest.

Merlin mustered his most mature voice. "We should avoid this queen's business."

"Agreed." Val looked them over one by one. "Another thing. If you want to stick around, you need to change. Plenty of shops here sell appropriate garb."

"*Garb?*" Kay asked, as if the word was making him as uncomfortable as the clothes inevitably would.

"Your fiery-haired friend can keep his robes," Val added. It took Merlin a quick beat to realize Val meant *him.* He kept forgetting his hair was red instead of gray. That bother aside, he felt more than a little proud that Val had singled him out— or at the very least, his attire.

"He's the only one with good clothes?" Kay asked, pointing at Merlin. *"Him?"*

"The rest of you look so…future-y," Val said in a distinctly pained way. "Come find me at the tournament ring when you can blend in."

&

Merlin waited in a small courtyard as everyone else got dressed in the public restrooms. The result was a buffet of Old Earth costumes. Kay wore highly anachronistic cargo shorts that would have made him look like any white American teenage boy of the late twentieth century if they hadn't been paired with a billowing linen blouse and bracers on his wrists. Lamarack looked slightly better in dark-blue leggings and a tunic that showed off how broad they were in the shoulders. Ari had picked a shirt with a crosshatch of leather cords at the chest, and a shiny leather pauldron.

"Hey, that thing on your arm looks cool," Kay said. "Let me wear it."

She dodged Kay's unsubtle grab. Merlin had never seen a Kay-and-Arthur pair act so much like true siblings. It was… refreshing, really. Ari patted the fitted and oiled scales of the pauldron, then drew Excalibur from the sheath on her back— another gift of the Lionel market. "At least *she* fits in," Ari said, staring at the sword with the sort of approval Merlin wished she would point at him.

"Yes," Kay said. "That's what I'm worried about. How your sword feels." He stomped around, facing Merlin. "It's new-face time."

"Pardon?" Merlin asked.

"We have new clothes," Kay said, slowing his explanation to an insulting trot. "Now give us new faces so Mercer won't be able to pick us out of the crowds."

"My magic isn't boundless," Merlin said.

"What exactly can it do?" Ari asked, sitting down on the stone wall of the courtyard, one knee up, casual in a way that made it clear she cared far too much about the answer.

Merlin put on his best all-knowing voice, dry and authoritative as the pages of an old tome. "I have the ability to warp existing physical realities. My magic can be drained, of course. Which means that after flying from Earth to moon, creating a lightning bolt, and making extra Kays, I'm a tad exhausted." He hummed again, and a small pink lizard appeared in his palm.

"Aw, cute," Lam said, patting the lizard with a finger.

Merlin's lips pinched. "I was trying to make a dragon." He shook his head, the lizard disappearing in a puff as Lam drew back. "That's the other bit. My magic is *temporal,* which means that anything I create has to be sustained by me."

"Sorry, Kay," Ari said, slapping him in the blouse. "No permanent face replacements."

Lam winked at Ari. "We shouldn't have gotten his hopes up for trading that one in."

"We'll just have to fight off Mercer the old-fashioned way." She leaped to standing on the stone wall and took a few practice stabs at the air. Light streamed along Excalibur's blade and her long hair, which she'd freed from its ties. Even if she hadn't been covered in golden rays, she would have looked heroic to Merlin. Arthur always looked most like a storybook hero *before* he had to face the true darkness of the cycle.

"Let's begin our training," he said nervously, trumpets lighting the air. It took him a moment to realize that the trumpets were not just in his head but thundering across the village grounds.

"Two hours to the tournament," Lam said, interpreting the horns.

"Hours, truly? I've even heard you mention years," Merlin noted. "Are these not time constructs of Earth?"

"Old Earth calendar," Kay said, fighting with the laces on his period-appropriate boots. "It's the standard on most planets and in space."

"And you all speak English," Merlin said. "Mighty interesting surprise there." Ari pointed her sword at Merlin and spouted a string of words he didn't quite catch, in a language he was only somewhat familiar with. "And you speak Arabic, apparently."

"I speak Ketchan," Ari corrected.

"We're speaking Mercer, dude," Lam said.

"Beg your pardon?"

"This language is called Mercer."

Merlin leveled his British shoulders. "It is *not*. Or at least it was not."

"Ketch is the only planet that's been able to hold on to their culture. We speak Mercer because that's the only language Mercer lets us access," Lam said, darkly. "Which is supposedly unifying."

"What a business, this Mercer. To co-opt cultures like a fish swallowing smaller fish..." Merlin shivered. "I don't like it." He glanced up at the spot where Ari had been sitting a moment ago. "Where did Ari go?"

"She's tricky," Kay said. "Impulsive. Impossible. And definitely not interested in your 'training.'"

Merlin hauled himself up and over the stone wall, falling down on the other side. Ari was disappearing between two buildings in the distance, and he followed her. He caught up with her behind what appeared to be horse stables. She stood, facing a blank corner, taking a picture with her watch. "Have you stumbled into a fond memory?"

"No," Ari said, whipping around. "An annoying one."

"I know your strength. It is a dedication to absolute truth. Quite Arthurian."

"Quit it with the Arthur stuff, will you?" Ari was taller— and possibly a touch older—than Merlin. But none of that changed what he needed to tell her. Merlin took a deep breath.

"You are the forty-second reincarnation of King Arthur." He kept going, ignoring the sharp cut of her doubting eyes. "You can wield Excalibur. Only Arthur can do that. The Lady of the Lake forged that sword for a hero. You *are* that hero, Ari. Or at least, you're the latest version."

Ari continued to stare.

"I won't lie," Merlin said. "This bit usually goes better... and you're usually younger." Most boys secretly believed they should be heroes: the stories told them so. Thus, when Merlin came along and delivered the destined news, he was usually greeted with something between nervous excitement and ecstasy. Arthur 2 had cried. Arthur 27 had cried. Most of the

Arthurs in between had at least thanked him. Ari was blinking at Merlin like he was a flickering lightbulb. "This universe needs help, Ari! Mercer is clearly cancerous, and people are suffering. King Arthur is destined to defeat threats to peace and unite all of mankind."

"Humankind," Ari said automatically.

The back of Merlin's neck prickled with embarrassment. He decided this was not the best time to mention that *he* needed Ari—needed an Arthur who could bring this cycle to a close. To stop him from aging backward before he required diapers.

Ari crossed her arms. "What if I'm not interested in living somebody else's life?"

Merlin nodded. He'd wanted to believe they would work together to defeat the cycle, but if that wasn't in the cards, he would play a different hand. He crossed his own arms—alarmed at how skinny they'd grown. "You aren't getting a bit of my magic for your parents' prison break unless you agree to train with me first."

That was for her own protection, as much as for Merlin's benefit. Ari would die if she went storming into a prison with nothing but love for her adoptive mothers.

"Fine," Ari said, waving her hand. "We'll train." Her eyes glimmered behind the casual acceptance. "But you should know I was a conscientious objector at knight camp."

They returned to the courtyard where Lam and Kay had begun sparring, the clash of cheap metal ringing out.

"Get this," Ari shouted over the din of poor swordsmanship. "Merlin wants to train me to be like your hero, Kay. King Arthur."

"I never said he was my hero. I said I liked his exhibit on *Heritage*." He turned his sword at his sister and Ari whipped out Excalibur to meet his blade. They tangoed for a little while before Merlin had all the proof he needed that swordplay was not Ari's weak point.

"No more bickering. Your training begins now. Step one, best Lamarack," Merlin ordered. He was surprised when Ari listened, spinning in a way that made Lam dive out of the way.

Instead of reaching for their sword, Lam caught Ari around the waist. "Hey," they said, head lodged under Ari's arm. "Has anyone ever told you that you look excellent from this angle?"

Ari blushed, hesitated, and Lam knocked her sword free, sounding a victorious cry.

"That was cheating," Ari huffed, amused but unwilling to admit it.

"Lam used their charm," Merlin said. "It's a perfectly good way to disarm someone."

"So, you want me to flirt past the prison guards? Make out with Mercer Associates?"

Now it was Merlin's turn to huff. "If you can get past someone you know, you will be able to bypass greater obstacles. It's harder to face down friends than enemies. Friends know you better and can use that knowledge against you."

Merlin didn't have friends, so he never got destroyed in that particular manner. Arthur was always hurt by the people he loved best. Gweneviere. Lancelot. His children—who had the unnerving tendency to kill him—starting with Mordred in that very first cycle. Come to think of it, Ari was a little too old. "You don't have any children, do you?"

"What?" Ari asked, blanching under her tan complexion. "*No.*"

"Geez, dude," Lam said.

Kay leaped in with his sword, too eager for a rematch, his black eye glistening plummy purple. He let out a blunt shout and charged Ari like an angry goat. At that moment, Merlin noticed a procession coming down the street that bordered the courtyard. A palanquin carried someone important—probably royal—toward the tournament.

Gweneviere.

The procession was headed right toward them. Merlin's magic sparked out of him in a frantic burst. Ari, Kay, and Lam froze on the spot.

Within the small, tented carriage, he saw a young woman in a blue silk dress with dark hair pinned in an elaborate, braided style. She was waving at her subjects and tourists alike, and Merlin found himself ducking to avoid her gaze, the one that ruled everything it landed on. He noted that—by the seemingly undying Earth standards—she was of mixed Asian and European heritage.

Something about her felt familiar, but then Gweneviere was always regal, beautiful, terrifying.

When the procession was well out of sight, Merlin unfroze his knights. Ari squinted at him. "What was that?"

"Sneeze," Merlin said.

Ari shrugged, then drove her entire weight into the softest part of Kay's belly. They wrestled without honor. Kay tugging hanks of Ari's hair, Ari yanking at Kay's belt, pulling his cargo shorts low enough to produce an unseemly crack. But it was a final kick to his shin and a few crunched toes that allowed Ari to run around him to the far end of the courtyard, doing a victory dance that was mostly knees and elbows.

Merlin shook his head, even as Ari celebrated. "You won, but you failed. You used your brawn, not your brain, Arthur!" She looked stung, and he corrected. "Ari. Your muscles will only get you so far. Your brain can get you everywhere. It can get you anything, if you *use* it."

"I do use my brain."

"Oh?" Merlin feigned. "Remind me, did you convince your brother to come save your friend, or did you beat him into submission?"

"I just needed him out of the way," Ari said with a bluntly honest shrug.

In that moment, Merlin discovered the weakness of his new Arthur. Ari wasn't a mindless brute or bully. But she *was* boldly impatient, and when she wanted to fix something she did it the fastest way possible.

"What will you do when your impulses aren't enough?" Merlin asked. "Not all problems are best solved alone."

The trumpets sounded again, and Ari's eyes hardened with challenge. Merlin was encouraged by this look, and a little frightened by it.

"Nearly tournament time," Lam said. "We have to go meet Val."

Merlin hesitated. Gweneviere would be at the tournament, but the likelihood of Ari meeting her face to face was minuscule. She would sit in the queen's box, and Ari would be one of a thousand commoners underfoot. Besides, Merlin hadn't seen a good joust in millennia.

&

The tournament ring was packed when they arrived. Lam used their watch to send a message, and a few minutes later Val appeared from the great churning mass of tourists, many of them wearing the colors of the knights they favored.

Merlin noted how many people sported black feathers. "The black knight is popular."

"Odds are always on the black knight," Val said.

"Remember *our* black knight?" Lam asked, their dark brown eyes glazing with nostalgia, and something a bit steamier.

"*So* hot," Kay crowed over the crowd.

"Oh, for heaven's sake," Merlin said. Lam and Kay went in search of turkey legs, and somehow Merlin and Val ended up walking down a row of stalls.

He steered Merlin gently, and Merlin felt five fingertips like a bright constellation on his back. "I don't know how Ari and Co. got you on board, or if you're planning to stick around, but if you're still here tonight, you should go to Knight Club. I'm always there after a tournament."

Merlin watched Val surveying the crowd. "Don't misunderstand, I love a pun as much as the next magician, but you have a nightclub? Here?"

"We're only as period appropriate as we want to be," Val explained. "For instance, not many queens in medieval Europe had black advisers, but that's no excuse to keep doing things the same old shitty way, now, is it?"

"That makes a great deal of sense. I'd still like to have a word with your sign painter, though. The dragons are wrong." Arthur 4 and Arthur 7 had both faced dragons—well, one had technically been a wyvern. "There should be less smiling and more scale rot."

Val ducked his head and laughed, Merlin's attention caught on the curve of his eyelashes.

"What's funny?" Merlin asked, his voice gruffer than he meant it to be.

Val leaned in as the rest of the crowd broke into cheers. They were so close their bodies were nearly brushing, and yet Val had to yell to be heard, his voice hot on Merlin's neck. "I asked you out and you're talking about scale rot!"

Forget constellations—Merlin's body lit up like the night sky.

"Hey," Kay said, reappearing, not seeming to notice or care that Merlin and Val had been talking. He'd squirted his blouse with turkey juice and shucked it off, revealing a "Lionel is for Lovers" T-shirt underneath. "My mouth is all salty. Where's ye olde water fountain?"

Val nodded to one of the servers, saying, "Official state business! Queen's adviser!" and tossed a coin to a person who caught it in ample cleavage and passed out a round of drinks. Cleavage was certainly a theme on this planet.

"Mead?" Kay asked, nuzzling into his cup. "Thanks for the free upgrade."

Lam downed one in less than ten seconds and started in on another. Merlin grasped a flagon, taking in the crisp-sweet smell and the deep golden tone. He had never been asked on a date, in any of his lifetimes. He didn't know what to do.

So he drank.

The first sip danced on his tongue. The second one turned his stomach into a festival.

Ari watched them all guzzle. "I'll take water."

Val leaned toward her like they'd reached a conversational bridge he didn't want to cross. "Truth is, we have a severe water shortage on our hands. Mercer is hovering at the outer edges of the system, withholding our latest hydration shipment."

"Wait," Kay said, holding up a finger before he swallowed a mouthful of mead. "You get your water from *Mercer?* What happened to 'absolutely no Mercer goods—'"

"If you have a better suggestion, I'd love to hear it," Val said, sipping from his own flagon, wincing as if the honeyed drink was sour. "Mercer is the only company with potable water to trade in the galaxy. They've made sure of it. In return, for their terrible water, we have to give them a small percentage of our natural resources. They want more, of course."

"They want everything," Ari corrected.

The crowds pushed them deeper into the tournament ring, and soon they were closed in, dozens of people on all sides. Val peeled away, calling out, "I'll find you after!" The mead that had seemed brilliant a minute ago was now buzzing through Merlin, turning him anxious.

"Were you flirting with my friend?" Ari shouted over the roar of the crowds.

"What?" Merlin asked, feeling as caught as a rabbit shivering in a hutch. Something about Ari demanded honesty—maybe because she seemed incapable of lies. "I don't know how to *flirt* with anyone," Merlin answered, which was the truth. "I'm too busy helping Arthur."

"So if I refuse this whole destiny thing, you'll go out with a cute boy?"

Merlin wished it was that simple. He opened his mouth to say so, but Ari was smiling her mischief at Merlin for the first time since she'd dragged him onto *Error*. Merlin could feel how real and valuable that smile was. It could have been currency on a lonely planet.

The trumpets hit their highest notes, and Merlin turned to watch as horses filled the ring. At first he worried he was drunker than he'd previously calculated. The creatures appeared to be made of metal, with stiff shining flanks, clanging hooves, and electric-blue eyes. None of Merlin's traveling companions seemed troubled by their presence, though, and Merlin tried to play along as the riders circled and a man with brass lungs announced their names.

"Whoa," Kay said, pointing out a girl with aggressively blond hair, black armor, and a hard seat, posting around the ring to deafening cheers. "That's her! That's the black knight!"

"The one who handed your asses to you at camp?" Ari asked, looking at Lam and Kay.

"Yeah," Lamarack said. "She's so...awesome." They sighed. Kay sighed.

Merlin had ungenerous thoughts about his F students. Especially as he watched the black knight break into a canter, soaring like an arrow from one end of the ring to the other. She swirled her sword through the air and the crowd cheered as if it had been lit on fire. How did Merlin get a knight like *that* for Ari's team?

The great doors around the ring closed. Merlin's cares felt as though they'd been left outside. The tournament began, and the black knight took down several opponents with ease: the green knight, the crimson knight, the rainbow knight. The crowd whooped. Merlin whooped along with them. He was just relaxed enough to hum a few notes and dance another flagon of mead from a passing tray into his hands. Ari gave him a sharp look. Merlin tried to look innocent as he sipped. The drink disappeared at an alarming rate. It stripped away the last of his worries. He even thought about asking Ari if they could stay long enough to visit this Knight Club.

Then a hard shadow passed over the crowd, and everyone looked up. "What?" Merlin asked. "Is it going to rain?"

"That was no storm cloud." Ari grabbed Merlin's flagon and downed the last few sips. The tournament had paused unnaturally, but now the clash of the fighters came back at full volume.

"What color is our doom today?" Kay asked.

"Want to take bets?" Lam asked. "Loser buys the winner another drink?"

"What are they talking about?" Merlin whispered to Ari.

"White Mercer ships are made to be seen. That's what they use when they want you to pay attention. Black ships blend with space. That's the nothing-to-see-here option."

"White," Lam said.

"Definitely black," Kay argued.

They all looked up—at a pair of enormous shapes taking over the sky. A white ship *and* a black one.

"That's...I've never seen that before," Lam said.

Betting dissolved, drinks suddenly forgotten. Ari turned to Merlin. "Can you hide me?"

The trick Merlin had used in the alley on the moon wouldn't work here—Ari could be seen from too many angles. He thought about trying to magic her straight out of the ring, but he couldn't see where she would land. Then again, maybe Merlin didn't need to get Ari *out* of the tournament. Maybe she needed to be deeper *in*.

He pulled her close and whispered, "I know a place no Mercer agents will look for you. And, what's more, you can continue your training. Think of it as a two-for-one special!" He hummed a harmony to the blare of the trumpets, sprinkled his fingers through the air—

And Ari vanished.

WINNERS & LOSERS

The cyborg horse between Ari's legs was close to overheating. That was her first thought. Her second was to wonder what was so heavy. Ari glanced at the long, unwieldy lance in her right hand and then the shield bound to her left forearm.

Merlin had magicked her into one of the knights' suits of armor.

In the jousting ring.

Shit.

She reeled back, trying to see the sky through the narrow eye slit of her helmet. The salt-and-pepper Mercer fleet was gone. A trumpet rang out, dragging her attention back to the ring. In the center, a hook-backed man dressed in green and gold jester fanfare dropped a red flag, and the crowd screamed their cheers. Kay's beloved former crush—the knight with the black plume on her helmet—spurred her horsebot into a sprint, straight for Ari.

"Did your horse short-circuit?"

"What?" Ari's voice banged around inside her helmet as she looked down at what she could only assume was her squire.

"Try the override," he said, touching a button on the horse's neck. In a rearing kick that nearly sent Ari tumbling ass over elbow, her cyborg steed bolted down the lane toward the black knight—who was still bolting toward her. The crowd grew louder, echoing in Ari's armor and making her bones rattle. The black knight was close. Ari could nearly see her eyes beneath her helmet's pointed visor. What to do? What to do?

Flinch. Ari turned sideways, dropping the lance and gluing herself behind her shield. The black knight's lance exploded in a shower of shards all over her, but she somehow stayed upright. Ari waited for the planet to quit vibrating, while her preprogrammed horse took her back to the starting point.

Her squire shoved the lance back in her hand, his eyebrows drawn low. "Come on, Pete. Remember how we practiced. It's one to one now. Next busted tip goes on to the final round, and don't make me remind you what you get if you win."

Somewhere in the still-vibrating corners of Ari's mind, she wondered what she would get if she won. She looked to the sidelines, unsurprised to find Merlin, Kay, and Lam cheering her on. Merlin waved and grinned, and she waved back. After all, that had been kind of...thrilling.

Ari adjusted herself within the armor, leaning into the joints at the elbows and shoulders. This wasn't her first time in full jousting gear. That first year at knight camp, Ari had been on the line with Lam, Kay...and Gwen. Val kept to the sidelines, tying on the tightest corsets until he nearly passed out. Ari had wanted to be a knight. She'd believed in the honor, loyalty, and comradery...until it felt fake. Like pointless pageantry. People like Gweneviere took it so seriously that Ari didn't want to play anymore.

Ari glanced at her brother and his shining black eye. Merlin's taunt about using her brawn and not her brain riled through her like a blast of steam through an engine.

Or was it remembering Gwen?

She was *watching* now, wasn't she?

Then you know what? Ari would give her something to watch.

When the jester dropped the flag again, Ari's horse was off the mark faster than the black knight's, sprinting toward grave injury, if not certain death. The black knight drew closer, the moment tighter, and the crowd louder—until lances *crashed*. Ari's erupted in a spray of wood, while the black knight's shot to the side.

Ari trotted around the ring holding her broken lance aloft and screaming a battle cry that felt oh so appropriate. The crowd ate it up. Her eyes trailed to the lofted pavilion in the center of the stands where Val clapped with a distracted expression beside Lionel's young queen—who had the audacity to give Ari an approving nod.

"You still love playing games, huh?" Ari's words soured the air in her helmet. She sat straighter in her saddle and watched as Gwen turned her face toward the sky. The Mercer ships were still missing. What game were *they* playing?

Ari clopped back toward her squire, who looked pretty disappointed. "Hey, didn't I win?"

"Get down and ready for the next round!" He pulled her off the horse, took her lance and shoved a sheathed sword in her hand.

Ari began to hand it back. The sheath was jeweled and distinctly not hers, but when she tugged on the pommel, she found that it *was* her sword. Apparently she and Excalibur were both hiding in fancy armor. "What am I supposed to do now?" she asked.

"Oh, Lord, Pete. How much did you drink before the tournament? This is the last time I squire for hopeless contenders." He grabbed her shoulders and swung her to face the center of the ring. "Now you've got to defeat the black knight. In hand-to-hand combat." He chuckled. "Good luck," he added, with all the sincerity of a middle finger.

Ari walked toward the center of the ring while the black knight waited with her sword poised at the ready like she could hold that huge piece of metal aloft forever. *Show-off.*

Ari knew enough about Lionel to know this was all about showmanship, but she was tiring. She drew her sword and tossed the sheath in the hard-packed sand. The cheers did not buoy her as she walked to the fight. Each step was heavier than the last, and she was sweating through whatever clothes Merlin had magicked beneath the suit of armor along with her skin and bones.

The black knight's eyes were hidden in the shade of her visor, and Ari thought that could only help. She didn't wait for trumpets or flags or fanfare. She swung at the black knight, loving the ringing clash of their swords connecting and surprising the knight.

How's that for brains, Merlin?

They fought in a tight circle, and Ari was fully aware of Excalibur's prowess. The sword directed her advances. Her retreats. Even her footsteps felt like a dance set to a strict tune.

Excalibur was enjoying this, but then, so was Ari—especially when she realized that the black knight had stopped playing. The girl's swordplay went from rigid to motivated to *on fire*. Ari's arms burned from the strain as they clashed and came together again and again. And she really—truly—wasn't ready when Excalibur went flying from her gloved hand and landed in the dirt.

The crowd went berserk, and Ari fell on her butt.

The black knight stood over her, sword point resting on Ari's breastplate.

"You people aren't playing to the death, are you?" Ari said between labored breaths.

The black knight cocked her head at Ari's voice and then used her sword to whip off Ari's helmet. Ari glanced around as the crowd rioted with what felt like psychotic joy.

The black knight removed her own helmet. "You are an impostor."

Ari took in the grown-up version of Kay and Lam's favorite bully. She was young, like all of them, but she wore it better. Her neck was thick, her hair brilliantly blond, and her pale cheeks flamed. She'd been Gwen's best friend—and yet she did not recognize Ari.

"Answer," she said, her voice tight.

"I'm the forty-second reincarnation of King Arthur," Ari said, surprised to find that those words left her lips with the weight of a truth.

The black knight squinted, as if she were trying to see past Ari's strange words. "I remember you. You're that girl with the awful brother. What was his name? Keith?"

"Kay?" Ari tried not to laugh. She couldn't wait to call him

Keith and see how well that went over. "He's going to be tickled you remember him."

The black knight squinted even harder. Then she looked up to the pavilion box. Ari glanced over her shoulder, too. Gwen was leaning over the railing, looking at Ari with either pleasure or *immense* disapproval. Funny how they looked related on her poised, beautiful face.

"Get your sword." The black knight turned her back, waiting for Ari to get to her feet.

Now that they were helmetless, Ari could feel the riot of the crowd more intensely. She dropped her leather gloves in the sand before picking up Excalibur. Her grip tightened around the already familiar handle in a way that centered her. This time Ari didn't attack first, but reviewed the blond force of nature.

All right, Merlin, I'll bite. What is the black knight up to?

"For my queen," the girl said quietly, snapping Ari's concentration.

She lunged, and Ari wasn't sure how to move, but Excalibur directed her, coming down to meet the knight's parry with extreme force. The black knight's sword shattered above the hilt, and Ari recoiled from the calamity of breaking metal. When she reopened her eyes, the black knight was on her knees before Ari.

The entire tournament ring had gone silent.

Ari looked at Excalibur and then what was left of the black knight's blade. She had won, but she had definitely *not* won. *Touché, Merlin.*

"Make way for the queen!" Val's voice rang out.

An aisle appeared through the crowd as people pushed

back, allowing the young queen to descend from her pavilion and cross the tournament ring.

Gwen came toward Ari with a steadiness that was unnerving. The last three years had given Gwen a substantial boost in the curve department, a lush sheen to her long brown hair, and a lavender gown undoubtedly worth more than a brand-new astro-class spaceship. The years had done nothing to soften her fiery brown gaze or alter the way Ari's blood rushed at the sight of her. Not necessarily in a good way. Not in a bad way, either.

Her steps took a hard right, veering from their direct path to Ari and choosing her champion instead. Ari gripped Excalibur while Gwen guided the black knight to her feet, kissing her sweetly on the mouth in a way that made Ari shove Excalibur into the packed dirt. Gwen was playing with her. Gwen was *always* playacting. And for the first time, Ari wanted to play as well. She reached into her knowledge of Gwen, into their tense past. What could she use to get through to her? To win Gwen's help with Mercer?

The black knight, Jordan—Ari remembered her name now—and Gwen conferred in hushed voices. At one point, they looked at Ari and then continued to whisper. Ari ached for the crowd to do *something*. Scream or cheer. Even boo. The silence felt like the weight of the dead.

Finally, Gwen turned to Ari, and the black knight stepped back.

The closer Gwen got, the smaller she became. More petite than Ari remembered, but then, Gwen hadn't shrunk; Ari had grown. If Ari's body matched Excalibur's in length and steel, this girl was a jeweled dagger. Treasured, yet dangerous. Concealed in a boot. Or a bodice.

Ari's eyes slipped to Gwen's glorious cleavage before she stared at the brown braid that wreathed the queen's head, hoping to mask her ogle. "Shouldn't queens have crowns?" Her nerves were turning her cocky. That wouldn't get her far.

"Shouldn't knights have armor that fits?" Gwen shot back, eyes openly on Ari's oversize breastplate. "I take it you've done something to the original contender. Unless you've changed your name to Pete, Ari."

There.

Right there.

Gwen's voice had faltered on Ari's name, and they'd both heard it.

"Long time, no see?" Ari said, using a soft hand to squeeze Gwen's shoulder.

"Are we pretending to be friends now?"

"We were friends," Ari said truthfully. "At the very least." Gwen's cheeks pinked, and Ari felt the better parts of Merlin's advice. She didn't need the brunt of her honesty; she needed the best edge of it. "We drove each other wild. That doesn't mean we weren't friends."

Gwen looked down, stepping much closer. "What the hell are you doing here? Three years and you just show back up in the middle of my tournament ring?"

"Trying to save Val from Mercer's wrath."

"And you put my entire planet in the cross fire?"

"What?"

"I doubt it will surprise you to hear that the Mercer force

now residing in our spaceport has issued a warrant for your immediate arrest. I've been ordered to turn you over." Ari opened her mouth, but the queen held up a finger. "What I want to know—and if you lie, I'll have Jordan stick you like a hunk of lamb—is *why* Mercer is after you. What have you done to incense the most persistent amoral force in this universe?"

Ari couldn't have lied if she wanted to, but she doubted Gwen was ready for all of her truths. "I snuck onto Old Earth. And I accidentally helped my friend over there break a moon colony. And I'm Ketchan...and I'm not behind the barrier."

The queen flared her eyes, a calculating look that was no small part intimidating.

"I've never lied to you, Gwen. Not even when you were lying to me."

Gwen sighed with a slight growl that slipped through Ari's armor and rubbed along her skin like a purring cat. The feeling amplified as the crowd began a methodic, expectant clap.

"What are they doing?" Ari asked.

"They're excited because I'm going to kiss you."

"That's what the winner receives for this tournament?"

"No, this is the final round. Only three contenders have made it this far. Jordan does not throw a fight unless I ask, and no one has ever beaten her. Including you."

"More pageantry," Ari said. "More lies."

"Pageantry isn't a lie, Ari." Gwen stepped closer, her heart-shaped face turned straight up, eyes afire. "It's a performance."

Ari was a fair amount taller. She would need to lean down to agree to this kiss, and she held on to that distance as if it kept her safe. "So, Gwen," Ari's voice frayed, pulled apart by the storm in her pulse, "for the sake of this performance, should we pretend this is our first kiss?"

"Damn you, Ari."

Gwen seized the neck of Ari's breastplate and drew her down in a swift move.

Ari expected something chaste, but she was wrong. She was always wrong when it came to Gwen. The queen's lips were soft but in charge. They pulled her further into the kiss with a seamless energy. And when Ari's breath slipped out in surprise, the queen's mouth stole her air.

By the time they parted, Ari had to remember how to stand upright, her entire body tilting toward Gwen. So, there were still sparks between them. Sparks that would give Merlin's magic a run for his money.

Gwen smiled, still holding Ari close by the front of her stolen suit of armor. "Do what I say, and I'll get you out of here and away from Mercer."

Ari glanced at where Kay and Merlin were cheering with the rest of them. "Just get my friends out of here, too. Including Val."

The queen took Ari's hand and lifted their entwined fingers over their heads. People cheered, louder than when Ari had been fighting Jordan. They shouted and shook the thin pillars that held the tent over the stands. A horn blasted throughout the stadium, and all eyes turned to Val, standing on the podium, staring at Ari with a gloriously shocked look.

Ari slipped on a smile, and her childhood best friend shook his head once before bellowing for the crowd, "To the queen and her new intended!"

Flagons and mugs went up in all directions as the people toasted them.

"Intended?" Ari laughed. "That's not something I've been called before."

"It means—to them at least—that I'm going to marry you."

&

Gwen never let go of Ari's hand as they traveled swiftly across the grounds toward the castle.

"Gwen," Ari started, "how could you let your people think you'd marry me?"

"I could hardly do otherwise at this point. You were quite the crowd favorite. My people would be furious if I rejected you on the spot. We can always tell them later that the marriage didn't go through."

Ari tried to drop her hand, but Gwen hung on as they approached the bridge gate. "See? Your pageantry *is* riddled with lies."

The queen sighed, and this time there was no enticing purr. "Great, now that we've pressed our lips together, let's do that other thing we're so good at—call each other names while you doubt my sincerity and I vow to never again get bashed against the rocks of your sense of right and wrong."

Val jogged to catch up, and Ari opened her mouth to argue back, but Gwen stopped her with a raised hand. "Val, go to the spaceport. Tell Mercer there's been a change of plans and that they will wait until I'm ready to meet with them. They will *not* venture into my territory without permission again."

"But they'll want..." Val's eyes darted to Ari.

"*They will wait,*" Gwen replied, her tone scorching. Val ran off in the direction of *Error* and the other small ships they'd seen when they landed on Lionel.

Ari looked down as she and Gwen crossed the bridge, eyeing the moat filled with swirling mercury—Lionel's chief natural resource. Once they were inside, they wound a quick path through the castle, and if Ari didn't feel so faintish and thirsty in her armor, she would have asked where they were going. Finally, they entered a large boudoir. Gwen kicked off her shoes and immediately began to unwind the strict braid from her brow.

Ari stood stiff and uncertain. Was she in the queen's bedroom? She totally was.

"Where're my friends?" Ari asked.

Gwen headed for a table bearing a large carafe. "They're fine. The crowd will take a while to disperse. In the meantime, I need to figure out how long I can stall Mercer before I have to hand you over."

"You wouldn't," Ari said, her voice scratchy with doubt. Gwen filled a goblet and handed it to Ari. Ari took a sip and spit it out. "No more wine or mead. I need water."

"No. My *planet* needs water." Gwen took the goblet back. She put it down with a sharp clap on the floor and beckoned for Ari to turn around. "I'll get you out of that."

Gwen began to undress her. There were thousands of buckles at every joint, holding together dozens of pieces of armor. Gwen collected a small mountain of leather, chain mail, and metal beside them while she spoke. "The Mercer fleet that flashed its superiority all over *my* tournament was only half your doing. The black ship is here for you. The white one is meant to mock Lionel. Every single month, Mercer nearly dehydrates the population before delivering our supplies. They want us to sell junk Mercer products, and allow Trojan building permits, *and* give them a higher percentage of our mercury reserves, but I will not be bullied."

Gwen lifted off the breastplate, and Ari felt a thousand pounds lighter. "I need to go to Troy and file a claim for mistreatment. The problem is, I don't have any bargaining chips."

Ari felt as if a piece of ice slid down her spine. "I'm your chip, am I?"

"Of course not," she snapped. "I don't trade in people." Gwen knelt to get the plates off of Ari's shins, throwing them aside before sitting on her heels. Ari felt all sorts of awkward with the queen at her feet, staring up with those hard, brown eyes. "I honestly dream of the days when all my people wanted was to marry me off. Constant tournaments to find a consort. I'm lucky Jordan is the best knight in the galaxy, otherwise I would have been married the day after my coronation to some oaf."

"That's bullshit," Ari found herself saying.

"It's era appropriate."

"It's a damn charade, Gwen."

"Yes, well, it's also my *life*. The life I chose. The one you couldn't even pretend to want for me when we were fourteen-year-olds." Gwen turned her back to Ari, motioning to the strings holding her dress closed. "Do you mind?"

"Um, sure." Ari pulled at the top one. It was really tight. She worked the entire cross-stitch free a few inches all the way down her back, before going through it all over again. The dress sprang open and Ari won a five-year-old bet. One tournament day, when Lam and Kay were strutting around in the desert-like heat, Val had insisted that the royals wore fancy underwear beneath those stiff gowns, and Ari bet there was no way. They'd be too hot.

Gwen's bare backside curved in a strikingly gorgeous way.

Ari's mouth turned into a real desert, her hands aching to move from strings to skin. Her infamous impulses were singing, a siren song that always accompanied run-ins with Gweneviere. "You could always marry me."

Gwen glanced over her shoulder. "Granted, martyrdom is *also* era appropriate, but why would we put ourselves through something that painful?"

"Because you don't want to be married off to some oafish knight who happens to catch Jordan on an off day. Because I am a bargaining chip, but if I'm your wife, I'm *your* bargaining chip. And Mercer won't be able to arrest me if I'm married to the queen of Lionel. I'd have—"

"Diplomatic immunity." Gwen turned, taking the intoxicating proximity of her skin away and leaving Ari's hands empty.

Gwen pulled the last piece of Ari's chain mail over Ari's head, taking most of the undershirt with it. Gwen didn't pull it all the way off, leaving Ari mostly topless, arms tightly tangled in her own sleeves. Gwen held Ari there, and smiled. "Are you fucking with me?"

"Excuse me?" Ari managed.

"You'd marry me. To outsmart Mercer. *You?*"

Ari examined her choices, her conscience. It didn't hurt that her nearly bared skin thought this was a great idea with such potential. "Yes, I would."

Gwen let go. Ari looped the shirt back on, and Gwen reached

back, pulling the strings taut on her dress in an impressively swift move.

"You're not getting changed?" Ari asked. "Then why did you have me untie you?"

Gwen sighed like Ari was missing all the important points, and Ari reddened from her toes to the tips of her ears. "I wanted to see if you're still afraid of me. You are. But don't worry, we'll keep this to politics."

Gwen sat on the edge of the bed. Ari couldn't tell if she was relieved or disappointed. "Seventy solar years ago, Lionel's founders negotiated a favorable arrangement with the Trojan government. It was no small feat. An era-inspired planet might sound attractive and lucrative, but it took a lot of convincing for Troy to relinquish the territory. Now they've changed their mind, and they're letting Mercer withhold hydration shipments. They hope we'll pack up and hand the planet back. Not on my watch. This is my home."

Ari nodded. Gwen had always been sincerely in love with Lionel.

"Tell me how you are the only Ketchan off-world I've ever heard of, Ari."

"I was found floating in a junked ship on the wrong side of the barrier, abandoned as space trash when I was seven. Kay's family took me in."

Pain flashed over Gwen's face, so raw that it didn't feel like polite sadness over a bit of Ari's backstory. But Gwen tucked away those feelings, putting her queenly expression back in place. "But why does Mercer want you so badly?"

"Maybe they think I bypassed their barrier, or they're still pissed at how outspoken Ketchans were about Mercer's galactic monopoly."

"Oh, it'll be more than that. The Administrator is infamous for his underground motivations, and for whatever reason, you're special. He's made a big stink about wanting you turned over. The whole galaxy is talking about it."

"This is why Kay wants us to go into hiding. And to take our friends with us, out of harm's way."

Gwen shook her head. "They'll find you easily. We have to face them."

Ari lined the pieces up, enjoying the daring, impulsive bits of this new plan. "We go to Troy, married, so that they can't arrest me on the spot. And you'll bargain for better treatment for Lionel."

"And you can demand amnesty for you and your friends, and find out why he wants you so badly."

"This could work," Ari dared, skipping over the whole *getting hitched* part.

"What about afterward, Ari?" Gwen pulled her knees under her chin. She had a way of looking young even while she looked old. Like her heart had been born at full maturity, and she was waiting for her body to catch up.

"What about it?"

"Will you run off again or will you stay with me? As my wife. Here."

Ari couldn't lie. Lionel was a weird, fun place. Her friends loved it, and she loved her earlier memories from camp, but to live here permanently when her true home was far away and just...waiting? "I'd have to think about it."

"That's fair." Gwen nodded, glancing away. "There's one more thing, and it's forward, but I don't care. I want a child. I'd already have one if my people weren't so intense about wedlock. If this marriage lasts, there will be one. Or more. Can you handle that?"

Ari's surprise left her slightly confused. "I love kids."

"You do?" Gwen's knees fell loose from her stranglehold on them.

"But in the spirit of honesty, I have to tell you Mercer is in the habit of punishing the people I love. *Badly*. My adoptive parents," Ari cleared her throat, "were arrested. We don't even know where they are."

Gwen straightened up. "That's easy. I'll find out."

"The information is restricted."

"Not for the head of a damn planet. We'll put it on the list of priorities when we meet with the council on Troy to argue Lionel's mistreatment. After the wedding, of course."

Ari looked at Gwen anew. They were both exhausted. They were both dehydrated. And even though Ari had been the one sweating her ass off in the ring, she had a feeling that Gwen had been thirsty for much longer. "So you *will* marry me? You've decided that fast?"

"Yes," Gwen said.

"A real marriage?" Ari shouldn't have been thinking about the curve of Gwen's back...and how it met her legs with such glory. Or that body flood of a kiss in the jousting ring.

"A political union," Gwen replied carefully, her slight blush the only indication that she was possibly remembering the way they'd melted together so well. "We'll have to do it before Mercer storms the city for you. Then we'll need to hightail it to

Troy and file our marriage with the galactic state department. We can't give Mercer an inch to get between us."

"I have a fast, albeit ugly, ship. We could be there in under a week."

"Okay."

"Done."

They were close enough to kiss again, and yet Ari knew there was an unbreakable barrier between them to rival the one orbiting Ketch. There always had been.

&

The night was strewn with crystal stars. The torchlight circling the tournament ring added a glow to the familiar faces around Ari. Beyond them, beyond the lights, she knew an entire planet was watching her enter the biggest lie of her life.

A political marriage. To Gwen.

Beside her, Kay and Lam stood...wasted. Val kept them upright with a hand on each of their shoulders. Merlin slid up to her in the shadows. "I can fix this!" he whispered. "I can make those ships go away. *Poof.* No problem. No one needs to marry anyone!"

"You can't take out the entire Mercer Company, Merlin. Plus, you're *really* drunk."

"There'snothingtodrinkonthisplanetbutbooze," he whisper-shouted.

Ari dug a finger in her ear. "Val?"

Val stepped forward and took Merlin by the back of the robes like he was a young pup. Ari couldn't even look at the magician; he was part of the reason why she felt like she was stepping into a lie. Ari hadn't told Gwen about Merlin, his King Arthur shenanigans—or this Morgana who was out of sight, but not out of mind. And she hadn't told Gwen that she was going to use whatever information the queen could get to break her parents out of prison.

Ari knew how well that would land.

"You look sick," Lam said. "Too much wine or too much reality?"

Ari leaned on Lamarack's shoulder, sighing.

Gwen came forward on Jordan's arm, wearing a dress of red silk and white, pinned roses—and a crown. Silver, simple, incandescent. It caught the torchlight like a mirror and cast it around her in a halo of sparks. Gwen smiled at Ari and then at the woman conducting the ceremony. She lifted her arm from Jordan's only to find Jordan unwilling to let go. The black knight was still in her full suit of armor as if she could wear it for a few more days without needing a break.

Gwen kissed Jordan on the lips sweetly, and the knight relinquished the bride with stiff, unwilling movements. The ceremony took mere minutes, but it was long enough for Ari's heart to race into a speed that left her gripping Excalibur, afraid. So bizarrely afraid. After an exchange of vows, Gwen pecked Ari on the mouth, and it was over.

Done.

Music lit up the tournament ring all around, while the planet began to dance and Gwen immediately started messaging Mercer. She took off her crown and dropped it in Ari's hands as if she were a handy end table. Ari examined the silver wreath. "Does this make me king?"

Val smiled at her, a little sadly, and plucked Gwen's crown out of her hands. "Your title is queen's consort."

Merlin peered from behind Val's shoulder, eyes large, and chanted, *"Love and Arthur. Oil and water."*

Ari put a hand on her friend's shoulder. He was her friend now, wasn't he? She hoped so; she'd need him to face Gwen's machinations, the corrupt government on Troy, and the gods damn Mercer Company.

Not to mention the voice inside that whispered—*You are one with King Arthur, and your destiny awaits.*

HEARTS
&
ACHES

Merlin hummed a bit of Handel's wedding march, flicked his fingers, and tried to scatter the tight knot of his headache. Alas, hungover magic was groaningly impossible.

He'd already spent a full day of the flight to Troy recovering from the royal wedding, and the wedding night celebrations that spilled over onto the ship. He wasn't the only one in rough shape. He remembered seeing Lam and Kay singing garbled versions of Old Earth songs before he passed out, but Merlin had more to get over than they did. It had been hard to tell what caused worse nausea: his eight...teenth cup of mead, or the sight of Ari and Gweneviere sealing their vows under the light of strange stars.

Not only had he failed to keep them from meeting, they had gotten engaged *and* married by nightfall on the same day he'd made his useless vow. And now the scene that greeted Merlin out the window was a fleet of six white Mercer vessels accompanying the newlyweds to Troy, where they would file their claim with the government and—hopefully—make it official.

The scope of this failure was staggering. Epic.

And as someone who'd lived through several volcanic eruptions and a Rolling Stones reunion tour, he didn't throw those words around lightly. He picked himself up from where he'd been resting, which turned out to be under the round table in the main cabin. Lam was down there, too, curled like a delicate leaf despite their size. Kay slept sitting up in a chair, boots stuck to the floor and mouth permanently open.

Ari—where was Ari?

Merlin staggered on magboots that pinched his toes, thinking thoughts that stung his brain. He was letting it all happen again. Not just the inevitable parts. He was going down his own worst paths. Heavy drinking? He hadn't imbibed this much in twenty cycles. He had lost entire Arthurs this way.

Merlin tramped through the tiny rooms of the spaceship but didn't find Ari anywhere. What he did find was Jordan, camped outside Kay's room in full regalia. The only thing she'd removed was her black-plumed helmet, revealing ruddy cheeks that shone in high contrast to her pale white complexion.

"Good day, *mage*," she said, her voice both strident and smooth. She appeared too delighted with this title, as if she had rampaging doubts about his abilities. Merlin was still annoyed that Jordan had somehow gotten on board *Error,* despite his drunken pleas to leave her behind. Gweneviere had insisted on having her champion by her side, and Ari hadn't been able to resist her new spouse's request.

Which was exactly what made Merlin's left eye twitch.

"Tell me they're not both in there," he said.

"My lady the queen and her consort have, indeed, claimed this tiny room. The queen is preparing Ari for their marriage examination on Troy."

Excalibur lay discarded in the hall, and he thought about carving his way through the shiny silver door and stopping whatever was going on in there. Instead, he caught sight of himself in the door's surface. He looked, if possible, even younger than he had when he'd woken in the Crystal Cave. It was hard to pinpoint what made the difference. Were his cheeks slightly rounder? He checked his stubble. Still formidably scratchy. Good.

Val came around the corner, stripped of his period costume, wearing an I ♥ NEW NEW NEW YORK T-shirt. He looked alarmingly awake and full of functions that Merlin lacked.

"Are the newlyweds sleeping in?" Val asked, nodding at the door Jordan guarded. "Or skipping the sleep bit altogether?"

Merlin made a sound somewhere between a dying cat and a choking dog.

Val frowned at him. He grabbed Merlin's arm and led him away, whispering, "You've been acting like we lived through an apocalypse instead of a fairly tame royal wedding. You should have seen Lionel's last planet-wide ceremony. The debauchery after Gwen's coronation went on for weeks. Gwen and I both lost our virginity. To the same boy, actually. Not at the same time."

Merlin blushed, changing color like a chameleon who had forgotten he was supposed to be blending in. This was probably how chameleons wound up dead.

Val settled into one of *Error*'s many nooks, this one looking like the skeleton of a kitchen. It had a few small cupboards, a tiny table and chairs, and a water filtration system that hummed like an old friend. Merlin dove for it, putting his face shamelessly under the stream, but most of it ended up on his toes.

"So, Merlin, why is this marriage a cause for mourning?" Val asked sharply.

"It's my fault," Merlin blurted, tongue still dry. "If I'd been able to defend Ari against Mercer, or even better, taught her how to defend herself, she wouldn't need this marriage." That was step two. *Train Ari.* And all he'd managed to do was get her to tackle Kay in a courtyard.

"This might be the best possible thing for Ari," Val said. "And before you object, I'm speaking less as a royal adviser and more as someone who's known her since she was seven. She likes people who know their own minds. And Gwen's mind is one of the most well-mapped on any planet. That girl does not leave things unfathomed."

"Of course she's smart and beautiful and wondrous," Merlin said. None of those traits had ever stopped Gweneviere from breaking Arthur's heart. In fact, her sheer amazingness only multiplied the pain when things came to an inevitable, crashing end. "You don't understand," Merlin said. "It's not your fault that you don't."

"Okay," Val said, leaning forward. "That's your cue to explain."

"Ari is the forty-second reincarnation of—"

"She told me that," Val said, startling Merlin. Ari had talked about being Arthur?

"What did she say?"

Val flashed him a smile so bright Merlin's headache flared. "All kinds of things while you were dancing with your robe pulled up to your thighs. Nice calves, by the way."

Merlin groaned.

"But I'm asking about *you*," Val said, finding two cups and filling them with water. "You're the real mystery here." He held one out and Merlin drank, playing for time. The truth was that he had no idea where he came from. He'd arrived in the first Arthur's era, old and magical, with a tiny wooden falcon clutched in his hand.

That falcon had given him his name. *Merlin.*

Remembering before that—or perhaps beyond it—was as impossible as seeing the future of this cycle. "Here's what you need to know about me," Merlin said, downing the last of the water. "I keep coming back and back and back, and I can't seem to make things better. You've heard of King Arthur?" Val nodded, curious and wary. "I'm the Merlin who serves Arthur."

Val cocked his head. "If you've been at this since the original Arthur, how old does that make you?"

"Seventeen, apparently," Merlin muttered.

Val refilled his cup, his slim back to Merlin. He had always dreaded talking about his age, and with every back step toward childhood, that dread doubled. "Is it possible your problem with Gwen and Ari's marriage is about you? Living that long sounds like a recipe for baggage."

Oh, good. A topic he liked even *less* than aging backward. "I sleep through entire centuries, so my burdens are lighter than you might think. And remember, I survived the era of psychology. You can't pull any tricks on me."

"I'm just trying to help." Val turned, his lips beaded with water and demanding all of Merlin's attention. "I thought I would only see you for a few hours yesterday, and here we are, sailing to Troy together. I've decided that's a sign we should be kissing, at the very least. If you're interested. But we should get to know each other first."

The combination of Val's matter-of-fact tone and the word *kissing* swirled together, making Merlin faintish. "What could you possibly want to know?"

Val sat on one of the tiny chairs, and when Merlin rushed to join him, their knees knocked. Merlin's pulse answered in kind. "Start with the good stuff," Val said, leaning forward with a smirk that could have killed Merlin, if Merlin was killable. "If you've been around that long, you must have fallen in love."

Merlin had held back the truth for too long, and it rushed out. "Once." It felt good to admit that—until it felt awful.

"What was this person's name?"

Merlin winced. "Art."

"Art?" Val said, with a deliberate blink. "You fell in love with one of your Arthurs?" He put a hand to his face, a grin shining between his fingers. "Oh, that is scandalous."

Merlin talked fast to cover the fact that he was shaking under his robes. "He wasn't the best of the Arthurs. He wasn't the bravest or the most heroic. He was clever, though. And he said the most bluntly ridiculous things."

So much about the cycles blurred, but Merlin could remember Art perfectly—a dark-haired man with melting brown eyes. They had kissed in the forest, under trees that seemed to hide them from an unfriendly sky. They had loved each other in a time when people pretended such things weren't happening. Weren't *possible*. And under the cover of that chosen ignorance, they had given each other words and promises and reasons to gasp.

"And then what?" Val asked, his much darker brown eyes wide and waiting.

"He died," Merlin said. But that wasn't true. Or at least, it was only half true. "I age backward, slowly. His death was all that could come to pass. So I...ended things between us."

Val shifted back and looked at Merlin from a distance. "You forced yourself not to care about someone because you thought it wouldn't end well? You really are old, aren't you?"

A dry sound of disapproval rose from Merlin's throat. "That's like saying you're eight years old because you used to be eight. I used to be an old man, but I'm not anymore. I'm aging, much the same as all of you are. I just happen to be the only one going in the opposite direction. And Ari is the last chance I have to stop getting younger," Merlin said, his voice cracking, and this time not because of blaring hormones. "I tried to train her on Lionel, but she was barely interested. And now..." Now she was stuck in Kay's bedroom, with Gweneviere of all people.

Merlin looked down again—at some point during this conversation Val's hand had taken up residence on his arm. "What kind of training?"

Merlin described the game he'd created for Ari with half of his mind, while the other half told him, over and over, about Val's hand touching the spot near his elbow, as if he didn't already *know*. Merlin shifted his entire body closer. The metal chair screeched under him.

"You say you've seen a lot of Arthurs," Val said, "but I've seen a lot of Ari. We've been friends since we were young enough to get into the mermaids' grove on Lionel for free."

"*Mermaids?*" Merlin asked, tempted to launch into a mini-lecture on historical accuracy.

Val rubbed his hand up and down Merlin's arm, and the lecture vanished. "If you want her to train, you have to give her something real to do. Games are fake to her, and Ari doesn't do fake. That's why she objected at top volume to knight camp."

"Hmmm," Merlin grumbled.

And then he started, gently, to float.

He wasn't the only one—Val was floating, as well as their cups and a few beads of water. "What's this?" Merlin asked, as Val propelled himself out of the tiny kitchen to investigate.

In the main cabin, Lam seemed to have woken up mid-float. Jordan's armor lifted away from her body. Excalibur had started spinning. "Oh, excellent," Merlin said. "A naked sword in free float."

"Dude," Lam said, their dreads floating above their face as they giggled. "Naked sword."

"What is happening on this cursed ship?" Jordan cried.

Kay clomped in on locking magboots, pointing toward the far door. "I turned off the gravity so my sister can't do anything in *my* bedroom."

"You mean, anything *else*," Lam said.

"You're going out the airlock," Kay promised, with a sharply pointed finger. "I had the weirdest drunk dream that Ari cut her hair, and she would not stop making out with Gwen." He glared at Merlin. "And you wouldn't stop hugging me."

"You two are being ridiculous yet again," Val said, crossing his arms as the rest of him drifted. "Gwen would never move so fast with a consort. This is a political marriage, first and foremost. If she and Ari do end up together in a romantic sense, it will happen in its own time."

Merlin's hope perked. "You think they might not be...?"

A sound spread from Kay's room.

An unmistakable, moaning, *gasping* sound.

"Sounds like the zero-grav just gave them a new challenge," Lam said. "Get it, girls!"

"No! Absolutely not!" Kay stomped for the ship's controls, and everything tumbled down. Merlin fell, chin first, on the hard metal floor, giving him a perfect view of Excalibur. The sword stopped spinning, the blade penetrating the round table with a slick *sheening* sound that left the entire spaceship in postcoital silence.

While the rest of Ari's knights snickered, Merlin groaned. "I loathe that sword's sense of humor."

&

When Ari and Gwen emerged from Kay's room, hours later, they looked a mess, and they acted like strangers. Gwen's long hair had been freed from its braids, rippling over one of Ari's old T-shirts, nearly reaching her tiny shorts. Somehow she looked even more regal—like a queen in the marketplace, trying to pass for a commoner. Ari edged around her, nervous.

Jordan greeted Gwen with a little feast on a tray. "You didn't need to do this," Gwen said sweetly as she seized a piece of toast and held it out to Ari.

Lancelot.

Jordan's name was wrong, but that happened—the cycle couldn't always give Merlin a 100 percent match, especially when cultural differences came into play. It wasn't reasonable to expect an Arthur and Percival and Lancelot in feudal Japan or Renaissance Italy. It was character that truly defined someone's role in the cycle. Lam had the undying loyalty of their predecessors; this Lamarack wasn't the first to lose a hand in the service of King Arthur. Val was the descendant of the driven, clever knight who had found the Holy Grail, though he'd never been quite this compellingly gorgeous. Jordan possessed the shining excellence, unbridled chivalry, and love for Gweneviere that added up to Ari's annihilation.

Gwen and Ari brought their breakfast to the tiny round table, a nearby window providing a scenic view of the Mercer ships. Soon they were all watching the fleet like it was a terrible TV show.

"What happens when we get to Troy?" Ari asked, eyes hard on the white vessels.

"They'll march us to the galactic state department like criminals," Gwen said. "Not my preferred way to make an entrance."

Merlin thought of what Val had said about giving Ari something real for her training—something that mattered. "*Unless* they can't get out of their ships," Merlin said. Everyone looked at him. "What if we sealed them inside of their vessels? Then you would arrive on Troy without their shadows looming over you."

"That's not going to change Mercer's game," Lam said.

Merlin had to prepare Ari for an inevitable standoff with Mercer. He might have failed to keep her safe from Gwen, but that made it all the more important to train her for this. "When you want to become a dragon slayer, you don't charge straight into the nest, swords swinging," Merlin said. "You sneak in and steal a few coins from his hoard first."

"What if the dragon worked hard for that money?" Lam asked. "You don't know his life. And how do you even know the dragon's a..."

"He's a boy dragon!" Merlin roared.

"Sure thing, *old* man," Kay said, slapping his arm.

"What?" Merlin asked. "Val, did you tell all of them that I age backward?"

Val shrugged. "It came up naturally."

"How does something like that come up naturally?"

"Ari knows dragons. Don't they have dragons on Ketch?" Lam asked.

"Taneens are really, really big lizards," Ari said. "I wouldn't call them dragons."

"They're totally dragons," Kay faux-whispered from behind his hand.

"I'm sorry, are we discussing dragons or Merlin's idea to fuck with Mercer?" Val asked, smiling at Merlin as if he'd found a way to be helpful. The group turned to Merlin—except Ari. She seemed to be considering his idea.

"It'll be safer to slip through Troy without a Mercer escort."

"Plus arriving under guard will undermine our marriage claim, which is definitely their goal," Gwen added.

Kay crossed his arms. "So, you're going to use your magic to seal their doors, right?"

"I believe I should save my magic for Troy, if this planet is half as horrific as everyone thinks," Merlin said.

"Yes," Jordan tutted. "You should save your 'magic.'"

Merlin felt his face screw up tightly like a small, affronted child. He had to turn her into a newt. He had no choice. He raised one hand, and Ari clamped it down to his side.

"Leave Merlin be. He proves his magic best when he waits for the right moment."

"I've seen his magic," Lam put in.

"Me, too," Kay grumbled.

"I'd *love* to see it," Val purred, causing Merlin to tingle and forget completely about Jordan.

"So a spacewalk," Lam said, bringing them back to the plan. "A dangerous one."

"I've been stuck in this ship too long," Ari said, standing with a grand flourish of a smile. "A walk outside sounds good."

"Ari…" Gwen said. Ari looked at her like she was waiting for Gwen's argument. An intense spark passed between them, until Gwen snuffed it out. "Seal those bastards in tight."

Through the window, Ari studied the Mercer ships attached to *Error* by a network of docking cables. They were caught like a fly in the center of a shimmering, metallic spiderweb.

"We'll use the cables," she said, making it sound easy.

"No one's going out there while we're moving," Kay said. "That'd be an ugly death."

Ari turned to her brother, and Merlin could almost *see* her brain scheming. "Can you break *Error*?"

"*What?*"

"Just a little," Ari said. "She has to be actually broken, though, so the Mercer ships will stop. Then you can fix her. After the doors are sealed."

"I would need someone on the ship's controls while I was in the engine," Kay said, putting a protective hand on the nearest part of *Error*.

"I can do it," Jordan said, standing at the ready.

Kay blinked. "You...fly, too?"

Merlin indulged in his first true teenage eye-roll.

"You think a ship like this is a challenge?" Jordan asked.

"It took me six years to learn her, inside and out," Kay shot back.

"Give me six minutes," Jordan said, shattering Kay's pride and flicking away the pieces. She strode toward the cockpit with her wide gait, armor clanking. Kay watched her go with renewed fire, as if somehow this exchange had only made her hotter.

"*Ugh, boys,*" Val said.

"I believe the phrase you're looking for is *straight boys,*" Merlin corrected.

"What is *straight?*" Lam asked, furrowing their brow.

"Oh, goodness," Merlin said. "Well, it's when a person has attractions to people who are on the other binary end of the... *ummm...*"

"They're messing with you, Merlin," Ari said, unable to keep the truth back, or maybe she didn't like watching him wriggle like a trout on the line. Merlin felt fairly sure he had just outed himself to everyone on the ship, something he had never done in all the cycles.

And it felt strangely, shockingly, *fine.*

"Gwen," Ari continued. "I want you in the cockpit with Jordan, ready to talk to the associates."

Merlin yelped, wanting to keep Gwen and Jordan apart at all costs. "I can stay in the cockpit and talk to Mercer. I'm well versed in villains." He thought about Morgana, his own personal, evil shadow.

"They'll be nicer to a queen than a fictional magician," Ari said. Before Merlin had the chance to bridle at the description, she'd moved on. "Besides, I already know what everyone is doing. Val and Lam, you'll work *Error*'s airlock."

Ari's leadership was emerging, as simply and powerfully as Excalibur being drawn from a sheath. Merlin watched delightedly as she proved that she could ace her training. Ari wasn't relying solely on impulse. She wasn't attempting to do it all on her own. She was planning, orchestrating—bringing people together to accomplish more than they could by themselves. It was a large part of what made an Arthur great. The first King Arthur's round table was the greatest legend he'd left behind, and all because he'd brought knights together like this. It had seemed improbable at first. A smile crept onto Merlin's face as he remembered the piping, runty boy who'd become the first Arthur.

Ari was curvier, and her voice actually a bit lower, but she had the same bright look on her face as she turned to Merlin. "You and I have the best job of all."

"We do?" Merlin asked.

"We're sealing the doors," Ari said, a hand clamped on his shoulder.

&

Merlin's stomach tightened into a complex system of knots as Ari dug through a closet. Soon Merlin was wearing a spacesuit that made him feel like a walking marshmallow.

A metallic catastrophe came from the engine room. Everyone jumped and winced as a wave passed through the walls, shuddering the ship to a stop. Merlin tipped over, his suit padding his fall.

"Should we be *on* this ship if it's so easy to break?" Jordan called from the cockpit.

Within seconds, the radio went live—just as Ari had predicted.

"What's your situation?" asked a blank voice.

"What's our situation?" Gwen hissed.

Kay yelled from the engine room, "Trydecker. *Kaplow.*"

"Our trydecker valve is broken," Gweneviere said in a voice that suggested the person on the other end should be reasonable. Merlin was impressed. "We're going to need..."

"Twenty minutes!" Kay yelled.

"Twenty minutes, at least," Gwen relayed.

"You have ten," the blank voice said.

"Ten minutes!" Gwen yelled throughout the ship, and Merlin felt how desperately small that number was. How many times had he lost ten years to a useless Arthur? Ten decades to a long sleep? Ten minutes was nothing...

"Ha!" Kay said. "I knew those Mercer bastards would cut the number."

"How much time do you actually need?" Val asked.

"Fifteen," Kay mumbled. "I didn't know they'd cut it that much."

"Let's go," Ari said, waddling with Merlin to the double set of doors that led into space.

"Have you ever spacewalked before?" Lam asked Merlin.

"Yes and no," Merlin said. "I self-propelled to the moon once."

"This is a dangerous walk for a beginner." *Or anyone,* Merlin read in the creases that appeared on Lam's usually smooth forehead. "Take it slow. You and Ari are tied together, and your helmet coms are on if you need to talk."

"You're also going to be tethered to *Error,*" Ari said. "I'll hook us up."

Merlin nodded, but his plan to train her was becoming less delightful with each moment. They moved through the first set of doors, which Lam and Val sealed behind them. Merlin mimicked Ari, taking hold of a bar as the second set of doors opened.

Space greeted him, endless and cold, the blackest of blacks.

I want to go home, Merlin thought. But he didn't know where home was. He meant the crystal cave, but that was just a way station on his endless journey. He seemed to understand space in a way that terrified him. Here was endlessness in its purest form.

At least Ari didn't seem to be worrying herself into oblivion. She sealed a metallic clip to the side of the ship, hooking a cable to Merlin's suit and one to her own. She pointed to the short tether that held them together.

Merlin picked a cable that would lead them to the first of the six ships. It wasn't thick enough to walk across. Ari let herself out. In her white suit, she was like a falling star. She caught the cable and started to move, hand over hand. Merlin thought, very seriously for a second, about canceling this whole cycle. Even if it was his last chance. But then Ari looked back at him with her eyes wide, thrilled. She was having *fun.*

Merlin let go.

His organs lurched as he propelled himself out, missing the cable. His fingers sifted through space. For a second Merlin thought he was lost—that he would be floating, forever.

Unable to die. Waiting out his time in a suit that kept him perfectly alone. Panic closed in on him.

"*Merlin,*" Ari said, her voice crackling through his helmet. That voice brought him back from the brink of nothing. Ari tugged him, one hand on the cable and the other on the tether between them. She was his lifeline out here, in more ways than one. Ari's laugh was sharp and bright. "I bet none of your Arthurs have done this."

"This is...unique," he said, pulling himself after her.

They reached the doors of the first Mercer ship, and Ari gave Merlin a can of something to spray. It released a puffy sealant that covered the edges of the door. Merlin watched it grow with a wondrous satisfaction. Magic was his personal cup of tea, but technology wasn't too shabby, either. They slid along the rest of the cables with growing ease, writing their defiance in puffy white goop. In his desperation to end the cycle, and his worry over turning Ari into Arthur, Merlin had forgotten how good it felt to strike a blow—any blow—against oppression.

They started along the final cable back to *Error,* and Merlin felt the first trickle of confidence he'd had in ages. Then one ship twisted, pulling taut against the cord that connected them to *Error.*

It would snap any moment, setting Ari and Merlin adrift.

He hummed a deep note, breaking the wire tied to the Mercer ship. Ari's surprise sent her teetering backward, and Merlin grabbed her hand in a firm grip. Arthur 42 would not die—not today. Not tomorrow. Not while Merlin was here to protect her.

"Thanks," Ari breathed.

"What is magic for?" Merlin asked.

When they made it back to the ship, Lam and Val hauled them in and sealed the doors behind them. Merlin ripped off his helmet, gulping *Error*'s blessed oxygen.

"Nine minutes, people!" Kay said, emerging from the engine room with grease smears all through his gray hair, arms lofted high.

"We're cleared to continue," Gweneviere said over the radio.

Error coughed her way back to life, but she flew smoothly enough. Merlin joined the rest of the crew at the window. The Mercer ships were no longer a sign of their impending doom. "It worked," Merlin said, shock lifting the edges of his voice.

"I thought you knew it was going to work the whole time," Ari said. "Aren't you my wise and all-knowing mentor?"

"I used to be." Now Merlin was walking without a tether, toward an unknown future. And it felt brilliant.

WIVES
&
ADMINISTRATORS

Error landed on Troy's sterile atmospheric docks, the shining silver platforms connected to the city by tethered elevators.

Ari's band of knights couldn't resist making a few faces in the small ship windows of their armored escorts. Ari tasted a wild humor at having trounced Mercer in this simple—and yet bizarrely satisfying—way. She displayed her middle finger for the shouting, shoving associates, while Kay dropped his pants and gave them the pressed ham on the glass.

"We only have minutes," Gwen said heatedly, drying out everyone's laughs. "Merlin, block their communications." Merlin complied, fingers dancing while various sensors and dishes crumpled on the outside of the Mercer ships. Ari's sense of lightness crumpled as well.

They dropped into the city in a glass elevator. Merlin's jaw hung open as he took in a planet that was entirely human-made. One enormous city covered the entire thing, without interruption. "Troy has no indigenous nature," Lam explained. "Just barren rock coated and recoated by skyscrapers. Bet you haven't seen anything like it."

"I have," he said. "This is quite like Mumbai or Tokyo or New York City in the twenty-third century, but even then, we had...sky." Merlin's eyes pointedly turned toward the pale atmosphere that glowed digitally, changing advertisements at swift intervals.

Ari put an arm around her magician. "It could be worse."

"It's worse," Kay said, pointing to a patch that lit up with Ari's picture. WANTED. DANGEROUS. KETCHAN. DO NOT APPROACH. The words scrolled beneath her scowling face, the image taken from too close—from when she'd used that couple's watch to take tourist photos on *Heritage*. She could see the visor of the knight's suit pushed all the way up. She should have kept the damn thing on to talk to them.

"Shit," Gwen said, and Ari looked at her wife, startled into a smile by how sexy Gwen sounded when she swore. "Val?"

"They can't detain her once you're inside the government offices," Val said. "It's a bizarre sanctuary loophole left over from when Troy had its own government, before Mercer swallowed it. You'll have to get there before anyone spots her, though."

"We move fast," Jordan said, her armor taking up most of the elevator. "The people here aren't strong enough to stand up to Mercer. They do as they're told. They'll report us."

Lam took off the purple scarf they were wearing and draped it around Ari's head. "And we'll go separate ways. We'll draw less attention if there are fewer of us traveling together."

Gwen took control with a succinct tilt of her head. "Jordan and Ari are with me."

Ari touched Merlin's shoulder. "You're with the boys and Lam. Take care of them?"

"No harm will come to them," Merlin promised, holding up two fingers as if making some kind of strange pledge.

She squeezed his thin shoulders and ruffled his red hair. "I trust you," she whispered. She never wanted to catch him staring into the void like he had during their spacewalk—as if he were about to be eaten whole by a cruel, pointless universe. Ari had felt like that after she lost her family, before she settled into life with Kay and the moms. "You're one of us now, got it?"

Merlin nodded with those large brown eyes that had grown on her so much that it felt like they'd always been familiar. The elevator slowed and stopped at the ground level of Troy. When the doors opened, they shot out into the city like a flock of birds from a tower window, splitting apart and yet staying in formation. Gwen knew the way, so Ari followed, and Jordan brought up the rear. Ari kept one hand near her shoulder, at the spot where Excalibur was strapped to her back.

The overcrowded nature of the planet helped matters. No one looked at Ari's face. They were too busy hustling—a rushing river of humanity that would not pause its flow for anything. The same force that was keeping her anonymous had a dark side, though. Troy had a history of terrible riots. People trampled beneath the heels of hysteria. Bodies strewn like litter in the aftermath. Which was why Mercer kept such a tight lockdown on the entire planet; she wouldn't be surprised if every single person was monitored.

Ari shivered as they wound down several streets and approached a wide, circular stone courtyard bearing an enormous gold statue of the Mercer Company logo. The gleaming building behind it wore the—much smaller—silver words GALACTIC STATE DEPARTMENT.

"They're not even trying to hide Mercer's control over the government," Ari noted. "They're bragging about it."

"Don't stop," Gwen said, nearly running inside. Ari followed but the doors blocked her entry. At first she thought she was busted, but then a red warning scrolled across the glass at eye level.

NO WEAPONS ALLOWED ON THE PREMISES.

Jordan was already unstrapping a number of concealed blades and dropping them into one of the lockers in the row beside the building. Gwen stood just inside the door, anxiously beckoning Ari to enter. Ari heaved Excalibur from her back, swinging it around in a way that cleared the crowd and caught some attention. Just then, the sky lit back up with her stark image and Mercer's ugly lies, and several people pointed and shouted.

She slammed Excalibur into the courtyard, the sword sliding through the metallic pavement as if it were as soft as earth.

Ari entered the building, leaving the crowd behind her. "We made it," she said, arms encircling Gwen. "It's going to be okay."

Relief and amusement tangoed in Gwen's expression. "Don't look now, Ari, but that was a bit of pageantry."

"If they already know I'm here, I'd rather not be shy about it."

"*Hmm,*" Gwen mouthed, a silky sound that sent Ari's mind and heart racing back to their naked, tangled hours on *Error.* "Ari," Gwen murmured, running her hands up Ari's arms. "I know what you're thinking about."

"How?" Ari asked, blushing and glancing at Jordan as the knight pushed through the thick glass doors.

"Because my body's been memorizing yours since the moment I met you." Gwen turned, pulling Ari along behind her with their fingers entwined.

"Fuck," Ari whispered, mouth dry. That statement didn't just satisfy Ari's addiction to truth. It set her heart on *fire*. "The things you do to me, lady…"

Gwen looked over her shoulder with a small, proud smile.

Minutes later, Ari and Gwen sat in the interplanetary marriage approval department. Ari eyeballed the people waiting to be interviewed and either granted legality or rejected. The white, sterile place criticized romance acutely, and everywhere she looked, Mercer had left its mark. Troy was no longer the democratic center of the galaxy. It was Mercer's favorite puppet.

Gwen was bent over a sticky, government-issued tablet, entering their information into the system with a typing speed that Ari had only imagined to be possible. She swept her curls over one shoulder, adjusting her silver crown the same way Merlin pushed his horn-rimmed glasses up his nose. The crown garnered a lot of looks. Most likely half of the new couples in the room had gone to Lionel for their medieval-styled honeymoons.

"You need one, too," Gwen said, tapping her crown without looking up from the tablet. "But don't worry. Consort crowns are smaller."

Consort. Ari would never get used to that.

"I imagine 'Helix' is your adopted name. Do you know your birth name?"

Ari peered backward into her memories. They ended in that dying water heater when Kay's chubby face peered over the edge. He'd cried when he saw her. She must have looked bad, but her brain seemed determined to protect her from the worst of the details—from whatever had come before, whatever had caused the shipwreck.

Ari shook her head. "I don't remember my last name, but Ari is a nickname. My birth name is Ara."

Gwen changed it on the tablet. "What should I call you?" she asked, her words poised but weighted.

Ari had given her nickname to her adoptive family. She'd never told them about Ara. She'd never told anyone until this moment, and now she wondered why it had come forward and where the rest of her old life might be hiding. "Ari. That's who I've been in both lives."

"And what about the other forty-one lives Val told me about?"

Wow, Gwen had chosen now to bring up the King Arthur stuff? "I haven't figured that out, but I know how off the wall it sounds. Merlin and Excalibur's magic are rather convincing, and confusing..." Ari shrugged. "I'm just trying to help my friends."

"We'll tackle that later, then." Gwen finished tapping on the tablet. "It'll be a few minutes. Relax. Both of you." Jordan's shoulders sank, clinking her armor. When Ari didn't follow suit, Gwen put a soft hand on the back of Ari's neck. "You might be Ketchan, but you are my wife, and the rules are clear. I will keep you safe."

Ari felt Gwen's confidence—or was it that soft touch?—lean through her, easing Ari's nerves. "But you're lying. You don't know that."

"I'm *hoping*. I'm trusting. That's not a lie. It's a leap of faith."

Ari always faltered when it came to hope; it felt like a lie that wanted to be a truth. "What about the boys and Lam? They're still marked for being my acquaintances and they're not great at blending in, if you didn't notice."

Gwen squeezed her fingers. "Lam's hand was not your fault. That was Mercer being"—she raised her voice pointedly—"tyrannical bullies!"

Ari glanced around. "Should you be saying that here?"

"A government that cannot handle criticism cannot handle governing. Isn't that right?" Gwen said, her voice floating across the room as if she were speaking to a stadium on Lionel.

Many, many eyes turned to her. They held shock and no small amount of fear.

"Besides," she continued with bravado. "This is the *galactic* state department. This is Troy. And it might be ground zero for the Mercer Company, but they can't own the government, can they? Or perhaps, they can't *admit* to owning it."

People were astounded. Ari was, too.

Gwen's tablet vibrated. "See? Always works. No one wants a salty queen in the waiting room stirring up trouble." She winked, stood, and pulled Ari toward the doors to the interior, their fingers linked in a sweetheart hold. "Stay, Jordan," she called over her shoulder.

Ari only had a few moments to categorize her impressed reaction. Gwen was not only playing a game with Mercer, she was enjoying it. "How do you do that, Gwen?"

"All the universe is a stage." She smiled. "The right spotlight pointed at the right place can make all the difference."

They followed the lighted signs on the floor toward a small interrogation room devoid of everything but a table and chairs. Ari and Gwen sat with their backs to the wall, waiting.

Ari crossed her arms. Her legs. Gwen was infuriatingly calm, and she knew that drove Ari nuts. The door opened, and a woman in a green suit held her hand out for Gwen's tablet. "Goody, a queen," she muttered. "You're going to help me win my bingo this month."

Gwen handed over the tablet, while the woman dropped into the seat on the other side of the table. She flicked through the first few pages of their information. "You were married nine days ago. On Lionel. So romantic. Consummated?" She looked up, one eyebrow high.

"Yes." Gwen looked at Ari.

"Yes," Ari said stiffly.

"Are you *sure*?" the woman asked.

Gwen inhaled in a pointed way. Val had just won the bet over whether they'd ask, and Ari couldn't help sinking back to Kay's room.

"But it's a political marriage," Ari had argued.

"Even those need physical ties, unless you'd like to say you are ace. I'm afraid it wouldn't work for me. Too many known lovers," Gwen admitted casually.

"Same," Ari replied, trying not to stare at Gwen with a brand-new kind of hunger.

"So you'll have to lie."

"I am not a convincing liar. When I lie I actually feel sick."

"Well, we can't have you throwing up in the galactic state department at the very thought of sleeping with me." Gwen had tried to cross the room, but Ari caught her around the waist, amazed at how merely cupping Gwen's hip made both of them inhale.

"You know that's not what I mean."

Gwen leaned in, pressing a soft leg between Ari's. "You really can't think of any way to solve this dilemma?" she'd asked, followed by a more challenging, "You're still afraid of me."

"I'm terrified," Ari had said, the words tumbling, pouring over Gwen's lips as she kissed a line down her jaw. "You rile me up. You always have. But I'm not afraid of your body." She proved it with her hands, her mouth, her limbs shaking until some nitwit turned the gravity off—only for them to discover that being pressed together in the air was even sweeter than the bed.

Hours later the pile of their clothes had seemed like a piece of art. Ari stared at it, took a picture with her watch. Then she turned to Gwen's sleeping form and edged closer. The queen's pretenses disappeared when she was asleep. And now, Ari knew, when she was making love.

"Four times," Ari said to the state department official. "It was exquisite. I can give you the play-by-play."

"Not necessary." The woman went back to the tablet. Gwen gave Ari an exasperated look that left Ari staring at Gwen's mouth—reliving the special talents of those lips.

"Born on Troy?" the woman asked Gwen, breaking their moment. "Welcome home."

Ari's desire flipped over into surprise. "I thought you were born on Lionel."

Gwen shifted in her seat and gave the woman a polite smile.

Oh, shit. Had Ari just given them away?

"No worries, honey," the woman said. "In my experience, the marriage is more legit if there are a few secrets. Otherwise it seems like you've been quizzing each other." Ari's nerves eased but didn't back off all the way. The woman kept reading and then looked at Ari. "Your birthplace is listed as Ketch."

Ari tried a smile. "That's gotta be the star center on the bingo board, am I right?"

The woman sprang out of the room as if she were fleeing Merlin's bizarre magic. In the corner, a red light went off soundlessly, and Ari heard the door lock in several places.

"What the—"

Gwen smiled at the red light. "Don't say anything, baby girl."

Ari ached to stand or pace, but Gwen kept her cool smile on the red light, holding Ari's hand tightly. Ari leaned back to Gwen's ear. "Did you just 'baby girl' me?"

"Too cutesy?" Gwen asked.

"The jury's still out. Buttercups."

"Vetoed."

"Understood."

Despite having spent a week trading pieces of their histories, sharing scars, and shedding clothes, this closeness felt new. It was highlighted by their fear. "Ari...listen," Gwen said, her words breathy, small. "We might have to deal with the Administrator. I'd hoped he wouldn't take notice, but..."

"The Mercer CEO?" Ari shot sideways out of her chair as anger, accusation, and rampant fear flamed through her body. "Gwen, he knows—"

"Stop," she whispered.

"—where my parents are locked up. He—"

Gwen tugged on the front of her shirt, with that *Damnit, Ari* look. They were kissing so fast Ari's internal fire sizzled. At first, it was a tender heat, but then the desperation of this entire trip built until Ari was holding Gwen as close as possible.

Gwen's face nuzzled against Ari's ear. "We can't let him know what we want. He'll use it against us. Trust me."

Gwen pulled back, her brown eyes bright, her lips flushed red. "Aren't we giving him a show?" she announced in the direction of the warning light. "Enjoying this with popcorn, Administrator?"

Ari felt sick at the idea of someone watching them. Not just *someone*. The man who ran the most powerful company in the galaxy—and therefore the universe. The door unlocked, and Ari reached emptily at the spot over her shoulder where Excalibur should be.

&

Gwen and Ari followed the flashing lights along the wall to an elevator on the dizzying top floor of a skyscraper. The Administrator's office was a circular room made entirely of windows, the décor solidly Mercer white with bold black accents.

Ari had heard stories about the Mercer Company's CEO over the years—and of course seen his face in his innumerable ads—but none of that prepared her for this meeting. He lounged across a couch, middle-aged with long limbs, his skin as white as if he had been grown in a tank of bleach. He was nondescript in the face, the body, the clothes. His hair was a white-blond thatch, oddly sparse. If Ari had tried to draw him, she would have managed a stick figure and given up.

He held up a bowl that had been resting in his lap. "Pretzels, not popcorn. What do we win for stumping you? Your planet? How about that awesome crown?"

When Gwen did little more than tighten her grip on Ari's hand, the Administrator shot up and crossed the room. "We kid, we kid." He hugged Gwen as if they were old friends, and Ari ached to dismantle the embrace with her bare hands.

Gwen allowed him to touch her and then breathed through her nose. "How lovely of you to drag me up here once again."

"Oh, my sweet and spicy Gweneviere. Tell us you missed us."

"No, thank you."

His eyes twinkled as he turned to Ari. "Ara Azar, how delighted we are to find you still living. And married to my favorite monarch! Should we discuss celebrity power couple names or let something emerge organically?"

Ari felt slapped.

Azar.

Her bones knew that name. Her heart did, as well.

Only her head was behind.

"How do you..." Ari started, trying to find the words.

Gwen bristled whole-bodily, tugging them to the couches to sit while Ari's mind stroked every single letter of *Azar* as if it were the greatest gift she'd ever been given...but that meant she was in debt to Mercer, which did not feel right. Her eyes dropped to the wooden coffee table, an elaborate chessboard embedded in its polished finish.

The Administrator lounged across the opposite couch. "Ara, please continue. You were going to say, 'How do you know my family name?' And *we* were going to say," he sat up, cold, dark eyes suddenly piercing, "from your mother's ship. Not your incarcerated adoptive mothers' ship. The first mother. Such a determined heart, that one." He leaned back again, seemingly bored. "But we won't say any more, so don't bother asking."

Ari's heart hammered so loudly she couldn't think straight. He was talking about her mother like he knew her. Like maybe she was still alive. Was she in one of Mercer's compounds, too? Was she a political prisoner here on Troy?

"We are only here for two reasons," Gwen said, making a grab for control of the conversation, looking keenly aware that it had slipped away. "One, you promised hydration shipments, and you haven't delivered. You have been late this past year, but this month's cycle you've been flat-out hovering in the atmosphere, refusing to land."

"Us? Personally, we never hover. Bad for the lower back."

"You know what I mean. What do I have to do to get Mercer to keep its word?"

"Sign over the planet," he said. Gwen snarled, and Ari gripped her wife's elbow. "We'll let you remain figurehead. You can even pretend to pass laws and whatnot."

"You know my answer," she said.

"As you wish. A few more weeks of dehydration and your people will hand over the planet willingly. For their troubles, we'll give each of them enough water for their own swimming pool. Two-day shipping on all aboveground pools." He held up a finger. "For a limited time, of course."

Ari leaned in, wanting to help Gwen. "What does Mercer have against Lionel?"

"Mercer?" the Administrator said as if he'd never heard the word before. "Mercer is a corporation, my dear rogue Ketchan. We sell things and solve problems; we do not have enemies." His eyes turned from Ari to Gwen, hardening. "But we do have customers who become loyal friends. Troy is such a friend. The same friendship Lionel has rejected repeatedly, and as you know, Troy is angry that it can't vent its overpopulated cities to Lionel, a largely underused planet."

"My people," Gwen interrupted, "require space to breathe, live, have families, and—"

"Ride robotic horses like medieval jesters? Wear cheap tin and call it armor?" He licked his lips, savoring his attack. "Or how about bow to a queen because they're too ignorant to figure out democracy?"

Gwen steamed. Ari didn't know that a person could actually do that, but she was certain that if she placed a hand on Gwen's arm, it would burn. "I'm fairly certain it's not a democracy if every electable politician is already living in Mercer's pocket."

The Administrator waved his hand. "Trivial points. Troy would like Lionel to be punished until you comply. Mercer is not your real problem. The overcrowded galaxy is."

Ari scowled and swiped the black king piece from the board. "Chess? That's not even bad-guy original. Don't you know that evil empires are overdone?"

The Administrator leaned forward, his elbows on his knees. "Finally, someone who gets us. It's boring to make people suffer. Good thing we don't have to do that *all* the time. We're the white team. The good guys." He moved a white pawn. "We connect galaxies' worth of goods to people in need. There are even planets where we are God." Ari tried to drop the black king, but the Administrator stole it out of her hand.

"Of course, we're also the bad guys when we need to be. You see, Ara, we're black and white. Right *and* wrong. And that never gets boring. What games you can play when you're both sides! Showing people what they need, and convincing them you're the only one who can possibly provide it. I'm sure you remember when we had to play bad guy and shut off Ketch beneath that barrier. Then again, they really had that coming. So much loquacious resistance. '*Mercer is evil. Band together, trade openly, provide for each other, blah blah.'* It's much better this way, with them keeping to their own planet. You're the only one out here, causing trouble."

Gwen pulled Ari back by the shoulder, away from the Administrator's slathered-on smile. "She's my wife. You can't touch her."

"Sadly, Troy is under the impression that this marriage is a sham. They're in the process of rejecting it. But not all is lost! Gweneviere, you are free to return to Lionel. The water will arrive soonish. And Ara, you're going to stay right here on Troy for a spell. Be our guest. Let us figure out what you... remember... about your dear old home planet."

Remember?

"Enough," Gwen said, her voice strong and yet scratchy. "First, you're going to make sure Troy signs off on our marriage. Then you're going to have the water delivered, or I'll sue. And interplanetary lawsuits kill the economy."

This was Gwen's strongest threat, but Ari could tell he wasn't fazed. In fact, the Administrator looked newly pleased. He nearly giggled. "You may have one of those things. Not both. The water or the marriage. How's that for good *and* bad?"

Gwen's body tensed, her breath shallow and quick. People would die if she picked Ari. Ari might die if she picked Lionel, leaving her in the hands of Mercer. Gwen looked at Ari, her desperation damn near heartbreaking. "Ari, I..."

She was going to pick the planet. She had to. Ari understood, but her mind felt tight and swift. She looked down at the coffee table. Made of wood. Actual wood. And from her time spent on *Heritage*'s observation deck in that stupid rubber knight suit, she knew there was only one planet where you could get wood. "Old Earth," Ari whispered.

A dead pause, and then the Administrator asked, "What about it?"

Gwen snapped to look at Ari, concerned. Intrigued.

"Nice table," Ari said, her tone cutting. "Imported?"

"Naturally," the Administrator said, all humor vanished.

"Recently?" she asked. "How does Troy feel about your side project?" She was bluffing, but a voice inside said, *Trust yourself.* "After all, there are, what? Hundreds of restrictions involved in a retired planet's preservation."

"You can't blackmail Mercer, my darling Ketchan. What proof could you even have?"

"There's an entire planet of proof. Or has Mercer grown so overconfident that you've forgotten where we *all* came from?" She scrolled two-fingered down her watch face and projected the video of the leveling machinery consuming half-dead trees.

"That's plenty, *thank you*." The Administrator placed his small hand over her arm, stunting the image, while his nondescript eyes took on a flinty edge. "Lionel can have its water. You can have your little fake marriage. Happy?"

Gwen was looking at Ari like she'd never seen her before. Ari pulled Gwen to her feet, crossing to the exit, but his voice stopped them at the door.

"Ladies, before you go, we have an offer that you will, of course, refuse, and yet it will be such a good offer that neither of you will forget it. For as long as you live in your cinderblock castle on your little medieval bubble land, you'll wonder what could have been."

Gwen tugged on Ari's arm. "Don't listen."

"As much water as you can store, whenever you want it," he called after them. "And you can keep the planet. No Mercer strings attached. You, Ara, can give your adoptive parents back to your brother, unharmed. Well, as unharmed as they've managed to remain. Prison is no picnic, after all. You could even fetch them today, if you like. Which would be ideal. I hear there's some sort of plague going around the cell block on Urite."

Ari pulled out of Gwen's hand to face the Administrator. "What price?"

"Just you." He smiled. "Just you for a whole planet and your *only* surviving mothers."

Ari saw through the Administrator's words. Her first mother—the one he'd started this whole conversation teasing her about—was dead, and he knew how, when, why...

Ari's mind burst with sudden memories. *Explosions.* Their spaceship was exploding, and she was alone, locked in a part of the ship far away from everyone she loved...

Where was the rest of that memory? What had happened before?

She grasped into the darkness and came up empty.

&

Gwen hauled Ari into the glass elevator with its panoramic, sinking view of Troy's capital city.

Ari was still dazed, trying to process the burst of memory and the Administrator's terrible offer. "Gwen, what if he's telling the—"

"No." Gwen paused the elevator, and they froze midair. "I don't know about you, but I'd rather not have our first lover's quarrel be about whether I should trade you in like a set of steak knives." She took a deep, shaking breath. "I know you're new to leading people, but you don't make deals with a company like Mercer. You move to the other side of the galaxy and scratch out a living without them. You're Ketchan, for crying out loud, Ari. Your people invented giving Mercer the middle finger. And *what* was that business about Old Earth?"

"Long story," Ari said. "That was...I was just trying to make him fear the truth."

"We have to get back to Lionel." Gwen reached for the button, but Ari caught her hand.

"Gwen, what if there is a plague on Urite? What if my..." *only surviving* "...parents are about to die? We have to save them."

"A prison break? Ari! Imagine what they'd do to my planet if I was associated with a prison break." Her brown eyes were fiery, and if Ari hadn't been steaming as well, she might have been entranced by how certain her wife always seemed. No matter what. Gwen knew her path. Her *home*. Ari would give just about anything for an ounce of that certainty.

Gwen's fire quieted as she looked at Ari's pained face. "Don't take this as me condoning anything, but why don't you talk to Merlin? Isn't he your go-to man for all things illegal and outrageous? Perhaps he can wiggle his fingers and transport them to a safer place."

At that moment, across the city, the sky exploded with fireworks.

Ari groaned. "Speak of the devil."

"He's shooting fireworks off in the city?" she yelled, hitting the elevator button.

"He can't help it," Ari said. "Dramatic soul."

Once at ground level, they found Jordan and filed out of the state department. A crowd had gathered around Excalibur, the sword still stabbed through the center of the square. They were taking turns tugging on it. Beefy people, kids, old and young. Ari pushed through to the center, elbowing aside a muscled woman who would have given Jordan a run for her money.

Ari lifted Excalibur, drawing the point toward the fake sky easily. She was instantly relieved by the weight of the steel, how strong and eternal and unerringly *good* this blade felt in her hands. The crowd hushed, fell back. They took her in strangely.

Ari's heart drilled a ferocious beat. This was the moment she'd feared since her moms had sat her down and explained that she was never to leave *Error* without them. That she was never to tell anyone she was Ketchan or speak her native language. When little Ari asked why, Captain Mom had seemed close to tears, and Mom answered, "Because too many people believe that difference is the enemy of unity."

Were they staring now because they knew Ari was Ketchan— or because she was wielding a mythical sword? And why did they look like they wanted her to *do something*?

Ari tilted her head back as she took in the mammoth statue of the Mercer Company logo's gold *M*. They'd stolen that letter, copyrighted it. Made it symbolic for everything and nothing. Hollow and yet harrowing. Like telling a girl that her mother had a determined heart—but that it hadn't saved her. Like teasing that same girl about how the women who had raised her were probably dying of plague at that very moment.

"Lady, being your wife…does that mean I can commit crimes without being charged?"

"Up to a point, yes," Gwen said, pinching her lips together. "Why?"

Ari sealed both hands on Excalibur, swinging it over her head and crying out as she brought it around her body and through the giant leg of the M. The statue did nothing at first. But then it groaned. And gave way to its broken side, the metal falling in a way that made Ari grab Gwen and pull her to safety. When it had finally flattened itself and fallen silent in the courtyard, Ari found Jordan's eyebrow hitched in a surprised and yet approving way.

"Let me know if you ever want to train," Jordan said with slight awe. "You have a gift."

"I'll keep that in mind."

Gwen was chewing on a few choice words. She held up an accusing finger, and Ari had the urge to kiss it. "The next time you goad me about being dramatic, I'm going to say, *Remember the M?* And you're going to apologize and kiss me like the universe is ending."

Ari's arm muscles pulled, a flash of nerves and desire that made it hard to drop Excalibur into the sheath at her back. "And what if the universe is actually ending?"

Then, from across the city, the entire planet started eerily chanting Merlin's name.

GOODS
&
BADS

"Merlin. Merlin. Merlin."

The crowd kept flinging Merlin's name at him, and not in a nice way. It cut into him, mocked him with a few millennia worth of regrets.

"Stop," he mumbled. *"Please."*

"MER-LIN."

Morgana smirked, her bony, bluish hands levitating to increase the intensity of the cheer. She twisted her hands, curled her fingers, and closed them, cutting the crowd off like she was strangling air from hundreds of throats. Everyone from small children to Mercer associates in white suits stood rapt, mouths slightly parted.

Granted, an open courtyard in the heart of Mercer country wasn't the best place for a magic battle, but he was making do. He would not let Morgana get to Ari. He would exhaust her cruel, cold magic on himself, if he had to. That was the plan. It was a terrible plan.

Merlin stumbled to one knee, shaking. He braced his head with his palm and closed his eyes...falling back to earlier that day, when he'd promised Ari he would keep her friends safe. He'd watched her walk away, striding after Gweneviere, as he filled with foolish hope that things would be different this time. That he truly was one of this band.

The hope was faraway now, a hazy thing he could no longer touch.

How had he gotten here? Leveled by Morgana...*on purpose*?

After parting from Ari, Merlin had followed the boys and Lam deep into Troy and found Mercer's influence smeared across the planet-wide city like white blood. The associates who wore bleached suits and blank features were the least of it. Every store was overstocked with Mercer products. Merlin wondered how anyone could breathe, and yet he also remembered the start of this. By the last cycle, heaps of goods and sundries had been considered necessary to life in almost every nation on Earth. Merlin had drawn the line at loofahs. They were puffy yet abrasive. No matter how many centuries he'd strolled through, he couldn't quite understand the appeal of needing to own *everything*.

"How are so many people shopping in the middle of the day?" Merlin asked. "Don't they have work? Families to tend to?" The people in the lines looked edgy, nervous, as they studied the contents of their carts and baskets.

"The government on Troy gives everyone shopping breaks," Val said in a gruff voice that Merlin was not acquainted with.

"That's...thoughtful?" Merlin tried.

Val shook his head and whispered in a way that tugged Merlin closer. "They put a quota on how much a person needs to buy from Mercer *every day* if they want to stay on Troy.

Anyone who doesn't meet the quota gets shipped to a much less livable planet. Anyone who runs out of money gets kicked off, too. It didn't used to be this bad, but when the Ketchans disappeared behind the barrier and took the last of the resistance with them, Mercer took it as their cue to ramp things up."

Merlin noticed someone at the front of a line whose basket must have been too skimpy. They were escorted away by Mercer associates, as everyone around them rushed from the scene. "Why isn't anyone speaking up? Stopping this?" Merlin asked, piping and reedy in a way that would have been mortifying if he wasn't so outraged.

"They'd get sent away for being agitators, of course," Val said, hooking his arm through Merlin's to keep them together in the pushing, hard-breathing crowd. "Did I mention that Mercer assigns a lifetime's worth of debt when they ship you off-planet? *Transportation fees*."

Merlin's magic prickled inside his hands, as if each finger was tipped with a stinger. He hummed a tuneless song—no time for pretty melodies—and blasted the Mercer associates holding the shopper. They flew backward, landing in a fountain with an impressive splash as the shopper ran off.

Would Ari be proud of him for doing that, or upset that he'd put her friends in danger by possibly drawing attention to them? Wheeling away, Merlin did his best to look like an innocent Trojan instead of an agitator. But oh, how he wanted to agitate.

Merlin went back to the promise of the cycle. Ari was in the galactic state department right now, being officially declared Gwen's consort. That was as close to a king as Merlin had gotten in a dozen cycles. There had been a civil rights leader, a president, a rock star—all kings in their own way. Soon Ari

would be cosmic royalty, which meant the next step was coming, head-on.

Defeat the greatest evil in the universe.

Mercer.

"Hey, guys!" Lam cried, as they passed a food stall that
emitted a sweet warm smell like melted heaven. "They have a
Honeybun."

Merlin was starving, and his feet hooked him around to the
end of the line with very little input from his brain. Two maple
cream donuts later, he had slightly revised his stance on Troy.
People did need to eat more than dehydrated packets of space
food, after all. Could he still think Mercer's influence was corrupt and oppressive while licking sugar off of his fingers?

Yes. Yes, he could.

"I can't believe you eat this stuff," Val said, tugging at Merlin, who had already gotten in line for another dozen to bring
back to the ship. "It was Lam's favorite on Pluto, and we didn't
have much of anything there, but still."

Merlin's curiosity prickled. Val had asked so many questions
about Merlin back on *Error,* and now he wanted to pose as many
in return. What had his childhood been like? Pluto sounded like
a hardscrabble planet, although Val had a sense of beauty and
refinement Merlin found rare in any time and place. Val also
had a way of rubbing at the back of his shaved head when he
was worked up over something, showing off the lines of his neck
where it shaded into his slim but strong shoulders, and then...

A sickly, electric rush flowed through Merlin's body.

Not hormones this time.

He had walked straight through Morgana.

"You really don't notice what is right in front of your face," she said with a low laugh that hit Merlin's spine like a crackle of static. She looked out of place in the daylight, but no one else seemed to notice the ancient enchantress on their commutes. People flowed around her as if she wasn't there at all.

Merlin sighed. "It was only a matter of time before you found me."

Morgana's forehead might not have been covered in real skin, but it could still knot with disappointment. "That's what lazy people say. *Time heals all wounds. These things take time. It's only a matter of...time.* You and I have been here long enough to know that's not true. Wounds fester, and time changes nothing."

Merlin would never admit it to Morgana, but she was right. Troy, for instance, might look and taste and feel like the future, but this was just a new kind of Dark Age. The path humans took through time was less the mythical arrow of progress, and more of a squiggle that doubled back on itself, curling and looping. A roller coaster designed by a drunkard.

If things truly got better, Morgana couldn't have given him a head full of the terrible happenings since the last Arthur. His brain served them up in king-size portions. Rampant fire. Choking floods. Clouds that smeared the sky with toxins. People trampling over each other to leave Earth, and then scattering so far and wide they could no longer help each other without a company like Mercer sliding in to fill the void.

This was why people needed Arthur.

"Are you two old friends?" Lam asked, stepping forward with interest.

She gave them a smile she had honed to a blade over the centuries. "I hate Merlin with the venom of an adder, the rage of a forest fire, and the vigor of a woman making love."

"So…no," Lam said. They stepped back, tugging Val and Kay.

"Go," Merlin said, flinging a hand to send the knights toward Ari, and safety. "Leave Morgana to me."

"I'd rather have them stay," Morgana said, and the words were like concrete pouring around the ankles of Val and Lam and Kay, sticking them in place.

"What the hell?" Kay asked.

"It's mind magic," Merlin barked.

"Really? It feels pretty damn physical to me."

"Don't worry, meaty little mortal. You have your own will," Morgana said, advancing toward Kay one step at a time. "It's what I'm using against you. Brute force will only get a person—a government, a company—so far. Dig an inch below the surface, and you discover what someone wants, which can be used to *nudge* them."

Morgana trailed her non-fingers along Kay's arm, and he shuddered as the air released a slight crackle. "The greatest power is a hand on your shoulder, a whisper in your head, gentle but insistent. These people don't want to see what's happening, so they don't see it. *You* don't want to find out what will happen if you threaten me, and that makes it easy to ensure you won't take a single step closer."

Morgana swiveled back to Merlin. Those pale lips, not dead, not alive, made him want to retch. "This isn't the whole party, is it? Where is your precious Ari?"

"You will stay away from her," Merlin nearly yelled.

Morgana chuckled. "Always trying to tell people where to go, what to do, what their destinies are." Merlin's anger pitched him forward, just as Morgana touched Lam's brow, making them writhe. "Where is she?"

Lam's eyes and mouth burst wide open, as if they were shouting without speech. "The Galactic State Department?" Morgana asked, reading their thoughts. "That way?"

Lam slumped to the ground, long limbs releasing as unconsciousness dropped over them. Kay and Val cried out, still frozen to the spot, while Morgana strode in the direction Ari had gone, ready to torture her.

Merlin couldn't let that happen to another Arthur.

He couldn't let it happen to *Ari,* who had caught him when he was nearly claimed by the blackness of space.

Merlin hummed a song from the climactic scene of his favorite boxing movie—this was going to be a magical showdown, wasn't it?—and picked up items from the nearest store, tossing them through the air, creating a whirlpool of goods. He threw them in Morgana's path. It wasn't much, but it stole her attention away from her purpose. He would make himself a nuisance. He would get her to fight him, exhaust her magic before she could get to Ari.

Morgana spun on a heel, hissing at him. Merlin almost cheered at how predictable her hatred was. Now he needed to keep her contained. He grabbed boxes and carts with his magic, trying to wall her in, but she strode through everything, her shimmering form emerging in front of each new obstacle.

Their fight was growing more obvious by the second to the people around him. Merlin needed to draw them in, to use *them* as Morgana's cage. He'd seen her avoid passing through people whenever she could, as if it left her with a bad aftertaste of humanity.

"What draws crowds?" Merlin shouted to Val and Kay, both still stuck in place.

"Music?" Kay suggested.

"Fireworks," Val shouted.

Merlin snapped his fingers in agreement. A tune by an old songstress known as Katy Perry fizzled to his lips. Fireworks exploded in the sky, red and yellow and green, causing everyone to gather around, looking up.

Merlin's smugness lasted only as long as it took to hear Morgana's laugh. It was as wispy as the rest of her, drizzling like cold rain. "How do you think Ari liked your little display?" she asked. "If she's as good an Arthur as you seem to think—and oh, yes, I can tell you like this one—she should come *running*."

Merlin faltered. His hands dropped to his sides. *Of course* Ari would come if she saw a show of Merlin's magic exploding across the city. Merlin's plan had been to distract Morgana with a battle. Instead, she had used his magic for her own purposes.

And now the crowd was chanting his name in a way that echoed through the unnatural city, calling out to Ari, no doubt.

"Merlin. Merlin. Merlin."

Morgana was barely expending magic with her paltry puppet tricks. He needed to get close. Let her poison him. Only, he was shaking. Afraid. And so tired...

"Leave him alone!" Val's arms wrapped around Merlin's chest, stunning him with closeness, tenderness.

Morgana swiveled, making Merlin's guts pinch. "Protective, are we? But you don't even know Merlin. I have the long view of his life, and I promise you, it's not pretty." She took a step forward and raised her fingers. "I can show you, if you like."

Val's face flared with worry and—was that curiosity?

Sickly fear sloshed through Merlin. He didn't want Val to have a box seat to his worst moments. But more than that, he didn't want Morgana to have power over his friends, like she'd always had over him. He filled both of his hands with green fireballs and tossed them at Morgana's feet.

She shook her head, like Merlin was both a silly child and a useless old man. "Have you forgotten our eternal stalemate, Merlin? Your magic can't hurt me, and unfortunately mine can't kill you." She walked toward Merlin at a stately pace, dripping with confidence like some women dripped with diamonds. He did have to give her points for that. She could have all the points she wanted, as long as she didn't win.

"Always so certain you're going to slither past me, Morgana," Merlin said.

"I have, several times," she said. "Or do you not remember your dead heroes? Do you let them fade as you go on forever, caring for no one but yourself?"

Morgana was so close now that he could see the unnatural smoothness of her skin, all the places where lines should have cracked her ancient face. "Are you going to paralyze me with what happened when I was asleep again?" Merlin asked. "It's not my fault you stay perpetually awake. You should invest in a good cave."

Ire scratched Morgana's face. Merlin had gotten under her icy demeanor, and it felt addictively good. "I don't need to show you that pain again," she spat. "Let's find something that *really* hurts. Let's visit the ways you've failed my brother in every lifetime, shall we?"

"This is ridiculous," Kay said, pushing between the two of them, his burly arms casting Merlin back toward Val. "She's not even human. How much can she actually do to us?"

Morgana was upon him in a second, a lightning strike of a

woman, fast enough to give the crowd whiplash. She pressed Kay's chest, and he crumbled like a handful of ash. He was on the ground, rolling and shouting, speaking in tongues. The only thing that Merlin could pick out was Ari's name...until Kay fell silent.

And Lam was still down a few yards away.

Merlin had promised Ari none of her friends would come to harm. How had he failed so fast? He kept his body between Morgana and Val, arms spread wide. "Stop pestering mortals and give yourself a challenge," Merlin taunted, his throat dry.

Morgana smiled at the invitation. Merlin knew she couldn't drive him into the grave like she could with his Arthurs. But she could make him hurt as deeply as possible. That should have been Merlin's motto for his role in the cycle—*all of the pain, none of the death.*

Morgana brushed her fingers over Merlin's cheek, sending a shower of needles through his skin, stabbing deeper until it reached his mind. He tried to catch a glimpse of Lam and Kay. To determine if Val was safe. To make sure that Ari was far away. But Morgana pressed a thumb to his forehead, the singe of her laugh following him into a vision.

He saw the Arthurs that Morgana had killed, the memories stacked high. Arthur 9, driven to insanity. Arthur 23, suicide. Arthur 35, reduced to frantic babbling about how a dark-haired sorceress haunted his dreams.

When the pictures faded, Morgana was smiling at him. Merlin could see through her face, his focus wavering in and out. She ran her fingers down his arm, leaving trails of white-hot pain. His vision went blank, replaced by the cruelest memory.

His lover's face so near it blurred his features, all except those bright brown eyes. The rush of Art's kiss, the welcoming darkness. And then Merlin was pushing Art away, saying, "We can't do this forever," meaning those words quite literally. When Art tried to argue, to kiss him again, when he broke down and cried, Merlin tightened his jaw and lectured on all the reasons they wouldn't work. He made himself sound wise, when all he truly felt was fear.

Merlin came out of that one lying on the ground, unable to tell if the bruising he felt was on the inside or out. He pushed up to his elbows. While he'd been stuck in his own head, Morgana had had plenty of time to cast Val to the ground, all three knights glassy-eyed. And there was more. She'd taken out the people around them, every last one.

Morgana had struck down Merlin's human shield.

"Merlin!" Ari's voice brightened the courtyard.

"No," he croaked, but his voice, like his heart, was in tatters. "Don't…" Merlin breathed hard. He didn't need Morgana's touch to unlock any more of his memories. She'd thrown the doors wide. Now he saw a castle in a chilled northern country that no longer existed, Arthur 12 listening as Merlin used visions of the future to help guide him. But it hadn't worked; he blamed Merlin for his heartbreak over Gweneviere and ran him through with Excalibur. It was the only time one of his Arthurs had tried to kill him.

Then that blistering day in a country far too hot for his robes, when Merlin grew so desperate to leave the cycle that he tossed himself off a cliff—only to wake up with seventeen broken bones and the rest of cycle 20 to finish.

And the moment he'd realized he was truly stuck on repeat. Arthur 6. Merlin had been so existentially seasick that he'd tried to sit that one out. He found the nearest monastery and argued with the monks until they decided he must have a demon for a mother. Arthur hadn't made it far without Merlin's help, dying with a thatch of arrows in his gut before he set foot near a throne.

"Merlin!" Ari shouted again as she crossed the courtyard, Excalibur held high.

"Stay away!" Merlin cried in a horribly soft voice. He tried to use magic to write it in the sky, but the sparks left his fingers and fizzled out.

"You've failed Arthur so many times," Morgana said, appearing over him, crouching until she was all he could see. The torn ribbons of her hair, the vicious mercy in her eyes. "Now it's time for this to end. *My* way."

"And what is that?" Merlin rasped.

"King Arthur needs to die," she said sweetly. "Once and for all."

Merlin tried to get up one more time but couldn't. Back to the black-and-white tiles of the courtyard he went. He couldn't see Ari, but he could hear the persistent pounding of her feet in the otherwise silenced city. "Maybe I'm weak, but Ari is stronger than the others," he said, conviction pushing the words out. "Your old tricks won't be enough this time, Morgana."

"Really?" she asked. "How about a new trick, then?"

Morgana vanished from her place at Merlin's side right before Ari reached him.

Ari fell to her knees, touching his face. "Merlin, what happened?"

Morgana reappeared with a cold smile, placing one finger against Ari's temple, and one against Merlin's. She sent them spinning into darkness and pain—together.

MEMORY
&
DEATH

"Where am I?" Ari asked, the words silvery and unattached to anything.

She had no body, no hands, no voice—only a view. She was in a shimmering cave lined in earth that smelled of ancient water. Reflected light formed a shimmering blue net on the walls.

"We are inside my worst memory," Merlin said, his voice beside her, and yet also far away. "Morgana has truly outdone herself. She wants you to see my deepest shame."

"I'm angry, bitter. Hungry," Ari said, confused.

"You aren't. I am...or I was. Once upon a time." Merlin's voice pointed toward two figures in the ethereal cave. One was a woman. Kind of. She was liquid grace and glowing edges, beautiful and terrifying.

"That's not Morgana," Ari said. Morgana felt vile. Evil. Although really those were the same words in a different arrangement. Either way, this felt deeper, like old rot or the roots of an ancient mountain, or perhaps the unfathomable darkness of space.

"That is not Morgana," Merlin agreed. "That is the Lady of the Lake. Nimue. To me, she called herself Nin. I have not seen her since this moment. Perhaps she is dead and gone. It was she who gave Arthur Excalibur."

"Does that make her good?"

Merlin's tone was so cold. Defeated. "It makes her a supplier of weapons."

"What about the other person?" Ari asked, squinting at the weathered, gnarled figure.

"You don't recognize him?" Merlin said, a splash of hope in his voice. "That is me. At my earliest. At my worst."

Ari took in the bold stars and moons on the cuffs and trim of his robe, unfaded. Old Merlin was the same height and weight as the Merlin she loved, and yet everything about this one was different. White, furious hair, beard, and eyebrows. A hooked nose and wrinkled lips.

And most of all, an insatiable, cold hunger that seemed to permeate Ari's heart.

"This interruption of yours is the worst yet, Nin," Old Merlin said with a dash of entitled impatience. Ari barely recognized the voice, *Merlin's voice*. It was so much older, the creases sharp. "I am needed by the king. He is in the midst of battle."

"If you go to Arthur now, you'll die," Nin said, her words flooding the cave and Ari's senses. "I can't have that."

"How can you be so sure I'll die?" Old Merlin asked. "Is there a prophecy?"

"Prophecies are for amateurs," Nin said, her watery voice freezing over. "You're not going anywhere, all apologies."

Old Merlin pushed up his sleeves, crooked, knobby fingers pointed at the Lady of the Lake. "Arthur needs me!" His voice cracked with desperation, and love, which overtook the anger of this memory. "Free me!"

"How about some more power, Merlin? To make up for your impending loss." Nin sighed. "You're not going to take this well. I haven't been looking forward to it. But I'm not so cruel as to send you spinning through eternity without a few perks."

The ancient magician's hands drooped. "What kind of power?"

"The ability to sense the future? To see forward a bit, the rough edges of events, anyway. It might help, given your... condition."

"Condition?" Ari found herself murmuring.

"My backward aging," Merlin elaborated from beside her. His presence had fractured as if the memory was breaking him into pieces. "I return to this moment often. *So* often. I want to crawl back through time and change everything. Stop it. Prevent it. Save Arthur...instead of treating myself."

"I accept your gift," Old Merlin grumbled, sounding bored.

Ari watched Nin press a kiss that beamed with light onto Old Merlin's head. Almost instantly, Old Merlin fell to his knees, sobbing, holding his brittle chest.

"What happened?" Ari asked.

"That was the first time I saw the future," Merlin said. "The end of that battle I'd just been stolen from."

"What did you see?" Ari asked, fear shimmering. Merlin didn't answer, and she wished she could hold his hand, frustrated that they were both simply wisps of consciousness tied to each other inside this trauma. "I'm here, Merlin. Tell me what you saw."

"I don't have to," Merlin finally said.

Old Merlin disappeared as the entire cave faded into a blackness that became night. The moon took forever to glow, and the stars were hidden. All around, Ari smelled death. Now she was relieved that she didn't have a body as her mind glided over countless corpses, following Old Merlin across the remains of a field washed with blood and death.

Thousands of soldiers, knights, and flags littered the field.

Broken and fallen. Without hope.

Old Merlin moved toward the heart of the misery, where one lone figure sat, clutching a body to their chest. Ari's shock almost overpowered Old Merlin's sadness in that moment. *Almost.* The person holding the fallen body was Morgana. Not the ethereal, bluish Morgana, but a woman of flesh and sorrow. The dead man in her arms was wearing a perfect suit of armor, his golden crown dimly glinting in the grass beside him.

"Merlin, is that..."

"My Arthur. The first."

Old Merlin's voice shook as sadness turned to anger. "So Mordred has murdered his own father. Stolen the kingdom of peace for his unrighteous purpose. I will find him and train him to do what is right." But even as he said the words, his eyes trailed to the body beside Arthur's—the one speared through by Excalibur.

"That's Arthur's son, Mordred," Merlin whispered to Ari. "They killed each other."

"Why?" Ari asked, shocked.

"Greed. Power," Merlin said. "What other answers are there?"

Morgana's voice pitched high and broken. "Camelot is as dead as the Pendragon line, you damned fool. There is no king. There is no kingdom. Already the remains of these armies torture every village and kill anyone loyal to your cursed crown. Your entire life is wasted. And I will punish you for eternity."

The night faded all around them. Ari felt nothing but Merlin's presence beside her as the darkness ached with depth.

"Well. She made good on *that* promise," Merlin finally said, a forced joke that fell like a stone through the nothingness.

"Why was Morgana so attached to Arthur?"

"They were sister and brother," he said, his voice faint, weak. The blackness around them became dizzying. "The anger that flows through her magic keeps the cycles in motion and tethers me to life, so she can give me yet more pain. At least that has been my best guess for a few thousand years."

"So we have to convince her to stop this," Ari said. "I can do it. I'll get through to her. I'm not afraid. We just have to get out of this memory, and then I'll convince her to help us."

Merlin laughed as though he loved Ari for her foolhardiness. "Ari, she's not to be trusted. And I fear I should warn you about Gweneviere before I lose my nerve."

"Gwen? What does Gwen have to do with any of this?"

"She is part of Arthur's story. A very important part. A rather...sad part. She will hurt you in the end, I'm afraid. So very badly."

"Bullshit," Ari said, sure of herself. "Maybe that's how it was with Arthur and his Gweneviere, but that's not how it is with Gwen and me."

"Ari..." Merlin said, as the endless darkness around them clarified with bursts of starlight. Constellations.

"Where are we now?" Ari asked.

"I believe you're meant to tell me that."

The view before Ari crystallized as a silver spaceship tore through the dark, coming straight at them, fleeing a red soiled planet that Ari's heart recognized even if her mind could not paint it. Ketch. The spaceship sped closer, and Ari could not stop a scream in the moment it overtook them and trapped them inside a control room full of warning lights and screeching alarms.

Ari stared at her mother: dark, straight hair hanging over one arm as her hands flew over the controls. "What is this, Merlin?"

"Your worst memory, I imagine."

Ari's father was there, too, at her mother's side. "We're marked. We only have minutes."

"We have to get beyond the static. Then the signal will reach the rest of the galaxy. And everyone will know. That barrier is going to make it hard to—"

"We're not going to make it. They're going to shoot us down," Ari's father said, and Ari started crying; the terror that came with this memory was too much. Her mind had blocked it for so many good reasons.

"They have to know the truth!" Ari's mother yelled.

"Ari," Merlin's voice pleaded from beside her. "Where are you? If this is your memory, you must be here."

Ari didn't have to answer because at that moment, her father heard small sobs and pulled a tiny Ari from beneath the control panel. Before little Ari could fit into his arms, she ran, out of the room, down the hall, nothing but her parents' strained shouts behind her.

Little Ari kept running, looking over her shoulder.

"You're so scared," Merlin said, as if he'd never felt such fear in all of his many lives.

"I was," Ari admitted. At that moment, the skinny girl stopped running. She halted in the hallway to look out the porthole at what seemed like solar flares headed straight for them. "But a voice in my head told me where to go. He said I was going to be all right. That was Arthur," she realized.

Merlin and Ari watched as the tiny girl ducked through the doorway of the hydration circuit just as the airlock clapped tight. A blast sent her across the room with a bone-dislodging shake before the gravity was gone.

Seven-year-old Ari floated, legs tucked in, arms sealed around her tiny body.

Alone.

"Stop this," Ari begged aloud. "Stop the memory." She could handle her parents' last moment. Even the blasts of fire streaking toward them.

But not this part.

The thirst came first, and tiny Ari fought to propel herself into a huge water barrel to swallow the last liquid bubbles floating inside it—but then she could not get back out. The walls were covered in coils of red-hot wires. She tried to push off, the heat so great she flailed and crashed into the other side. And blacked out from the pain. Every few days she tried again, her body stung all over, etched with hundreds of razor-fine circle burns across her back, her arms, her chest.

"*Ow*," Merlin mouthed each time she was burned, feeling the agony that came with the memory. "Ari—"

"Quiet," Ari whispered. "He's coming."

A boy's round face peered over the edge of the barrel. Nine-year-old Kay's reddish hair was already turning gray, and he cried when he saw Ari's clothes burned to tatters, her frame frozen in pain, her eyes as wild and glassed as a dying animal's. He cried so hard he could not help her, but the women who were with him floated in and down, one tethered to the other. The woman closest had a young, kind face and silver hair.

She reached a hand to little Ari, and Ari took it.

The memory began to fade to black, but Ari fought it. Her past misery was a blade, but she would not let go until she'd grasped the handle of her hope. She found herself reaching for the two women, even as they turned translucent. "They spoke to me in a language I didn't understand, and yet I knew they were saying I would be okay. I couldn't believe them at first, and when they took me on board their strange, tiny spaceship, I found a podlike bed that swung like my mother's arms. I never wanted to move. I wanted to die there. But I didn't."

Merlin and Ari were in the black nothingness again. He was silent beside her for a long moment. Too long.

"When will we escape these memories?" she asked.

"When Morgana's magic has worn off." Merlin sounded distant as if he were busy tucking his feelings into his deep robe pockets, trying to hide them from her.

"Why did she want us to share this, do you think?"

"Because she is cruel." There, again, Merlin seemed cracked. Ari felt resolved, more determined to defeat this reincarnation

thing. This King Arthur cycle. This Mercer nightmare. Whatever it was, it was going down.

"Merlin—"

"He saved you. King Arthur saved you. He told you where
to hide on that ship. Like he knew what was going to happen."

"Yes. Does that mean something?"

"Perhaps."

Ari felt warm. Something pressed against her, tugged and
whispered. She could feel her lips again, her breath, her heartbeat. "Merlin, something's happening to me. How do you feel?"

"Scared," he whispered into the moment that ripped them
from each other. "Alone. Like always."

Ari felt herself shouting from the pain of their paired consciousness detaching. Her breath cut in fast and sharp, hampered
by lips on her lips.

"*Gwen,*" she groaned, and Gwen gasped with relief, tugging
Ari into a sitting position.

Ari opened her eyes. She was on *Error,* on Kay's crumpled
bed in the pilot's cabin. "What happened?"

"That ghost woman attacked you," Gwen said, smooth-
ing Ari's hair back and kissing her cheeks, her jaw, her neck.
"You're okay. Thank the stars, you came back."

"Is everyone else okay?" Ari murmured, her eyes adjusting
slowly and painfully to the light in the small room.

"Lam, Kay, and Val woke up days ago. They said they'd
been stuck in their worst memories. You and Merlin...We
were starting to worry that you wouldn't wake up."

Ari pulled away from Gwen to face the small body next to
her. Her hand was clasped in his as if they'd been that way out

of raw necessity. She squeezed his fingers. He didn't squeeze back.

"Merlin," Ari said, leaning over him, shaking his shoulders. "Merlin!"

When that didn't work—when his thin, young face stayed pale and still—she leaned over and pressed her cheek against his. "Wake up, old man. We've got a universe to save."

His eyes fluttered open, and Gwen let go of a huge breath. Together, the girls helped him sit up. They gave him water. When his gaze finally came back into focus, he looked at Ari— and then away, shame turning his cheeks red. "You know now. I chose more power over Arthur," he hiccupped. "I caused his death. *And* the cycle. I never—"

"Merlin," Ari said. "We're not back there. We're here now. Together. Gwen," she turned toward her girl. "Can you bring the others in?"

Gwen nodded and left the room.

Ari put her hands on his shoulders. "Whatever the hell Morgana wanted to happen backfired. I don't hate you. I don't blame you. I want to help." She pressed a hand to her chest. "I want to help Arthur. We're going to end the cycle. I'm so fucking fired up now, that damn blue witch has no idea. So, what do we do?"

"The steps," Merlin murmured. "The next step in the cycle is to face the greatest evil."

"Mercer. Wonderful. And then?"

"Unite humankind."

"And then?"

Merlin shifted. "I've never gotten that far. Not even with

the first King Arthur. He died before his vision of Camelot could spread and help others. Well, you saw."

Ari blew out a huge breath. "So, defeat Mercer. Unite humankind."

"Ari's already on her way with that," Kay said as the room filled with relieved faces. Her brother crossed his arms before the end of the bed. Val pounced on Merlin, smothering him in affectionate squeezes that made his pale skin bloom with the best shades of pink. Gwen came back to Ari's side and folded herself into the corner of her arm and hip.

Lam and Jordan stood by the door, gorgeous and gloriously different sentinels, one in purple silk, one in silver armor.

"What did you say, Kay?" Ari asked.

"Ari is a damn hero. Isn't she?" Kay looked at the others, and they nodded.

Gwen sat forward and sort of batted her eyelashes. "Don't freak out, baby girl, but the situation with Mercer has gotten a little operatic."

"Oh, I love where this is going."

"Honestly, this entire situation is a damn miracle," Val said. "We all could have been arrested by Mercer and sent to Urite."

Urite. Ari couldn't help going cold as she remembered the Administrator taunting her about her parents. That felt like years ago, but it had only been a few days, hadn't it? "Tell me what happened after Morgana messed with us."

Jordan stood forward. "She disappeared after she attacked you. We had to get you all out before associates descended like carrion flies."

"Gross, Jordan," Gwen said, holding up a hand to her

knight. "People on Troy came to help us. They carried all of you back to *Error* and made sure that we could take off."

Ari could hear the mournful undertones in Gwen's voice. "What happened to them?"

"They were arrested. Some were killed. But not before sending out these rebellion beacons. They've reached every Mercer-controlled system. The entire galaxy is waking up, and they want you to lead them."

Ari blinked. "Excuse me?"

Val held out his watch. An image leaped forth of Ari pulling the sword from the stone courtyard and destroying the Mercer Company logo in front of the galactic state department. And then the image cut to Merlin throwing magical green fireballs, fighting off Morgana. The scrolling text beneath it read:

KING ARTHUR HAS RISEN. MERLIN HAS RETURNED. RISE UP WITH HOPE.

"Oh!" Merlin explained. "I've never made the highlight reel before!"

Ari looked to her magician and found his wide-eyed expression matched hers. "Did you know this was going to happen?"

"I've never seen it done so efficiently," he said. "And while I slept, no less!"

"But it's part of the cycle," Ari said, trying to clarify. "I have to do this. To help you."

"To help everyone," Gwen added. "We have a chance to break Mercer's stranglehold. To help billions of people. First we have to—"

"Save Ari's parents on Urite," Merlin said loudly.

Kay's arms dropped, and he stepped forward. "My parents are on *Urite*?"

"There's plague on Urite," Val said, face falling. "It was all over the media on Troy."

Ari stood and went to her brother. She grabbed his elbows. He was shaking his head, but it was more than that. His whole body trembled with a potent combo of fear and anger. "I know, Kay. We'll help them."

"I don't think that's a good—" Gwen started to say, but Ari whipped around, causing Gwen to drop the rest of the sentence.

"Think about it!" Merlin said. "You want Ari to stand up to Mercer? An act of resistance for the universe to rally behind? Imagine if we spirit the parents of the new King Arthur away from a Mercer prison! I've never *had* parents, but they're generally considered important. And Ari's parents..."

Ari looked to Merlin. She could see in his eyes that he now knew why her parents' freedom meant so much. They hadn't just adopted her. They'd saved her from a torturous death in the void. It was time to return the favor. It was a freakin' quest.

"How?" Jordan repeated. "Urite is inaccessible."

"Easy," Merlin said, standing up on wobbly legs. "Drop me off at the next Mercer-controlled colony. I'll get arrested, and you'll have an inside man for the job. *With* magic."

"What about the plague?" Val asked. "No way."

"I can't die."

Everyone in the room looked at Merlin. "At least, I haven't figured out how to die yet."

"Those are two very different things," Val said.

"Why can't you die?" Gwen asked, startling Merlin so that he looked at her. Ari had to echo her wife's curiosity. Why couldn't Merlin die? Was it his magic? His backward aging?

And why did Nin have such a sharp interest in keeping him alive during King Arthur's final battle? The Lady of the Lake might have been silent since Merlin's time at Camelot, but she was a part of this. Ari could almost feel her watching. She sent a mental middle finger in the general direction of the being called Nin—and shuddered when an icy laugh clouded her mind.

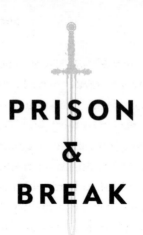

PRISON
&
BREAK

Merlin found it quite easy to get arrested.

Error dropped him on a tiny blip of a planet. Larger planets loomed bright in the sky as he stood in a city square and raved about the evils of Mercer.

"These corporate greedlords have made themselves indispensable, spreading the lie that you could not possibly live without them!" Merlin's voice peaked and twirled, fear sending it to new heights as the ubiquitous Mercer associates closed in on the square.

Merlin's fingers flared up, ready to spark them into a fried state.

"No magic," he muttered. "Not even a flicker."

Footage of him slinging fireballs had been shared with the universe, and Ari had made him promise to keep his identity and abilities under wraps. He'd invented a face and a set of fingerprints. Nothing showy. He was now a different teenager, as scrawny as ever, but with nondescript features, short brown hair, and overlarge feet he kept nearly tripping on.

Not looking like himself was strange enough, but not using magic was like putting a muzzle on his heart. He raged against the powerless feeling as large figures pushed their way through the crowd, casting people to the ground, cracking them with heavy sticks, stepping hard on their hands, crunching finger bones for the crime of listening to the truth.

Merlin's fingers sizzled so hard with magic that he had to suck on them to cool their unspent fury. "There is someone coming to save you all from a Mercer-shaped fate," he cried. "Her name is Ari, and she is…" Did he dare cry *the forty-second reincarnation of King Arthur*? Would he lose the crowd?

"Ari," someone whispered. "The girl with the sword."

"No such person," someone else shouted. "She's a Mercer invention. They want to sell us a hero and merch to go with her."

Merlin's heart knocked around in dismay. It seemed that Mercer was even in the business of manufacturing false hope for those who hated them, and then snatching that hope back. "The monsters are getting smarter," he mumbled.

"I've seen Ari myself," he added for the crowd. "On Troy." Oh, how he wanted to say that he'd fought alongside her, that he was Merlin. *Her* Merlin. But he kept his nondescript mouth shut. "She pulled Excalibur, and there is only one explanation. She's the hero we've been waiting for." Little did these people know just how *long* he'd been waiting—but the need on their faces was as sharp as the one in his gut.

The guards got their gloves around his arms, locked him in, and dragged him away from the square.

"Rise up with hope!" he cried, holding a pretend Excalibur aloft. It probably made him look like a mad puppeteer, but the crowd loved it. They cheered, and then dispersed as more associates poured toward the square. Just as Merlin's triumph lost its giddy, adrenaline-inspired edge, a guard did him the favor of knocking him out cold.

When he woke up, Merlin's head was pulsing, pushing dread through his body. From the cold perspective of a packed prison transport, all of this felt stupidly dangerous. He looked out the tiny porthole window and discovered an unwelcome truth. The prison wasn't *on* Urite. The prison *was* Urite.

The land was a broken scene of toothy rock and haggard ice. Prison buildings hewn from that ice stretched all the way to the curve where land met sky. They were mostly white, blinding and harsh, with vivid blues, salty greens, and mysterious purples trapped inside the frozen walls.

The landing of the ship jarred Merlin. A guard came by and kicked at the prisoners with a dutiful swing of boot to stomach. "Get up. Get up." It was Merlin's turn. He hummed a single note before the boot made contact with his gut. The guard howled with pain and drew back his foot. Merlin smiled up at him, all innocence.

A broken toe wasn't much on the grand scoreboard against Mercer, but he would take it.

Another guard came and hauled Merlin to his feet, wrapping him in a coat that would have made an Arctic parka feel inadequate. Outside of the ship, the atmosphere was gasping-thin, and everywhere the air met Merlin's skin, he thought it would crack into cold splinters.

"Why bother bringing prisoners here?" Merlin asked. "It hardly seems hospitable."

The guard must have been bored, or overly used to keeping

company with prisoners, because his response was almost friendly. "It's a great place to dump the dead. No predators here. No summer thaw. No spoilage or surprise diseases. Prisoners here are serving life sentences without parole. Easier to keep the pre-dead where they all end up eventually."

Merlin looked into the placid face of the guard as the winds attacked them from all sides and his worries attacked from the inside. He had thought he was going to leave this place easily—now he wasn't so certain. Were Ari's parents really worth the possibility of getting stuck here? Living out endless tortures on this bastard glacier?

Yes. He'd seen Ari's memory. He'd been *inside* of it. Those women had saved his Arthur, kept his last chance at ending the cycle alive. But this wasn't just about him. It wasn't even *mostly* about him. He'd felt Ari's painful hope at her rescue. Her ache at the impossibility of being loved so much, after her birth parents died.

Merlin had never had parents of any kind. Arthur was the closest thing he'd ever had to family. And now—Ari. She'd seen the worst of his past, and she hadn't hated him like Morgana had hoped.

They passed by a troop of guards dumping bodies into an icy chasm, a dark deep slit in the ground. He found himself straining to see if any of those people looked like Kay's mothers, if they bore traces of Ari's mischief and pride. But there were too many bodies, and they were being rolled down into the darkness quickly, without any respect for who they had been in life.

The guard pushed Merlin along, until they neared the great doors of the prison, yet another slab of ice. "In," the guard said, dropping his chatty nature and hitting Merlin in the back with the butt of his shiny black gun.

Merlin stumbled forward, then turned. "How does that work in this temperature?"

"Ahhh, that's the trick, isn't it?" the guard said.

As the doors closed behind them, the guard aimed his gun toward the disappearing view of the frigid expanse and fired. Literally. What came out was not a stream of bullets but a blast of white-hearted, molten heat.

"An impressive death toy," Merlin muttered.

The doors shut with a hollow boom, restoring order.

Pre-dead inside. Properly dead outside.

The guard marched Merlin away from the doors. The interior of the prison was not far off from what Merlin expected. The cell they shoved him into reminded him of one he'd inhabited when Arthur 18 was alive, and Merlin was put on trial for witchcraft. He remembered giving his accusers an earful. "Witches prefer candles and spells and herbs. I detest herbs." But the Inquisition didn't seem to care about such distinctions.

Once he was inside the cell, Merlin noticed that another person was in there, a human-ish lump facing the wall. He'd never had a cellmate before. Maybe he could recruit this person to help on his quest.

A new guard appeared with a small packet of fabric. "Undress."

"What?" Merlin asked, already cold at the thought.

"Those are going in the incinerator," the guard said, pointing at everything Merlin was wearing.

Merlin looked down at his robes. He'd insisted on wearing them even though Val had argued that they were unique, too Merlinesque. But that was why he'd needed them so badly. They kept him anchored in who he was. In *what* he was—a great magician. He touched the stitching of crescent moons, the worried cuffs. They'd started to fall apart after a dozen cycles, and he'd been mending them ever since.

"*Now,*" the guard said.

"No." The word flew out, small and stupid and stubborn.

"What?" the guard asked.

Merlin couldn't explain it. No one but Ari would understand. She didn't have many pieces of her past left, either. "They're mine."

The guard raised the butt of his heat gun and cracked Merlin across the back of the shoulders. He fell to all fours. The man struck him again, as if every second he didn't comply was a new crime against Mercer.

Merlin's back erupted with pain. Bruising ran down to his bones. His hands gave out, and he landed facedown on the floor, the man's boot stamped into his back. The pain shaded into numbness as his body decided he could no longer handle reality. Magic didn't matter. He couldn't stop this.

What was he going to do? Take on the entire prison? The entire planet?

His breath came in short, shameful pants. His mind created a new set of steps. *Find Ari's parents. Make a plan. Get back to Ari.*

Nowhere in there did it say, *Keep your robes at all costs.*

"Fine," he said, rolling away from the gun and getting up.

He shrugged out of the sleeves, then ducked out of the neck. As he pulled them over his head, he realized that this was the last of him—the final vestige of the Merlin from the old stories.

He was a naked, shivering teenager.

The guard checked his watch, confirmed something, and said, "We'll be back for you soon enough. Don't go anywhere."

A short laugh rose from the lump known as Merlin's cellmate. The guard left them, sliding a panel of ice into place, a clear one that Merlin could see through like window glass. He pulled on the uniform that had been left behind. It was warm enough to keep him alive, but not nearly warm enough to give him that sparkle of comfort he'd started to feel on *Error*.

"My name's Hex," Merlin's cellmate said, swinging around to greet him. This person looked barely twenty—which seemed young until Merlin remembered he was seventeen. "What did they pick you up for?"

"Disturbing the thing that passes for peace," Merlin spat. "And yourself?"

"I stole seventy-two piñatas," Hex said, deadpan.

Merlin's lips pinched with fresh puzzlement. "Why did you need seventy-two piñatas?"

"I didn't," Hex said. "I just needed to do…*something,* you know? Stealing Mercer goods was what my hands decided on. And a dozen of the piñatas were done up to look like the Administrator, so my friends got a good crack at him before we got caught."

"You would fit in well with my new friends!" Merlin said.

He wanted to explain about Ari, and how she was going to save them all from Mercer. But there was no time to waste—if plague had come to Urite, the contagion would move faster than Merlin ever could.

Setting his hands against the burning-cold ice, he hummed a warm bit of a lullaby, and watched as the cold gave way to his blazing anger. Water puddled at his feet, and soon he could crack his way through the thin, paltry remnants of the ice.

"That's something I've never seen," Hex said, cocking an eyebrow as if that was all he'd give Merlin for *melting the damn wall*. "You still don't want to go out there, though."

"What could possibly make 'in here' a better option?" Merlin asked, wiping his hands off on his crinkly uniform.

Then he heard the sounds from the hall, ricocheting off the cold walls.

The coughing, retching, whimpering that added up to death.

&

Merlin walked up and down the hall, touching the ice panels that separated him from the *pre-dead*. They lay there behind sheets of ice, their pain so complete that few of them even looked up as he passed. Their eyes were clouded, throats swollen closed, lymph nodes so shiny and inflamed they looked like grapefruits—except for the ones that had already burst. Plague spots turned tender flesh dark.

Pain, everywhere.

So much that Merlin felt it in his own skin.

He had seen plague, and believed that he'd outlived it. There were so many foul ways to die, and this was one of the worst. Merlin knew that his magic could do nothing to stop the sickness. He'd never been a healer. His physical magic was blunt, external. He couldn't reach inside a person and untwine sickness from their cells.

He ran back to Hex.

"The guards must have vaccines. Or a cure that can be used

in the event of infection," Merlin added, already thinking of how he could steal from their stores to keep himself healthy. And Ari's parents. Hex, too. He wished that he could find enough to go around, but he highly doubted it. The idea of leaving so many people to die raged through him like another form of sickness.

The guard who'd confiscated Merlin's robes came around the corner with two others. They registered the melted door at the same moment. Merlin and Hex ran. Two of the guards rushed forward, grabbing Hex and Merlin before they could make it down the hall.

The third guard was right behind them.

He pricked Merlin with something—a deep, lasting jab.

And that's when Merlin understood. This plague wasn't passing through contagion. It wasn't the uncontrollable sickness of yesteryear. Mercer had tamed this vile death like a pet, and they were giving it to these prisoners, one by one.

And now, they'd given it to Merlin.

He cried out as the needle pressed into muscle, a hollow soreness.

Hex was grunting and twisting. The guard hadn't jabbed him yet. Merlin spun the sound of his pain into a song, shouting the lyrics to "You've Got a Friend" at the top of his lungs—a turn of events that made the guards stare. Or maybe it was the fact that Merlin's red hair was growing back into place, falling down in front of his eyes. His face shifted, nose thinning and cheeks turning rounder.

Sparks flew from his fingers.

He apologized for breaking his promise not to use magic as he took down the guard with the needle. Then another apology—"sorry, quite sorry"—as he zinged the one hold-ing Hex.

"Why are you being so nice to them right now?" Hex asked.

"I'm British!" Merlin cried. Some things were hard to shake, even after centuries away from home.

He turned his fingers on the guard who'd been holding him, and the guard leaped back, his hands up in surrender.

Good. Merlin needed someone to play along.

"Would you like to take another swing at Mercer?" Merlin asked Hex. "Grab his heat gun."

Hex trotted over and took it from the guard's side, play-ing with the features until a long spout of flame came out, inches from the guard's face. "Oops," he said, not looking repentant.

"Where are Lian and Vera Helix?" Merlin asked. He would never find them on his own in this icy labyrinth.

"Let me look," the guard said, cagily, as he reached for his watch.

"Grab that!" Merlin shouted, but before Hex could torch the watch, the guard had pressed a red button on the inside.

Every guard in Urite had been alerted to their presence.

Merlin took out the guard with another finger-spark, and ran. But he had no idea where he was going, and this place was impossible to navigate, every hallway the same, each one lined with the dead and dying.

And now Merlin was starting to feel ill, sweat cropping up in all sorts of places. The bubonic plague had taken a week to incubate, but judging by the way his insides felt like they were swelling and withering at the same time, Mercer had sped that process up a bit.

"I won't die, I won't die," Merlin chanted on thin breaths as he jogged.

"Yeah, buddy," Hex joked. "Keep telling yourself that."

He had saved Hex, at least. Ari would be proud of him for bringing her a new rebellious knight. Maybe Val would make Merlin some chicken soup, or whatever fake medieval stew they made on Lionel when people got sick. And they would have Ari's parents back. All he needed was to find them.

And get them out.

And...

And...

There were always so many steps. His feet slowed, his wheezing starting to burn his lungs, his throat crowded with pain. He remembered now just how miserable quests had always been.

"Don't go down that way," Hex said, grabbing Merlin by the back of his uniform like taking a puppy by the scruff of his neck. "That's the guard station and med bay. Tons of Mercer types."

Merlin nodded. And then, through the haze of sickness, he thought of another step he had to add to his plan. He couldn't leave all of these people here to die, at the hands of Mercer. This company did not care what happened to the people of this universe as long as they had their power. And Merlin was finding, with each day, he cared more and more.

Ari was the hero. But Merlin was *here*, and he could help.

He hobbled toward the guard station, the exact direction he wasn't meant to go.

"Hey!" Hex cried. "Did you hear me?"

Guards rushed at them, a whole battalion. At the same moment, Merlin caught sight of what he needed. A room with the words MED BAY written on the door, and behind the ice-walls, case after case with medical warnings stamped all over them. He hummed and pointed and splintered the cases. The guards looked back at the med bay as if a bomb had exploded behind them—and were met with the sight of a thousand plague needles flying straight at their faces.

Merlin stopped the syringes an inch from sticking anyone.

"Now," he said. "I need the location of two prisoners. Lian and Vera Helix."

The guards traded looks, but none of them made a move. They didn't have Mercer telling them what to do, and Merlin could see how dependent they'd grown on their orders.

"The Administrator would let you die, you know. You're not worth any more to Mercer than these prisoners are. They've trapped you inside of their decisions and their poorly cut suits. You know that if you cross them, you're already a forfeit in their game. But today, you get to decide. Tell me where Lian and Vera Helix are, and you can pretend I found them on my own. Mercer will be none the wiser."

One of the guards stepped forward, her hands up, as if placating a feral child. "They're in cavern four along the west wall. Now... put the needles down."

"Of course," Merlin said, crashing them to the floor, breaking them open so the plague juice ran in toxic yellow streams, sliding over the ice. The guards yelped and tried to avoid it at all costs as Merlin took off.

Cavern four along the west wall turned out to be several miles away, and when Merlin and Hex made it there, a rogue guard was waiting.

Hex hit the highest power setting on the heat gun and blasted his way forward.

"No!" Merlin cried, but the guard was already firing back. Merlin raised his hands and twisted the heat ray away from Hex, using it to melt the doors along the hallway, one by one. Some prisoners leaped out and ran on limbs half-rotted with sores. Others were too sick to move. While Merlin was distracted, another guard ran up behind them and hit Hex square in the back. He went down, hard, with a smack against the ice and the smell of sizzling flesh.

Merlin tossed fireballs from both hands—one at each of the guards—too late. Hex stayed motionless, his face frozen in a moment of victory. He'd gone down believing they would escape. Merlin had doled out hope, and then let him die, which somehow felt worse than giving him no hope at all. Hex wasn't coming back to *Error*. He would never be a knight of Ari's round table.

"I'm sorry," Merlin said, one last apology.

And then Merlin saw two women emerging from their cell, slowly, to see what the commotion was. Their arms were locked tight around each other. If they were going down, they were doing it together.

One of them faced Merlin with an unusual sharpness in her eyes. He recognized the shine of filigreed silver hair that didn't seem to have anything to do with age—and this woman's hard blue eyes.

Kay. She looked like Kay.

"You must be Mom," he said to the quiet woman in her arms, Lian. She looked glassy, her skin taut and shiny. They'd stuck her with plague. "And you're Captain Mom," he finished, looking straight into Vera's hard eyes.

He *knew* these women. He had seen them float into the water heater and save young Ari.

Vera's already pale face took on the sheen of ice. "What did you call me?"

"My Arthur is your daughter," he said, aware of how sick he looked, how strange he sounded. "Your Ari is my Arthur."

"You know Ari?" Lian exclaimed, tears flooding her eyes.

Vera shifted her hold on her wife, so she could raise a finger to Merlin. "If you are messing with us, I will end you."

Merlin surprised himself with such a deep sigh. "As if endings were that easy…"

The dehydration that he'd been fighting sent him to his knees, dizzy and weak.

"I think this boy is sick, Vera," Lian whispered.

"I'm much, much better," he said with the small burst of an unexpected laugh. "I'm here to save you from Mercer, like you saved Ari so many years ago. My name is Merlin."

"Merlin…like the bird on Old Earth," Lian offered, and Merlin would have been overcome with tears if there had been a bit of water to spare in his body. As it was, his eyes just felt gritty and pained as he thought of that tiny wooden falcon— the only possible sign he'd ever had parents of his own.

"How exactly are you going to save us?" Vera asked.

Merlin had no idea. He was too sick to have ideas. He coughed out half of his confidence, and Vera stepped back reflexively, but Lian rushed to his side, dabbing sweat from his forehead with her sleeve. She smiled down at him. Ari had told him she was the sweet one, the one who kept them all from losing hope.

Even with her death coming on fast, she was still trying to comfort a stranger.

Mom was *dying*.

Merlin coughed harder, and a plan came out. "We're going to leave the only way that Mercer will let us. As dead bodies."

Lian pulled her fingers back, cringing.

"Not actual dead bodies." Merlin shook his head. "I have... magic." For the first time in history he was afraid he wouldn't be able to explain things. He needed a small demonstration. Something that wouldn't take up too much magic. Merlin hummed a few notes of a lullaby. "This is the color of your son's hair," he said, twisting one of his own reddish locks into a silver-gray. He opened his palm. A red circle etched itself across his skin. "And this is the shape of your daughter's scars."

"Vera..."

"I see it, Lian. I should have known this little ginger was trouble from the second he said Ari's name." She paused. "Maybe a few seconds before that."

"We told them not to come back for us," Lian said.

Merlin thought of Ari and Kay, their strange bond that defied the cycle. "Kay's heart is as hard as porridge, and Ari is loyal to a fault. *You* taught them to save people. This is a cycle of your own making, and simply getting arrested won't break it."

"He's right," Lian said, releasing a dry cough.

Merlin made a silent promise—even if Lian was dying, she would see her children first. This vow wasn't on his list of steps. It wouldn't change the story. And yet it mattered so much that he could hardly breathe right.

"All right," he said. "Ready to take a little nap?"

Vera nodded staunchly. Lian grabbed her hand and kissed it once, twice, as Vera watched her with so much love. Merlin hummed the calming tones of a meditation and touched Lian on the forehead with one thumb, and Vera with the other. They stiffened and turned a distinctly gray-ish color.

Then Merlin touched his own forehead with his thumb. He froze, his mind the only moving thing inside of his sinking stone of a body. He told himself one thing over and over again.

Stay awake.

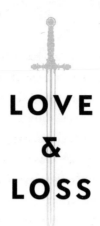

LOVE
&
LOSS

Ari couldn't sleep as *Error* crashed and shuddered through the unstable nebula surrounding Urite's solar system. Everyone was laying low, preparing for what was sure to be a costly prison break.

Gwen lay beside Ari, on her stomach, her curls cascading over her back, revealing a shoulder that Ari was too fond of. She wanted to draw it. Or bite it. But Merlin's warning returned sharply. Gwen would hurt her; it was canon.

"I won't believe it," Ari murmured, running a hand over Gwen's skin, smiling at the way it made Gwen's nose wrinkle in her sleep. Before she could enjoy the still, warm moment, her thoughts returned to Merlin. She couldn't shake the idea that he was in trouble. A lot of trouble.

"Ari," Gwen said sleepily. "Merlin is going to be okay."

Ari's fingers froze on Gwen's elbow. "How do you always know what I'm thinking?"

Gwen sat up, tucking the blanket over her breasts. "Because

you're translucent. You always have been. It's not just your words that beam honesty. It's everything about you. It's why people in a universe controlled by Mercer's lies look at you and see King Arthur. A true hero."

Ari squinted playfully. "I could have secrets, if I wanted to."

"But you don't want to," Gwen said, riffling in a drawer beside the bed. "You're nakedly brave. Courageously stalwart."

"And how do you know that?"

"I told you. Translucent. My own personal stained-glass window." Gwen sighed with a small smile. "You're going to make the *worst* politician in Lionel's history. Or perhaps the best. We'll have to wait and see." She held out a small velvet bag, pouring two silver rings in her palm. "I have a present for you."

Ari inspected one, finding it heavy. "Jewelry? Are we that far into our marriage already?" she teased. Teasing made sense; being married did not.

Gwen placed one on her delicate fourth finger and one on Ari's. "People wore these to denote married status on Old Earth. Antique thinking, but one of the more romantic gestures in the heap of barbarity my planet is trying to resurrect. You should read some of the ancient texts we've uncovered. It's all, *Bow to the men, you wicked females!*"

Ari took a moment to soften her honesty. "If it's that bad, why do you want to be their queen?"

"Because the queen controls the barbarity," she said, not dismissive, but on the border of it. "On Lionel, we have the chance to revise the more backward aspects of the culture. And we have each other now." Gwen's always confident voice frayed a little. "I mean, I'm not letting you take on this anti-Mercer mantle all alone. Lionel is behind you, one hundred percent."

Ari stared at Gwen. Her brown eyes were entrancing. Velvet, almost. If Ari had been any other girl, she might have stayed in this moment of hope with her new wife.

"We're going to fail," Ari said, the truth slipping out like a dagger laid upon a table. "Mercer is a hundred times stronger than Lionel. Maybe if we went to Ketch, and got some real backup..."

Gwen looked stunned. "You want to go to Ketch?"

"If I could find a way through the barrier, we would have strength in numbers. There were billions of Ketchans before the barrier closed. The planet is huge." Ari didn't have to add that going to Ketch would mean leaving Gwen's Lionelian responsibilities...and therefore Gwen. This was not something they could do together. This was an Ari and Merlin mission for sure.

Merlin. Oh, gods, he better be all right.

Gwen slipped on her robe, sliding past the subject of going to Ketch. "I'll check with Jordan and see how close we are."

Ari watched her leave, the queen's shoulders squared, her hair somehow more glorious when it was a free tangle of curls than perfectly pinned up. They weren't fighting all out; they just weren't lining up at the moment, either. Ari twirled her new ring on her finger, catching herself smiling at it. For all their weirdly tense history, the idea of Gwen in her life, for the rest of her life, did make her damn happy.

Val cleared his throat from the doorway.

"Are Lam and Kay getting ready for the plan?" she asked.

"Plan?" Val said with firmly crossed arms. "There's no plan. There's just 'Merlin will give us a sign.' We are literally flying into a maximum-security planet looking for *anything*."

"Watch it, Val," Kay said, passing by in the hall. "Your boyfriend is helping my parents."

"Excuse me, he's *not* my boyfriend," Val said, whirling around. "But he would be by now if all of you hadn't let him get himself arrested."

Lam popped their head in around Val. "Mercer put atmosphere alarms around Urite, the bastards. Jordan just picked up the signal. We'll only have a few minutes once we land before Mercer is headed straight for us."

Lam disappeared into the main cabin. Ari turned back to Val's hard frown. "I'm sorry, and I feel pretty terrible about Merlin being arrested. I'm scared sick for him."

"I don't want apologies, Ari. I want him back." He rubbed his neck. "Merlin is the only person I've connected with in years. Do you know how hard it is to find someone weird enough for me, even on Lionel?"

"That's why I'm going planet-side. To do what I can for all of them," Ari said, squeezing Val's shoulder. "Don't forget, I'm the only one on board who can wield a mythological sword. Excalibur and Merlin's magic are the keys to beating Mercer. I have no doubt about that."

And Ketch, she thought wildly. For some reason, ever since her memory pairing with Merlin, Ari could feel King Arthur inside of her, tugging her like he had on that day when he'd led her to Excalibur in the oak…and he *really* wanted her to go to Ketch.

"What about the one who attacked us on Troy?" Val's expression narrowed to a point. His experience with Morgana had left a mark. "Whose side is she on?"

"Not Mercer's," Ari said. "At least I don't think so."

Val left, and Ari started putting on her pants. Her boots. Her belt.

"Oh, no, you don't," Gwen said, returning with a hard scowl. "It's far too costly for you to go down there. If you get caught you could die. Or worse, Mercer could use your felony as grounds to take over Lionel and dethrone me."

Ari squinted, still clicking her belt in place. "How is the second one worse than the first?"

"In the first reality, I lose you. In the second? All Lionelians lose their home. Thousands of my people will die because they can't relocate to Mercer-controlled planets. They'll be refugees."

"Gwen, as the supposed savior of humankind, I'm pretty sure I have to get my hands dirty."

Gwen slid her palms against Ari's, entwining their fingers. "I have other ideas for those hands."

Ari growled in a pleased way. She couldn't help it. Gwen pressed closer without reservation. Body to body, lips to lips. Ari's thoughts swung in tighter and tighter circles until they vanished and she was lifting Gwen into their kiss.

Ari's knotted muscles released, her insides melting. She fell into the bed, pulling Gwen on top of her. Their hips connected in a way that made Ari tear at Gwen's clothes, and it wasn't until Ari had pulled Gwen's delicate shoulders out of her robe and left a trail of kisses from her neck to her lovely nipples that she came back up for air.

Ari dropped her head on the bed, dizzy, gasping. Red hot. She sat up on her elbows. Gwen's beautiful, rich skin was all she could see. Ari made herself look into Gwen's eyes. "I have to go down there with them."

"Trust your knights." She squeezed Ari's hips with her thighs. "Stay with me."

Perhaps it was Lionel that made Gwen refer to Ari's friends as her knights, but it only reminded her of Merlin. Of King Arthur. "Do you believe what everyone else believes, Gwen? That I'm some magical, long-dead king?"

Gwen sat up, straddling Ari like a winged mythical creature. She shrugged her robe back onto her shoulders. "I think people need heroes. I think you're a hero. It's that simple to me. And that important. And I'm not going to lose you on stupid Urite."

"They're my parents, Gwen."

"Your parents are…important. They're just not more important than beating Mercer."

Ari sat up, pushing Gwen away. "Are you *serious* right now?"

Gwen was steaming. "I have parents, too, Ari, but you don't see me dropping everything I care about to save them."

Ari felt Gwen's words in strange places. "You told me your parents were dead." Gwen slid farther away, now more of a delicate bird perched on the edge of the bed. "*And* you were born on Troy and never told me. Why do you keep lying? What else are you lying about?"

"Stop."

"How am I supposed to trust you if you're still keeping secrets?"

She will hurt you in the end, so very badly, Merlin had said. Gwen turned, surprising Ari with bright tearful spots in her eyes. "*Still* keeping secrets? Are we fourteen again, making out behind the stables while you demand to know everything about me, and when I don't tell you instantly, you *run away*?"

Now that was a harsh truth. Ari sat up, shoulder to shoulder with Gwen, unable to look at her. "We're not exactly the same. We have sex now."

"Is that supposed to be funny?" Gwen's eyes flared. "Why are you acting like I'm about to dump you?"

Ari didn't look away. She couldn't. "Merlin says you're going to hurt me. Like this is part of the cycle."

"He *what*?"

"I don't want to believe it, but he's been weirdly right before. And you said it yourself that this King Arthur stuff has some merit to it."

"You believe him? You think I'm going to hurt you because some skinny puppy wizard said so?"

They both fell silent.

"I'm sorry," Ari finally said.

"About what, Ari? That you believe Merlin is telling the truth and that I'm lying because I won't tell you everything? You've twisted me up inside all over again, except it's worse because I'm not fourteen anymore and I know that I love you."

Ari tilted on the bed, surprised.

The door opened, and Kay appeared in the aftermath of Gwen's L-bomb like an octopus at a picnic. Gwen stood up to yell. "Can't you knock, you buffoon?"

"This is my room!" He glanced from Gwen to Ari, sensing the frayed ends of their argument. "I need clothes." He picked up a balled shirt out of a drawer and left, tossing back a few words over his shoulder. "Landing in five. Suit up!"

They stared at each other silently for a long moment. "I have to go with them, Gwen."

"I know!"

It was a quiet shout, and Gwen pressed her hand over her mouth in such a wounded way that Ari stood and pulled Gwen tight.

"Don't you dare say a word about love," Gwen mumbled, her mouth against Ari's neck. "I brought it up, and you didn't respond, and now anything you say is ruined because you've had time to feel bad."

"My brother rammed into the room."

"There was a decent pause before that." Gwen's tone wasn't iciness but plain old pain. "Look, I put myself out there, and you don't want the risk, so it's fine."

"I want to be with you, but..." Ari admitted. *There's so much I have to do.*

"I don't think I want to hear that *but,*" Gwen said.

Error shuddered as though they were entering heavy wind. They held on to each other while Ari's magboots kept them rooted to the spot. When the shuddering grew worse, Ari loosened her grip on Gwen, raising her voice over the roar outside. "We're in the atmosphere. In the storm. This is going to happen fast."

Gwen balanced through the ship's shudders, strapping on Ari's pauldron and the sheath she kept across her back. She tightened the buckles. Looped the extra leather in tightly.

Ari watched Gwen's bowed head and soft, curved neck. Her hair was down in beautiful waves. "People think there are only two ways to react when someone brings up love," she started so quietly that Gwen pulled herself against Ari to hear.

"The first is to say it back. The second is not to. But if you don't say it back, you have to compensate. Soften hurt feelings with, 'Oh, thank you' or 'That's so sweet.' I didn't do either."

Gwen tightened Ari's belt, which was unnecessary, unless Gwen was aiming for the tiny groan she managed to tug out of Ari. "You're telling me there's a third option?"

"To not say anything. To look like a confounded idiot. To wonder why your heart has turned into a hurricane and how love could be possible when you're supposedly a cursed, dead king in the presence of a very powerful, very alive queen."

Error slammed into the icy ground of Urite, and Ari and Gwen held on to each other again, this time desperately. When the ship finally slid to a stop, Ari picked up Excalibur and thrust the sword into the sheath. She dug in her memories, all the way back to knight camp. She took Gwen's hand and pressed her lips to her knuckles. "Upon my honor," Ari said.

Gwen nearly laughed. "Upon your honor...what?"

"See? I suck at this stuff," Ari tried not to burn with embarrassment. This was why she'd stopped playing knight at camp with the rest of them. The game wouldn't ring true, no matter how hard she tried. "I'm supposed to promise you something, aren't I?"

Gwen nodded. She turned her face up to Ari's, waiting to be kissed. Ari touched her cheek, looked over her eyelashes, nose, cheekbones. Her chin and mouth and slight, slight smile. Gwen had forgiven her. It was tucked right there in the turn of her lips. Why was that as endlessly attractive as their arguments?

"I'll come right back," Ari promised. She slipped off her watch and put it on Gwen's wrist. "There are some pictures on there. Something to look at until I get back."

&

Kay, Lamarack, and Ari made slow tracks through the frigid tundra. They wore thick, wool Lionelian horse blankets around their shoulders and heads, but it wasn't nearly enough. The endless rows of graves could barely be seen through the icy black night and whipping cold, but they were everywhere, threatening each step.

And falling down on this planet meant shattered bones.

"This isn't a prison break!" Lam yelled over the roar of the wind. "It's grave robbery!"

Kay led the charge through the freezing gusts. He walked too fast, erratically searching. They worked their way to the section that boasted the fresh mound of a mass grave. A slit in the earth beside it revealed a new chasm for those who were currently dying inside the prison walls.

"Fucking Mercer!" Lam stumbled. Their face didn't look right, and they were from Pluto, used to this sort of deep freeze. "Kay! We can't stay out here much longer. We're going to die. Your moms wouldn't want that!"

"I'm not giving up!" her brother shouted. "Something sparkled over there like one of Merlin's stupid fireworks. We have to keep going!"

Ari clawed her way closer, took his face in her hands and tried to warm his cheeks with her breath. "Kay, calm down. We have to think about what we can do next."

"There!" Lam's voice was weak, but they both heard their urgency. They were pointing at a small, bony hand sticking up out of the mound like a damn nightmare. Ari rushed to it, peeled her gloves off, and clasped the hand.

It clasped back.

They dug at the ground without luck. It was frozen solid, and Ari could see in the distance the laser devices that they must use to dig out the soil—but the machines were far away, and there were definitely prison guards over there.

Ari flung the horse blanket off her shoulders and unsheathed Excalibur. She screamed in frustration as she stuck the sword into the earth around Merlin's pale, limp hand, using the blade to pry up the ground in great crumbling sections.

When they'd uncovered half of him, Lamarack and Kay took the young magician by the shoulders and hauled him out of the earth with screams of their own. It had become so painful to move—to breathe—that Ari felt like all was already lost. Particularly when Merlin didn't open his eyes. They rested him on one of the horse blankets, and he looked as far from his bombastic, ridiculous self as possible, his blue flapping robes replaced by a torn, gray uniform.

He bled from a jagged cut on his shoulder that had undoubtedly been caused by Ari's enthusiastic use of Excalibur as a shovel. She knelt beside him. "Merlin! Merlin, you damn fool, wake yourself up." She held his cheeks, kissed him on each side. "Come on!"

Ari held his hand up for him, remembering that moment on the moon when he was so terribly beaten by Morgana—and yet still had a little lightning in him.

Merlin's mouth formed a word Ari couldn't hear. He pointed one finger toward the howling, black night and managed a small flourish.

In a blast of orange-red, dazzling heat, the entire setting transformed. Kay, Lam, and Ari hid their heads beneath their arms as a sudden, searing light burst forth. Warmth fell over her like a soft rainstorm. They were in a tropical bubble. The frozen ground had turned to warm, yielding sand, and above, a hot, beautiful sun shone. There was no wind here, but—did Ari imagine it?—there seemed to be music. A classical guitar strumming somewhere nearby. There was even a damn palm tree next to Lam.

"What the hell is this?" Kay blustered.

"Bermuda," Merlin said with a small shrug that made him stumble. "My happy place."

"We should hurry," Lamarack said. "I have a feeling that everyone on this sad frozen rock is extremely interested in what's happening right now."

"Where are my parents?" Kay yelled.

Merlin motioned to the spot in the mound beside him. "I had to turn them to stone for a little while. Easiest way to fake a frozen death."

Kay and Lamarack began to dig at the now melting earth, uncovering a mass grave that made them turn their heads away and curse at the staggering loss of life.

Merlin tried to sit up, but his shoulder was a bleeding mess. Ari pressed the wound firmly between her hands. "Bermuda?" she asked, trying to distract him from his pain.

Merlin closed his shadowed eyes. "Just a little piece of it I stole a long time ago."

She *tutted*. "You shouldn't steal, Merlin. Didn't your parents ever tell you that?"

"Parents? I was born a few thousand years old in a cave made of crystal." He slid into a distinctly musical way of speaking that Ari had grown to care for, albeit against her will.

"Besides," he said, his tone sinking, "there are worse things to steal. Like children from their families."

Ari pulled him to his feet, held him tight. "You're out of your head, old man." He clasped her back with a whimper that made his injury even more obvious. "I'm sorry. I shouldn't have sent you. I'm so sorry," she murmured into his ruined hair. "You're never going to have to do anything like this again, okay? I promise."

For once, Merlin the magician didn't fight back. He nodded furiously and kept his face tightly against Ari's chest.

"I've got her! I've got her!" Kay yelled, unearthing Captain Mom's rigid form. He pushed the dirt away from her eyes and hair. Lamarack excavated Mom at the same moment. Ari wanted to run to them, but Kay's groans kept her locked in place. Or was it Merlin's arms still around her?

"Fix them, Merlin. Now!" Kay growled.

Merlin took a few deep breaths. He kept one arm around Ari's waist and wiggled his fingers through the air. Nothing happened. He tried again, leaning even heavier on Ari. Finally, a bit of magic trickled out and struck Captain Mom.

Her stone visage softened until she gasped for breath. Kay didn't give her a moment to recover. He grabbed her with both arms and sobbed. He was much bigger than Captain Mom, and that was new, wasn't it? When they had been arrested, he'd still been short.

"Kay," Captain Mom said. "Calm down, baby. I'm okay."

He couldn't stop crying. Couldn't calm down. Not even when the sirens blasted over the soft melody of the invisibly strumming guitar.

"We have to go!" Lam yelled. They'd pulled Mom out of

the sand. She was still stone, and unlike Captain Mom, she seemed to have been frozen on her side, curled up.

Captain Mom and Kay got to their feet. Kay looked at Mom's tiny, frozen form. "Change her back, Merlin!"

Merlin jumped at the threatening heat in his voice. He opened his mouth to speak—to tell Kay that he was too weak. It was obvious to Ari, but Captain Mom beat him to it.

"She's safer like that. We should wake her up when we're away from here. She needs medical attention." The no-nonsense command in her voice reminded Ari of Gwen, which was strange. Captain Mom straightened her shirt and looked at Ari for the first time. She reached one hand out, and Ari looked at it for so long, remembering that moment in the water barrel.

Finally, she stepped forward and hugged her.

"Look at you," she whispered in Ari's ear. "My hero."

Ari felt frozen pieces cracking off her. "Mama," she whispered, pulling her even tighter. "We missed you *so much*."

Lam cleared their throat, lifting Mom higher in their arms. "The whole planet has been alerted to our presence, and we've got to get out of here."

Error swept low, just visible outside of the dome of brilliant, tropical light. In the next moment, a fiery blast shot through the bubble, breaking the world with furious cold.

"Run!" Ari screamed.

A second blast caught Lam in the leg, and they went down, shouting in pain. Kay shot forward to catch Mom, and Captain Mom helped Lam toward the spot where *Error* had landed.

"Go!" Ari yelled to Merlin, turning to face the prison guards streaking toward them. "I'll be right behind you!"

Merlin whimpered as he stumbled toward the ship, and Ari

swung around, Excalibur bared to face the guards running at her. The one in front fired, and she swung at the blast as if it were a game. The fire hit Excalibur, turning the entire sword blazingly hot. Ari dropped it, shocked, and was instantly surrounded by Mercer associates who battered her to her knees.

"It's the one from the vid feed!" one of them crowed. "We're going to get promotions!"

"Kill her," another one said. "She's too dangerous to take alive. We'll get the same perks if she's dead." The guard raised a large weapon and pressed it against Ari's head.

Ari felt it charging up, crafting impossible heat.

"No!" one of the guards yelled. "She has to be recognizable. Do her in the chest."

The guard moved the weapon lower, and Ari kicked out, taking their legs out from under them. In a heartbeat, three guards were on top of her, holding her down on the ice while the one she'd knocked over got up, angry and spitting. They stood, pointed the weapon at Ari's chest, and Ari felt King Arthur come through her, urging her to call out one word.

"Morgana!" she cried.

"Arthur," a familiar voice purred through the wind, making the guards pause and look around. They could not see Morgana in their midst. But Ari could.

The associates froze as if she'd turned them to ice, and Ari kicked them away. Morgana came so close that Ari felt the specific cold that belonged to this ancient enchantress.

"I hear my brother in your voice," she said. "He controls you well."

"It isn't control," Ari managed. "It's alliance."

Ari picked up Excalibur, fingers numb. She would not die

unarmed or without a fight. "Thank you. Although I'm worried you stopped them just so you could kill me yourself."

"Most likely," Morgana sneered. Her eyes trailed the long, silver blade, gleaming so much more than the metal ever could. When she came to the deep red spot along the edge, she paused. "My dear, what is that?"

"Merlin's blood," Ari said, the words sticking in her throat. She couldn't feel the residual warmth of Bermuda anymore. She was freezing solid where she stood. Morgana looked ready to laugh. To scream with delight.

And Ari's mind fractured as Morgana moved *through her*.

IMPOSSIBLE

&

UNACCEPTABLE

Merlin stared out into a blinding rash of snow. "Ari!" he cried. "Ari?"

Everyone else had run aboard *Error*. She had to be close behind. And yet waiting another minute gave him nothing but white spots in his vision as the frozen wind cut through his prison uniform and plague-touched skin. There was also the matter of his shoulder, which Excalibur had taken a bite from. Blood was crystallizing in the wound, gritty and painful.

But none of that could stop him from searching for Ari. He'd been stumbling along with Ari right behind him—and then she was gone. Merlin had told the rest of the knights to run onward, trusting his Excalibur sonar to find her when the rest of his senses failed. But he was too sick, too drained.

And Excalibur did not sing back.

"Get your ass in here, magic-boy!" Kay shouted from inside. "And bring Ari with you! They're about to fire on us!"

The snow cleared just enough for Merlin to see heat cannons

revving up—the grown-up versions of the guns that the prison guards carried. They were pointed rather directly at his face. He turned and ran into the ship, seconds before the door slammed closed.

"Where is Ari?" Kay asked, looking around Merlin as if he might have been hiding her.

"I…I couldn't find her," Merlin said, the words stirring up all the ways he'd lost Arthur. All the failures Morgana wouldn't let him forget.

Kay raised the heat gun he'd brought on their rescue mission. This one was *definitely* pointed at Merlin's face.

He cringed. He cowered.

It was a horrible showing, and shame paraded through his body. What was worse, he didn't have any magic to stop Kay from shooting him. And the absolute worst of all? A small part of him believed he deserved this fate.

"Hey!" Val shouted, getting between the two of them. "Shooting the person who just saved your parents isn't a good look, Kay." He grabbed the gun by the barrel, yelped at its heat, and tossed it across the cargo den.

Jordan caught it in one hand.

"No time for boyfights!" Lam shouted from where they sat, leg mangled and black. "We have to go." A blast of heat rocked the ship, as if confirming Lam's words. Everyone tipped on their feet, and Val fell hard.

"How long will the heat-skin hold?" Gwen asked Kay, as an uncomfortable warmth seeped through the walls.

"*Error* is still mildly damaged from when *someone* broke a planet," Kay announced.

"It was a moon," Merlin muttered.

"We must take off, my queen," Jordan said shakily as another gust of dragon's breath hit the tiny ship. "This moment demands bravery and decision. If we do not meet it with both, we will perish."

"Ready to jettison Ari already, are you?" Merlin asked wildly, pointing his accusations at this would-be Lancelot. "Think it will give you more time alone with your beloved queen?"

"We're not jettisoning anyone," Val said, fighting his way back to his feet. "We're saving our lives now, so we can still save Ari. Those guards on your tail must have grabbed her."

The knights fled toward the main cabin, and Jordan and Kay took up residence in the cockpit. Merlin stood at the door, heart strained to the breaking point. Had Ari gotten captured by Mercer? Would Mercer see more value in her as a prisoner—or as a dead hero they could wave around to destroy everyone's mounting hope?

"No one is leaving this frozen wart of a planet until we get my sister back," Kay said, knocking Jordan away from the controls just as another heat ray hit them hard. Captain Mom appeared beside Merlin at the cockpit—she must have been securing Mom for the journey.

"Ari?" she asked, looking around at the crew.

Kay looked back and shook his head once. He hesitated for a second too long, and another blast hit them.

"HEAT-SKIN COMPROMISED," *Error* said in a stilted voice.

Jordan grabbed the controls from Kay—and he didn't fight, only sat back with a thud. The ship soared as blast after blast hit them, making it impossible to turn back.

Merlin couldn't stop any of it. Merlin couldn't twist this moment into something better. Without magic, or hope, the only thing left to do was lie to himself. Ari had come up with some kind of scheme while the rest of them packed into the ship. She was promising, but still too impulsive for an Arthur.

Unacceptable, Merlin told himself as he spun on his feet. When he found her, he'd give her a good talking-to about keeping close to her knights and not striking out on her own so much. *Error* burned through the atmosphere, rattling so hard that Merlin thought his bones might liquefy.

"We'll find her," he said to anyone who was willing to listen. Sickness and exhaustion swelled to take up every inch of his body. "We'll find Ari. I promise. I always find my Arthur."

But that was the biggest lie of them all.

And with that, he fainted into Captain Mom's strong arms.

&

When Merlin woke up, the confusion of his body told him that he'd been out for days. He no longer felt horribly sick—only a bit stiff. He was settled into one of the canvas hammocks in the bunk room, his back permanently curled.

He tipped himself out of the fabric and onto the floor, where he sat for a few minutes, staring at his faded plague sores.

When he heard a voice at the end of the ship, he ran toward it.

"Ari Helix, also known as Ara Azar, a Ketchan criminal, has been found dead in the Avelo solar system," said a slightly delighted, disembodied voice.

Ari's knights—minus Gwen—were sitting at the round table in center of the ship, their eyes pinned to their watches, which were streaming video of Ari. Fighting on Troy. Winning the tournament on Lionel. Kissing the queen.

All while the Administrator announced, over and over again, that she was gone.

"No," Merlin said. "No, no, no, no."

"Does saying that five times bring her back?" Lam asked. "Because anything else is just useless."

"She was *found* dead?" Merlin asked as the video looped and started over, tiny Aris everywhere. She looked so real, so furiously alive.

"It's from the tyrannical textbook," Val said, anger spilling over as he pressed his watch to stop the news stream. "They don't want to brag openly about killing her. It might rally more people to Ari's cause. They made it sound like she tripped and fell on her own heroic ideals. Nobody's fault. Nothing to see here. Move along."

"They're lying!" Merlin said, hopping from foot to foot like he was standing on hornets. "They want people to believe she's dead, to cut off the universe's hope at the knees..."

Val shook his head slightly, as everyone else's eyes magnetized to Merlin.

"You missed a lot while you were asleep, old man," Lam said, getting heavily to their feet, their knee bound up tight. Despite their obvious pain, they put an arm around Merlin and guided him toward the cargo area where Kay was staring at a long box, gray-faced. "Mercer delivered her body this morning," Lam said. "Free two-day shipping on all deceased loved ones," they added, with a hard crust to their mocking tone.

Ari was laid out in a person-sized shipping crate, the brittle plastic version of a coffin. There were no wounds that Merlin could see—but she was still in a way that only meant death. Had Mercer cornered her and then waited for her to freeze?

Had she fallen into one of Urite's icy chasms? There were no traces, no wounds to tell the story. Ari's lips were bleached, so far from their living shade Merlin couldn't imagine them back to the right color.

"You got to rest," Kay said, voice cracking. "Now fix her."

"I can't," Merlin croaked. "Resurrection is a nasty, heartless business. My magic couldn't reanimate her for more than a few minutes, and she would be a zombie, not...not your sister."

Not my friend.

Merlin's palms leaked sweat and his brain seethed as he tried to find a loophole. Maybe this wasn't Ari at all—maybe some horrible magic was involved. But Morgana's power was in the mind, and Nin had been out of the cycle for so long and never bothered to interfere like this before. Merlin was the only person who might have been able to craft a fake Ari, but she would have faded as soon as he stopped holding the illusion in place.

There was only one explanation left.

Ari was dead, and this cycle was done. Failed. Like all the others.

Merlin picked a point on the ship to stare at, a rivet, so he wouldn't have to keep looking at Ari's body. At his failure. At the impossible future. He narrowed the moment down until he could deal with it again. He whittled and shaved until it was only a single rivet in a single seam in *Error*'s belly.

Val cleared his throat. "Lam, do you want to say...?"

"You're better at it," Lam said.

"You're older," Val argued.

They had never sounded more like siblings. Merlin snuck a glance and found their shoulders set in hard lines, their broad faces taking on the dim light of the cabin, their dark-brown skin glowing with overtones of gold.

"Ari Helix," Lam said, "may your body rest softly where it lies. May your spirit follow the path of the nearest moon to a softer place. May there be nothing but ease for you now, and always."

"Ara Azar," Val corrected quietly. "That was her Ketchan name. If you don't say it right, she won't go where she needs to be."

Ara Azar. It flowed like a swift bend in a river. It shone like a coin in the sun.

It belonged to her.

And so did they.

Captain Mom drifted to the cargo area, drawn by the sound of Lam and Val's prayer. At the sight of Ari's body, she hunkered against the doorjamb and covered her face. Kay moved beside her, one arm on her back. Jordan put both hands on the pommel of her sword, head low. Without anyone saying a word, it became a vigil, with starlight streaming through the portholes instead of candles.

Merlin felt slightly out of place. Everyone else here was family—Lam and Val, the moms and Kay. Gwen and Jordan weren't strictly related, but their closeness spoke of a lifetime spent together.

He was the only one left alone now that Ari was gone.

Jordan drew her sword. It was thinner than the broadsword she'd fought with on Lionel, the edges so sharp they seemed to punish the air for being in her way. "Ari was a warrior. I honor her death by helping the people she fought to protect. Her mission becomes mine."

Merlin couldn't help thinking of the other things that

should be Ari's that might soon be Jordan's. With Arthur out of the way, Lancelot would no doubt step in and comfort the grieving Gweneviere.

As if she'd heard Merlin thinking about her, Gwen walked silently in from the main cabin, wearing the T-shirt Ari had lent her on their wedding night. Her face was red and creased where she'd been pressing it too hard into a pillow, trying to bury her grief, no doubt.

She walked to Ari's side and put a hand on the clear surface of the coffin, as if it might convince Ari's eyes to open. "You said you'd come right back," she said. "You didn't. You *lied*." Gwen balled herself up, stiffened her body, and closed her eyes, as if part of her was joining Ari, dying in the cargo hold.

Merlin didn't know what to do.

He touched the rivet.

It was cold. It was lifeless. It was a circle. Merlin started tracing it, but his finger was finished almost as soon as it began, and then the journey started all over again.

&

The portal to the crystal cave shone black and oily, like tea steeped so long it had grown evil.

Merlin had to go back to the beginning. He would sleep, and wait for the next Arthur to wake him up. He just hoped he wouldn't grow too young in the meantime.

He'd closed the door to the bathroom to conjure the portal. All he had to do was take a step. But his dark reflection stopped him—dead-eyed, sickly, much too thin, still wearing a prison uniform.

Mercer had done this to him, and somehow he was still luckier than so many people they had hurt. Lian, still frozen like stone to keep her from dying too fast. Hex, dead. Ari...dead. So many people with lost families, splintered love. Merlin had a nice warm cave he could run to, but that wouldn't stop Mercer from killing the rest of Ari's knights. Whether they did it quickly or slowly, they would murder each of them while Merlin slept. Not being able to see it didn't stop it from happening.

Morgana was right on that count, if nothing else.

He upset the portal with a fingertip, turning it back into the plain bathroom mirror. Then he threw open the door and called through the ship. "Val? Val?"

He came quickly—no doubt beckoned by the nervous tremble in Merlin's voice. "What's wrong?"

Merlin drew a shaky breath. He couldn't believe how close he'd come to leaving. "I need help. These clothes..."

"You're right." Val fingered the hem of Merlin's prison shirt. "This is a problem."

In one sleek motion Val lifted the shirt and tossed it to the floor. Then Val pulled his own shirt up, revealing a tank top that showed every line of his body as clear as the boundaries on a map. Merlin's body went warm and helpless. This wasn't why he'd called Val in, and yet, it was.

Val ran his fingers through Merlin's tangled hair, tugging gently at his knots. "You can't go anywhere like this. This look is entirely too 'I've escaped from prison to murder everyone.'"

"They took my robes," Merlin said, not wanting to admit how much it bothered him.

"I liked your stars and moons," Val said softly, "but maybe it's for the best. Think of it as a complete Merlin makeover."

"You mean like in those teen movies from that hideous decade with the hairspray?"

"I have no idea what you're talking about," Val said, his pressed lips teasing and kind, two things Merlin had always assumed didn't go together but with Val were interlocking pieces.

Val slid Merlin's glasses off his face and set them on the edge of the sink. The lines of the room went swimmy.

"I need those," Merlin said.

"Don't worry," Val said. "I like these old-fashioned frames. The darkness brings out the bright in your eyes." Merlin let out a spatter of surprised, nervous blinks. "But I need them off to work." Val slid a first-aid kit out from the cupboard and clicked the box open, picking out a small pair of scissors. He went back to running his fingers through Merlin's hair, wetting it with water from the sink, pulling it smooth, snipping at the ends.

"It feels like you've done this before," Merlin said.

"Oh, I've done *everything*," Val said, with that sudden spark of flirtation that made Merlin desperate to know what the fire would feel like. "Before I was Gwen's chief adviser, I used to do this for newcomers to Lionel. People go there to change their lives, and that usually means changing their looks."

"Why did you leave Pluto?" Merlin asked, surprised that the question still mattered. Surprised that *anything* still mattered, with Ari dead.

"I wanted to make a difference in this ridiculous universe." Val paused to brush hair from the tops of Merlin's shoulders. Merlin stiffened at the soft work of Val's fingers. "Other than Ketch behind its barrier, Lionel is the only official Mercer holdout. There are underground movements on other planets, resistance efforts. Lam wanted me to stay on Pluto and help there. My parents knew I was angling to be a diplomat, and they basically said 'anywhere but Lionel.' But that planet was calling my name." The smile dropped out of Val's voice. "We're heading back to Lionel now, and Mercer isn't going to play nice, but even if I lose the place I loved so much, I'll have to go on living." He slowed his work, the slice of the scissors falling quiet. "Just like you have to."

This was all wrong. Val was supposed to hate him. "I let Ari die. I lost her, back on Urite. I failed her, just like Morgana said I would."

Val laughed. He *laughed* at one of Merlin's dearest worries. "Oh, that self-punishing bit. I used to do that, too. How's it working out for you?"

Val shook his head as he snipped. And snipped some more. Merlin started to worry about what he'd look like when this was all over. He spun Merlin to face him, and they were standing close enough that Val's face was beautifully clear, the rest of the room melting into softness behind him. "Do you want some eyeliner?"

"Do I…what?" Merlin tried to answer. Val's face was *right there*, with its smooth planes and tempting smile lines. But Ari was dead, and it wasn't the right time. There was no right time for Merlin. It was a concept that didn't exist, like a negative square number.

"Not really an eyeliner boy," Val said, misreading Merlin's silence. "But you have to let me shave *this*." He ran a hand down Merlin's jaw, and Merlin's lips parted, before he realized what Val meant to do.

"No," Merlin said. "Absolutely not."

"It's so scruffy!" Val said, rubbing the line of prickly hair.

"These are the last remnants of what used to be a glorious beard," Merlin argued. "People spoke of it for centuries! It was even a curse! *Merlin's beard*!"

But what he really meant was that it was the last thread holding him together. The last sign that Merlin might be able to fix things before it was too late.

Or too early, in his case.

"Fine," Val said, in a way that made Merlin imagine that Val would try to convince him again later. "But here...just let me..." He smoothed Merlin's eyebrows and tucked his hair behind his ears. Merlin ducked his head forward just a bit.

And then they were perfectly close. So close that it would be easier to kiss than *not* kiss.

Merlin hummed a little. It was the only way to stop himself from doing...everything else. He shook his hands, and magic rained from his fingers in faint lines of color, wrapping them together in indigo and rose and buttercup and grass-green, all of the beauty that would have gone into a kiss flowing into the air, filling it.

"How did you know I needed something pretty?" Val asked.

"I thought you were making *me* pretty," Merlin said.

Val smirked briefly, then tilted his neck back to watch. Wonder and relief and happiness overtook his face, and Merlin had done that. He'd made something good happen, for once. Val smiled, and Merlin had to stop his fingers from slipping over the soft skin of Val's neck.

Ari was still in that plastic coffin. Ari was still dead.

Val pulled his shirt back on and reached into a tiny drawer, procuring a T-shirt and pair of old, perfectly worn-in jeans. Fashion came and went, but Merlin had always believed that jeans—like cockroaches—would survive into any possible future.

"Change," Val said, half slipping out of the bathroom, before adding, "Merlin, don't forget to look at yourself." He pointed to the mirror and shut the door.

Merlin pulled on the new clothes. He found his glasses, settling them back in place. The haze of color faded, and Merlin saw himself clearly for the first time in ages. He didn't look like a great or fearsome magician, but he wasn't horrified by what he saw, either. He had an artful snarl of reddish hair, brown eyes glinting in frames of black and silver, pale skin that clung to a skinny body.

The Merlin who abandoned friends and enemies for the safety of the crystal cave was gone.

&

They dropped Ari's mothers off at the nearest medical station that would take a plague victim without too many questions. After Merlin melted Lian from her fake-death state, Ari and Kay's moms were gone, and silence reigned over the small, cracked kingdom of *Error*.

It lasted until they reached Lionel's solar system.

"I've been away too long," Gwen said, worrying through a dozen different emergency scenarios. "We'll be facing lack of water. Dehydration. Riots, possibly." Now that she'd taken off the overlarge T-shirt and put on her queen's garb, she didn't say a word about Ari. She was as focused on her planet as Merlin had been on that metal rivet.

The only thing that stopped her recitation of possible horrors was the sight of Kay coming in from the cockpit. "We're about to hit Lionel. Where do you want me to put down?"

Gwen shook her head in frowning wonderment. "You're... here. I assumed you left with your parents."

"I thought you might need help," Kay said, crossing the twin logs of his arms.

Jordan stood, getting squarely between Kay and her queen. "All you've ever cared about is your own life and your kin."

Kay shrugged. "Yeah, well, Ari married Gwen. So that makes us..."

"What?" Gwen asked, sidestepping Jordan. "That makes us what?"

"People who don't leave each other headed toward a fucking mess," Kay said, pointing out the window. The low orbit of Lionel was filled with ships, every one of them Mercer Black— a shade that demanded all the light and gave nothing back.

Mercer wasn't just here to make Gwen's life difficult. They were going to punish an entire planet.

"Message came through," Lamarack yelled from the cockpit. "A diplomatic detachment from Troy landed about ten hours ago and said Mercer is repossessing Lionel because the queen is in debt for a criminal charge against her wife."

"So they did approve your marriage," Val said. "How suddenly convenient."

Gwen rubbed a ring on her hand, one that Merlin hadn't noticed before. "We should have come straight back to Lionel. We never should have gone to that damn planet."

The words were out, and Gwen didn't try to take them back, though she did recoil. Merlin expected Kay to have a serious allergic reaction to the suggestion that his parents should have been left to die. Instead he swept an arm around Gwen that she surprisingly took him up on. He lifted her into a hug, and she dangled like a small child from his arms.

Val cleared his throat. "Gwen? What do we do?"

Kay put her down, and she pressed her face on his shirt. "You smell like her," she said. Kay gave Gwen a strange, twisting look, as if she'd said both the best and worst possible thing at the same time. "Thank you for staying," Gwen added, her composure back in place—like armor.

"I'm staying, too," Merlin said.

Gwen slayed Merlin's excitement with a glance. "I thought you'd made it clear that you don't care for me."

"Ancient grudges die hard," he admitted. "But I never should have treated you as Ari's enemy. The enemy is obvious enough."

Merlin looked out over the field of ships. He wasn't Arthur—he wouldn't defeat the greatest evil in the universe, or unite humankind. He couldn't stop the cycle by himself. But he thought of Val's home, about to be invaded. Val's words. *I wanted to make a difference in this ridiculous universe.* Merlin looked from knight to knight, each of their faces echoing the doom that he'd felt when he thought about going back to the crystal cave.

Magic prickled back to life in his fingertips.

The most imposing bit of Beethoven he could remember slipped through his lips. His hands rose and conducted a frantic composition. A web of crackling, golden energy bolts sprang into existence between the black Mercer ships and the surface of Lionel. A single ship advanced, and was zapped so hard that it looked like a finger stuck in a heavenly socket.

"Let's get you home," Merlin said, poking a tiny hole in the web so *Error* could fly through, energy snapping wildly around them. They sailed toward Lionel, and Merlin mended the tear in the web, the Mercer ships stuck behind them—for now. Merlin imagined Ari at his side, slinging one arm over his shoulder and saying *"Not bad, old man."*

For a single second, he let himself believe she was still with them.

HOME
&
DRAGONS

Ari was still on Urite...except she wasn't.

She spun inside while Morgana rummaged through her memories, feelings, and fears as if the enchantress were a burglar pillaging the jewelry store of her mind. Ari couldn't stomach a second more of the smash and grab sensation.

She grasped at an image Morgana had tossed aside.

In the memory, Captain Mom was teaching Ari how to park *Error* on a crowded space dock, two hands on the controls, squared shoulders, clear eyes. The keen memory of success and pride overwhelmed Morgana's theft for a moment, and Ari didn't hesitate. She latched on to another memory, winding up with that time on Tanaka when Kay and Ari had gotten into fisticuffs over a girl with forever legs who'd given both of them her ship's call code.

From there Ari searched until she found it, knowing it would drive Morgana mad: the recent snapshot of Merlin's cracked-egg smile after they'd come out of their worst memories together, closer, united. Hands joined.

Morgana's voracious spirit paused, her voice issuing from inside Ari's mind. *You're fighting me. Stop.*

Not a chance, Ari responded, digging deeper, tumbling into the bedsheets of her new favorite memory, the one that spun through her when she was doing everything else, making her flush, dizzy, and spread with a warmth that fought the cold of infinite stars. Gwen was naked, chest heaving, curling fingers into Ari's hair while her legs trembled, whispering, *You're going to leave me again. I don't trust you. I can't . . .* Ari kissed up her thighs, hips, to the smooth plane between her breasts. Ari tasted Gwen's fingers, promised that she would stay . . . that this time belonged to them and could be no one else's. Not Lionel's or Mercer's. Not King Arthur's or Merlin's.

And Gwen had cried like Ari didn't know how much Gwen needed to hear those words, and Ari had found surprising tears because she hadn't known how much she needed to say them.

Morgana withdrew as if she'd been burned by the fire of the memory. *I don't want your mortal passions! If you stop fighting, I'll give you what your heart desires.*

Ari knew a trap when she heard one, and yet her longings burst forth as if a door had been thrown open—possibly by Arthur himself. Did he want this to happen? Wouldn't he stand with her against Morgana?

At first Ari's desires were a neat arrangement of her knights, Merlin, Gwen, *Error,* but the surface rippled like a mirage on blistering sand, revealing a deeper ache. Ari wanted to go home, but then, Arthur wanted it, too. She could feel his guiding hand as if she didn't just want to go back to Ketch; she needed to.

Home, Ari whispered.

Morgana made an exasperated sound and chucked Ari like a stone.

Ari landed hard on the frozen ground, face first, still gripping Excalibur. By a miracle, she hadn't impaled herself on her own sword. She gasped, sore all over. And opened her eyes.

Ari *wasn't* on Urite.

She was on a crystal-clear shell. Some kind of thick glass. And below her—a solid death drop below—lay an intricate, crenellated city made of red stone with wide-arching windows.

"Omaira!" Ari sat up, reeling around to take in her surroundings. Beyond the capital city, a red desert spread out below her, highlighted with magnificent oranges and yellows. Large animals crawled in the distance, bragging of life. Tears stung Ari's eyes and at the back of her throat where she could taste how much she'd missed Ketch—a sensation swiftly soured by a logo stamped into the glass barrier. The Mercer *M.*

Morgana hunkered beside Ari. "Interesting. My magic cannot get you through this."

"Great." Ari dusted her hands off and stood. "I didn't actually ask you to bring me here."

"But you did. And Arthur did as well." Her dark eyes gleamed, and Ari hated that she was right. The fact that she hadn't spoken her desire out loud was true, but also a technicality. "He is close to speaking with me, I can tell. I've waited several millennia for this."

"Morgana, my friends are back on Urite. They—"

"Left that planet as planned, without you. I saw them escape the molten cannons myself."

"Cannons?" Ari almost yelled. "Did Mercer go after them?"

Morgana leaned closer, a little too close, squinting at Ari's face. "You are home, you insignificant string bean. That is what you asked for. *Home*. Focus on that."

Ari was dizzy from the height and also maybe from the thin atmosphere. She looked down at Ketch. "Right, home. Down *there*. How am I supposed to get through the barrier?"

"My power is internal. So is time travel, although the physical aspects of space travel do require a little blood from a certain scrawny, self-aggrandizing—"

"Morgana."

"Yes, well, we probably needed Merlin for this. An oversight on both of our parts, come to think of it. I don't have any physical magic. Technically, I cannot even touch you." Ari felt a chill that might have been Morgana's fingers. "All of you waste your bodies. You have no idea of their power, of what you'd be without them. If I hear Merlin complain about his frail, backward body once more, I'll lock him in the cell of his worst memory and be done with it."

Ari couldn't help herself. "I've seen his worst memory. It isn't a prison. He's going to face his fears. Even if that means facing down Nin herself."

"How could you be naïve about the Lady of the Lake?" Morgana asked, stunned. Ari didn't like that she'd shocked her; it felt like sipping spoiled milk. "You say her name like she's one of your friends or enemies. She is neither, and you would do well to remember it."

Ari sheathed Excalibur at her back. "Fine, but you're jealous of Merlin's *frail* body. Admit it."

Morgana cocked her head. "Imagine going through existence as a ghost. An unwelcome whisper. A living curse." She huffed. "You would be jealous, too. Even of that gangly—"

"I bet he could make you a body. You could work together to solve the cycle. You could join us instead of being a huge damn intangible thorn in everyone's side."

"He *could* make me a body. This I have recently proved to be true." She smiled evilly.

"You did something on Urite, didn't you? I saw how you looked at Merlin's blood."

That evil smile grew.

"What did you do?"

"I bought us some time to be together. To get you to Ketch and find a way to talk with my brother. If you wish this chat to be over, give me access to Arthur. If he's not in your head, perhaps he's in your heart. Trickier. Such a fickle organ. So fragile and easily...stilled."

Morgana pressed closer, and Ari stepped backward on the glass, her magboot sliding on the surface.

"Wait," she tried, holding one arm across her chest as if that might keep the woman from reaching inside her blood and muscle, clawing through her very pulse. A hundred feet beneath her, she saw the crenellated top floor of the city's largest tower. A central meeting place called Ras Almal—where her parents had worked. Memories poured in, and she couldn't help smiling.

Home was so close...and yet still impossible to reach. Unless she could send out a signal.

Ari grasped at her bare wrist, swearing. She'd given Gwen

her watch, her only way to communicate with *Error,* or anyone else. *I'll be right back,* Ari'd said when she stepped off *Error* on Urite. Gwen had known something would go wrong; Ari hadn't listened.

"I'm going to die up here. Alone. Or with you, but that's the same thing, isn't it?"

Morgana's face showed the first sign of humanity. "Perhaps. You can't break this barrier with your hands, can you? Wouldn't it be a kindness then, to let me inside to see my brother with your last breaths. You do seem kind, albeit brash, silly, and boastfully truthful. All of Arthur's best—and worst—traits."

Morgana reached toward Ari's chest, and Ari drew Excalibur, pointing the blade at this wisp of a human. "I am *not* your long-dead king."

Morgana laughed, choking the air with a sudden sadness. "I knew no such being. Arthur is a pawn in a magical, self-fulfilling torture, devised by Merlin in either his powerful ineptness or his purposeful corruptness. I cannot tell which."

"Merlin isn't evil. He's overenthusiastic and shortsighted, I'll give you that," Ari said. "But he loves his Arthurs. They give him purpose."

"Merlin's purpose is calamity. His love is hollow. *Fake.* A plastic plant. A garbage mountain. A lazy lover." Morgana's anger lifted her voice. "All these countless years, *my* Arthur is undead, unrested. His soul flits in and out of reality like a bird with a broken wing, landing on small creatures that might have the fortitude to help. Those beings get distracted by quests. By Merlin. By a love story that confuses tragedy with triteness. I loathe the very—"

"What is it about this doomed love story?" Ari interrupted,

her hand straying to the ring on her index finger. "Merlin seemed terrified of it."

"I could *show* you things that Merlin keeps secret. I could change your understanding of what it means to *be* Arthur. Merlin has fed you the morality and grandeur. I could show you the tragedies that fall in the wake of such foolhardiness." Morgana's whisper dwindled. "These endless years Merlin has played hero games while my little brother's soul lingers, suffers, *fractures*."

"I get it," Ari tried. "I have a brother, too. I'd do anything for him."

Morgana paused. "You do not seem surprised to hear that King Arthur is my brother. Merlin told you, did he? Perhaps he is maturing as he ... *immatures*." She tittered at her own joke. "Still, I'm surprised. My brother's creation is Merlin's greatest shame. The living proof that his heart is corrupt, that in the end, Earth's great magician is no more than a demon."

Ari wanted to thumb off Morgana's anger, but her curiosity edged forward. "What?"

"He created the rape of my mother."

Ari narrowed her eyes, confused.

Morgana sneered. "You are trying to imagine young, prancing, what is the phrase?—*gay as a maypole*—Merlin committing such an act. I would have you picture him as he was in the beginning. Ancient, gnarled, miserable." Ari knew Morgana spoke truly. She had seen Old Merlin firsthand in that memory, his dark hunger, his insatiable need for power. "On the night my father was murdered by Uther Pendragon, Merlin used his magic to make Uther identical to my father. And in that guise, Uther entered my castle, my home, and violated my mother."

Ari's mind smacked into the memory of wearing Kay's

body—and Merlin making her promise that she would do no harm with it. Ari glanced at the tower hundreds of feet below her magboots. "Maybe Merlin didn't know what that psychopath was going to do, Morgana."

"Maybe he did not *care*." Morgana curled her hands into fists as if she were imagining squeezing the life from Merlin. "That would be enough to loathe him, but there's more. When that violation turned into my beautiful brother, Merlin *stole* him. He corrupted Arthur with his trainings and self-aggrandizing importance. The once and future *king*. The unifying force of mankind. Merlin convinced Arthur to give himself to the machinations of warring men. And he has been lost to them ever since."

Ari looked down at her hands, clutching Excalibur. She could feel a limp, bird-boned Merlin in her arms, newly pulled from the frozen ground of Urite. His words had been as brittle as flecks of ice.

There are worse things to steal. Like children from their families.

"You believe me," Morgana said, "because you know no woman would create such lies. Perhaps the cycle has finally solved one problem."

"We are close to figuring out how to end the cycle. And you're going to help, whether you like it or not."

Ari's drive came from somewhere deeper than a long-dead king. She turned her sword point down and cast the blade into the crystal casing, through the damn Mercer logo like a bull's-eye. Ari imagined ice breaking, fracturing, and snapping apart around her.

That wasn't what happened.

The barrier popped like a glass bubble, and she fell mercilessly toward the surface of the red planet.

&

Ari didn't let go of Excalibur, even if it made her fall faster, harsher, spinning. And the sword had its own ideas, guiding her toward that skyscraper of a tower, snagging on the top edge. The blade slammed into the sandstone in a way that yanked Ari's arm in its socket. She swung from a height that was impossible. Improbable. *Insane.*

Ari instantly tried to get a second hand on the pommel, but twisted and nearly fell.

"Help!" she called out.

No one came—perhaps because she was speaking the wrong language.

"Musaeada!" she called, the word smooth and strong.

Still, no one appeared.

Ari's teeth gnashed, her whole body began to shake, and there on the edge of the tower, Morgana appeared, sitting with her legs crossed, elbow on knee, chin in palm. "Death by gravity? Interesting choice. I admit you are my favorite Arthur thus far. I honestly didn't think my misguided brother with his antiquated beliefs would ever choose a girl. Still, why you?"

"I don't know," Ari said, each word loosening her grip on the sword. "Help me."

"Why?" Morgana asked, no longer cold or dangerous. All of a sudden she seemed like a girl who'd gotten the worst fate in the world. Worse than Ari's. "If you fall, I'll simply have to wait for a new Arthur. Another chance. I think that's the best choice at this point in the game."

"Merlin is dying. What do you think will happen to your cycle when he's gone?"

Morgana shook her head and—was Ari imagining it?—she seemed angered by the idea of losing Merlin. "He's too stubborn to die."

"He's getting too young. He's scared. Terrified." Ari's grip burned. "And you're not going to let me die like you did to all those other Arthurs. The ones you killed."

Morgana leaned closer. "I killed the ones who were poisoned by Merlin. I release my brother's spirit so he might take flight again, find a new creature to mend his broken soul. So tell me, *forty-second King Arthur,* do you believe your fate is to unite humankind?"

"My fate..." Ari gasped, "...is mine."

Morgana vanished.

Ari swung from the sword, the wind pressing her closer to the tower in a way that helped her wedge her feet against the stone. She adjusted her grip in a moment of sheer terror that left her heart firing off its beat. All she had to do was climb.

She kicked into the tower, lifted herself—and Excalibur wobbled in its hold.

She froze.

Something caught her eye from below. A large four-legged creature scaled the tower at rapid speed. A giant gods damn taneen—the desert lizards Kay always called dragons— scurried up to meet her with the hungriest look on its face.

Ari scrabbled against the tower, not caring if she fell. Falling would be better than being eaten alive.

But when the lizard came up underneath her, nearly half the size of *Error,* it lifted her up with its scaled head, dropping her off on the roof of the tower. She sprawled, shaking. Excalibur was still stuck in the stone, out of reach, as the taneen started sniffing her. Admittedly she didn't remember much about Ketch, but she was certain these creatures weren't supposed to be this big... or inside the city.

A primal fear took over. The kind that wasn't organized and complicated like her fear of Mercer. It was bold and raw. A pounding, resounding, *Oh, holy shit.*

Taneens were only dangerous when they were hungry; that's what her father had always promised. She glanced along the harsh, platelike scales folded into a hard ridge down its back, ending in a long, alarming tail. The large triangular head made its way to her face, huffing dry, hot breath into her hair. Its eyes were a bluish red that blazed purple when the sun lit on them.

The taneen backed off, cowering oddly before it shook like it was ridding itself of rain. Ari watched with a sort of horror as Morgana seeped out of its scales, shaking her bluish body, straightening her ethereal dress. "What a creature," she whispered, seemingly enamored. "Powerful, savage, like the wolves of Earth. Hard to convince. She very much needs to eat you."

"Were you... inside of it? Controlling it?" Ari asked, still breathing hard.

Morgana held her palms up. "You asked for my help. Are you, or are you not still dangling from the ledge of certain death?"

Ari scrambled to her feet, backing toward a doorway as the

taneen regained its sense of self. Its scales lifted high, a hissing breath making it bare fine, sharp teeth.

"She's in a mood, desperate to mate. Only there aren't many of her kind left. She's rather lonely, truth be told. Her last few hatchlings have died of hunger."

"While that's fascinating, Morgana, right now she looks pissed."

"Not pissed. *Starving.*"

"Why didn't you take her out of the city before you let go of her? She's going to attack me any second!"

"Because you need to prove yourself. I'm not Merlin, who'll give you chance after chance to fail on your way to success. With me, you lose once, and then it's game over." She laughed as if she'd finally, in all her long years, started to have fun. "Go on, Ari, King of Your Own Fate. Slay a dragon. Let's see it."

Ari gaped. This was like training with Merlin, only completely bonkers and deadly. "What do I get if I win?"

Morgana ticked her answers off on her fingers. "One, you survive. Two, you earn my help, and three, I'll give you all the truths you crave. Every detail. All the foul answers and dark paths of your predecessors that Merlin is too scared to reveal."

The taneen was taking Ari in, tasting the air with a forked tongue.

"Deal." Ari searched out Excalibur, finding the blade lodged in a notch on the stone balcony—on the other side of the dragon. Because, holy shit, Kay was right; taneens were totally dragons. Ari called for help again and rattled the doorknob, but it was locked tight. *Where is everyone? Did they go into hiding when I broke the barrier? Is Mercer on its way?*

Ari made the terrible choice to glance at the sky. The taneen shot toward her and snapped its powerful jaws at her left leg. She jolted sideways, leaping onto the rim of the tower edge, only to reel backward from vertigo. Jumping down, the taneen twisted around itself in the tight space, trying to reach her, and she used its momentarily knotted limbs to climb over its back and dive for Excalibur.

She grabbed the handle and tugged—and nothing happened.

"You've got to be kidding me! You don't budge *now*?" Ari yelled, yanking harder. The taneen took that moment to bite her shoulder. Luckily, it was the shoulder bearing the pauldron. The leather held back the sting of sharp teeth, but not the immense pressure of those powerful jaws. Ari howled with pain as Excalibur released from the stone.

She whipped the sword around with one hand, smacking the taneen on the large plated head. The top scale cracked, and the dragon gave a loud howling moan. She backed up, shaking her long neck while blood seeped out from the crack and down her wide face. Backing up, the creature lowered her whole body, crouched, eyeing Ari with those blue-red irises, almost... affronted. Sad.

Ari didn't know what to do with the wildness in that expression. She wondered if she'd had that same overwhelmed, neglected look in her eyes when Kay's family had found her in that junked bit of ship, starving. "Did you honestly think I'd let you eat me?"

Her mouth opened wide, and she licked the blood dripping down her snout. Then the great lizard shook her head as if ridding herself of a thought, leaped over the edge of the tower and sailed down through the city, four legs splayed, revealing webbed skin between her limbs and body that was, Ari had to admit, more practical than dragon wings.

Ari stared at the gliding taneen, amused to have won, and yet troubled. From beneath the barrier, Omaira didn't seem as colorful or lively as she remembered. It was also silent. Maybe everyone had gone into hiding, fearing Mercer. She didn't blame them.

"I have to explain how I broke the barrier. How I can help," Ari said, mostly to herself, although she knew that Morgana was still listening. Ari used Excalibur to pop open the door to the balcony, then sheathed the mighty blade at her back. "This tower is Ras Almal. The Maj, the elder council, meets here. My family was one of the founding families."

Ari didn't know why she was spouting facts except that they steadied her. And she needed it. It felt like something far worse than falling from the heavens, battling an ancient enchantress or even a dragon, was waiting for her in the city.

So she didn't wait.

Ari flung the door wide and flew down the ornate, spiral steps of the tower. Her feet slipped several times. The stones were coated in sand, as if the wind had swept it inside over many years and no one had swept it back out.

Ras Almal...unkempt? Abandoned?

At the bottom of the tower, she rushed into the street, only to find more sand shifting out of open doorways, coating everything. Shutters were torn, speckled with taneen teeth marks. Ari rubbed her aching shoulder. *"Marhabaan!"*

There was no answer; and Ari was wrong. The people hadn't hidden at the sight of the barrier's destruction. They hadn't been here for a very long time.

"What has happened? Where is everyone?"

Morgana appeared beside her, nearly opaque for once. "You know. You've seen this before. You've chosen not to remember."

Ari stared at her. "I know what happened here?"

"Human minds are delicate, and yet complicated. Like trees. I was an oak when you first met me, remember? Pinned by Excalibur since the last Arthur ran me through. In the centuries I spent there, I learned that whole branches can be cut off when the trunk is in crisis. A necessary dismemberment." Morgana glanced around. "What you know about this place might stop you from being Ari altogether. Would you risk it?"

"I faced the dragon. I won. You promised to give me all the hard truths." Ari stared Morgana down. "I'm not afraid. I need to remember! If I know what—"

Morgana tapped the side of Ari's head.

And Ari was lost.

She was small again, skinny, tiny, enamored with twin brass racehorses, one for each hand. Her family had been off-planet, speaking out against Mercer's blatantly higher taxation on the poorer planets, while all the economic incentives were heaped on places like Troy. Ari understood more than her parents thought she did when it came to Mercer, but she pretended not to. It wasn't any fun to feel sick about the cancer of unchecked capitalism.

But then her family returned to Ketch, Ari running to show her cousin Yasmeen her new horses—only to find the entire city silent.

And there were . . . sleeping figures in the streets.

Ari's parents screamed at her to stay on the ship while they ran from body to body, crying out. Crying for help. Ari thought they wanted her to help, to do *something,* and she took light steps away from the empty space docks, toward the small figure of a boy younger than her. Ari told herself she didn't know him, but the lie made her stomach knot.

He played down by the mosaic fountain sometimes, the one with the jeweled camels. Yasmeen probably knew his name. Ari would ask her cousin when they met up again, and his name would most likely wake him. That always worked in the best stories.

But when she was only a few steps away, she let go of the dream that he was sleeping. His green eyes were thrown open at the sky. Green and gone.

And yet she swore she saw movement in him. A sign of life. A twitch in his throat that might be a held breath. She knelt beside him and shook his shoulder with a careful hand. His mouth dropped open, pouring black flies into the desert air, into Ari's eyes and hair.

She screamed and screamed, her father swooping her up as they ran back to the space docks. Ari dropped the racehorses. Maybe they were the bad luck. Maybe they'd caused this to happen. It was the only thought that made sense.

Ari's parents' ship took off moments later, running from the sight of Mercer bots in the sky, building something, while a Mercer patrol screeched after them, sounding alarms in the ship that made Ari hide beneath the control panel and bite her knuckle until it bled.

Ari lifted her head. She was on her knees, alone. Morgana was gone. The sun was setting, blue-and-orange fiery light lining the horizon. Even the siren birds were lilting through the air. It was a familiar nightmare that had masqueraded through her hopes as a dream.

Ketch, the entire planet, was a tomb.

She had to get out of here.

She ran first to the space docks, but they were stripped bare. Mercer had poisoned the population somehow and then taken every conceivable ship in case there were survivors. Then they'd sealed the planet away, and when her parents had tried to tell the galaxy of Mercer's massacre, they'd been murdered.

Ari's thoughts skittered back to the conversation about Lionel's treatment with the Administrator. How close was Mercer to repeating its genocidal history?

"Morgana!" Ari swung around, yelling at the skies. "Get me out of here!"

Morgana didn't appear, the coward, but her voice slid along the wind. "I'd need Merlin's blood to make another portal to push you through. Why don't you call your friends?"

Ari looked at her blank wrist again, missing her watch, her only direct com link with *Error*. Now that the barrier was broken, she should be able to get a message out, but how? She ran back to Ras Almal, up the stairs to the balcony where she'd battled the taneen. She swept the sand off the stone and pressed the hidden buttons, bringing the system online. It still worked. She typed in the fourteen-digit strand of *Error*'s call codes— the only number she'd memorized in the whole universe. Kay would answer. And Merlin and Gwen would bring them here. They'd pick her up. Save her from this dead place...

Ari pressed Enter. The signal spun and spun until it ended, cut off. THE SHIP YOU ARE TRYING TO LOCATE IS OUT OF RANGE OR NO LONGER IN SERVICE, the system told her.

Ari turned, her back sliding down the console until her butt hit the hard stone. She looked at her hands, stained red from the gritty sand. She'd dreamed of this moment so many times, the blood desert of Ketch coating her skin once again. Now this red seemed to symbolize the heights to which Mercer would rise to wipe out rebellion.

The color of cost.

"They'll answer," Ari said, her voice unrecognizable in her own ears. "My friends will be looking for me. They're safe somewhere. I'll keep calling until they answer."

"How could you know that?" Morgana said, sitting beside her. She was not so all-powerful for once, as lost as Ari in her own ways. "They might think you're dead. I might have—"

"Arthur wanted me to see this place, so this is part of it." Ari covered her face with her hands. *You wanted me to know what Mercer is truly capable of. Is that it, Arthur?*

No answer.

"You are an admirable creature," Morgana said, clearly against her will. "Your entire planet is lost, your people extinct, and you are scratching around for hope like that ravenous dragon, as if perhaps one more meal will make a difference in your starvation."

"You're insufferable." Ari felt herself crumbling in. Morgana had been right; Ari was not the same person, not with these memories unlocked. This truth unfurled her fury. A woken dragon. "Morgana?"

"Yes?"

"Show me everything. Everything Merlin doesn't want me to know."

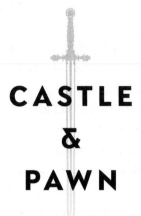

CASTLE
&
PAWN

One Year Later

Merlin was awake in the middle of the night again, walking the ramparts of the castle, checking his magical barrier for weaknesses.

The web of energy lines he'd created to keep Lionel safe from the Mercer ships required constant upkeep, and a year of staring at the sky had left his face permanently pinched, his neck aching, his eyesight worse than ever. His magic was always on the verge of being drained. But he did what was needed. He hummed and sent up a few crackling threads to repair a small breach—not big enough for a ship to fit through, but he couldn't let it grow.

"Nicely done," Gwen said, her voice bleary. She patted Merlin's shoulder. "Lionel thanks you for your service." Gwen rarely slept, always afraid that the next day would bring doom to her people. Merlin worried that the ever-glowing lights of his barrier wasn't helping, but at least Gwen and Merlin had found common ground on their nocturnal castle-walks. She was the first Gweneviere he had ever befriended. She had even named him Lionel's official mage.

Of course, not everyone was delighted with Merlin's barrier.

"Do you think the tourists will ever forgive me for sealing them in?" Merlin asked, as the energy lines reconnected in the night sky, the glowing cage repaired, and Lionel safe—or trapped.

"There are worse places to be stuck than Lionel," Gwen said, her brown eyes brightening with argument. "Even when it's under siege."

"They burned me in effigy. They even put a scruffy little red beard on the thing."

"It *was* strikingly accurate," Gwen agreed.

Merlin didn't know why it bothered him so much. He wasn't used to being popular. That was Arthur's job. But for some reason he wanted these people to understand he was on their side—maybe because he'd cast his lot with them in a way that he never truly had before.

"You saved all of us from death at Mercer's hands," Gwen pushed on. "Including me, and for that I will always be grateful."

"Saving people is woefully temporary," Merlin muttered. Mercer was still up there. And Ari was still dead in the hold of *Error*. Now that they were planet-bound, the ship had become a sort of tomb. Merlin could barely see it, docked past the edge of the city, a dark lump in the desert, glowing softly with reflected light.

Lam spent hours kneeling at the side of Ari's plastic coffin, filling her in on what was happening with her friends. Kay swore he visited so often to keep the ship in flying order, but he

always came back with a red, puffy face. The Lionelians went
to have their hope brought back to life after long days of dehydration, exhaustion, and fear. Even in death, Ari was a symbol
of pushing back against Mercer's tide.

Gwen and Merlin didn't visit.

Merlin couldn't face his longing to have Ari back at his side.
Every time he saw her lying in that Mercer box, the sensation
felt ineffably *wrong*. It was even worse for Gwen, he suspected.
Her wedding ring never budged from her finger. She still wore
Ari's watch, and she lit the thing up now, staring at one of the
pictures she often returned to. As far as Merlin could tell, it
was a pile of laundry.

He wanted to comfort Gwen—but what did he know about
love?

"I'm going to bed," Gwen announced. The old Merlin
would have muttered, *Whose* bed? But he kept his mouth shut.
It was none of his business, even if this truth would have made
Ari's heart split into mismatched pieces.

"Good night," Gwen whispered. She seemed to be saying it
to her watch. Perhaps to Ari herself. Gwen cut off the display
and padded down the stone hallway.

Merlin's fingers roamed over a small wooden falcon in his
pocket. He'd found it in the abandoned marketplace, half finished. It reminded him a little of the one he'd had when he was
very, very old. The one he'd woken up with in the crystal cave,
clasping as if it were a lifeline to an unknowable home. And
that really was the problem, wasn't it? Merlin had begun to
think of Lionel as his home. He looked out over the tournament rings and the marketplace, the houses and the shops. He

loved this place in a way he'd never dared to love anything in ages.

Merlin turned his attention back to the skies. Barrier maintenance was never-ending, and if he wanted to keep this place, he could not falter. He could not fail his friends the way he'd failed Ari. When he felt like his neck was going to snap, he sang every Earth song he could remember, not for magical purposes, just to keep himself awake. The truth was that his mind clung to the catchiest tunes, which meant a disproportionate number of nursery rhymes and pop songs. After bumbling his way through a few half-remembered K-pop hits, Merlin heard soft footsteps behind him.

"Up again, your majesty?" he asked.

Long, strong fingers settled on the back of his neck, rubbing at the sore muscles. Merlin melted into the feeling.

"I am not the Queen of Lionel," Val said. "Though I do look good in her clothes."

"Yes," Merlin said. "Yes, I can confirm that you do."

Merlin had seen Val dressed up in Gwen's clothes more than once and found it distractingly exquisite. Everything about Val delighted him. He calmly organized, keeping everyone alive in the face of this painful, drawn-out siege, and yet he also insisted on beauty. He planned little picnic dinners out of the meager portions of food, making a show of the last of the Lionelian mead. Merlin was also in love with that burning, bold way Val stared across a crowded room. And the times when the weight of the siege was too much, and Merlin's hand found a home on Val's arm, or the small of his lower back, and Val murmured in appreciation of the touch.

They had been flirting mercilessly with each other for months. But there was absolutely nothing more that Merlin could do about it unless he wanted a heartbreak as grand as anything on the Arthurian scale.

"You have a nice singing voice, have I ever told you that?" Val asked, his hands still searching out the tension in Merlin's neck.

"No one's ever told me that," Merlin said. People were often awed by his magic—never by *him*. "I do have quite a bit of practice at singing."

"Should we practice other things?" Val asked.

Merlin looked down, abruptly taking his eyes off the barrier and finding Val's glowing brighter than the magic overhead. "I've told you all of the reasons why I keep my distance," Merlin said, his voice perilously thin.

Val nodded, ticking them off on his fingers as, somehow, their bodies drifted closer. "You're getting younger. I'm getting older. I'm probably going to die soon. You might never figure out mortality. These seem like small issues, really," Val said, teasing Merlin like it was his life's work. "If you can come up with a good one…"

"The barrier," Merlin said. "If I take my eyes off it for too long, we'll all be dead."

You'll *all be dead,* Merlin's brain corrected. *And I'll be left alone to mourn you.*

Val put his arms around Merlin's neck, lacing his hands there, keeping Merlin's eyes at ground level. "If you did die tomorrow…"

Merlin's finger flew into the air. "I can't—"

"*Theoretically,*" Val said, gently rolling his eyes. "What would you want people to say about you, Merlin?"

"Once upon a time, he had a very nice beard," Merlin said. "He was the teacher of forty-two king Arthurs. He never gave in to tyrants."

"Your fear is a tyrant," Val shot back.

"Are you saying I'm as bad as Mercer?" Merlin asked, his offense only mostly feigned.

"You're worse," Val said. "Mercer doesn't tease me and then leave me alone at night to . . . what's the Old Earth phrase? Take *care* of myself?"

Merlin coughed. Violently.

"Are you all right?" Val asked, his smile spreading wide.

Walk away. Leave now. Abandon all hope, ye who flirt with Val.

But Merlin stayed exactly where he was, with Val's hands looped around his neck. His body was making its own decisions, and they were questionable at best. "You've been . . . because of me?"

"Yes," Val said, taking a step forward. "How do you deal with it?"

"I lecture myself, mostly. Long, dry lectures." Merlin's palms were prickling. His hands were still at his sides, forgotten and awkward. "But sometimes . . . yes. Sometimes I indulge in other methods. My imagination is rather potent. Shall I show you?"

Oh, celestial gods. What had he just offered?

"You're killing me," Val said, his smile as wide as ever.

"Then at least we're dying together this time." Merlin raised his hands to the place they most longed to be—Val's chest. He slowly, slowly, started to explore, fingers moving in circles, rippling outward. He pulled their bodies together, fitting Val's slightly longer frame with Merlin's smaller one. Val had muscles that didn't look prominent like Kay's or Jordan's, but they were there, shifting under his skin, glowing blue-purple in the barrier's light.

Even with so much time to anticipate what this might feel like, each moment of contact surprised Merlin. The slip of hands under shirts. Their faces brushing, cheeks and jaws sliding along each other, lips soft on skin, a long slow preamble to kissing.

"Ohhhhh," Val said slowly, standing back.

Merlin leaped. "What? What?" Had he ruined everything in some unforeseen way?

"You knew this was going to happen tonight," Val said with a pleased, satisfied smile.

"What do you mean?" Merlin was genuinely puzzled.

"You shaved for me." Val ran a finger along Merlin's jawline, rubbing his curiously smooth countenance. "How did you shave this close during a planet-wide drought? You're baby soft."

Those words unlocked a deep fear. Merlin had never so much as set a razor to his skin. *Baby soft*. This was the proof of Merlin's backward aging. He would never have a future with Val.

Shut it down. Shut it all down.

He violently cut off the feelings running through his body. The emotions blasting through his heart.

Everything.

The night went dark, and Merlin and Val gasped. For the

first time in a year, there was no barrier, no brilliant web of light in the sky.

"Did we just doom the planet by almost kissing?" Val asked.

"No." Merlin had shut down everything inside of himself—including his magic. Technically, they had doomed the planet by *not* kissing.

And Mercer ships were already raining down.

&

Merlin tried to put the barrier back up, but his magic was too weak to create the entire thing from scratch. Besides, Mercer ships were swarming the atmosphere, and now Lionel had an invasion to deal with.

Val and Merlin ran through the castle, waking everyone up, shouting down the stone hallways. They were all going to die, as Merlin looked on, unkillable. And all Merlin could think was that it was a damn shame he'd stopped himself from kissing Val before it was too late.

All he could picture was Ari's disappointed face.

Everyone gathered by the light of a few stubby candles in the great hall, pulling on clothes. "Merlin, what happened to the barrier?" Gwen demanded. "Why is it *gone*?"

"I experienced a slight...malfunction," Merlin whispered, guilt rolling inside of him like great sea swells. "Please, if you'll let me apologize..."

But before he could grovel, Gwen's watch lit up, ominously blue. For a year, not a single message had been able to get in or out of Lionel. Merlin's web of magic had been down for less than five minutes, and here was someone who wanted to talk.

The Administrator's head popped up. Everyone else looked so different after this year, but he was exactly the same, with his smooth face and bland eyes. "Good-bye, dearest Gweneviere," he said in a vinegar voice. "We'll always wish you had accepted our offer on Troy. We miss your wife *so much*, don't you? Good news, you'll be reunited soon—"

The signal cut out.

Killed. On purpose.

"His sense of drama is getting stale," Val muttered.

"The Mercer ships are landing," Gwen said. "We've sealed the castle doors. Jordan is outside on watch. Hopefully she's waking people up and gathering her knights."

Merlin knew that the Lionelian tournament knights had been training for this all year. He also knew that they were dehydrated, exhausted, and didn't stand a chance in a full-blown fight against a Mercer attack force outfitted with the best killing machines money could buy.

"What now?" Merlin croaked.

Gwen and Lamarack exchanged a glance. "We evacuate the planet," she said. "Go."

Lam took off, with a quick kiss of her hand.

"Evacuate?" Merlin echoed. "How are we going to do that with a tiny ship that was far from spaceworthy in the first place?" His voice sounded pinched and hysterical in his own ears. His guilt reached a fever pitch. "*Error* isn't even close. How are we supposed to get to her with Mercer forces pouring through the city?"

The cannons boomed, and everyone jumped. "I thought those were ceremonial," Kay said.

"They work in a pinch," Gwen said. "We have to keep the

invading forces distracted for long enough to get off the ground. Lam and I have it all worked out."

Gwen grabbed a candle in a stamped tin holder and approached the wall of tapestries in the dining hall. Most of them showed pictures of knights on horsebots. Not exactly traditional, but Merlin had grown to love the anachronisms of this place as much as everything else.

Jordan appeared, pounding down a flight of stairs, looking so red and strained with exertion that Merlin thought she would tip over on the spot. "Are you quite all right?"

"How did you even get inside?" Kay asked.

Jordan knelt before Gwen, her loyalty spotless even under such stress. "I had to get to my queen. I swung over the mercury moat on a hidden rope and scaled the castle walls by starlight."

"Of course you did," Merlin said, rolling his eyes.

Gwen ignored the jab. "I didn't want it to come to this, but with the ships landing, we have no choice. There *is* another ship in our colony, Merlin." She pulled aside a tapestry—one of the previous queen at her coronation—and revealed a metallic door that looked strangely like the ones on *Error.* "You're standing inside of it."

Kay spun to her, his face gratifyingly blank. "The castle is *a spaceship?*"

"The towers, crenellations, and most of the façade were added later," she said, which explained Merlin's observations about the additions to the odd metallic base of the castle. "The core of the building is a generation ship that the original colonists converted."

"But it hasn't flown since Lionel was established seventy solar cycles ago," Val said.

"You want me to revive it with magic!" Merlin shouted, hoping he could still save the day, even though he was the one who'd put them in so much danger in the first place.

"We need you to save your strength. Besides, the ship has to fly on its own if we're to have any real chance." Gwen's eyes skipped over him, to Kay. "Let's have the only person in this company who's lived in a spaceship since birth take a look at the machinery."

"What?" Kay asked. "No." Gwen's brown-eyed stare was weighty, a weapon that bludgeoned Kay better than any words. "I can't fly your castle!" he insisted.

"Sounds like a personal problem," Val muttered.

"You three," Gwen said, her gaze picking out Val, Merlin, and Kay. "Come."

Jordan frowned openly at Gwen's choices. "My queen, I could help—"

"I need you to lead our people to safety. We have precious little time. Mercer will have to drain the mercury moat before they invade, but that still only gives us minutes," Gwen said, cutting off the knight with a hand to the back of her neck. She set her forehead against Jordan's. "Today is the death of our dream, old friend. We can't let everyone die with it. Get our people to the evacuation points."

Jordan gave a deep nod and rushed away.

Gwen pulled open the hidden metal door, revealing a set of stairs. The rest of the party descended into a set of close chambers that Gwen navigated with quick, nervous steps, the light of her candle throwing shadows on the metal walls, while the cannon fire above grew apocalyptic. Gwen finally stopped and shoved a box of tools in Kay's hands. The hope on her face was the most aching thing Merlin had seen since Ari's death. "Please," she said.

"I can't promise anything, spaceship-wise," Kay said carefully. "*Error* is the biggest thing I've ever flown. And I'm not going to say a word against her, but...she's no castle."

"More like a flying broom closet," Val said.

Gwen pointed Kay in the direction of the main console. It looked like all of the computers Merlin had seen over the course of a very long lifetime had been melted together. "The principles are the same," Gwen promised.

"Yeah," Kay said. "But doom is in the details."

Twenty minutes later, Kay was swearing at a wall of metal. Gwen and Val had disappeared to check on the castle attendants and get a progress report.

"I've gone through the motions, and she won't start." Kay punched a few buttons with a sudden ferocious energy.

"Is it really so different from *Error*?" Merlin asked.

"My baby," Kay said longingly. Then he swallowed with the grim determination of a man about to embrace his last resort. "Whenever *Error* gets fussy, I, uh, sweet-talk her a bit. Could you maybe turn around?"

Merlin spun in a half-circle before he fully understood what he'd agreed to.

"Hey there," Kay said. "I know we don't know each other so well, but we're in this together so...let's make it happen. Okay?" He paused, and Merlin could only imagine that he was pressing buttons. Or caressing them. "Yeah. That's a good place to start, you pretty castle."

Merlin's cheeks flared with the kind of heat that would kill a lesser mortal. This felt like a fitting punishment for shutting off the barrier and refusing to kiss Val…listening to Kay sweet-talk a spaceship was the kind of mortification he deserved.

"All right, that's good," Kay said. "Yeah. Now we're getting somewhere."

Merlin thought he would faint from relief at the sight of Gwen and Val running down the stairs with several attendants in tunics and leggings and soft leather boots. His reprieve was short-lived, however.

"Mercer drained the moat," Val said. "We have about two minutes before the whole castle is crawling with associates."

Kay coughed.

Merlin stepped forward, somehow becoming the ambassador for the most embarrassing mission ever. It had gone from an absurd possibility to their only shot at escape. "We have a bit of an issue," Merlin said. "The ship is in need of… encouragement."

"Did you *hear* me say two minutes?" Val asked.

Kay let out the sigh of a condemned man. He turned back to the consoles. "Hey, sweet thing. *Heyyyy.* Don't be jumpy like that. You're doing fine. Just tell me what you need."

Shock pried Gwen's mouth open.

Kay pressed a string of buttons. "Okay, so I think I've got you configured, and since your main system generates its own power, you just need a spark, baby." He looked to Merlin.

Merlin fired up his fingers, hummed a slow jam to fit the mood, and hit the spot Kay was pointing to with a weak, sickly bolt.

The room fell silent—the cannons had stopped firing. Merlin cast a look around at Gwen and Kay and Val, trying to memorize their faces so he would remember them as well as he remembered Ari when they were dead two minutes from now.

Then the consoles gave off a dusty-hot breath. The spaceship lifted from the surrounding rock with a catastrophic crash, and everyone was tossed to the side. Merlin grabbed a hard metallic corner, wishing it were softer and Val-shaped.

"You're going to be the first castle in space, baby," Kay said, patting the nearest panel. "That's pretty hot."

&

There were five meeting points outside the city, each one holding a well-concealed pocket of a hundred or more Lionelians. In the distance, they watched the Mercer forces overrun their city, burning the marketplace, shelling the tournament ring.

At the final meeting point, *Error* waited, a dark speck against the honeyed sunset. This place was so beautiful, and Mercer had just ripped out its beating heart so that its loyal customers could have luxury condos on stolen worlds.

"Should one of us stay with the evacuees?" Val asked as the castle doors swung closed, everyone safely inside and the controls handed over to Gwen's most trusted tactical adviser.

"We'll lead them from *Error*," Gwen said darkly. Merlin could tell that she was worried about the Administrator's next moves. Gwen might still be marked, even though they'd taken Lionel. She was keeping her people safe by keeping her distance, and it stung her as acutely as losing the entire planet, he could tell.

Error soared through the clear skies. Apparently, Mercer

didn't care about chasing them down as long as they won and took what was wrongfully theirs. Gwen sat in a tight ball, her knees meeting her chest. This was the other part of choosing to be on a small, private ship. She didn't want to show her people her grief.

"I'm sorry," Merlin said, laying his failure at her feet. "My magic shouldn't have faltered."

Gwen shook her head bitterly, and he thought she was so mad she couldn't speak, but then she looked up, her eyes devastated and yet filled with fire. "Our little planet lasted against Mercer for a *year* because of you. We gave everyone in the universe hope that it could be done. We never folded. And we got out alive." She sighed. "That's what resistance looks like, Merlin. It's not one glorious, shining victory. It's a torch that you keep burning, no matter what."

It was a beautiful speech—and by the end of it, Gwen was crying.

As soon as they were out of Lionel's orbit, Kay called Jordan into the cockpit to take over for him. He went to Gwen, wrapped his arms around her and led her toward the little kitchen for a drink of water. This was what Gwen and Kay did best together ever since Ari died. They pooled their grief, swimming freely in it. Merlin wondered if they would go to the cargo bay and stare at Ari's sealed coffin together.

Val sat at the round table in the center of the cabin, looking for someplace to take them all now that Lionel belonged to Mercer. Not even an hour after he'd lost his home, Val was already deep in thought, doing the necessary work, saving everyone in a hundred small ways.

That was his magic.

Val's long fingers worried the edges of a star chart. He tapped endless coordinates into his watch and sighed. They would be facing another doom tomorrow, with nowhere to go and supplies so low, and Merlin finally understood the math.

He needed to kiss Val before that happened.

He needed to kiss Val *now*.

Merlin stood up, breaking the calm of the tiny cabin.

"Where are you going?" Val asked, worry running through his words like a current.

"I'll be right back," Merlin said, holding up a finger. "With ideas."

He wanted to scout out a place beforehand. When Merlin finally kissed Val, it would be with all of the focus and purpose he usually saved for ending this blasted cycle. But Error was so *tiny*. Merlin rushed from room to room. Kay's cabin was locked up, and Lam was in the bathroom. Merlin felt dizzy with indecision and lack of food. "Snacks!" he cried, remembering the one place on the ship that no one else had access to.

The pantry. He'd unlocked it with Kay's retinal scan once. He could do it again. He bolted toward the back of the ship, imagining Val up against the dry goods, the rustle of boxes mingling with soft breath. Merlin had just enough magic left. He put his fingertips to his chest and shocked himself with a burst, his body swelling into Kay's. He used Kay's large, blockish hands to open the pantry.

And shut it.

Merlin tried to un-see Kay's pale, fully undressed backside. The twin logs of his legs, the squared-off cheeks of his buttocks, his mussed silver hair. And behind him, pressed against the shelves, her dark curls raked with sweat, her sighs dashing Merlin's hopes, was Gweneviere.

This was the other new part of Gwen and Kay's relationship, post-Ari. They grieved together...and then they slunk off somewhere to have sex.

Merlin slammed the door, emphatically. He understood the strength of their grief, but that didn't mean he wanted to see Kay's naked pantry dance. His magic melted away, leaving him Merlin-shaped.

He whispered a single word as if it were a curse. *"Kay!"*

Val ran in. "Kay what?"

"Kay and Gwen," he mumbled.

"Are they in there?" Val asked, disgusted. "Oh, celestial gods, please tell me he wasn't doing the sexy talk."

Jordan lumbered in.

"I thought you were in the cockpit," Val said. "Who's flying the ship?"

"I discovered something when I turned on the com line," she said. "I must tell my queen."

"Not now, Jordan," Merlin said, flicking her away with his fingertips. Her presence only reminded Merlin of how wrong he'd been about the Lancelot situation. Merlin thought the same impossible thing he'd thought so many times since Ari's death: *Kay is Lancelot.*

Merlin had wasted his time worrying about Jordan's ferocious-blond brand of loyalty. Kay had failed knight camp, but he was stubborn and true. And he had given up everything to be Ari's brother. He was her most loyal knight.

And now he was bursting out of the pantry, dressed in red boxer briefs. "You have to stop stealing my face!"

"Stop stealing Ari's wife!" Merlin shouted.

"Ari is dead!" Kay yelled, a vein appearing on his forehead like a bolt of angry lightning.

Gwen emerged from behind Kay, tugging her dress back together.

"No judgment, no judgment, no judgment," Merlin muttered under his breath.

"Really?" Val asked. "I vote judgment."

Jordan sighed. "My queen, I've found something."

"No one is queen anymore," Gwen said, her voice low and shadowed. "What is it, Jordan?"

The black knight paused. Her potent silence told Merlin that she was in possession of a factual grenade and was about to drop it. "The ship has four thousand, three hundred and seventy-two missed messages," she said. "And they're all from Ketch."

PAGEANTRY

&

REALITY

The stone-paved main street was a battlefield.

Ari rode up to meet the line of Mercer associates astride a damn dragon. "That's right, you corporate assholes!" she called out, sword high, sun glinting off the blade. "He might not breathe fire but he does eat dumbasses for breakfast!"

She sounded her war cry and spurred her great green steed into a scurrying charge. Ari meant to flip off his back, cutting through the Administrator's front line of defense with one fell swoop from Excalibur. Instead, her taneen sank on its hindquarters to scratch its shoulder with a vigorous thumping from its back leg.

Ari launched off him sideways, taking out the front row all right, but not gracefully. The stuffed associates' shirts exploded, spilling rice everywhere, and Kay dove at the sight, lapping up the uncooked grains.

"No, no! Kay, stop!" She grabbed him around the neck, nearly thicker around than both of her arms, and pulled the young taneen back. "Remember the last time you ate a bunch of uncooked rice? Your belly ached for a week. Sit, Kay! I said, *sit*."

The dragon, who was only a few months old and yet already bigger than the horsebots on Lionel, sat back on his haunches, whipping his tail around and kicking sand and rice everywhere. Ari laughed, digging out a piece of lamb jerky from her pocket and tossing it into Kay's mouth. Her favorite taneen hatchling was exactly like her brother. Obstinate, obnoxious, smelly, and always thinking with his stomach. That's what had made him the easiest to train. And fall in love with. She gave him a thorough rub along the soft skin between the plates across his back. Kay made a moony, happy sound—which also sounded like her brother.

"Stay…" Ari said, backing up. Kay began to wiggle out of place, and she gave him a stern eye. He sat back down, but continued to create chaos with his tail. "Okay, one more. This is the big one, remember?" Ari eyed Kay, who was already more interested in whatever might be in her pocket than her command. "Play dead!" she called.

Kay grinned, triangular mouth hanging open, tongue hanging out to the side.

"Does Big Mama know you're playing with her baby again?" Morgana said, appearing out of thin air like an annoying ghostly know-it-all.

"Big Mama is fine as long as I feed them both. Besides, Kay doesn't like being secluded in the hot, boring desert. Do you, buddy?" Ari rubbed down his hard nose, getting licked on the cheek. "Now, play dead!"

Kay squatted low and playfully. Big Mama's howl echoed down the street, and the sight of the enormous taneen turned

Kay into less of a trained dragon and more of a toddler, wiggling with delight to perform for his mom. He rolled on his back, legs in the air, and lolled his tongue out. Big Mama came scuttling down the street, dwarfing everything in sight, including her baby. She sniffed at Kay's position and then growled disapprovingly.

"He's just playing dead, Big Mama." Ari stuck two fingers in her mouth and whistled. Kay jumped back onto his feet. She pulled out two pieces of lamb jerky, tossing one in Kay's mouth and the other up to his mom. Big Mama swallowed it whole and turned around, pounding the rice-associates into the sand with her large, clawed feet as she went. Kay slobbered on Ari's arm for a minute and then scuttled after his mom.

Ari climbed the street sign, unwinding the camera tied to the post. She reviewed the footage they'd made. "There's some good stuff, I think. Not a complete loss considering it took two weeks to build those dummies."

"I still can't understand why you're doing this," Morgana said.

"It's training." Ari hopped down and swung Excalibur with a loose wrist. "Practice for the real thing."

"Assuming you ever get off this rock."

"Optimism, Morgana," Ari said, even though she was starting to feel the opposite. Two dry seasons had come and gone on Ketch. The next rain season was due any day, and that meant at least a year had gone by on the Old Earth calendar. She moved to the line of dummies she'd made of her friends. Val wore a homemade corset. Merlin, Ari's mother's favorite green robe. Lamarack was one-handed and bragged the best mauve thawb she could find. Kay wasn't there because she had the loutish taneen for when she missed her brother.

The Gwen dummy had been a bit of a disaster. Ari had gone through seriously dark moods while she worked on it, and eventually given up. It didn't help that Ari could now recite the dozens of Arthur-Lancelot-Gweneviere heartbreaks from the previous cycles, complete with the video-quality memory playbacks Morgana was in the habit of gifting when she didn't think Ari was taking the matter seriously enough.

Morgana's training had been nothing if not thorough.

Which had inspired the Jordan dummy—Ari's favorite opponent. It was covered in pots and pans turned into armor; even though Ari had found a suit of armor, she'd kept the ragtag version instead. It was less formidable, easier to bang against. Ari sent Excalibur singing through the air, *dang*ing across Jordan's breastplate. It wasn't enough, so she turned, using her full body to throw the sword into the dummy.

The handle wavered in the aftermath—sticking out of Jordan's head.

"Oh, yes, that reeks of optimism," Morgana said.

"You said I should vent."

"*I* said you should give up on Gweneviere. It's a poisoned love story. You said you could 'vent' your 'feelings.' "

"I never should have taught you how to use air quotes," Ari muttered. She went to pull the sword out of the dummy, but Morgana beat her to it. Her ghostly fingers closed around the handle without gaining purchase. "It's not going to work. Excalibur won't let you."

"It let me once. On Urite." Morgana heaved an annoyed sigh. "But then Merlin's blood was on it. What I wouldn't give for just a few vials full of that heavenly liquid."

"Ugh, no more waxing poetic about Merlin's magical

blood!" Ari hauled the sword free and shoved it into the sheath at her back. "And don't think that I—"

A simple, glorious tone sounded. As loud as the city was large.

At first, Ari couldn't move. "That's the signal beacon. *Error* is calling me back!" She sprinted for Ras Almal alone, climbing the steps two at a time, used to this workout. Ten flights and her legs barely burned anymore. If this had been her normal training, she would have set a personal best by dozens of seconds.

On the tower balcony, Ari silenced the signal alarm and stared at the blinking com light. From the number, she could tell it was *Error* calling. *Who* was calling was still a mystery. What had happened to her friends while she was here? Were they all right? Were some of them dead? Why had it taken so long for them to call her back? She'd run through these thoughts so many times over the last few seasons that her brain short-circuited. This could even be the Administrator bragging about his latest victory over her friends.

Ari answered. "Ari here."

At first no one spoke on the other line.

"This is Ara Azar on Ketch," she tried. "Who is this?"

"Ari?" Merlin's voice crackled with static and hope. "Is that truly you?"

"Merlin!" She pressed a knuckle against her tearing eye, holding back a windstorm of sudden emotions. "Where are you? Are you okay?"

"We're...adrift. Lionel was taken over. I couldn't stop it, Ari. We all tried, but we've nowhere to go, and Mercer won't permit us to land anywhere."

So it was time. Ari had been placing the jigsaw pieces of a plan together since she'd fallen like an angel into the remains of her destroyed home. Arthur, in all his absent wisdom, had been pressing her toward this, as well. Preparing, training, readying for battle.

One step at a time. No impulsive decisions.

After all, this was the Administrator's game of chess. And Ari was taking back the offense. That's what her time on Ketch had taught her. You don't ride a taneen in one day. You spend months getting them to simply eat out of your hand. And you couldn't bring Mercer down in one accusation, but with a few well-placed moves, you could change the game.

"I have a plan, Merlin. Listen close." Ari gave him instructions for what to do with the Lionelian refugees—and then where they would meet. She tried to remain as unemotional as possible and hung up. She managed to stop herself from asking about her friends. How Gwen was. Why her brother hadn't come on the line. All those things had to be pushed aside for now.

"Check, Administrator," Ari said, finally pressing Send on the file she'd been compiling for months. A tell-all about what had happened to Ketch, sending it out on all open channels, for the great, wide universe to see.

&

The second step of the plan was a whirlwind of action. The generation ship—*the fucking castle*—stunned the hell out of Ari, falling through Ketch's atmosphere and into the sandy desert like a barely-reined-in meteor. She helped the several thousand Lionelians into the least known city on the planet, the one built into the sandstone mountains in the south, where the taneens didn't tend to venture. She made sure the refugees were stocked with food, water, medicine.

And she left.

Piloting the only working emergency life pod from Lionel's castle, she powered, full throttle, to the very solar system that first sent humans into the cosmos like a constellation of consequences. From Mars, she caught a glimpse of *Heritage:* skulking, watching, unnerved no doubt by the space waves alight with anti-Mercer chatter. The communications coming through her console were a gratifying tangle of discussion about Ari's video.

She hadn't held back. She'd shown the collections of human bones, piled high by the taneens who'd feasted when the planet went lifeless. And she'd shown the excruciating death of the hatchling. The one that drank from a Mercer barrel of "water" from the shipment that had poisoned everyone. Big Mama had lost her mind that day, and that was on the video, too. The enormous grieving mother howled into the desert wind as the seizing little one finally went limp. She'd knocked her own head into a stone wall and bitten Ari three times before they'd both collapsed in a pile of misery.

Of understanding.

That's how Ari had learned *how* Mercer did it. They'd waited for the dry season—and then struck. A cowardly, spineless move. But they hadn't just murdered Ketch; they'd swept their crime under that barrier. Ari was pleased to hear so much speculation across so many worlds about what else Mercer might have covered up.

Ari kept her eye trained on the swiftly approaching, gaudy moon, and requested a docking space. Then she began the—honestly exhausting—decision of picking out what to wear. Something to blend in but, obviously, also look nice. She took in her appearance in one of the silver walls in the pod. Her skin had darkened under the Ketchan skies. Her hair was nearly twice as long, the ends gracing her hips, and her muscles were banging from the constant training.

What would Gwen think of her now?

Ari's heart did an embarrassing drop beat as she straightened her clothes. "Be cool. She's been with someone else. No big deal. Maybe several people. Maybe even…probably…huge, muscular, perfect, ridiculous fucking Jordan." Ari pulled her belt tight as she imagined the black knight with her impeccable chivalry and gleaming armor—and had to unhook the leather and start again. She narrowed her eyes on her reflection. "You're in trouble, Ara."

"Permission to dock in Dodge Colony LK-189," a docking guard voice floated in from the console. "You aren't a Mercer affiliate, are you?"

Ari squinted and hit the com. "Do I look like a Mercer affiliate? This ship is barely running."

"Have to ask. We kicked the bastards out."

What did that mean? Good news, maybe? Well, it was good for this secret meet-up, although Ari still wasn't going to flash her face around. She used the controls to drop the pod through the pinhole in the thermal shades. Then she docked and brought the drape of her shirt over her head and tucked her long hair in.

Setting off across the colony, Ari noted that Dodge had a brand-new dome, even if the town didn't seem to have changed an iota otherwise. There was still the loud market full of incessant peddling of used Mercer goods at slashed prices. Still the flicker of caustic neon signs. The air was too slim on oxygen, while the gravel was too ashy to be any kind of soil. All the same. Apart from one thing.

Instead of Mercer patrols there were Mercer protests.

A clutch of people on a variety of street corners had scrolling digital signs and harsh chants. One carried a replica of Excalibur that made Ari ache for her sword. For once she'd left it behind on the pod. Excalibur was too easy to spot, too impossible to conceal.

Plus, Ari knew how good she was at *not* using the sword.

"No impulsive moves," she murmured, turning down the alley where she'd first met Morgana. The ancient enchantress hadn't reappeared since she'd talked with Merlin. Pouting, no doubt. Ari didn't know if Morgana had followed her to Dodge, although she would have put quite a few credits on that wager.

Ari ducked through the back door of Dark Matter. The place hadn't changed, and it transported Ari to the beginning of her King Arthur journey, to begging the bartender for a whiff of oxygen. When he refused, she'd stabbed her funny new toy in the middle of the dance floor as a *Thanks, asshole.* And then shortly after, Merlin had gyrated over to her.

Ari swept her eyes through the crowded, dark place. The pulse of the music pulled on her growing nerves. If her friends were here, they were being discreet for once. Imagine that. Maybe Ari wasn't the only one who'd had to grow up in the last year.

Ari leaned on the counter and pressed a coin down without making eye contact. She took a deep, steadying breath from the mask the bartender held out and it felt like her starving brain was getting more than it could handle.

When she turned back to the dance floor, Ari saw her.

Dressed down in a baby-blue flight suit that had once belonged to Kay's mom, Gwen danced in a way that was anything but era-appropriate. Her head was thrown back, long neck exposed, while her curls were braided to the side and wound tightly into a knot. Ari had never seen that style on her before. She'd never seen Gwen in a flight suit.

And, shit, she'd never seen Gwen *dancing.*

Gwen gave her entire body to the swollen music. Her full hips were a fluid swing, her hands not afraid to slide over every curve on her frame. Stomach, breasts, lips...although Ari could still pinpoint the exact spot where Gwen gave herself away. Her eyes were closed, her expression deeply tense in a way that passed as exertion amidst the other dancers.

But Gwen wasn't tired; she was terrified.

So she was dancing.

Oh, lady.

Ari used the heel of her hand to secure her heart and gave in to Gwen's riptide. The flash burn of oxygen in Ari's veins abetted her confidence as she crossed the dance floor and met the back of Gwen's body with her front. Gwen froze for the tiniest moment as Ari's touch slid down Gwen's arms, sealing the tops of Gwen's soft hands with Ari's callused palms. Their fingers wove, matching rings clinking in a way that made Ari slip on a relieved sigh. Gwen was still wearing her wedding ring. That had to mean something, didn't it?

They danced for the rest of the song, Ari's hold on Gwen unyielding, Gwen's body pressing into Ari's with a kind of urgency that reminded Ari how long it had been since she'd been this close to another person…and lit up in this way. She was nearly dizzy, at the mercy of the rhythmic bass, and Gwen's feverishly intense hold on her fingers.

And still, they hadn't even faced each other.

As the song ended, and a new one began, the music dwindled to nothing in Ari's mind. Gwen turned around in Ari's arms. Her eyes were bright, her tears barely masked. Ari felt herself blinking back her own overwhelming feelings. For so long, this kind of moment had seemed impossibly far away. Unreachable. A star that Ari would only ever stare at…and wish upon.

"If you're one of the Administrator's monsters, he's made a huge mistake," Gwen said, her icy voice cutting across the music, surprising Ari. "And you better not be a ghost."

"What?" Ari asked just as Gwen jabbed a needle in Ari's hip.

The shadows of Dark Matter rose like a mouth and bit down on her all at once.

Lights out.

&

"She's waking up."

Ari reached a stiff hand over her shoulder for Excalibur, but the sword was absent, left in that escape pod. Her stomach was folded hard over someone's shoulder. She recognized the scent of their dreads and the bass of their heaving breaths. Lam was carrying her—had been for a while by the way they flagged. "Lam?" she said, her mouth cottony.

"I've got you, girl." They shifted her weight. "Although you are a lot heavier than you used to be. Been working out?"

"She looks too different." Gwen's voice...or was Ari dreaming?

"If she looked the same, that'd be more suspicious. People change after a year, Gweneviere."

"I know that," Gwen said, mild panic in her tone. Ari managed to lift her head, her long hair falling over her eyes and framing the view of Gwen trailing behind Lam through the docking bay. Gwen stared at her guiltily for a moment, and then looked away, crossing around Lam so that Ari couldn't see her.

"What is...happening?" Ari managed.

"Mutiny," Lam said. "At least that's what it feels like."

Ari recognized the sound of *Error*'s door opening, and Lam walked in and dropped her to the ground. They weren't trying to be so harsh, but she landed hard all the same. In a flash of tight jeans and sassy hair, Ari was leveled backward by a hug. She gripped her friend, although when she sat up, she was surprised to find Merlin in her arms, not Val.

"I knew it," he said, an adorable haircut showing off his cherubic ears. "I knew it, but some days it felt downright cruel to hope."

"King Arthur always returns when he's needed. Doesn't he, old man?" she said, rubbing the lag out of her eyes. "Although I don't remember the part when his knights fucking drug him!"

Merlin snapped a look at Gwen. "You didn't. You said you wouldn't!"

"She made me nervous. And she doesn't have Excalibur, so how could it be her?"

"Excalibur is in the escape pod. Too recognizable." Ari pressed her feet under her, trying to stand. "Why don't you believe that I'm Ari? Why did you attack me?"

"Because you are dead," Val's voice cut in. Ari raised her

head to look at her oldest friend, only to find him standing next to a Mercer casket. He pointed down, and she stumbled toward it, knocking into the plastic container.

The dead person inside was Ari, vacuum sealed like space food. Ari's shock of nerves helped clear her head, although not fast enough. "Oh, gods…"

"Who are you? What happened to Ari? Are you a Mercer clone? A human droid?" Val fired off so fast that Ari's head spun. Jordan stood behind Val in full armor, looking very much like a palace guard about to cut her in two.

"I'm Ari. I don't know who…or what this is." She pointed at the body in the Mercer-stamped coffin. "Except…" Slowly— *too* slowly—Morgana's nagging words from Ketch filtered back through her mind. "Morgana!"

Merlin jumped as Morgana materialized with a sincerely annoyed look on her face.

"Explain," Ari barked.

"I killed you, or really, I turned one of the corpses on Urite into an exact replica of you. It was an astounding bit of magic, to be honest. Merlin's blood is delightful and—"

"*What?*" Ari and Merlin yelled together.

"Your friends think you died on the prison planet a year ago." Morgana spoke quickly, eyeing her fingernails as if she were debating their length. "I needed them to not come looking for you."

Ari blinked. "Why didn't you tell me?"

"I thought maybe it wouldn't come up."

"How would *killing me* in the eyes of everyone I know and love not come up?"

Morgana gave Ari that *Yes, fine, I've been a bit evil* look and disappeared.

Ari propped herself up on the closest thing she could find, which unfortunately was the casket. She took in each person in the cargo bay. Gwen's face was flushed, her eyes cast to the floor. Merlin's expression was all folded up like an angry little kid's, and Val was staring with big, brown eyes. Jordan stood at the door, arms crossed.

Only Lam swept over and gave her a hug. "At least I have one friend," Ari said into their shoulder.

"Give everyone a minute," Lam said. "We took your death hard."

Jordan cleared her throat. "My queen, this could still be a Mercer trick. She could have been brainwashed. Or worse, perhaps she is merely a manifestation from that vile enchantress."

"Not happy to see me, Jordan?" Ari snapped. "Or should I call you Lancelot?"

"*Umm,*" Merlin grabbed her arm. "That's not a name I've ever spoken in your presence. How do you know about—?"

"Morgana's told me everything, Merlin." Ari couldn't keep her gaze from darting toward Gwen. "Everything."

"We should vote again. I remain on the team of those who don't believe she is real," Jordan butted in, one hand on the sword at her belt, ready to draw.

"Vote? Wait, there are divided teams? Over whether I'm actually dead?" Ari shook her head with disbelief. "Truly well done, Morgana!" she shouted into the air. All of them looked around the cargo bay. Particularly Merlin, whose attention shot up like one of the taneen hatchlings when Big Mama was incoming. Nothing happened. "We don't have time for her games." Ari swiveled, taking in the crew once again. "Where's my brother?" The question came out louder, sharper than she meant it to; she'd been holding it back too long.

"Kay is the captain of Team Dead Ari," Val said with an impressive amount of attitude.

"He's in a lot of pain," Lam said, placing their hand on Ari's shoulder. "He's confused..."

"And you still haven't proved that you are Ari."

Ari faced Gwen, amazed that those words had come from her. "What else do I have to do to prove it to you?" Ari asked, her question as heated as their bodies had been when they were dancing. She stepped close and managed an impish smile that had the gratifying effect of making Gwen blush from her cleavage to the tips of her perfect ears. Ari lowered her voice, but everyone could hear—and she wanted them to. "I know how to make your breath hitch. I know that right now you're torn between holding on to me and pushing me away—like always. And I *know* that while I've been alone this whole year, with no one but Morgana and my murdered people, you haven't been on your own. Have you?"

Gwen's face pitched down, although she was not ashamed. She was admitting it, a graceful confirmation fit for a queen. This was part of Ari's plan; get Gwen to admit it fast. Then it wouldn't be a weird secret thing between them. Ari wouldn't let it tear them apart like it did with the other Arthurs and their Gwenevieres. They could move on, together.

"You didn't do anything wrong. I was gone. Dead, apparently. We weren't...Maybe we aren't even..." Ari surprised herself by getting flustered, tied up in her own need to erase the weirdness between them. *There's no time for a love triangle. No time.*

Ari's gaze traveled over her shoulder to Jordan and her voice iced. "Put your blade away, knight." Everyone turned toward Jordan. She'd drawn her sword a few inches out of its sheath. "You don't want to see how much I have trained over the last year."

Jordan looked to Gwen and with one nod, Jordan relented, tucking the sword away.

Ari cleared her throat. The look on her friends' faces was just another confirmation she didn't need. And where was her brother in all of this? She didn't realize how much she needed the balance of his idiocy in this band until it was missing. "Besides, Gwen, if I'm not Ari, who took care of all those Lionelians on Ketch?"

Gwen gripped Ari's wrist, more desperate than tender. "They're okay?"

"Frightened and hungry, but I made sure they were safe and hidden."

"Thank you. I..." Gwen's hand dropped along with her voice.

"You do look mightily different," Val interrupted. "You've been through a lot. We put the pieces together from that footage you sent over. Although we don't know how you got from Urite to Ketch. And *all* the Ketchans are...dead?"

"I'm the last."

That, at least, Ari'd had plenty of time to come to grips with, even if it was a wound she'd carry for the rest of her life. "Morgana abducted me on Urite. Arthur wanted me to see Ketch." Ari shook her head. "*I* needed to see what had become of my planet. But once I was there, leaving wasn't possible. I'm sorry about Morgana's treachery. I didn't know. And I didn't know Lionel was under attack. I called you thousands of times." Her gaze returned to Gwen's for the last of that speech. "Thousands."

Gwen looked torn in half, and Ari couldn't tell if she hated that look or if she wanted to bandage Gwen together with an embrace. Val spoke up again as if determined to iron out the tension between them with facts. "Merlin created a barrier to keep us all safe from Mercer. It worked, until it didn't," Val said, mildly guiltily. "That's why your calls wouldn't go through."

"That's in the past." Ari cracked her knuckles. "My broadcast has done what I wanted it to, stirred up doubt in Mercer. It's given those with a drive to fight something to fight about. I heard that several planets have even kicked Mercer out for the time being. Now we have to swing that momentum into the next step. We have to go to Old Earth, show the universe what Mercer has done to the cradle of civilization. And I will call the Administrator out to face me."

Merlin cleared his throat, a parched sound. Ari realized just how much younger he looked since the last time she'd seen him. Somehow rounder in the cheeks and skinnier in the shoulders. "What's the end goal of this plan, Ari?"

"Unseat the Administrator. Defeat Mercer. Unite humankind. You up for it, old man?"

"Well, but I hadn't thought that now..." he blustered. "Yes, certainly!"

"Good. We do this." Ari couldn't stand the stiff face-off in the cargo bay—or the absence of her brother—a second more.

She pushed into the main cabin, shouldering past Jordan, and looked around. The ship was as weathered and junked as ever, and yet still beautiful in its lived-in, homey appearance. "Kay!" she called out. "Kay!"

Her brother appeared in the doorway of the cockpit. "Hello, impostor."

Ari bit back relief and severe pain as she looked at his silvery-gray hair and broad shoulders. He was thinner than she'd ever seen him, gaunt almost. "Answer me this, Kay. Can dead people punch?"

She charged, and he was more than ready. They went down in a heap, wrestling, tearing at each other. Ari slammed him in the ribs a few times, terrified by the new imbalance between them, how weak he was in comparison to how strong she'd become.

"You're dead!" he yelled. "You're not real! You're here to torment me!"

"Does this feel real?" Ari bit his arm and kneed him in the side. He kept struggling, rejecting her with weedy protests that ate at her confidence. "You're hurting me," she yelled in his ear, even though she had his arm pinned behind his back.

How could he act like this? Why hadn't he been the one to meet her at Dark Matter with Gwen? She hit him again, again, making him feel the pain that was rolling over her, proving with every breath that they weren't fighting like they used to. Like siblings. This was different.

They were all different—driven apart.

Ari pushed him onto his back and was about to pop him in the nose when her fist froze.

Kay's face was a miserable purple-red. He was crying. "We

thought you were dead!" he hollered. "We had your body! I couldn't... You don't know what that was like!"

"I can imagine. I was on a planet full of bodies." Ari lowered her fist, although she was still pinning his chest with her knees. "But I'm here. I'm right here! Why is that such bad news?"

Kay's head turned away from her, searching the crowd of their friends in the doorway. "How do we explain, Gwen? She'll never forgive either of us."

Ari looked to Gwen. Her face was in her hands as if the sight of them fighting had broken something open. She was... weeping. Ari had never seen that before. Never.

No.

Ari jumped up, back, slammed against the wall by her own surprise.

"I know it's a shock," Merlin said, picking careful steps over Kay, hands outstretched as if approaching a starving dragon. "I made the same mistake. Lancelot is always the best knight. That's true enough, but maybe more important, he's the knight Arthur trusts... most of all."

Ari's eyes moved past Merlin to Gwen, who was now on her knees beside Kay. She pulled his miserable crying face into the softest spot on her chest, whispered in his ear, combed back his hair with those fingers that belonged to Ari.

And Ari's heart cracked.

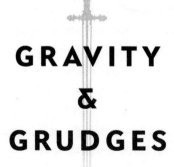

GRAVITY
&
GRUDGES

Morgana was going to pay for this.

It was *her* doing that Merlin had believed Ari was dead for a year. *Her* fault that Ari was brokenhearted and her knights torn asunder just as they were about to head into a great battle. After the Gwen-and-Kay revelation they had flown in brittle silence all the way to Old Earth. Now Merlin stumbled away from the grove where Ari was broadcasting a signal, showing the universe how devastated the cradle of humanity had become at Mercer's hands.

And calling the Administrator out to face her.

"Oh, dear," Merlin said, trailing blood.

He'd asked Jordan to punch him in the face, hard enough to spout a nosebleed, and she'd been all too happy to oblige.

"This is for dropping your magic at the cost of my planet, Mage of Lionel," she'd said, before unleashing her fury on his face.

"*Ow,*" he muttered, truly in pain, before returning to the rather broad playacting that was meant to lure the enchantress into his trap. Morgana was many things, but subtle had never been one of them.

"So much blood..." he said, honestly a little concerned as another gush poured through his fingers. Ari had told him that Morgana had used his blood to create the dead body on Urite. Merlin knew Morgana far too well for his own comfort. After a sampling of his power, she'd be eager for more. "I'm just bleeding magical blood everywhere!"

"Merlin, Merlin," she said, appearing in a haze, looking even more ominous than usual on the ruined forest of Old Earth. "Can't seem to keep your happy little band in line, can you?"

Merlin ran at her, growling—and passed through her in a cold, staticky rush.

Which was exactly the point.

"What are you doing, old man?" she asked. It was a name she must have picked up from Ari, and hearing it come from her lips made Merlin dizzy with the strange familiarity. He turned to find the lines of her body turning solid in the half-light. Her pale skin became opaque, and her cheeks filled in with a faint blush.

"Aha!" Merlin cried. "You used my magic to create a body. Now I've done the same to you!"

Morgana looked down at herself. She touched her arms, her chest, gave her breasts a quick but thorough groping.

"I'm not letting you keep lurking from cycle to cycle, snatching my Arthurs," Merlin said. "Now you're on equal footing with the rest of us." He pointed at her bony, bare feet. "Quite literally, in fact."

She looked at him slowly, her eyes on fire, but not with hatred for once. She looked confused, nearly grateful.

"Why would you gift me such a thing?" Morgana asked faintly. "How long will this last?"

"Considering that body you created is still in *Error*'s hold, I'd say it's going to stick. Surprisingly enough, we make a good team. Or at least our magic does." Merlin's heated words were cooling. Morgana looked younger than Merlin had remembered. And smaller, even though she was technically the same size she'd always been.

For a moment, she was no longer the hag who had been visiting revenge on him for centuries—she was a young woman with a very famous kingly brother and the magic of Avalon running through her veins.

"I've longed for this day." Her spite flooded back as she looked Merlin over. "You've been whining about your body for so long you've forgotten how glorious they are."

Merlin shook his head, incredulous. "Bodies come with wants and pains and warts and toilet breaks. Don't even ask me about erections."

"I will consider it a most solemn vow," Morgana said.

Merlin nearly laughed. It sounded like a joke. Morgana didn't make jokes. She only twisted her cruelty into knots of sarcasm. Had Ari changed her during their time together on Ketch? She had certainly changed Ari, Merlin thought, as he regained the solid footing of his anger. "I gave you a body so you can't *poof* away from the situation you've caused. No more *poofing*!"

"What exactly have I done, Merlin?" Morgana asked, advancing on him slowly. She seemed to savor the way the earth felt under her bare feet. "Have I stolen your Arthur?" The shadow of old pain passed through her eyes, but she chased it away with a smirk of righteousness. "Now you know what I have felt, these many ages. What have I done but shown her the truths you fear?"

"*Hmm,* let me write you a list. You've torn Ari away from the girl she loves. You've induced the worst heartbreak in the cycle by convincing everyone she was dead. AND you've broken up Ari's band."

Morgana was getting uncomfortably close.

Merlin started backing up. "Don't you remember how Arthur's knights kept him alive? The round table wasn't just a decorating choice, Morgana. We'll never finish the cycle if she falls today." He nodded to the grove. Ari's voice rang out, carrying at a heroic pitch. At this very second, she was calling on her allies to unite against Mercer.

"I don't care about your little hero games," Morgana said.

"You want to put your brother to rest," Merlin said, and Morgana's eyes went wide. Merlin could see the whites. She was really getting in his personal space.

"Ari told you," Morgana said, looking a bit betrayed. She swiped at Merlin with her nails, and he leaped back. So it had come to this—a plain old catfight.

"She always tells the truth," Merlin said. "Haven't you noticed?" Morgana lashed out at Merlin again, and he caught her forearms in a weak grip. "You want peace for your brother, but the cycle must be completed first! Nin gave me the steps. Find Arthur, train Arthur, nudge Arthur onto the nearest—"

"How much is the Lady of the Lake bound up in this?"

Morgana interrupted, looking properly afraid. "And why did you never see fit to mention it?"

"Maybe because you never asked nicely," Merlin said, pushing Morgana away and running to put some distance between them.

"I'm not *nice*," Morgana hissed from where she fell to the ground, her ancient dress now covered in dirt. "Nice is for women who haven't had their bodies taken away and replaced by the eternal torture of people-watching. They're so terrible to each other, Merlin." She put her head to the ground, heavily, and keened as if she was tortured by the same images she'd given him so many times on waking from the crystal cave.

"You're really feeling it, aren't you?" Merlin asked, his empathy springing up in unsuspected places, like flowers out of season. "You haven't had a body to feel their pain in so long…"

"It's…it's unbearable," she gasped.

Merlin rushed to her side. He kneeled, one hand on her bony back as she tried to pull in air. He couldn't have her dying now. How would he punish her if she was dead?

"Think of something good," he said. "That…might help."

"Nothing good has happened to me in so long," she whispered, the words slick with pain.

"Think of Ari!" Merlin cried. And, as much as it hurt him to admit it, he added, "I know you two must have developed some feeling for each other on Ketch. She's your Ketch buddy!"

Morgana shook her head, her dark hair hanging in tatters around her face. "Ari hates me for deceiving her. For killing her in the eyes of her friends."

"You can fix that," Merlin said, still surprised that he was comforting Morgana. Still worried that she was about to spring up and stab him through the heart. He patted her back gingerly.

"There is no taking back what is done," Morgana said, staring up at Merlin with the kind of accusation that never wavered. "You, of all people, should know that."

Merlin took a deep breath. If Ari was out in the grove taking on the future, perhaps it was time for him to finally face the horrors of the past. "There are times when I think I should not have taken your brother," he admitted. "But your stepfather was treating him as a dangerous bastard, and I…"

Merlin dug up the truth by its roots, one word at a time. "I believed I could create a kind of justice for Uther's actions. I never should have given that man the magic to appear in your father's form. Uther was violent, as so many were then, but I never…I never imagined he would do such a vile thing." His voice broke into a thousand pieces. "I was a fool. I left his service at once and raised your brother to change the ways of men. To prove that might does not equal right. To show the world that alliance is more powerful than violence."

Morgana keened, and Merlin could not tell if it was from his words, or from the memories seething through her mind.

There was one more truth, and the story would never be finished without it. "None of that changes your mother's hurt. Or your own loss."

And in that moment, Merlin understood. He wasn't going to make Morgana pay. She *had* been paying, for centuries, the toll the cycle took on her soul as great as the one it took on his. They had both done awful things in their time. They had both suffered. But no single human could hold the pain of all the terrible things in the universe.

Merlin touched Morgana's temple, and memories flowed between them, a river running back to its source.

Arthur, magically changing into a squirrel, scampering through the trees as the green leaves danced.

Arthur, his scruffy hair and bright-blue eyes, the freckles that hadn't yet faded peeking above the top of a tome Merlin had given him.

Arthur, crowned king when he was still a nervous young man, while a young woman watched from the crowd, a pilgrim from Avalon, wearing priestess robes and sharing Arthur's faded freckles.

"What are you doing?" Morgana asked, gasping as if she were surfacing from a deep lake.

"I'm giving you what you missed, Morgana," he said.

It was what she had done so many times, when Merlin woke up, except she'd only shown him the worst of humanity.

He put his arm around her, helping her up. She felt solid in his grip. Terrifying and true. "There are more memories, and you can have them," he promised, "but first I need your help."

&

Merlin brought Morgana back to the grove where Ari had just finished her message to the universe. She stood in the center of a ring of sickly trees, hacking at the ruins of a stump with Excalibur.

"This place is desecrated," Morgana said, as she struggled to breathe Earth's chemical-strewn air. "What has become of our home?"

"Humans did not take care of it, but Mercer delivered the

killing blow," Merlin said. "That's one of the reasons Ari...
and your brother...have chosen to stand against them."

"My brother needs peace," Morgana sniffed.

"Then why did he choose Ari?" Merlin asked. "Why did he
save her from the attack on her parents' ship? Why did he wish
for her to see Ketch? Could it be that he needs *both*?"

Morgana glared at him, but at least this time she didn't try
to take out his eyes with her long, eternally untrimmed nails.

Ari's knights were watching the skies, nervous, and distant
from one another. Merlin longed for the banter they'd once
filled *Error* with and the playful way they'd tackled each other
on Lionel.

"Did Mercer respond?" Lam called out.

"They picked it up, but no response," Kay shouted from
Error, where he was transmitting Ari's message in the hopes
that their allies would pick up. "Now we'll see if that bastard
shows his face."

"He'll come," Ari and Gwen said together, before exchang-
ing glances and looking away.

"Can you make another one of those nets to be certain only
the Administrator's ship comes through? The last thing we
need is to be bombarded by a fleet."

"Certainly," Merlin said. He hummed an old tune he'd
learned from a Roman centurion. It had a stiff yet drumming
beat. Perfect for oncoming battle. When he was done, and the
skies were neatly webbed in gold, he grinned at his band. Not
a single one of them were looking at him. Not a single one
impressed. Not even Val. They eyed the ruined planet, wincing
with each chemical-laden breath.

"They're a mess," Merlin muttered. "We can't win anything in this state."

"That one is rather pretty," Morgana pointed at Val, whose hard-set face was, indeed, lovely even when most worried. "Is he the reason you so desperately wish to stop aging backward?"

"Ari told you that, too?" Merlin croaked.

"She's honest, as you've observed," Morgana said.

Merlin fiddled with the hem of his T-shirt. "Well, there are lots of reasons to wish for the cycle's end. That's only one small—"

"Have you kissed him yet?" Morgana stroked her own lips with a gentle finger. "I remember kissing…"

Merlin's stomach tugged. It was one thing to lose his Arthur to Morgana, but Val was entirely off-limits. "Stay away from him," Merlin barked. "And before you go on a kissing spree, we need to pull Ari's knights back together. No one needs a martyr right now. Your field trip to Ketch turned Ari into something of a heroic loner."

But Merlin knew it was more than that. When they first met, Ari had believed, on some deep level, that she was alone in the universe. That was why she'd tried to solve all her problems by herself. It had been getting better, but her time on Ketch with Morgana had made her backslide. He watched Ari from a distance, noting how alone she looked even surrounded by those who loved her most. She'd shut herself off again. Withdrawn.

"You're writhing with jealousy," Morgana said. "I've trained Ari better than you ever would have."

Ari did look quite impressive after her stay on Ketch, her

muscles long and curved, her deepened brown skin shining. Ever her hair had a new sheen to it. Merlin suspected that she'd discovered the secrets of Ketchan hair care. But there was also a hardness to her features, an impassable distance in her eyes. She'd returned to a home that had been violated, long-lost family and friends murdered. She'd gone home to find connection and found herself more alone than ever. And she'd been made to bear the weight of a planet-wide massacre by herself. No one should have to face that—no matter how strong.

"She needs her friends," Merlin said. "And her friends need to work their problems out before those problems trip them up and get them murdered. You must admit that Arthurs do tend to have trouble with their nearest and dearest, and it never ends well."

"Agreed," Morgana said, grudgingly.

"What if we lock them all together on *Error* and let them fight it out?" Merlin asked. Morgana looked at him like he had been huffing paint, or perhaps drinking it straight from the can. "Well, what's your brilliant idea, then?" he asked, more than a touch defensive.

"People aren't brought together by fear, Merlin," Morgana said quietly. "They're torn asunder by it. If you want to unite this small and scraggly band, you must give them something to love together. A moment of shared hope and beauty."

Merlin clapped. "Yes! Perfect! How do we do that?"

Kay reappeared in the doorway of the ship, looking gray and weathered. "Mercer definitely picked up our signal."

"How do we do that *quickly*?" Merlin corrected.

Morgana's smile spread like a dark stain, and Merlin's heart chilled. The fear that he'd so often felt in her presence was back. Apparently, it would never leave him alone for too long. "I'll need your blood," she said.

Merlin touched his nose and found that, while it was still tender, the nosebleed Jordan had so generously given him had dried up. He tried to dab a bit of dried blood and hold it out for Morgana, but she was already rummaging in the folds of her dress. She brought out a shining silver dagger, twisted and glittering.

"Have you had that on you this whole time?" Merlin cried.

"A priestess of Avalon is always prepared."

She stabbed Merlin in the thigh with a little too much glee. The pain was sudden, and it doubled when she pulled the blade out, his blood flowing in a gushing river. He yelped and hopped away on the other foot.

"What's going on over there?" Ari called warily, shielding her eyes from the sun. "Morgana, is that you?"

"It's all right!" Merlin said. "We're, umm, collaborating."

The wound in his thigh screamed that maybe he'd made a mistake.

Morgana reached down and touched her hand to the blood, kneeling to bring her red palm down to the ground, and then holding it up to the sky. She walked, painting the trees in the grove with bloody handprints as she went.

Val ran to Merlin's side and held him up as Merlin hopped. "She stabbed you?!"

"It's for a good cause," Merlin said in a strained whisper. "I think."

"I'm so glad she's on our side now," Val deadpanned.

"How real is she?" Lam asked, eyeing her with a sly, interested smile, which Morgana returned over her shoulder.

"Real," Merlin confirmed while Val huffed.

"Seriously, Lam? Sinister enchantress cannot be your type."

"Sexy in a slip dress certainly is," Lam said.

Merlin watched Morgana's strange magic bloom around them. Everywhere she brushed his blood, the ripped ground healed itself, the bark of the trees knitted and the branches grew, springing open buds and then uncurling healthy green leaves. Flowers sprang up in the wake of her bare feet. Merlin's blood was watering a garden of new growth. Morgana had used the magic that had given her a body to give Earth back its life.

And the knights were watching, gasping.

Kay climbed down from *Error*. Gwen emerged from her hiding spot. Val looked up, taking in a deep breath of air that no longer tasted so tangy or metallic.

"This is what it could have been..." Ari said, looking around her.

"This is what it can be again," Merlin said, hopping toward her with Val's help. "If we stop Mercer. Together."

Morgana looked back from the distance she'd just traveled, filled with grass that rose and fell like gentle breath. A lake glittered and beckoned them. After a year of drought on Lionel, it was the most beautiful thing Merlin could imagine. He looked around at the freshly changed landscape and was surprised to find it familiar. This was a park that, in its day on Earth, had been rather famous.

Lamarack ran through it with joyful abandon, a sort of wild hope to replace the grim waiting. Ari let herself turn in circles, taking it in. Merlin could see, in her rediscovered smile, the girl he'd met on the moon. The one who had come back from

Ketch, hopeful for Gwen's love. The orphan who had lost as many homes as Merlin had—and kept fighting.

She nodded appreciation. "Nicely done, old man."

Val tugged him deeper into the magical landscape—not too quickly, because his leg hurt like the dickens. Still, the moment was almost perfect.

But at the very edges, Merlin could still sense the ruin. And in the skies, *Heritage* loomed as a reminder. Mercer had been kicked, but they were not down.

CHECK
&
MATE

At last, Ari had a real battlefield.

Merlin had called it a park, but the rolling acres of green, dotted by the strong profiles of old trees, looked perfect for a last stand. Even the sky was the kind of blue that jeweled the heavens. Ari reassured herself that she had the upper hand— and that Excalibur was sealed in it.

The second step in her plan, to show the universe what had befallen Old Earth, had gone perfectly. The universe had received her messages. Several planets had even kicked Mercer out like Dodge colony had, a fact she'd rubbed in during her open message to the Administrator. And yet, she was also absolutely positive that something costly would happen when he showed his face. She glanced at the sky. He hadn't sent a snarky return message, which Ari took as a sign that he was scrambling to meet her demands.

Any moment, the tide of right would beat down the mountain of wrong. She only wished Kay was with her. Dragon Kay, that is. Her brother could fuck right off this planet, for all she cared.

"Liar," Ari muttered. She was failing to assemble a kingly outfit from the pile of cast-off armor Jordan had dumped in the green grass. A rubbery piece caught Ari's eye, and she lifted Kay's old knight training suit from the mound, the one he'd threatened her into so they could pick up supplies on *Heritage* a lifetime ago. She sniffed it, wincing, and yet overwhelmed by how her brother's fear had always proved he loved her. Ari was going to be okay about Gwen and Kay. She was going to stitch her heart back together until she could manage *okay*.

"Tomorrow," she grumbled. "Today is for Mercer."

Ari sat back on the grass beside her ragtag collection of knights. In the near distance, Merlin was getting fussed over by Val. The newly embodied Morgana was smelling a disturbing number of things, including Lam. And Kay and Gwen were fighting, which would have felt great, maybe, if their arguing didn't reek of long-standing intimacy.

Ari's eyes found Jordan, sitting on the other side of the pile of plates and chain mail. The black knight admittedly had the best armor and kept it in the best shape. For once, her blond hair was down, crimped from being unbraided and spread around her wide shoulders. She wore a plain tunic, polishing her shoulder guards with a rag that looked older than *Error*.

Ari picked up a dented breastplate and held it to herself, but there was no way to hook it on. Knights didn't dress themselves; they had squires, or they helped one another. She dropped it.

"You'll need someone to assist you," Jordan said. "It's not going to be me."

"I could have guessed that much."

Jordan glanced up and caught Ari's eye. "If you had lowered yourself to ask me one question about my personal life—one—you wouldn't have suspected me of stealing your love. None of you would."

Ari stood. If she was going to be lectured by Jordan, she was doing it on her feet. She walked closer, casting a shadow across Jordan's polishing. "What's that supposed to mean?"

"I don't take," her eyes traveled to where Gwen and Kay argued, "lovers."

"You're ace?"

Jordan looked up at Ari with a *how could you be so slow* expression. "Of course." She held up her armor. "This is my passion. *This* is my love."

Ari tossed herself down in the grass, lounging back. "I'm sorry, Jordan, but—it's better if I don't try to lie. You see, I've never wanted to like you."

"The feeling is mutual."

Ari surprised herself with a smile. "I'm glad I have you on my side, though. You are a great warrior."

"And you," Jordan said, returning to her polishing, "have no way of winning this duel you've challenged the Administrator to." Ari sat back up. "Mercer will not have honor. Not swords or shields. They will most likely drop a flash bomb. Something quick, efficient, and deadly."

"And the universe will be watching. If we have to be martyrs, so be it."

"Like Ketch?"

"What?"

"You shared Ketch's death with the cosmos as if their loss

was a kind of sacrifice, but that was ten years ago. Mercer covered up their crimes, their honor, their loss. And it changed nothing."

"That won't happen here today. I've made sure that the universe will care. That others will come and help," Ari said, although she wasn't certain. How could she be? She glanced at the golden-webbed sky and then reached for her security blanket, pulling Excalibur out of the leather sheath. The blade was tarnished, filthy.

"Oh!" Jordan exclaimed. "What have you done?" She tossed a polishing rag at Ari. "Spit and circles. Tight ones."

Ari began to polish while Lamarack crossed the field to them, hunkering to examine the pile of armor. "Slim pickings," Ari said. "We won't exactly look the part of heroes when Mercer storms down."

"Heroes we will be. Lords and ladies? Not so much." Lam tossed a broken gauntlet. Their smile came up to meet Ari's in a way that had her daydreaming about years and lives ago, when Lam was the first person to catch her eye.

"Help me get outfitted?" Ari asked. Lam nodded, and Ari hopped up, grabbing the breastplate and holding it in place. Lam fastened the back while Ari asked, "How come we never got together, Lam?"

Jordan muttered, "Unbelievable."

Lam enjoyed themselves thoroughly with a sexy chuckle. "Because your brother would have thrown a fit." Their voice faded with careful kindness. "And because, for those of us who were paying attention, there was only ever one person for you. Even back when you two were only known for your shouting matches."

"Not obvious to everyone," Ari said, chewing each word, staring at Kay. Her brother looked at her—and then away.

"You were dead," Lam said. "Besides, they're not the kind of couple you think they are. It's more convenience and grief, and a very odd request on Gwen's side—"

"An honorable knight would ask *them*," Jordan shoved in.

Ari didn't have to decide how to answer. Kay was stalking toward them.

"A word, Ari," he said, "before we get dive-bombed by Mercer?"

"Leave the sword," Jordan growled.

"I'm not going to stab him!"

"So I can polish it! You're doing a terrible job. No wonder you failed knight camp."

"These two flunked out. I was a conscientious objector!"

"Yes, and what are you now?" Jordan asked, never fazed by Ari's temper.

"King Fucking Arthur, that's who!"

Lam busted out a full-bellied laugh. Ari's own smile cracked as she stuck the sword in the earth before Jordan. Kay looked like he wanted to smile but was afraid that if he did, the sky might crumble down around him.

Ari walked deeper into the heart of the glorious field, her brother at her heels. When they were out of earshot of the others, she made herself speak. "First, tell me where our parents are."

"Tanaka, last I heard. They've been on the lam for a while, but they check in regularly. They took your death hard. Especially Captain Mom. She blamed herself."

"That's enough." Ari burned. "Now tell me what you two lovebirds were arguing about."

"How much to tell you about us."

Okay, perhaps it *was* wise that Jordan made her leave the sword behind. "So? Do I get lies? Half-truths? What's the verdict?" Ari paused. "I assume you're the one who wants me to know. Gwen has always been a labyrinth of careful fiction. Did you know she was born on Troy? She told me she came from Lionel. She—"

"Was abandoned by her parents, Ari. Sold to the Lionel School for casino credits when she was five. Can you even imagine how hard that would be to admit?"

Ari stopped walking. The sun was so strong, she had to shield her eyes to take in her brother's. "She could have told me that."

"You're not always easy to talk to," he said, rubbing the bite mark she'd left on his forearm. "And you have no idea how close she came to being one of those Mercer kids. Raised by them, *owned* by them. She's into this kings and queens life because it is her family." He started to pace, and Ari knew her brother well enough to know that he was working himself up to something. "She's been on her own her whole life, dreaming of what it'd be like to have someone. A *real* person. At least you and I had each other when our moms were taken."

Ari reached out and caught his arm, making him face her. "Fine, Kay. You're right, but none of that explains how or why *you* would step in when I was...unavailable."

Kay's eyebrows notched. "Gods damnit, Ari! You've flown in and out of her life like a space rat boyfriend, you know that? Appearing, disappearing. You've hurt her so—"

"Stop, I know!" Ari's eyes crossed the field, reaching for the place where Gwen stood, one hand on her belly, her face a cloud of emotion as she watched them.

One hand on her belly.

"A very odd request," Ari murmured, remembering Lam's words...and then Gwen's confession about wanting a kid back on Lionel. Ari's eyes widened on her brother. "She's not..."

"Not ever going to be alone again. Even if both of us get killed."

Kay held his head higher, proud of himself on some level Ari couldn't even begin to line up. And she couldn't breathe. Gwen was going to have a baby. *Kay's* baby.

The Gwen and Ari who had danced yesterday—pressed together as if every force in the universe was binding them— were gone. Vanished. Her head rushed, and she doubled over, hands on her knees, hair falling in her face. "Okay," she said. "Okay, okay, okay." The word was broken, on repeat. This was not *okay.*

"Ara."

Ari paused. Gwen had never used her real name before. She looked up to find Kay much farther away, replaced by an apprehensive Gwen. Apparently, it was her turn to offer apologies. Or explanations. Or excuses.

"Gweneviere." Ari lifted herself to her full height; she needed to be stronger than this. Even if it was the biggest lie she'd ever embraced. "I think I'm to congratulate you."

Gwen sighed, her shoulders slumping. "I need you to understand—"

"We can talk about this later." Ari aimed for calm understanding, but it came across as plain old hurt, her tone stinging. "I have to focus on what we're doing here." She crossed back to Excalibur, ripping it out of the earth where Jordan was trying to bring it back to a glorious sheen.

Gwen followed. "No, we have to talk now. We might not have a later."

The black knight growled and left them alone.

Ari looked over the newly polished sword. It was easier than looking into Gwen's deeply brown eyes. "What..." She cleared her throat. "What are we supposed to say, Gwen? You picked the one person in the universe I wouldn't be able to..." Forgive wasn't the right word. Forget wasn't either. There was no right word. "The one person that would end my feelings for you."

"End?" Gwen snapped in that commanding queen voice Ari loved and roiled against in equal measure. "What, did you take up lying while you were gone?"

Ari kept staring at her sword, the newly polished places a harsh contrast to the tarnished lines. She could be mad at Kay, surly to her knights, but she was nothing but wounded with Gwen. "I *can't* feel this way, Gwen. I have to bring down the Administrator today."

"That's bullshit, Ari."

"But it's not! And this," Ari motioned between them, "proves it. Arthur's heart gets ruined by Gweneviere. That's the legend. *You break me,* and I'm so destroyed I bury myself in the cause. Defeat evil, maybe even unite humanity this time. Until he..."

Ari's thoughts nosedived as she recalled Arthur's death at the hand of his son. She glanced at Gwen's stomach.

"Ari, you're talking about yourself and King Arthur like you're the same person."

"We are. Sort of."

"More lies," Gwen said. "Have they all brainwashed you?"

"You want to know the truth, Gwen? This feels worse than the loss of my people." Ari winced, one hand over her face, hoping the rest of her friends didn't know how close she was to being worthless. "That's insane, isn't it? This should be nothing." She attempted a small smile, sniffing back the storm. "People get their hearts broken every damn day."

Gwen stepped closer to Ari, her hands running up Ari's arms, massaging her countless scars, and Ari lost a bet. *If Gwen can hurt me, I'll stay away,* she'd snapped at Morgana on Ketch. *I'll rise above it.* Morgana had laughed.

No one was laughing now.

And no matter what, Ari wasn't going to be able to walk away from Gwen. She would stay right here, in the riot of her pain, for even a chance at this closeness.

Gwen's fingers took hold of Ari's dented breastplate, and Ari had a steaming flash of the tournament when Gwen had pulled Ari into that kiss so confidently Ari had taken to it like gravity. Gwen pulled Ari close again, but instead of kissing, she pressed their faces together. Gwen's lips found Ari's ear. "It had to be him, Ari. He was the closest I could get to you."

She let go, pushed Ari back. And walked away.

At first it felt like the cosmos were on fire. Ari took a deep breath. She closed her eyes, searching for the place inside where King Arthur stopped, and Ari started. Gwen was right; it was becoming harder and harder to find.

Merlin jogged over, pulling a robe over his T-shirt and jeans. "Back in uniform, old man?"

"It's—what do they say?—*game time*!" He was grinning, but the look slipped, no doubt because he could tell how torn up Ari had become. "Are you all right?"

"I am…not." Ari dropped Excalibur into the sheath at her back. "But that's the way it's supposed to be, isn't it? This is all part of the story?" Merlin's acute sadness shone through, his baby-smooth face a reminder of how much he lost with each passing day. "Come on. We're going to end this. I promise, Merlin. I'm going to save you."

They embraced, and Ari held on to him too tightly.

"This feels like it's really happening all of a sudden," Val said, linking an arm with Merlin's. "Not that I was doubting it, but well, of course I was. So what do we do when the Big Bad arrives?"

"We blow up *Heritage,*" Lam said, staring up at the huge starship parked past the moon. "I have explosives."

Merlin waved his hands. "Blowing up the Death Star always seems like a good idea, but it only leads to bigger Death Stars."

Morgana took in the crowd with a growing curiosity, her physical presence a bit strange. She tilted her head back and pointed. "There. They come."

In the deep reaches of the blue sky, Ari saw the first sign of Mercer, a vessel that dropped like a dark insect. Just *one.* "Open up the web. Let him in, Merlin."

Merlin obeyed, and the ship zoomed close. At first Ari hoped it was the Administrator, coming down to meet them with some honor. Then she woke up.

"Take cover!" she yelled, as it zoomed by. Its bay doors opened, and Ari imagined bombs or associates or poison falling on them.

Instead something wrapped in Mercer packaging fell from the vessel. It was as large as the escape pod she'd stolen from the generation ship. And yet it didn't hit the ground like metal.

It hit like flesh.

Ari recognized the shape. And yet, she stood stock-still, gripping her sword.

"What is it?" Jordan asked. "A weapon of some kind?"

Ari waited for the large lump to move. When it didn't, she walked toward it, slowly at first, and then faster and faster. Her friends followed, but they were not quick enough to stop her from pulling the tarp back, revealing the dead taneen hatchling. Kay's green head was battered and bloodied. His long, forked tongue swollen and stuck out, his eyes a murdered black.

"Kay!" she screamed. "No, no, no!" Her legs gave out, and she was all aching fists against the side of the dragon's hide. The real Kay appeared, dragging her back from the body.

Overhead, the vessel disappeared.

"What the hell is this supposed to mean?" Lam asked, voice tremulous.

"It's the dragon from Ari's video," Val said, his voice biting. "The Administrator wants us to know that Mercer has been to Ketch."

Gwen started to scream about her people, hysterical as Ari was turning coldly numb. Jordan fought to hold on to the queen.

Ari's words tumbled from her lips. "Not Kay," she whispered. "He's just a baby."

Her brother held her face with both hands, making Ari look into his blue eyes. "Kay is…the dragon? You named a dragon after me?"

She closed her eyes. "Missed you too much. Had to find a way to say your name every day." Ari started to burn again, boiling with feelings that left her fingers clawing into her brother's starved frame. The Administrator had done this. Taken their home. Their lives. He'd found the one thing that had brought Ari happiness on Ketch, and he'd murdered it.

"I'm going to kill him, Kay. I'm going to rip a hole through the Administrator."

"You're not a killer, Ari," he said, pulling her tight. He smelled exactly like *Error,* like their moms, like the best parts of their lives together. "None of us are. That's what never adds up. We can play battles and knights and kings, but in the end, we just want to exist."

The Mercer vessel reappeared, hovering a few hundred feet above them. Ari's band pulled in a tight circle, shoulder to shoulder. But the Mercer ship didn't move.

"What is it doing?" Lam asked.

Ari was distracted, looking around at the battlefield. They were broadcasting what was happening from *Error,* but how easy would it be for Mercer to kill the signal? Explain it away to the universe as a minor, silly uprising? She had flashes of Ketch, destroyed without the universe even registering a blip. This was a trap. A terrible idea.

"Time for you to do one of those fantastic party tricks, Merl!" Kay called out.

"Merl?!" Merlin sputtered. "Unacceptable."

"Seriously, friends, what is that ship waiting for?" Lam asked, voice riled.

"I second Kay," Gwen commanded. "Some magic would be great right now."

"Merlin!" Val cried out. Ari whirled around to find Merlin limp in Val's arms—as though his consciousness had been stolen straight out of this galaxy. Val struggled to hold him upright. "He just...went down. Like someone unplugged him."

Ari turned to Morgana. "What happened to him?"

Morgana shook her head, her black hair snaking about her shoulders. Sudden fear had etched her into a timeless, terrifying beauty. "We're doomed."

A series of clicks issued from the great body of the taneen. Jordan threw back the rest of the packaging as smoke pumped from the belly of the dead dragon. Jordan cried out to move back, but it was too late. They were all gagging, falling down and into each other. Ari's eyes burned so hard she had to close them. And then she couldn't open them again.

&

Ari was aware of a bizarre, chattering drumming that reached through the darkness. She looked around slowly. An earthy and yet metallic smell left her uneasy. Mildly nauseated. She was on her feet, propped up by associates, and beside her a massive creature stamped anxious hooves into hard-packed soil.

She glanced around at a wall of Mercer associates. No, not a wall.

An entire army.

Only, they looked different. Their white uniforms seemed to have been tailored on Lionel, double-breasted with stiff collars. And they wore swords at the hip instead of their usual guns. Ari swung back around and into the pawing creature that was so much taller than her.

"It's a horse," the Administrator said, stepping around the front of the beast, stroking its velvet nose and feeding an apple with the Mercer logo genetically engineered on the skin into its wide, clomping mouth. "Damn near impossible to find these days, but we have our ways." His nondescript eyes met hers and he gave Ari a pleased smile. Even more intimidating was his outfit. Instead of his traditional Mercer-white suit, he wore a golden robe that smacked of spiritual significance; Merlin might call them *dress robes*.

He noticed her stare and smoothed his hands down his front. "We are quite a sight, but we had to dress up for your coronation. Honestly, we've been playing with pawns for so long, we forgot how fun it'd be to throw a little sovereign drama in. The people are just gobbling it up."

"What?" Ari's voice came out scraped. She glanced down at herself. She was wearing a suit of armor that was etched with glorious gold and silver filigree, a ferocious red dragon emblazoned on the chest.

The Administrator pointed to it. "The family crest of the Pendragons. A nice touch, isn't it? That one was our idea, since you're so determined to go all King Arthur with this little rebellion."

Ari regretted longing for proper armor earlier; she should have remembered that wanting things led to Mercer. She touched the sheath on her hip. At least Excalibur was at her side, although she doubted the sword would have allowed them to take it from her. "Where am I?"

"On *Heritage*. It's only been a few days since your stunt on Old Earth. Your little band was in a state. Took us quite a while to shine you all up." He winked. "To make you presentable for the festivities."

"Where are my friends?"

"You mean your *knights,* King Arthur...King Ara? Whatever." He flourished a hand behind her, and Ari looked over her shoulder to find five more horses in a tight formation. On one side, Gwen sat, side-saddle, gagged, wearing the most beautiful dress Ari had ever seen. It was shining even in the low light of this strange, closed-in space, a million diamonds riveting the seams—none of them as bright as the fear in Gwen's brown eyes.

Behind her, Jordan sat with her head slumped forward, unconscious. Her armor had been polished to a mirror sheen, and Ari watched in a sort of slow-motion terror as a Mercer associate shot something into Jordan's leg and her eyes began to flutter open.

On the other side of the formation, Kay sat astride a chestnut horse that seemed extra nervous. Ari tried not to stare too long into her brother's dark expression. He was flame-cheeked and furious. The kind of furious that could be a problem.

Beside him, Lam sat with their dreads perfectly placed, a leather suit of armor to match Jordan's metal one. They were not gagged, but a purple bruise down one side of their jaw implied that they'd already learned not to speak. Val was behind them, on the smallest brown horse. His face was streaked with tears, an unnerving juxtaposition to the finely pressed tunic of the queen's adviser.

But where was Merlin?

Ari remembered him going down...Morgana's prediction...

"Merlin," Ari said, spinning back to face the Administrator. "Morgana. Where are they?"

"Your magical duo is under surveillance. We don't quite know what they're capable of, so best to keep them sedated.

Don't you think? We wouldn't want anything to ruin the big day. Your *victory,* Ara Azar."

Ari echoed his word as if it were her greatest crime. "Victory?"

"Indeed. You so desperately had to be alive and tell everyone about our Old Earth exploits...and our Ketchan one. Ugh. It's been a human resources disaster." He waved his hand. "But we're rolling with it. Are you ready?"

"For what?"

He sighed and threw in a slight growl. "For the big event! All three Mercer galaxies are watching via our pay-per-view ceremonial channel, as well as a packed arena of a million of the most loyal Mercer customers." He pointed toward the wall they were facing. Ari could tell now that it was a series of rolling doors, the kind that would open grandly and spit out Ari and her friends into the middle of a universe-wide televised pageant.

So that was the chattering drumming she kept hearing. A *million* people.

"You, Ara Azar, are about to be crowned Mercer's king. As much as I don't enjoy sharing the role as figurehead, we admit when allowances must be made." His eyes moved to Gwen's. "We're even giving you Lionel to rule from. It'll be restocked, a Mercer-sanctioned medieval planet, where all our customers will be encouraged to vacation. A taste of rebellion! Of hope and the past, and the one true king. Blah, blah. You know the story they're feverish for. Give it to them."

"Why would you do that? Why not execute me and send your message of unchallenged dominance?"

His eyes flashed with impatience. "Because martyrs kill the economy. This is a mutually beneficial arrangement. Why must we always *convince* you of what you need to do?" His fury lit up Ari's nerves like a circuit board of warnings. She'd never seen him approach a snapping point, and all of a sudden, she did not want to know what that looked like. He clapped his hands once. The crowd of associates parted for a few guards bearing two bound women. Ari's moms.

They had not been prepared for a televised ceremony. Their clothes looked unwashed, their skin sallow, their expressions dim, maybe even drugged. As if Mercer had had them for a *long* time. "But they were supposed to be—"

"Safe? Did someone tell you that?" He took a deep breath. "We had them tell your brother they were safe, of course. We had to keep an eye on all of you. Do you know how much we watch you all, Ara?" He laughed. "Let me demonstrate. We were watching you in that rubber knight suit in the middle ages section last year. We were watching you in that disco when you met your magician. We were watching you weep over those piles of Ketchan bones, and we saw you planning our demise. Every square inch of it. We are *always* watching. That's what a good provider does. That's how we anticipate your needs."

He poked her with one finger on her shining suit of armor, and smiled. "See? We even knew you needed this. Doesn't it fit perfectly?"

Ari would never admit that truth. She looked beyond him, to where her parents seemed ready to die. "So you're going to make me do this by threatening my parents?"

The Administrator looked offended. "Oh, no. They are here to keep your brother in line. He's been a handful. The lives of the entire population of Lionel will keep Gwen in line. And we have those two to keep each other behaving." He flicked his fingers at Val and Lamarack. "We've got something on everyone. We always do."

"And what about me?"

"Oh, you're easy. You'd do anything for *any* of these people. The fact that we have them all as leverage is a bit greedy, but you're such a family, aren't you? We'd hate to split you up."

Ari's nerves tightened her stomach, her grip. "So, all I have to do is... be your king?"

The Administrator held out his hand, and an associate stepped forward to place a gaudy gold crown on it. Jeweled Mercer logos circled the band while the points rose ferociously into knife-sharp blades. A dozen of them. "Isn't it beautiful? And quite a bit sharp." He mimed pricking himself on one of the points, and then sucked his finger.

Ari didn't have a chance to respond.

Kay was *laughing*. A hard, loud laugh that she'd heard a million times over the last ten years. The *what a fucking idiot* laugh.

"Kay—" she started, but the Administrator was faster. He snapped his fingers.

Two associates pulled Kay off the horse and dragged him over. He was still laughing, her dumbass brother. They released him, threw him on the ground and held his shoulders down with boots—and still Ari's brother kept laughing. "Your entire plan revolves around my sister being able to lie? Oh, gods, you people really are morons."

Ari surged between them, but associates dragged her backward, keeping her arms pinned out of reach of Excalibur. "Kay!" she growled. "Shut up!"

The Administrator laughed, too, a high sound to match Kay's defiant humor. "Ridiculous! We know! But here we are." He flipped the gaudy crown over in his hand and leaned close to Ari's brother on the ground. Too close. "On behalf of the Mercer Company, we appreciate your role in this collaborative conquest."

He smashed the long, dramatic points of the crown into Kay's chest.

Kay's mouth overflowed with red so fast he coughed instead of crying out, and Ari screamed while the Administrator gave one final shove that stole the laughter—and life—from her brother's eyes.

Ari couldn't move. This *wasn't* happening. She stared at his shredded chest, urging herself to wake up. *Wake up!* She couldn't tear her eyes away, not even as she heard the heart-rending cries of her parents' grief.

"There," the Administrator stood. "A demonstration always smooths matters. Now we'll have no more resistance. The show must go on, yes?"

On the other side of the sliding doors, a massive creature howled in pain and anger.

Ari closed her eyes, recognizing that call.

Big Mama.

"Now," the Administrator said, wiping his hands on a towel. "There's a large dragon out there who is rather furious that we filled her baby full of holes. Your first job as a Mercer employee is to entertain the masses. Go shove that beautiful sword through her thick skull. Or die trying. A fake king or a dead rebel? Both are brilliant crowd pleasers. What will it be? Honestly, the suspense is just killing us! And, Ari?"

He put a hand on her arm. His nails bit through the chain mail, and he drew her so close that his terrible, hot breath was all over her neck. "Checkmate."

CAVE
&
SPARK

Merlin screamed, as if that would help. As if anyone in the universe could hear him.

He was suspended inside a Merlin-sized bubble in the Lady of the Lake's deep, shining waters. Dark-blue surrounded him on all sides, as far as he could see. The sides of the bubble were slippery, and Merlin couldn't keep his footing. He kept sliding, betrayed by the leg that Morgana had stabbed. When he could no longer move, he pinged the sides of the bubble with magic, but whatever enchantment Nin had created held up.

"Ari!" he shouted. "Ari, I'm coming!"

He was hoarse from hopeful lies. The truth was that Merlin had no idea how much time had passed since he fainted. Nin had taken him out of the story—ripped him away right at the moment when Ari needed him most.

And trapped him here.

Like last time...when King Arthur...when he...

Merlin banged and banged and *banged* because apparently the one thing Nin couldn't stand was being disturbed.

"*What is it now?*" she asked, her voice a watery ripple moving through the lake.

"I need to leave this cursed place," Merlin said, his heartbeat frantic.

"*No, Merlin,*" Nin sighed. "*I'm doing this for your good. If you had unleashed your magic, Mercer would have killed you, and I haven't waited all this time to watch you cut down by a CEO with a blank soul and an unfortunate haircut. You're safe here.*"

Merlin snorted. Benevolence from Nin was highly suspect. The only helpful thing she'd ever done was give Arthur a sword.

"She's a supplier of weapons," Merlin whispered, remembering.

There had to be magical weapons around here. A few notes bobbed under Merlin's breath as he sang about all things good and pointy. Then he watched the deep-blue water, trying not to look too eager.

A moment later, a sword sailed through the lake, deep-gray and aimed at Merlin. The bubble popped, and the inside flooded, earthy lake water rushing in. Merlin grabbed the sword as the whole thing collapsed inward.

Opening his eyes to peer through the murkiness, he swam toward the only source of light, a faint glow in the distance. All the while, the Lady of the Lake fought him with a sudden riptide, the kind that belonged in a great, salty ocean.

"Stop fighting me," she said, her voice trembling the water. "You're making this into a battle that it doesn't need to be."

Merlin kept swimming at a hard pace even though his stabbed leg sent out rays of pain. The feeling was almost unbearable, but at the same time it brought him strange comfort. It was a connection to Ari. If he was in pain, he was alive. If he was alive, there was still a chance of getting back to her.

The water churned to nearly white, tossing him viciously. He felt as if his lungs would fail, giving up before his heart did. He emerged on the underground shores of the lake, dragging himself out dripping wet, chest on fire. Merlin held up the sword he'd summoned, trying to look fierce, or at least not entirely waterlogged—and waited.

He should have felt better now that he was no longer a bubble prisoner, but this place was even worse. The light in Nin's cave shone vaguely blue. The sounds muted, as if someone put a finger to their lips and shushed the entire world.

He'd been here before. This was the home of Merlin's worst memory, the one he'd relived with Ari. Shame flooded him, even darker and colder than Nin's lake.

The Lady of the Lake glimmered into being. Her outline burned gold, the rest of her body wavering like a reflection on water. "Welcome back, Merlin," she said, her voice rippling through him like his body was a plucked string. "Are you ready to stop this childish, one-sided fight?"

He raised the sword higher, his arm weak, his body faintish with hunger. Nin had forgotten that Merlin having a body meant she needed to feed him if she was going to keep him as a magical pet, and their time together had already felt like a mad stretch of days. Anything could have happened to Ari and his friends by now. He took a step forward, even though his leg protested with throbbing pain.

"I will not let Ari die," Merlin said, pushing out the words. "I just got her back! And I will not let Arthur down. *Again*."

"What will you do instead?" she asked idly. "Kill me?"

The Lady of the Lake looked sternly at the sword in Merlin's hands and said a few words in a language that sounded older than the water and earth around them. The sword shot out of his grip and landed in Nin's gut as she laughed.

"Now," she said, speaking to him while impaled, as if she'd settled their debate and hoped they could move on. "What happened to you, Merlin? I haven't had to keep you from dying in many cycles. I thought you had mastered the art of self-preservation." She frowned mildly. "Go back to not caring, please. It was saving me so much trouble."

Nin's words scratched on the door of his deepest questions. Was she the reason he couldn't seem to die? He pushed the matter aside with a great deal of effort and focused on what he'd been torn from.

"What has become of Ari?" Merlin begged. "Let me see what's going to happen. You've allowed me that much before." Nin had given him that power the last time he was in her cave.

"I had to take your future-vision back," she said coldly. "Some vows are older even than your magic, and I promised I wouldn't interfere with this part of the story." Nin studied him through eyes that were silver as mercury, except when they were blue as flame. In that moment, he saw Nin clearly—and was struck by how little she cared.

He used to be more like her. He used to be able to turn off parts of his empathy, put his soul on mute. But he couldn't go back to that, even if he wanted to.

"Show me what I'm missing," he demanded.

"You want to know what Ari is facing?" she asked, with a sigh as weary as time. "Fine."

She removed the sword from her abdomen with one clean sweep. Then she stirred the air as if it were water. The rippled texture gave way to a picture of Ari in armor, in the center of a sand-filled tournament ring. She looked harried, exhausted, and she was holding Excalibur in a flagging grip as an enormous dragonlike creature circled her. Its jaws descended with a vile metallic crunch. Ari winced at a spot where the dragon's teeth had caught her between armored plates. Blood was *everywhere,* darkening the sand, spilling through the vision in a way that seemed to turn the pools of water around Merlin red.

"No," he whispered. "No, no, no."

It was happening all over again. History had doubled over on itself. Ari was going to die as he stood at Nin's side, powerless. The picture of Ari's battle faded, but the pain stayed with Merlin. "She needs me," he whimpered. "We're...friends."

"Friends? That's an interesting word for your relationship," Nin mocked. "Besides, when have you ever had *friends*? You have Arthurs who outgrow your help. Pretending you are part of their lives will make things far more painful, Merlin. You're just...passing through."

Even though Merlin couldn't see the future, he could still fear it. He imagined the horror and disgust on Val's face when he realized that Merlin was too young for him. He saw Ari growing into her power—and leaving him behind.

Even if she lived past this day, they were doomed to lose each other. Merlin's shaking leg gave out, and he fell to the rocks. Nin studied him with a cocked head, a finger to her perfectly formed chin. "You know, I thought watching you age backward would be more fun, but we've gotten to the point where it's mostly ridiculous and mildly shameful."

"*You* try being a teenager." Merlin pushed to his feet, looking for a way out of this place, even though he doubted one existed. But if Nin had thought showing him Ari in a tournament ring would be enough to mollify him, she didn't know him. She only knew the Old Merlin.

He hummed, warming up his magic.

Nin's ethereal face turned slightly frantic. "If you stop being a child about all of this, I will end your backward aging."

"You... what?"

Nin took a step closer to Merlin, closer than she'd ever been, crowding his thoughts, pushing out Ari with her all-consuming glow. Nin reached out, her bright fingers touching the wound on his leg.

It faded, just like the picture of Ari had.

"The time has come," Nin said. "You've gotten close enough, and frankly I don't want to watch this show anymore. It's become so formulaic. The good ones always do." Anger clawed its way into Merlin's thoughts. All this time, through all of this tragedy, the Lady of the Lake had been watching as if his life were some cheap form of *entertainment*?

"You've *watched* those Arthurs die, and you did nothing?" His questions took a hard left into the personal. "You watched me kiss Art and... walk away?"

"That bit was quite sad," she said, putting her fingers to her lips as if she still savored the memory. "Now, dear Merlin, let me return you to your parents. You'll be done with your backward stroll through time. You won't be alone, and you'll never have to be a squalling infant. Everyone gets what they want."

Her words pierced Merlin's mind like a lance, shattering his determination to return to Ari into a thousand tiny shards.

"I have...parents?" he asked blankly. There were no parents in his memories, even the earliest ones. He'd searched them endlessly, looking for the smallest clue of their existence. With so many centuries at his disposal, he'd had plenty of time to torture himself over it. The only bit of physical evidence that he'd even had of a life before he first awoke in the crystal cave had been that tiny wooden falcon. He stuck a hand in his pocket, suddenly afraid that he'd lost the one from Lionel. It was still there, small and solid and rough at the edges, tethering him to his new life.

"Did you think someone made you out of sticks and robes?" Nin asked with a laugh. "Of course you have parents."

"Who are they?" Merlin's voice was hoarse, twisting, strange in his own ears.

"That I can't say. They're quite powerful, and I doubt they would like me being the one to give you the news of who you really are, where you come from, et cetera and so forth."

"Or you just don't want to lose out on the dramatic potential of watching me confront my secret, magical parents," Merlin spat.

"Oh, well, yes. That's part of it," she said with a mild, infuriating grin. "Tell me you're ready, and I'll return you to them. They are so nearly ready to see you again." Nin folded her hands, waiting for Merlin to accept her offer.

He let himself sink into that sweet, tempting possibility. He didn't have to keep inching toward childhood. The loneliness that had kept his life separate from everyone else's could be over. The special oblivion that waited for him at the end of this would be banished, with one word.

Yes.

"What will happen to Ari?" he asked, unable to stop himself. "Will she defeat Mercer? Unite humankind?"

"Oh, Merlin, uniting humankind under one banner?" She tutted like a grandmother, even though she looked eternally twenty-five. "That sounds like imperialism, doesn't it? *The suns never set on the Arthurian empire?* Do you remember how many problems that impulse caused in the past? What about the future? Doesn't this Mercer Company want to unite everyone, too? How can any single entity know what's best for all people? These humans keep making the same boring mistake of demonizing difference, but believe me, if unity for all worked, I would have gotten into the deity game a long time ago."

"But...you're the one who gave me the steps," Merlin said. "That's the last step. And Ari will be the one to finally do it. She knows that bringing people together doesn't mean making them the same." Merlin felt everything inessential begin to slip away. "She's more like the first Arthur than any I've trained. I can't leave them."

The Lady of the Lake's smile curled like a burning page. "What makes you think Ari will live through the day? You could be giving up everything for a dead girl and a wisp of ancient spirit."

The idea that Ari might be dying only made Merlin more desperate. But what Nin had offered still glimmered like diamonds on water in the dying sun. Merlin wanted to stop aging backward so much he could taste it. It was a meal with his family. A kiss finally shared without fear. Only that kiss wouldn't be with Val, and that family would be far away from Ari—if she even survived.

Merlin had made this mistake before. He'd taken Nin's bargain, and let Arthur die.

He might not have started the cycle, but if he wanted to end it, he was going to have to stop making the same mistakes. It wasn't just a question of plodding through the steps, again and again and again.

Merlin had to change the story.

"Let me go, Nin," he said, the depths of his commanding old-man voice returning for a single moment. He had one card left to play, and he would throw it down. Nin had brought him here *twice,* and both times she'd bargained with him to stay as if he *did* have the power to get himself out if he wanted to. Merlin pointed his magic straight at her. A song came to him: he hummed the sprightly tune to that old *Camelot* musical.

"What are you doing?" she asked, narrowing her eyes.

"Using the power you've already given me," Merlin said, her doubt encouraging him. After all, Nin had only started bargaining when Merlin looked for a way out of the cave. If he was truly trapped here, she would not have offered a deal.

"Do you believe you can touch me with magic?" Nin asked, her voice fading into the air as her form vanished.

"It's like you said before, this isn't a battle." The first sparks flew out of Merlin's hands and hit the cave wall, crumbling a section, letting in the blinding light of pure time. "This is a prison break. Fortunately, I have some practice with those."

More magic flew out, and another great chunk of the wall fell, rocks hitting water with a great crash. He didn't need to give Nin a body, like he had with Morgana, if he wanted to use his magic on her. The cave *was* her body—it was her physical creation.

All he needed was a way out.

"Stop that," Nin said, her voice shaking the ground.

"Let me go!" Merlin cried.

The cave blasted white as all of his magic came out of him at once.

&

Merlin returned to a room filled with medical equipment and Mercer associates, all of them scattered in a rough, broken circle. The ground was covered with jagged white scorch marks.

So the explosion had done more than release him from Nin's cave.

When Merlin stood, his body weighed several thousand pounds, and his brain might as well have been a briny pickle in a delicate glass jar. "I've been heavily sedated," he said, but it came out more like, "I'be en hemily sebated."

He hated the thought that Mercer had been taking his blood and running tests, but he didn't have time to destroy whatever evidence of his magic they'd collected. He needed to get to Ari before Mercer killed one of his friends.

Merlin gave himself a tremendous smack, which succeeded in shocking away the worst of the sedative. He began to stumble out of the medical facility, but one of the bodies on the floor caught his eye. This one had been locked to a chair—and taken down along with it. Scorch marks had fileted her skin with white burns. Merlin pushed the black hair back from her face and whispered her name, "Morgana?"

Nothing.

In a moment that melted the color from the body, Morgana materialized beside him, freed from Merlin's corporeal gift—and no small amount pissed.

"That is the *last time* you kill me, old man."

"Apologies," Merlin said. "Truly, it was collateral damage."

"There are worse ways to die, I suppose," Morgana admitted. "Those people," she cast dirty glances at the dead associates around them, "would have taken apart our cells, if allowed. I locked several of them in the asylum of their worst memories, but more just kept coming."

Merlin wanted to tell Morgana about his run-in with Nin, but there was no time. He asked the only question that mattered. "Where are the others?"

"They were speaking of a ceremony." Morgana's body faded back to its familiar transparent state. "This way."

Merlin chased after her, stumbling out of the medical facility, into…a mall, of all places. The white lights made him blink while the sterilized air left a dead taste in his mouth. At first he spun around in the hall, but then he caught the sounds of a great, cheering crowd. He followed it to a huge set of double doors just as a great roar went up from behind them. Were they cheering on Ari—or the dragon she was fighting?

"Tickets," a Mercer associate asked, barring the way and pushing out a hand.

Merlin didn't have tickets. He did a quick bodily check—no magic, either.

Morgana had already slithered past the associate and was

watching him with frantic impatience. Even she was terrified on Ari's behalf.

Merlin gave the Mercer associate a high five, and then used his momentary confusion to run past him into the stadium. "A trick as old as time!" he cried as he took off, hoping the associate wouldn't fire his gun straight into a crowd.

As he ran into the massive tiered stadium, the vicious cries for blood summoned his worst fear. He could only hope that this time, he hadn't reached his Arthur too late.

COST
&
CROWNS

Big Mama's jaws snapped tight on Ari's thigh.

A half-moon of pain pierced the chain mail, sinking into Ari's muscle and causing her to scream. She brought Excalibur's pommel down on the taneen's nose, knocking the dragon in what she knew to be a sensitive spot.

Big Mama snorted and reared, letting Ari escape. She limped across the red sand floor of the massive arena, warm blood sweeping down her leg from a dozen new punctures. Ari ducked behind a large stone dais in the center, trying to catch her breath.

To make a choice.

All around, the endless screams of the crowd and the flashes of thousands of cameras kept Ari's heart thundering and Big Mama's roars furious. Mercer had spared no expense for this show. The million-seater auditorium rose up for half a mile around them, the uppermost tiers barely in sight. It felt like being at the bottom of a well—and just as hopeless.

Big Mama didn't care who Ari was or how long they'd known each other. Like Ari, Mercer had piled the dragon heavily with armor. They'd starved her strategically. They'd killed her baby in front of her. Ari had half a mind to let the grieving taneen eat her, but that wasn't the game, was it? Ari had to win.

That was the only eventuality the Administrator would allow. If Ari died, there would be no king to place a cursed Mercer crown upon. Her friends would be erased from existence like Ketch had been. And yet none of that truth made it easier to kill this dragon.

Big Mama scuttled around the dais, head bleeding from two spots, the red washing the taneen's vision. Ari scaled the stones, swinging one-handed when Big Mama's teeth snapped at her arm. Once she'd rolled over the top edge, she kept herself in the center. Big Mama was as tall as the dais, but she couldn't fit on it. She spun around it a few times, roaring in disapproval, Ari just out of reach.

Ari had to find a way to get the taneen to remember her. If she could, *maybe* there was a way to avoid turning the dragon's death into a spectacle for an uncaring, unfeeling universe. Maybe she could show them that this was not a senseless beast to destroy...

Ari wished she still had some lamb jerky as she ripped at the pieces of the King Arthur armor Mercer had fitted her with. Nothing would budge but the helmet, so she tore it off and held her sword behind her back in one shaking hand.

Big Mama had her front legs on the edge of the dais, jaws snapping at the air.

"Hey...it's me. Remember me?" Ari mimed taking a piece of jerky out of her pocket. Big Mama's dark, liquid eyes roved over Ari's empty palm. "I don't have anything for you. They've taken everything from me. And you. They..." Her voice choked up as the words rose out, broken and excruciating. "They killed Kay."

Both of them.

"And we can't...we can't beat them all. Neither of us can." Ari moved closer, sword arm still held back. Her other palm was held out emptily, offering nothing but friendship to the enraged dragon.

"Do you remember how Kay would play dead?" Ari snuck a few steps closer. The taneen was taking in the tears in her eyes, the flush of pain in her words. Ari had wondered how much she could understand. Kay had been limited, but then, he was just a baby. "Do you think you can do that, Big Mama? Can you *play dead*?"

The taneen's jaws closed, her head cocked. She understood Ari, maybe.

"I'm going to shove this sword through that terrible armor. I'm going to get it off of you. But you have to stay down afterward. Do you hear me? *Play dead.*"

Ari couldn't tell if this would work. She doubted it, and yet, what choice did she have? She closed her eyes and took one last step closer. Big Mama could have snapped her head off, if she wanted.

But she didn't.

Ari swung Excalibur around, slicing across the terrible armored plates Mercer had tied to Big Mama. The armor fell away at the same time that the dragon teetered upright on her hind legs—and then fell backward with an enormous, bone-crunching crash that shook the arena and left it in silence.

Ari rushed to the edge of the dais, unsure if she'd convinced the dragon, or if Excalibur had been too sharp. The taneen's long, thick neck, now free from the armor, was bleeding into the red sand. Were those injuries from the armor or Ari? She couldn't tell.

And Big Mama didn't move.

The crowd went berserk, and the great rolling doors at the end of the arena opened, filling the floor with an army of Mercer associates, as well as her friends on horseback, and the devil himself, the Administrator.

&

Ari knelt against her will.

Her eyes were stuck on the sand smeared across the stone dais. Rusted red. Ketchan sand; she would have recognized it anywhere. Stolen from her planet and spread across this sick arena. This touch of detail was so cruel, it made it hard to breathe. To be killed on soil that had been stolen from her murdered planet was one thing.

To be made into a puppet figurehead upon it was something else entirely.

The Administrator's performance was one of gracious words and swelling musical accompaniment as he placed the cursed crown—Kay's blood erased from its shining points and jewels—on Ari's head.

Beside her, Gwen was wearing her old crown from Lionel. They had been positioned together as dual sovereigns. King and queen. A pair for the Administrator's living chessboard.

The crowd erupted in polite cheers while the Administrator

began to talk...and talk. He spoke of Ari's life like it was an inspirational book he'd read, and Ari could do nothing but suffer the weight of that crown. It truly was heavy. At least ten pounds. Maybe even lined in lead; she wouldn't put it past Mercer, after all, they wanted her to know she was under their yoke. Everything she did, believed, chose, breathed was because they allowed it.

At the foot of the stone dais, too far away, Ari could feel her friends' heartbeats as if they were her own. Lamarack's resistant pound, Jordan's loyal drum, and Val's tenor. In between those beats, she heard the silence as well. The voided places where the people of Ketch now resided, shadowed by Mercer's lies. Her birth parents, too, were in that silence, blasted into it.

And Kay.

Ari couldn't remember him with thick shoulders and shaggy hair. She saw only the chubby nine-year-old who'd sat outside her hammock after she'd been saved from the crash, unable to speak their language and frozen by hundreds of stiff, slowly healing burns. Young Kay had poked food through a gap in the zipper, one chip at a time. For hours, for days. None of his words had meant anything, until they started to. *Kay, kay, kay. Kay.* He had said it until little Ari whispered it back, and then he'd crowed throughout the ship like teaching her his name had been the highlight of his entire life.

It had made Ari smile...after the trauma of her birth parents' murder, after the torture of the water barrel. An impossible feat.

A gasp slipped out as she returned to the present, head bent beneath the scorching lights of the arena, bearing the suffocating armor. Gwen stirred beside her, and Ari returned to the idea of heartbeats. Gwen's was so close, so steadfast, and it wasn't alone, was it? There would be a baby. A new person who would come into this ruined universe, who'd grow up to look at her and ask, *Why? Why would you want me to exist in such a broken place?*

The Administrator's voice droned on, and Ari squeezed her eyes, trying not to imagine his vile heartbeat along with the rest. Loud and cruel, fast and stabbing.

How do we fight back, Arthur? she asked that deep, silent voice inside.

No reply.

"How do we fight back?" Ari whispered through gritted teeth.

"Ari?" Gwen answered, the smallest whisper of a voice.

"You'll die." Ari glanced at Gwen's face, her stomach. "Both of you. If I fight now, you'll die. All of us will. I can't…"

Gwen slid her hand over Ari's. The Administrator was still regaling the crowd with images and videos from Ari's life. The moment when Jordan had thrown the fight on Lionel. When Gwen had come down from the stands with the unwavering look in her eye and had kissed the daylights out of Ari.

Gwen had been getting her back for leaving all those years ago, without so much as a good-bye. It had been such a delicious punishment; everything Ari'd missed out on, every heated moment she'd lost, shining through those brief seconds. And all of a sudden, Ari wanted a long life with millions of disagreements; she wanted Gwen to punish her like that forever.

The crowd in the tiered arena was just as entranced. They watched the 3D video of Ari and Gwen's marriage on massive screens, and Gwen leaned in close.

"He is not giving us our lives, Ari. He's taking them from us. Like he stole Kay's." Gwen's grief was so new, a shine on her skin, a light rain that had fallen over her.

For Ari, his loss was a knife twisted into her side by the Administrator himself. Her eyes teared up miserably. "Please, don't. I can't talk about him now. I can't... We have to take the deal. Go back to Lionel. Find some spark of hope and—"

"No matter what Mercer lets us have, it won't be ours. We will be possessions. And *we*," Gwen motioned down at their friends far below, also on their knees, heads cast down, "would rather die. Here. Now. With the universe as a witness."

Ari felt herself looking up into the dazzling, bright lights, whispering the Administrator's embittered words, "Martyrs do *kill* the economy." She turned to Gwen, the terrible stone of a crown biting into the side of her head. She felt a sting and a warm spot. The edges of it were so sharp it was making her bleed. Gwen touched the side of Ari's face, fingers coming away red.

As red as Kay's mouth in his last laughing moment.

Ari shuddered, pain spiraling outward at an alarming rate. "I have an idea, but I need your help. You know I'm no good at pageantry."

Gwen smiled, ever so slightly. "You are miles from where you used to be, dragon slayer."

Ari winced, casting a quick look at the enormous mound of Big Mama beside the dais. She hadn't moved, and Ari's scheme to keep the dragon alive seemed less and less realistic. "I have an idea, but we have to win the crowd. We need to surprise them. Something simple but attention grabbing."

Gwen stared at Ari, biting her lip, cheeks flushed.

Was that a suggestion?

"Gwen..." Ari stared at her pink mouth and the bright pain behind her eyes. The crowd was still eating up the video of their wedding. Even the Administrator had his head tipped back, staring up at the entranced crowd, pleased, no doubt, by the mounting roll of incoming credits.

"It would surprise them," Gwen whispered.

When Ari was marooned on Ketch, she had dreamed about kissing Gwen again. She'd set the stage in her mind thousands of times. There were swooping embraces. Passionate, swirling lifts. Soft, drowsy bedtime kisses. Fierce, needing, rolling, gasping ones...

All of those longings faded now, turned to something so fractured she couldn't see the image through the shards. She didn't know what was still Ari and Gwen. There was so much Mercer now. So much Kay. So much King Arthur.

Ari turned away, thinking back to that moment behind the stables when they were young. They'd never gotten along, Gwen and Ari. They'd argued through knight camp so heatedly that their teacher had paired them up as a punishment, and yet it had flipped their magnetism. That moment against the wall, out of view, they'd started to fight about something pointless. Gwen's shoulder was slipping out of her dress—always slipping out—and Ari had bitten in. A full-on attack of hormones and desire that tumbled them into a knot of unending kisses and hands and hips, skin feverish to meet skin.

It hadn't stopped their arguments, but it'd inspired new ones. Beautiful ones.

A few million light-years in space and time from those two girls, Ari found herself staring at Gwen's shoulder. This time her clothes weren't slipping free; this dress fit like a corset, so tight it left angry red marks where it was pressing in.

But it was also strapless.

Ari's face dipped low, closer, closer. Her mouth found Gwen's shoulder, breaking the barrier between them with a playful nip, destroying it as swiftly as Excalibur had demolished the one around Ketch. Gwen cradled Ari's face, bringing their lips together in a way that seemed to make the whole gods damn universe tremble.

Or maybe that was just Ari.

Gwen bruised things in Ari's heart. She always had. Her closeness was a continuous tender ache because what would Ari feel, do, be afterward?

New.

Every kiss with Gwen left Ari new.

They pulled each other to their feet—no more kneeling in front of the Administrator—and kept kissing. Their history served them, but so did their pain, knotting their bodies together in a way that could not be faked. Or pulled apart. Ari was only barely aware of the moment when the arena noticed their passion, the applause turning riotous and raw. Screams of joy from so many people who wanted to be this entangled— which only encouraged Ari to deepen the kiss.

After all, love was one of the few things Mercer could not sell.

The Administrator's elevated voice filtered through Ari's ears. His *aww shucks* turned into impatient chatter. "Break it up now. We have business to discuss!" he tried playfully.

Finally, breath slipping fast between both of their lips, Ari asked, "Are you ready?"

Gwen nodded and ripped the crown off of Ari's head, throwing it into the stands with an impressive arc for its weight. After the brief flash of delight from the crowd, the Administrator's cold stare chilled the entire arena.

"Nobody puts a crown on my girl but me," Gwen said with a pleased smile, her voice echoing for miles. The Administrator's jaw popped like it had right before he'd smashed that crown into Kay's chest, and Ari felt the mere seconds they had to live, right as the arena exploded with an arcing rainbow of fireworks.

Gwen glanced up. Everyone did—except Ari. She searched the stands, feeling him. And he was there, several sections up, and yet she would have recognized his skinny power stance from a few hundred light-years away.

"Merlin," Ari whispered, tears threatening.

His expression and rapid gesturing seemed to say, *Well? Get on with your revolution.*

Ari grabbed Gwen and pulled her down the steps that had been pressed into the side of the stone dais for the Administrator. They fled toward their knights while the crowd continued to marvel over Merlin's special brand of distraction.

Jordan—wonderful, noble fucking Jordan—was already taking out an entire line of Mercer associates with one swing of her broadsword. Ari and her knights huddled together, using the horses to create a shield between them and the small army of Mercer associates.

"What are we doing?" Val yelled. "Running for it?"

"We're fighting!" Lam said.

"I'm already fighting!" Jordan yelled over her shoulder, taking out a rogue associate with a hard elbow to the face.

"We're…" Ari couldn't look into their soon-to-be-dead faces. "We're…"

Gwen's fingers slipped between Ari's, strengthening her hold. "We're making our stand."

"We are the truth the universe has to see. We will show them the lengths to which Mercer will go. Everyone wanted a king. A coronation. A spectacle. We're going to show them the tragedy behind such wishes." Ari's voice broke as she thought about her brother. "There's only one door on the arena level, the one we came through, and we only have a chance if we don't let reinforcements in. Even if that means we are locked in here." She turned to the black knight. "Jordan, keep the door shut. Lam—"

"Figure out how to blow it to splinters when we're ready to escape. Got it." Everyone stared at them as they untied the bracer from their left wrist, revealing a secret lining that held a series of vials. "Told you, I have explosives."

Jordan squinted at the small glass tubes of bright-blue liquid. "Is that what I think it is?"

"Yes, it is," Lam said proudly.

Ari blew out a breath. "All right then, but hold off until I've gotten to the Administrator. Lam, will that stuff be enough to take the whole starship apart?"

Lam shook their head. "No, but it'll make it uninhabitable, to say the least. Should give the spectators plenty of time to get back to their vessels and blast away. Us, too."

"We should make them go down with the ship," Jordan said. "Mercer-owned cowards."

"Some of them are, yes." Ari looked up into the stands. The crowd was still rioting over the fireworks. "But some of them are like us, waiting for a time and place to make a stand. We might be surprised," she said. "But hold back the associates as long as you can. Give me time."

The associates were forming ranks around the knights, while the Administrator had started to holler orders down from the dais. "Where are you going?" Val asked.

"To get my magician!" Ari's hand sealed around Excalibur while she used the other to bring Gwen's knuckles to her lips. "We end this together," she promised Gwen. "For Kay."

Lam pushed one of the horses toward Ari, but she shook her head. "I don't need it. I'm going to ride my dragon."

She put two fingers in her mouth and whistled as hard as she could.

And Big Mama roared back to life.

&

Ari flew around the arena on Big Mama's back, scattering the Mercer ranks into screaming, trampled piles. She fought to get her bearings, to find Merlin again, and then she sent the taneen up into the stands.

Big Mama scaled the tiers of the stadium as easily as she'd once climbed Ras Almal. Ari found her magician trying to make his way down to the arena by climbing over row after row of seats, the cushions flapping.

"Good to see you, old man!" she hollered, hauling him onto the back of her dragon.

He held her around the waist, and yelled in her ear, "Thank you for being alive! Again!"

Ari couldn't help but laugh as she turned the dragon around

and returned to the arena. The raised stone dais was now the Administrator's stronghold, and he'd barricaded himself in the middle of an array of associates. Ari could just barely make out his terrible thatched hair.

That was fine; he could stay up there, hiding. As long as he couldn't leave or call for reinforcements, she had a chance to make an example out of him before—well, before it was all over. She was relieved to see that Jordan was on her task and the massive sliding door was tightly closed, no new Mercer reinforcements coming through.

Ari charged Big Mama back toward her knights, scattering associates in every direction. The taneen took a few tentative nips of flesh here and there, and Ari let her, jumping off her back with Merlin and into the spot where Lam and Val were fighting the good fight. Lam looked amazing in their leather armor, leveling associates with furious one-handed swings, but Val was bleeding from the shoulder. Merlin and Ari took down the half a dozen associates closest to them, and Ari held on to Lam, catching her breath to ask about their progress.

"The explosives?"

"In place." They pointed to the seam on the sliding door. "We have about five minutes before it becomes caustic."

Ari was exhausted, her body shaking. "Get this off of me," she yelled, turning so that Lam could unstrap the miserable Pendragon breastplate. As she turned her back, her eyes fell on two boys, madly making out. "Hey!" Ari yelled. "We're in the middle of a battle!"

Merlin waved a dismissive hand and kept on kissing Val.

The breastplate fell away, and Ari stood taller. She was ready to finish this. She had to be.

"Where's Jordan?" Ari asked, whipping around. "Where's *Gwen*?"

Lam pointed up at the stone dais. "They grabbed Gwen. Jordan went full knight rage. I've never seen anything like it."

Ari's heart stormed as she squinted up to where the Administrator stood, holding Gwen, just *waiting* for Ari to notice. "Bastard," she breathed. "He's using her as bait. That's still not bad-guy original," she cursed, remembering their first meeting.

Ari turned back to Merlin, shaking him out of the deepest kiss she'd ever witnessed. "Merlin, where's Morgana?"

"I accidentally killed that body I gave her. She's...around."

"She'd better be."

Ari's brain hummed as she tried to imagine a way to get close to the Administrator. She could get close to him, but not armed. He'd make sure of that. "How much magic do you have left, old man?"

Merlin chewed his lip, and Val tugged it free as if he couldn't resist. "My fireworks were not easy, because I had this run-in with an old friend who zapped all my—"

"He's got nothing," Val said. "He's staying with me. What do you want us to do?"

Ari picked up two ornate Mercer swords and shoved one in Val's hand and one in Merlin's. They both looked at them like they were odd hairbrushes. "You two stay with Lam. Help them get those doors open, if it's possible. Find a way out of here, if you can."

"*Error* should be in the docking garage," Lam said. "When you were unconscious, they were retrofitting her with a bunch of Mercer gadgets. Turning her into a sort of chariot to parade their fake king in. It's what made Kay lose his cool before...."

Ari swallowed hard, trying not to picture that scene. "Find her, and get my parents, too—"

Morgana appeared, wispy and miserable. "They are sealing us in from every angle. Escape is improbable."

Ari apologized to Merlin and slid Excalibur along his arm. Val shouted and Merlin cried out, turning pale. A line of blood shone along the blade, and Ari looked at Morgana, hard. "Optimism, Morgana."

"Ara Azar," the Administrator said, voice booming from the surround sound speakers in the stadium. The entire place went dead silent. All of the associates stopped fighting at once, and even Big Mama quietly feasted in the corner.

"King Ara, please return to the dais to collect your queen," he tittered.

Some people in the crowd actually laughed.

The still-armed associates cleared back as Ari began the long, slow walk toward the dais. When she neared the stairs, she found Jordan, down on her side, bleeding into the red sand. Her helmet was thrown off and her face was full of righteous aggression. "No quarter, no mercy," she whispered, wincing.

Ari nodded and approached the steps.

"Unarmed, thank you," the Administrator called out.

Ari dropped Excalibur in the sand and climbed the steps to face the Administrator. She tore away pieces of the clunky, punishing armor as she went until she was just Ari, standing in a shirt she'd stolen from her mother's room on Ketch. He sent his associates away like a fool, but then, he really didn't fear Ari. He never had. That was the first thing she needed to change.

The Administrator held Gwen's dagger to the inside of Gwen's hip in a way that proved to Ari exactly how much he knew—and that he was threatening two lives at once.

"You're going to knife a pregnant woman?" Ari asked, voice carrying to the cameras, the projection above their heads still trailing the best of the action. "That's evil, Administrator. I thought Mercer wasn't evil, or good. They just *are*."

The crowd stilled, all eyes on them.

He released Gwen slowly, a strangely savage look on his face that left Ari spinning with fear. The dagger moved away from Gwen, and he held it up as if he were relenting.

And then he pushed Gwen off the dais.

She fell with a small scream, landing hard on the sandy ground in a crumpled heap.

Ari surged forward and caught the Administrator by those terrible ceremonial robes, pinning him to the altar that only minutes ago he'd tried to use as evidence of his ordained right.

The Administrator's slick expression didn't waver. "You forget that they don't care if I'm evil. No one stands against us, because they need us." He turned his look to the stands. "Without Mercer you'd die, hungry, thirsty, squawking at each other. You all need us too much, don't you?"

The silence was answer enough.

Mercer owned the universe, but it was more than that. Mercer made truth irrelevant. As long as they were in control, atrocity would always be excused in the name of convenience and greed.

Ari's fingers latched on to his throat. She wanted to recoil from his bleached skin. His hollow eyes. The Administrator had nothing inside of him. No hate. No caring. There was only the cold balance of cost and trade. A bank account of sterilized numbers. A mass grave of figures.

Ari pulled away.

And he laughed. "We did not think you would choke us to death for the entertainment of the masses. Didn't your brother already tell you? You're no killer."

Kay's truth coming out of the Administrator's mouth was the worst kind of salt on this new wound, and Ari stung all over. She looked over the side of the dais to where Gwen was still crumpled, unconscious or worse. The crowd followed her gaze, murmuring with longing at the sight of the fallen queen. This was proof. They did want more than Mercer crap. They wanted love. Hope. Truth. They were starved for it.

The Administrator flashed a cold smile into the arena, unaffected. "Moving. Truly. How much for the movie rights?"

"I'm not for sale, Administrator. And that's why you should have been afraid of me a long time ago."

Behind her, Lam's explosives cracked the arena wide open, and the place turned into a screaming rush of fleeing people. Morgana shimmered into existence beside Ari, bearing Excalibur. Ari took the sword and drove it through the center of the Administrator's chest. He slumped, pinned to the stone altar by an antique token of hope.

"It's true. I'm no murderer," she said, pulling the blade free. "But I do have an impulse-control problem. And a sword."

FIRE
&
SPACE

After Ari ran the Administrator clean through, every-thing was a blur of crowds and running and shouting until Merlin was back on *Error,* watching the mall explode. A brilliant cloud of red swallowed itself as quickly as it had appeared, the oxygen burned out in a flash, the fire quenched.

And just like that, the flagship of the Mercer Company had been destroyed.

Error was one of thousands of ships that had fled the mall only to pause and take in the beautiful destruction. Merlin was grateful for this moment. Not only was *Heritage* being torched, he finally had a chance to look over his band of ragtag survivors: Val had taken a stab to the back, Jordan and Lam were bleeding from a few dozen places, although none looked life-threatening, and Gwen had a severe concussion from her fall, and a purple knot on her head that looked troublesome.

Merlin was tired. More tired than should have been possible unless one was mildly immortal. *Mildly.*

Nin had confirmed it, then. He would die of young age.

And Kay? He was dead. The kind of dead that you didn't come back from. Val and Merlin had tripped on his body during their mad escape. Merlin had lost precious minutes checking his pulse, hoping for a miracle. But Kay's heart stayed silent.

Val had had to get Merlin back on his feet as he leaked surprised tears—over Kay, one of his least favorite characters in this over-spun tale. Wonders never cease.

"Good-bye, Kay," Merlin said. "You were an odd hero, but a good one."

His friends stood taller as the devastation of *Heritage* turned into the best Viking funeral he'd ever seen. And he had seen quite a few in his near-endless days. Unlike Merlin's backward eternity, Kay had been given twenty short solar years, a cruelly brief calendar based on a planet where humans no longer lived.

Merlin turned to Ari. She stood to the side, looking more Arthurian than ever. Grief had been a sizeable part of this story since the very beginning. It made Ari seem like she'd aged all at once, calm and resigned as if she could fight everything except this moment. Excalibur's point bit the floor of *Error* while her hands rested on the hilt, majestic—particularly with the soundtrack of the roaring dragon stuffed into the cargo bay.

"Are we safe with that thing in there?" Jordan asked.

Ari chuckled sadly. "She's stuffed on associates. We're safe."

"I thought you said you were only going to blow up the mall a little bit," Val said to Lam as pieces of *Heritage* began to separate, floating free of one another.

"Minor miscalculation," Lam said, with a look that convinced

Merlin it was no such thing. "At least Kay is going down with the ship."

"Gods damn it, he loved that fucking mall," Val insisted. "Even in all of its Mercer-inspired awfulness."

"A fitting tribute for a warrior's death," Jordan said, folding her arms with a kind of deep understanding.

Ari crossed the cabin and shut the door to the hallway, no doubt hoping she could keep her grieving, injured parents from having to relive their son's death. "Kay wasn't fighting when he died," she said, sadness etching her words. "He was telling the truth. About me."

"And you were the thing Mercer feared most," Gwen said, her voice reaching across the rather notable distance between them. "A girl they couldn't control, who wouldn't stop talking. That's the scariest damn thing in the universe."

Another huge explosion silently lit up the space outside *Error*'s largest window. Debris went free-floating everywhere. "What is all that?" Lam asked.

"Looks like food," Val said. "Billions of snacks. That must have been the grocery section."

"A twenty-one-snack salute," Merlin murmured with surprising joy.

Ari gave a sad laugh. "Well, now it really is his funeral. And at least we saved Kay's baby," she added, running a hand down *Error*'s riveted wall.

The baby in question was Kay's ship, of course, but the words conjured up another meaning. Everyone's eyes went to Gwen's stomach, including the queen's.

"Truly?" Jordan asked, wiping her brow in tired disbelief.

"I knew it," Val muttered. "You can't get something like that past a good adviser."

Merlin felt slightly ashamed that he hadn't noticed Gwen's pregnancy, though of course he'd been trying to ignore the reality that Gwen and Kay were together in the first place.

Gwen and Ari looked away from each other. Merlin ached for them, in exactly the way he'd feared he would. They were bound together in all of this, and yet, they were also forced apart by the details.

The knights continued to watch as *Heritage* broke into large pieces of space trash, spreading out like a supernova of consumerism. This time Mercer was not chasing them down. No one was chasing.

The Mercer faction on *Heritage* had exploded as efficiently as the ship. The moment the Administrator died, the associates abandoned their posts, their weapons, their uniforms. Merlin had seen many of them bartering for passage on civilian ships. It reminded him of some of the more infamous beasts of his past. Cyborgs, kraken, white supremacists. None of them were much of a threat without their head. And Ari had decapitated the Mercer Company.

Now the universe needed leadership. A breath of life to answer this much death. Merlin would help Ari get everything in place, of course.

Ari moved to the cockpit. "We're going to Ketch." She paused in the doorway, looking back over her shoulder. "I want to set up a new kind of government from there. One where every planet has a voice."

Well, perhaps Ari didn't need quite that much guidance.

After all, she had always been stronger than Arthur. And when she stopped letting her loneliness guide her, she was a much better listener.

If she was prepared to lead the universe to a new age of peace, did that mean Merlin could live *his* life? What was left of it anyway?

"If anyone wants to go somewhere else, I'll drop you off. But know that my home is your home. You're all welcome." Merlin watched Ari's eyes lock on Gwen's. They were the figureheads, after all. Half of this band belonged to Ari. Half to Gwen.

"I've always wanted to see Ketch," Gwen said, slipping to Ari's side. "If you want to stay with me, that is where I'm going. Let's just hope that the Lionelians are still there and safe."

"If they aren't, I'll find them," Ari said solemnly. "Every single one."

"I know," Gwen's fingers slipped between Ari's.

Val slumped into Merlin's shoulder. As much as Merlin wanted to get back to their fiery mid-battle kissing, there was a more pressing matter.

"You're hurt," he said, touching Val's back lightly. Val winced. Merlin wavered between pride at having saved Val's life with a sword to an associate's gut, and distress that Val had still gotten stabbed in the process.

"May I wrap that for you?" Merlin asked.

"Shirtless fun *is* shirtless," Val said, his eyes half open. He sank a little, dragging Merlin with him, seeming to feel his injury all at once.

"Use Kay's room," Ari said. "It's yours now."

"But…don't you want…?" Merlin sputtered.

"I can't go in there," Ari said.

Merlin looked to Gwen. And her stomach.

"I'm in much better shape than Val at the moment," Gwen said. "And my baby has already survived a battle, so if you start treating us like we're two delicate flowers, I'll happily stab you in the other thigh." Gwen ducked into the cockpit, leaving Merlin to wonder where the original thigh-stabber had gotten off to.

He hadn't seen Morgana since the height of the action. She'd vanished, like she always did. At least she'd turned up when she was needed. She had helped Ari, even if it wasn't a direct route to putting King Arthur to rest. Maybe that body he'd given her—and accidentally taken back—had done Morgana some good. He made a mental note to drop her back into corporeal form the next time she resurfaced.

Merlin stood with great care, pulling Val along with him into Kay's room. It felt a little strange to claim it, knowing that Kay would have hollered at him for putting so much as a foot over the boundary. "I promise not to go in the pantry without permission," he whispered to Kay's ghost.

As Merlin reached to close the door, Ari appeared, catching the latch. "Don't make us turn off the gravity on you two."

"Wh-what?" he sputtered.

"My childhood best friend and my magician...it's official?"

"Stranger things *have* happened," Merlin pointed out, his cheeks flushed as hard as a sunrise. Ari smiled, a stiff, small curve of her lips that promised she would come back from her losses. That they had not defeated her, and that there was much left to do, and see, and feel. Merlin smiled back, trying to infuse his heart with the same sort of hope.

&

Merlin bandaged Val's wound while he was still semi-conscious, and then sat at his side for at least a day, until Val awoke, eyelids fluttering. He pulled the blankets down, as if he needed to get up at once. As if he'd already missed too much of the action.

The great sweeping-away of blankets revealed Val's chest. Merlin had seen it while he was wrapping Val up, but out of politeness and a sense of self-preservation, he had tried not to linger. Here it was again. Lovely and smooth. Merlin gave a cough as dry and crumbling as an old book.

"Is that how you look at everyone who gets stabbed?" Val asked, a sleepy smile sliding over his face. "Or just me?"

"Is there something I can...do for you?" Merlin asked. "Do you need anything?"

Val nodded. "I'm thirsty."

Merlin picked up a glass of water from the table near the bed, hands shuddering. If he'd had a whisper of magic left in his body, he would have used it to stop them. Steady them. But he'd used it on leaving Nin's cave of anguish, and now all he had to offer Val was himself. And the water.

He raised the rim of the glass to Val's mouth and tipped it. When he pulled it away, Val's lips glistened. "This is the sort of terrifying I usually run from at top speed," Merlin whispered.

Damn Ari with her damned inspiring honesty.

Merlin waited for Val's lips to bloom with disappointment. "But you're not running," he said. "You're right here." He pushed back to make a space for Merlin on the bed. Merlin sat, forming an instant catalogue of every place that he *almost* touched Val.

Damn body with its damned feelings.

"Yes, well, I've had some forced epiphanies," Merlin said.

Val propped himself on an elbow to look at Merlin better, letting the blanket slide farther down his chest, revealing the line that cut toward his hips. "What happened when you passed out?"

Merlin found he couldn't wait another moment to tell someone. And the someone he'd been waiting for—so very long—was Val. "I was trapped by an ancient enchantress who—"

"*Another* one?" Val asked. "How many magical women have you pissed off, Merlin?" There was a softness under his mocking, like the silky sheets that shifted beneath their bodies.

"Nin isn't a woman, really. More like…a force. Not even a force of nature. She's somehow outside of nature. Or beyond it. I can't quite tell. Turns out, she's the reason I'm no good at dying. She's been protecting me."

Val grabbed the water from Merlin, too thirsty to wait for his carefully administered sips. Merlin told Val everything that had happened between the moment he left Val's side and the moment he came back. "And then Nin gave me a choice. She offered to stop this aging backward mess."

The cup paused against Val's lips.

"But it meant leaving Ari. And you." That last one was not easy to say aloud—it nearly tugged Merlin's stomach up his throat. "I couldn't do that."

Val put the glass down so slowly that Merlin thought something was wrong. Then he placed a hand on Merlin's face. The touch had a confidence that pinned Merlin in place after so much wandering through places and times that didn't belong to him. The bright stripes in Val's dark eyes brought him back to Earth.

Val's face moved closer, and Merlin closed his eyes. On Lionel, Merlin hadn't wanted to kiss Val because he feared they would slide past each other, aging in different directions. Now he wanted to kiss Val because he *knew* that was bound to happen, and he would lose his chance.

They had so little time.

Their lips touched and pushed that feeling away. There was no time inside of a kiss, nothing but soft, dark sensation. Hardness came next, in the tousle of their lips, in the insistence of Merlin's hands on Val's neck. And in other, very obvious, places.

Val's hand drifted under the blanket, and found an unnamed spot between Merlin's hip and the zipper of his jeans. Merlin startled at how intense that small touch could be. Val's fingers pushed against the thick cloth, making his nerves *flare*. No wonder jeans had survived the apocalypse.

"What are you doing?" Merlin asked, his voice low and trembling.

"Thanking you," Val said. "For choosing this over..."

"A future?" Merlin asked. Panic ignited in him, turning him to a falling star, blazing to a crash. He couldn't do this. He didn't know how. Or he'd forgotten. There was no hope for him, nothing but a handful of ash where his bravery should be. "You're injured," Merlin said, sounding like his old self, the one who fussed and bothered.

"Rest is another kind of magic," Val said, with a flourish of a smile.

"You need *more* rest," Merlin said. He knew the tumble of this argument. The quick downhill of talking himself out of things. "I should..."

"Be gentle?" Val asked. "Yes. You should."

He pulled Merlin closer, and this time when they kissed, there were bright crackles of feeling. Need welled up, pouring into each kiss. And the *sound*. The music of them trading breath for breath, the slide of fingers on skin, groans deep in their throats.

When their bodies met under the pile of blankets, Merlin was on the verge of something as vast as time. He watched the twist of Val's muscles the same way he would watch the play of stars in the deepest night sky. And then Merlin couldn't just watch. When he reached for Val, he was rewarded with a gasp and a sweet, melting sigh. Val's hands also vanished beneath the blankets.

And after lifetimes of saying no, Merlin found himself saying yes, and yes, and yes.

CIRCLES
&
CURSES

Joy had a way of surprising Ari. She never expected it, never sought it out, and some days it felt nonexistent—and yet it found its way in like sunlight through the cracks of a closed door.

Showing off Ketch to her friends and parents was full of joy. She flew them over the red, rolling deserts in *Error*. She took them to the mountainous city where she'd hid the Lionelians, only to find that they were safe and unharmed. Apparently a fleet of Mercer vessels had stood sentinel in the sky for days, but they'd disappeared after the Administrator's demise.

Next, Ari and her friends took Big Mama back to her sandy nest. Big Mama dug up three large eggs, mooning loudly over their uncracked, cold forms. For a twisting moment, it seemed impossible that the unhatched taneens had survived so long without their mother's heat, but Morgana appeared, reaching ephemerally through the shells to confirm that two of the three still bore beating hearts and growing bodies.

Gwen surprised all of them, pushing toward Morgana to ask her to check her baby. The knights, Merlin, and Ari held their breaths while Morgana laid a bluish-clear hand on Gwen's stomach and pulled it away sharply.

"Alive," she said. "*Loud*, and healthy."

Ari was alight with joy. She could not stop herself from embracing Gwen while Jordan muttered a thankful chant and Lamarack lifted Val into the air, shaking him with happiness. Gwen shivered in Ari's arms, her fear releasing in trembles and significant exhalations. Ari felt the constant heat between them fade to warmth. Less like a flash burn, and more of a hearth.

"This baby will be Lionelian, but born on Ketch. An important piece of both of us." Ari found herself whispering in Gwen's ear before she remembered Kay's last parting wisdom while they were on that imaginary green field of Old Earth. "Even if you're from Troy, originally," Ari said. "We create our families. We choose our homes, don't we?" There was no challenge in her voice—only curiosity and a need to understand why Gwen had held back from her.

Gwen sighed, melting into Ari a little more with each breath. "My parents lived on Troy, and I was born there, but I don't remember it. My first memories are of Lionel. We moved there when I was small, but my parents..." She moved back and stretched, holding out her arms in the bluish-gold sunlight of this vivid planet. "It was too hard to play Middle Ages. They went back to Troy."

"They left you...alone on Lionel?" Ari asked, slight anger leaking through her words.

"Never came back. Never even sent a message." Gwen's

words slid into place—her worries about being left behind by Ari taking on the weight of her past. "The only good thing they ever did was gift me to the training school. I fell in love with Lionel. I found my first loyal friend." Gwen smiled at Jordan. "She's also a left-behind, and we made a vow to each other that someday one of us would be queen."

"I could have so easily been given to Mercer," Gwen added. "They would have owned me."

Ari felt angry for not understanding sooner. She felt like pacing, like raging out. "Our baby won't have those terrible realities poised over their head. I will not rest until—"

Gwen took her arm. "It's okay, Ari. Everything we've done this past year ... losing each other and then Kay ... well, she will not grow up under Mercer's control."

"She?" Ari asked.

Gwen nodded. "Mother's intuition."

Ari didn't say anything, but she hoped Gwen was right. According to Morgana and Merlin, King Arthur's progeny, especially the boys, tended to cause far more trouble than they were worth. Of course, this child wasn't Ari's on a strictly genetic level. Was that enough to avoid the retelling of Arthur's death at the hand of his son?

Mordred.

What a frigid name.

"You said *ours*," Gwen murmured, pulling Ari close by the arm, interrupting her doomed thoughts. "You said *our* baby."

"That's presumptuous, I know—"

Gwen stopped her lips with a kiss that was so soft and sweet, Ari couldn't help but glow with joy—as if that door had been thrown open and now the sunlight was just pouring in.

Her moms made their way over, asking with all the subtle patience of a hungry taneen if they were going to be grandparents. When Gwen said yes, Mom roared with Big Mama levels of excitement, while Captain Mom wept.

Lastly, Ari took her friends to Ras Almal in the capital city of Omaira. She brought them to the huge amphitheater where the seven founding families of Ketch once met to discuss Mercer, their planet, their galaxy.

"I made this," Ari said, slightly bashful as she pointed to the center of the large room. "Well, I had a lot of time on my hands the last time I was here."

Merlin's eyes nearly popped. "It's a..."

"Round table," Ari said, brushing sand off the stones she'd cut and hauled into place with her own hands, one brick at a time. "When I first heard about King Arthur, I thought this bit was the shining jewel of hypocrisy. How could there be one true king who then gave everyone an equal voice? Then, when I was here with so much time on my hands to think things through, I realized that humanity will never give people an equal voice. It's not in our nature. That's why King Arthur had to decree it."

Merlin's eyes stung with unbottled tears.

"Are you all right, old man?" Ari asked, smiling and slapping his back.

Merlin started up a low chant of sorts. "Find Ari. Train Ari. Nudge her onto the nearest throne. Defeat the greatest evil in the universe. Unite all of humankind. I've never been this close to completing it."

"Will you stop aging backward if we sort this out?"

He opened his mouth, but then shut it. "I have absolutely

no idea," Merlin said. Ari wondered if he was waiting for some kind of great clicking, a way of knowing that this was over. "I've always believed that when this was through, I would stop aging backward. Recently I've learned that there might be... other factors at play."

Ari clapped his shoulder. "Whatever stands in the way, we will meet it and surmount it. I promise." She was still feeling slightly unbeatable after taking down Mercer.

Her friends had made their way around the entire table, and they came back to her. Ari cleared her throat to tell them the good news. "I was dreaming we'd get to use this one day. And now, we will." She looked around at her friends, taking them in one at a time. "I put out a call that anyone who wants to help create a new future should send delegates to Ketch. One hundred and forty-seven planets have responded favorably, including Troy. They are headed here to sit at this table right now. To discuss what kind of universe we want to live in. To figure out what we do with the remains of Mercer."

"Even Pluto?" Lam asked. "Are our parents coming?"

"They sent word that you would be the ideal representative," Ari said. "Do you accept?"

Lamarack winked, silvery-mauve eyeshadow glittering. "Of course."

Ari turned to Gwen next. "I'm assuming you'll speak for Lionel, I will speak for Ketch, and Merlin?"

Merlin had been staring across the table disbelievingly. "What?"

"Forget it. He's lost in an epic shag flashback," Lam joked.

Val looped his arm around Merlin's waist. "Don't tease my boyfriend."

Merlin's hand rested on Val's arm as he smiled at Ari. "What is it you need me to do? I could be court mage. I rather enjoyed that position on Lionel...and Camelot, once upon a time."

Ari gripped his shoulder. "I'd like you to be the representative from Old Earth."

Merlin burst into tears, and that, too, was its own strange joy.

&

"Eighteen days," a harsh voice barked across the round table. "That's how long my planet can survive without Mercer supplies. You keep saying that you don't intend to cost people their lives, but a Mercer boycott is *not possible*. Not without great losses."

Ari leaned forward, elbows on the stone table, exhausted. They had been at this for hours with such little progress. Her eyes twitched first to Gwen, who shook her head lightly, and then to Merlin who was bouncing in his seat as if he was about to send fireworks at the next person who declared that a universe without the Mercer Company was *not possible*.

"No one is saying we don't need suppliers connecting a variety of worlds, but do we need an all-encompassing, tyrannical company with monopolistic power?" Lamarack countered, looking rather impressive in their leather armor. "This summit is about finding new laws, regulations that will keep companies like Mercer from taking over the universe—literally."

Ari had found a strong voice in Lamarack. They were equal parts well-spoken and unfettered with the rebellious reputation that held Gwen back.

The same naysaying voice, a hard-edged, elderly woman

from Tanaka, spoke again. "That is all fine and good, but will these things be resolved before the month is out? Before my people are dying of starvation? I think not. We need to talk about working with Mercer in the meantime. Bridging the gap, installing immediate regulations that—"

The woman was cut off by the sudden appearance of a matronly, beautiful figure. Her image was projected in the middle of the table from the speaker they had been using to allow everyone to hear. The woman wore an ivory dress that rolled over soft curves, and a smile that was just as kind and inviting.

"Greetings, wounded universe. My name is Terra, and I'm speaking to you on behalf of the Mercer Family."

"Mercer!" several dozen people shouted, a rejection that emboldened Ari to stand and face the projection with Excalibur in hand.

"What do you want?"

Terra continued to smile, so grandmotherly that Ari winced at her sincerity. "To deliver an olive branch. The Mercer Company is no more. We are rebranding, reassessing our role in the universe and our position as a supplier of great needs. We are the Mercer *Family*. We are here to support you, care for you." She spread her soft arms and glanced around the room.

"You offer this aid by hacking into our private meeting," Gwen said, raising herself beside Ari. "That sounds *exactly* like the old Mercer."

"We apologize, but we did not feel that we could appear in person, what with your rather murderous leadership."

Ari slammed Excalibur down on the table. "I executed the man who ordered and oversaw the genocide of my people. And I would do it again."

"We understand your actions in the arena, Ara Azar. The former Administrator had lost his way and become power hungry. We all know the constant threat of that, don't we?" Her eyes fell on Ari in a chastising way that was entirely too effective.

Gwen gripped Ari's arm, a warning.

"We did not come here to argue fault, but to look to the future. We are aware that several planets have fallen under intense hardship since the destruction of the starship *Heritage* and the cessation of trade across the Mercer-connected galaxies. We would like to offer food and medical supplies at no charge, to all of you. Furthermore, we will agree to any regulations that this summit feels necessary to enact."

Terra fell silent, and Merlin stood. Everyone looked at him.

"That is too generous. What is your price?" he asked. "I have lived long enough to know that no empire eats crow without getting something in return."

The matronly smile returned. "We ask only for you to return what you've taken from us."

"Taken?" Ari nearly yelled. "What have we taken from you? Other than that monstrosity of a starship."

"The last Administrator, as wrong as he was, was important to us. You will provide us with the next Administrator." Her hand waved toward Gwen.

"I would rather die than work for Mercer," Gwen said, chilling the whole amphitheater.

"You would rather see to the near-instant deaths of fifty planets' worth of people?" the woman asked, and for the first time, her voice had a no-nonsense edge. "No matter," she said, softening. "We could not use you. Administrators require a rather special upbringing. We need a child. A baby is even better."

Ari's body went numb.

"The heir to the Lionelian and Ketchan throne. Give us the baby, the embryo. We will grow it with such care that it will be stronger, healthier, and smarter than it could ever be in your malnourished womb."

"This is outrageous," Merlin hissed.

Terra turned to face him. "It is rather medieval, but Mercer didn't pick the theme, now, did we?" She smiled with fragility, sadness. It humanized her in astounding and horrible ways. "Give us this physical reminder of your loyalty before the rest of the galaxies, and we will make sure that not a single person dies in the aftermath of your rebellion. One life for so, so *many*. We will give you the night to accept our offer."

She disappeared without another word. For all this new Administrator's differences, she had the same sense of drama.

The long silence in her wake meant a lot of things. That some people *would* accept this offer. That many more were considering *how* to accept this offer.

Ari's voice shook out of her. "If you believe Mercer, that they will agree to regulations and help the needy in this time without profit...if you believe that Gwen handing over her child as payment for my wrath upon the former Administrator is just, leave now."

Ari didn't mean to be so clipped, so harsh—but she was about to lose her Ketchan mind, and she did not know what else to do. A dozen people stood. No, it was more than that. Far more than half. It was so many, in fact, that Ari dismissed the rest of them without even taking count. In a very small corner of her consciousness, she understood. They were thinking of this one child—barely the size of a thumb—that could give the entire universe a chance.

In the aftermath of the exodus, Ari stood before her knights, Merlin, and Gwen in the amphitheater.

Gwen's face was ashy, her eyes vacant. Ari helped her into a seat.

"This is vile," Jordan whispered.

"I'm going to be sick," Val added.

Ari searched Merlin's face. She couldn't bring herself to turn to Gwen, although she was still gripping Ari's elbow. "Merlin, what do we do?"

He shook his head—and kept shaking it. "You cannot give that child to your enemy, Ari. It's the recipe for another Mordred. *We cannot allow this.*"

"Of course we can't, but we only have until morning to come up with a plan," Ari said faintly. "Or we will have a few starving galaxies to answer to..." Ari shook with the ultimatum Mercer had served up in the middle of her first round-table summit. The heir to Lionel and Ketch, the family Gwen had always wanted, the last piece of Kay—and the baby that Ari had already not-so-secretly started to love—in exchange for "peace."

They all stared at one another, as if that could change anything.

"No plan in the universe is going to fix this one," Val whispered. Ari violently hated how right he was. There was nothing they could do to keep this child safe when Mercer still held so much sway over every habitable planet.

The speaker in the center of the stone table fizzled and

popped. Lam ducked while Jordan drew her sword. There was a sputter of digital noise, and suddenly the group was staring at an object of some sort. Old bone-colored pottery, lined with a gold rim.

"What the hell is that?" Val shouted. "More presents from Mercer?"

Merlin moved to the edge of the round table, leaning in as he inspected.

"It's coming from Arthur," Ari said, placing her hand over her chest, breath tight. "And it's hurting him to show us this. I think he's in some kind of prison."

"It looks like a grail," Jordan said. "The Holy Grail? The one that appeared to Arthur and his knights, igniting their quest for it?" Ari—and several of her friends—shot Jordan a look. "Am I truly the only person here who found out we're reliving an ancient medieval myth and looked up the story?"

"Ouch," Lam said.

Merlin waved his hand at Jordan. "But the Grail was wood. This is...Arthur's chalice."

As if its name had broken its spell, the image vanished. Ari slumped into the chair beside Gwen, still trying hard to breathe. "What just happened, Merlin? What was that?"

Merlin slumped into the chair beside her, staring into space. "I almost didn't recognize it. I have so few memories of that time. Of that place."

"I remember," Morgana said, voice deep and yet riled. "Arthur's chalice was a gift from the enchantresses of Avalon during his eighteenth birthday season. It compelled those who drank from it to see the truth, the truth that is hardest to face. Arthur used it to compel obnoxious, young, would-be kings into becoming his knights. It went missing in Arthur's lifetime. Lost."

"Arthur spent years looking for it," Merlin said in a whisper, looking up at Morgana. "The loss of that chalice felt like the beginning of his end. He did not have it when Mordred came of age...when he began to rage against his father..." Merlin's eyes drifted to Gwen's stomach, and Ari stood up, crossing between them as she paced.

"A cup that makes people believe the truth? If we had that—" She flew back toward Merlin, taking his shoulders. "If we had that, we could make this Terra see the horrors of her ways. We could change the Mercer Company from the *inside*."

Merlin stood, pushing her away. "And how would we get it by tomorrow, Ari? I couldn't find it when Arthur's kingdom was in the balance. What makes you believe we'll just pluck it out of the air before Mercer comes back?"

"Because we aren't going to pluck it out of the air," Ari said, eyes and heart on fire. "We're going to steal it from the past."

ONCE
&
FUTURE

Merlin stood at the edge of the red desert, just after sunset. He found himself breathing the dry air deeply, savoring the rampant colors of this place. Particularly the siren birds whose screams underscored this terrible—and by that he meant *absolutely horrible*—idea to return to Camelot.

But Merlin had not been able to reject it because of the baby. The child could not be ripped away from Ari and Gwen as payment to Mercer. It would not become another Mordred, not while he stood by and watched. He hadn't broken away from Nin, and possibly incurred her wrath, just to let that happen. King Arthur had picked this moment so there was no way Merlin could refuse.

"You chivalrous ass," Merlin muttered.

Morgana appeared so suddenly and so close to Merlin that he screamed.

"*Why* must you do that?" he said, dusting himself off as if the shock of seeing her was clingy as sand.

"You do see the poetry in this, don't you?" Morgana said with a slick smile. "You couldn't find Arthur's chalice all those years ago to save his kingdom because future you stole it right from his table."

"We don't know that that will come to pass. Or *did* come to pass. We don't know anything apart from my solid gut reaction that this is a terrible idea."

"Easy for you to say," she said, more than a touch of sadness in her voice, reminding Merlin of what was about to happen. "You will have to be the one to do it. Ari is too fond of me, despite our arguments. The act will harm her."

Merlin's face mussed up, a combination of being annoyed that Morgana was right and a little heartbroken about how casually the enchantress spoke. "How will we make sure we find the right time *and* place?" he asked. "Camelot was a mere blip of a moment. We could easily end up on Old Earth now, England sunk in the Atlantic, or Britain during the time of the Spice Girls, for heaven's sake." He couldn't help himself; "Wannabe" started to hum through his lips.

Morgana held a wispy finger to his mouth. "If you get one of your damn pop songs stuck in my head, I'll come back to haunt you."

Merlin tried to smile. "That would be reason enough, old enemy."

Morgana gazed at the same last streak of desert sunset that Merlin had just been admiring. "We have to use Nin's magic, Merlin. That's how we find the right time and place. You know what that means."

The sight of Excalibur flashed in Merlin's mind. "I do. Ari will be heartbroken."

"Such sacrifices," Morgana whispered. "Is all existence riddled with such sacrifice?"

Merlin sighed. "It certainly seems that way."

Ari's knights appeared, tramping away from Omaira, leaving the lights of the city behind. Together the small, quiet band followed a stone road to the spot where the desert opened up like a dark-red sea. Merlin had spent the afternoon inspecting their outfits and dressing them in the remnants of Lionelian fashion on *Error*. He'd been so successful that they now appeared as if they'd fallen out of a distant time, even if his fashion demands had turned slightly... ominous. Particularly when he apologized profusely and put Lamarack in men's clothes to match their leather armor—and made them scrub off their makeup.

"Did you say good-bye to your mothers, Ari?" Merlin asked.

"I did," she said grimly. "I told them they couldn't ask where we were going, in case Mercer tries to get it out of them."

"Not that anyone would believe them," Gwen added.

"Or be able to follow us," Ari said, holding tightly to Gwen's hand.

"They can't chase us to the past, but they can certainly wreak havoc while we're gone," Merlin said, thinking of the Lionelians they'd fought so hard to save. Big Mama, sitting on her eggs at this very moment.

"I don't trust the rest of the representatives to hold out against Mercer for long, especially if we're missing," Ari said. "How long *will* we be gone?"

Merlin didn't have an answer to Ari's question. They would find Arthur's chalice as quickly as they could, but it wouldn't be an easy task. For a flicker of a moment, he didn't believe that it could be done. As they marched, that flicker grew into a burning, blazing fear. "If we get lucky, we could be back tonight, so to speak. We can return to any time we want to. The trick is figuring out *how* to get back."

"How much farther are we going?" Gwen asked, looking dangerously exhausted.

"Not far," Merlin said, nodding to Jordan, who swept Gwen up in her broad arms and carried her like a baby.

"She'll be a terrible target," Merlin whispered to Ari. "If it's obvious that she's pregnant and not married to a man, they could stone her."

"Stone her?"

"Beat her to death with stones."

"*What?*" Ari blurted, alarming every single person in their company. She grabbed his arm and yanked him close. "Tell me you're joking."

"How could someone joke about that?" he asked, bright tears blurring his vision. "I'm trying to warn you. Back then it's not Mercer you have to worry about. It's *murder.* Sexism," he said, glaring at Gwen. "Racism." His eyes bounced across the group. "Homophobia!" he croaked.

"*Homo* what?" Ari asked.

"You must listen, Ari," Merlin said. "King Arthur was special because he rose from the ashes of one of the worst times in human history. That's why it was called the Dark Ages."

Ari's grip fastened on Excalibur. "Merlin, this isn't just to stop Mercer and save the baby. We're going to look for a way to save you, too, to stop your backward aging, before…" She didn't have to finish her sentence. Merlin felt his own ending looming up like a doorway to oblivion. He didn't tell her that he'd started to give up on having a future, that he couldn't afford that hope any longer, although he suspected she sensed it in his resigned silence.

This would be Merlin's last quest, and so he had no choice but to make it his greatest.

"Here," Morgana's voice rang out, causing everyone to stop. At first, there was only the night, but then the light-blue shimmering soul of the ancient enchantress appeared before them.

"How do we make it happen?" Ari asked.

"We combine our magic. As much as we can gather," Merlin said, closing his eyes and humming. He took Ari's magnificent sword, leaking incandescent energy into it, making it shine like a bright star. When he was done, his singing voice dwindled out, and he sagged slightly.

Ari eyed the glowing sword, and Jordan set Gwen down. "Now what?"

"Give me a moment." Morgana threw her dark head back, taking in the silver stars. "How will you return? The opening will only hold for a moment."

"The elegant nightmare makes a great point," Val muttered.

"We'll find a way. That place sounds like it's overrun with magic." Ari turned to Gwen, dark doubt in her voice. "Do you trust me? It'll be my goal to bring us back to this time, to fix this future, but who knows if that's possible."

"Of course," Gwen said, her honesty as brilliant as torchlight.

They faced Morgana. The enchantress held a hand to Ari's cheek, and one on Merlin's. "The people of that time and place will seek to kill you, while their savagery and ignorance will break you. You, because you've never imagined it," she said to Ari, and then she turned to Merlin, "And you because you believed you'd escaped it."

Merlin felt a chill in the desert wind, but he hardened his stance.

Morgana positioned herself with the tip of the sword on her chest. "Aim for my heart, old wizard."

"It's *magician*," Merlin coughed.

"Wait, you're going to...kill her?" Ari asked, horrified. "No, I—"

"Farewell," Morgana said. She reached for Merlin's shoulders and pressed close in a rush. Merlin felt the impending death magic rattle through every single atom. Morgana screamed with the kind of pain that ended worlds, Excalibur rushing straight through her.

And the night exploded with blue light.

They were thrown back into the sand, nothing left of Excalibur in Merlin's palm except for the handle and hilt. Nothing left of Morgana except for a contracting web of gray mist. Merlin had killed Morgana, so it wouldn't leave a hole in Ari, but he felt one open up, unexpected and ragged, in his own heart.

"Go!" he yelled. "Before it closes!"

Lamarack shouted a warning, but Merlin's eyes were already set beyond this time and place. He struggled to his feet, one arm locked around Ari. They moved as one through ice-cold mist, away from this end and into the cursed heart of the very beginning.

Don't miss the epic conclusion
to Ari and Merlin's cycle in

THE
SWORD
IN THE
STARS

COMING IN 2020

ACKNOWLEDGMENTS

First, we would like to acknowledge King Arthur for maybe (but probably not) existing, and Merlin, for getting past that awkward part of history where people thought he was just some magical demon spawn. Also, a shout-out to Gweneviere for surviving centuries of patriarchy, slut-shaming, and way too many spellings of her name.

T. H. White, thank you for the retelling that sparked our retelling. Thank you for showing us that the Arthurian legend could be high-spirited, funny, sad, *and* resistance literature all at once.

Thank you to the queer authors who came before us and paved this road to a more inclusive future. Thank you to the readers of these books, and the LGBTQIAP+ heroes of the real world who so rarely see themselves reflected on the page.

Thank you to the outspoken, the people who stand up to injustice. Who strike a blow—any blow—against oppression.

Thank you to Cori's Lebanese family, whose struggles against cultural assimilation inspired much of Ari's journey.

Thank you to our brilliant writing group, SAGA, and Mr. Daum for inspiration and light during a very dark time.

Thank you to Queer Pete, our kindred rainbow spirits.

Thank you to Emily Andras for the show *Wynonna Earp,*

the nerdy, feminist, stuffed-with-queers adventure we always needed to watch. And you know, Emily, if you'd like to turn this into a show...

Thank you to Imagine Dragons, because whether they knew it or not, they wrote the soundtrack to *Once & Future*.

Thank you to our agents, the Sara(h)s, who never once faltered when we said we wanted to write queer King Arthur in space.

Thank you to Aubrey Poole, our knightly editor astride a green space dragon, for making this book fiercer and funnier and truer.

Thank you to James Patterson, our unexpected champion, for believing in this story and seeing a place for it on the shelves.

A huge HUZZAH to the entire JIMMY team for a cover that made us swoon and such shining, unbelievable support.

Thank you to the booksellers and librarians who hand this book to all kinds of young people. You are our heroes.

Thank you to Maverick, who is as loving and wild as a baby taneen.

Thank you to our families for embracing us for who we are.

And finally—this is just Cori here—thank you to Amy Rose for the kind of love that fills the cosmos with hope.

P.S. This is just Amy Rose! Thank you, Cori, for inviting me to be part of the story I fell for *almost* as hard and fast as I fell for you. Let's write so many more together.

ABOUT THE AUTHORS

Cori McCarthy had been dreaming about retelling the King Arthur myth set in space for several years, but something always held them back... until the day they asked their partner in life and words, Amy Rose Capetta, to write it with them. Such is magic. One day, an idea is only an idea, and the next, it has arms, legs, and space dragons.

Amy Rose Capetta (she/her) holds a BA in Theater Arts from UC Santa Cruz and an MFA from Vermont College of Fine Arts. She is the author of the space duet *Entangled* and *Unmade,* as well as a love story wrapped in a murder mystery, *Echo After Echo,* and the vibrant Italian-inspired fantasy, *The Brilliant Death,* and its forthcoming sequel. She identifies as a queer demigirl. Find out more about Amy Rose and her books at AmyRoseCapetta.com.

Cori McCarthy (they/them) earned degrees in poetry and screenwriting before falling in love with young adult literature at Vermont College of Fine Arts. Cori is the author of two science fiction thrillers, *The Color of Rain* and *Breaking Sky,* which are respectively about human trafficking in space and futuristic queer teen fighter pilots. They are also the author of two contemporary novels, the mixed media urbex adventure *You Were Here,* and the feminist romcom *Now a Major*

Motion Picture. They identify as an Irish-Arab American, as well as a pan demi enby. Find out more about Cori and their books at CoriMcCarthy.com.

In 2015, Amy Rose and Cori cofounded Rainbow Boxes, a charitable initiative to send inclusive fiction to community libraries and LGBTQ+ support shelters all over America. In 2018, they cofounded the Rainbow Writers Workshop at the Writing Barn in Austin, Texas, an annual event where aspiring queer writers can come together to learn craft and launch their careers. The couple lives together in the mountains of Vermont where they raise a magical child who may very well be the next King Arthur.